WHITE LINES

WHITE LINES

Mel Stein

HEADLINE

First published in 1997
by HEADLINE BOOK PUBLISHING

10 9 8 7 6 5 4 3 2 1

British Library Cataloguing in Publication Data

Stein, Mel
    White lines
    1.Soccer - Fiction 2.Thrillers
    I. Title
    823.9'14 [F]

ISBN 0 7472 1392 5

Typeset by
CBS, Felixstowe, Suffolk

Printed and bound in Great Britain by
Mackays of Chatham PLC, Chatham, Kent

HEADLINE BOOK PUBLISHING
A division of Hodder Headline PLC
338 Euston Road
London NW1 3BH

To the Queen, from her loyal consort.

PROLOGUE

September 1992

'I want those rights,' said the man at the head of the board-room table, and, as if to leave no chance of any misunderstanding of his intentions, he hit the polished wood with his clenched fist.

The three men to his right said nothing, but merely nodded. Although they were all directors of Jet Productions, they knew their opinions, collective or individual, counted for little or nothing once their chairman, Nathan Carr, had set his mind on a particular project. Of the three to his left, the only one to speak was the sole woman in the room.

'I want, Nathan, I want . . . You must have been a horrible child.'

Nobody else present would have dared to test his mood and humour in this way, but then none of the others had slept with him. Alissa Bland had been his mistress for some five years, back in the mid-eighties, and although the affair was long over, although she was on the board as Project Development Director on her merits, she still demanded some licence in their relationship as the price he had to pay. Alissa was nearly forty now, yet as stunning as she had been a decade earlier. Nobody before or since Nathan Carr had ever terminated an affair with her until she had been good and ready to bring it to an end.

There were times when Carr was alone with her when he had the odd pang of regret. The blonde hair that he knew to be natural, as soft to touch as spun-silk, hanging loosely down to her shoulders, the high regal forehead, the skin so clear and smooth that it was impossible to believe she had ever suffered a blemish as a teenager, the perfectly arched eyebrows that needed no attention above eyes that could be described as nothing else but gentle blue. Gentle! Carr knew she could be gentle, but not many people who had dealt with Alissa in business, as she clawed

1

her way up the profession, would have described her as anything else but diamond hard.

Yet, however tough and ambitious she might be, she was nothing compared to Carr himself. Sometimes, it was difficult to believe he was only in his early forties. He looked older. His hair, once so jet-black, was almost entirely grey, he wore steel-rimmed spectacles all the time, and there were tightening lines around his mouth. He was still a good-looking man for all that. He probably always would be, and in the occasional weaker moments, perhaps those same moments when Carr was wondering why he'd brought it to an end, Alissa would wonder whether she could bring it all back to life.

But then he'd left her for another woman and, worse, he'd actually married her. Alissa knew the exact date. Carr had met his wife-to-be at a film premiere on May 27 1986. By June 10 he'd abandoned Alissa. On September 4 Nathan Carr married Miss Susie White and now it was September 1992 and they'd been together for six years and it looked as if it were going to last. The only thing that kept Alissa going was the fact that there were no children. Maybe the bitch couldn't have them. She knew that she, herself, could. After all, there had been that abortion a year into the affair. She'd never told Nathan about it. She was scared at the time that he might think she'd got herself pregnant deliberately, that she was trying to entrap him into marriage. It was another hand dealt to her that she could see with hindsight she'd played desperately wrong.

'It may be five years down the line, but when it happens I want to be part of it,' Carr continued. There was a set determination about his mouth that Alissa knew could be converted into a winning smile at will. Oh yes, she knew that smile, the flash of perfect teeth, the controlled crinkling above the grey-green eyes that showed no real sign of humour. Any minute now he would run his hand through his thick hair. There, he did it, that gesture of reassurance that everything was still in place although the colour might be different, that he was seemingly impervious to age, that mid-life might be beckoning him, but he was ignoring the signal.

'Tell us again, Nathan, exactly what it is you want,' Alissa said. 'After all, we girlies find it a bit hard to follow you men when it comes down to sport. Or at least the sort of sport you play on the field rather than behind the bushes.'

Carr shot her a look that said he knew she was winding him up, that the explanation would be for the other board members present; for Colin Turnbull, for Murray Cameron, for Philip King, all of whom had a slightly glassy look about them. It was the same at every meeting, as Carr hit them with bound volumes of figures, eschewing all chances of discussion. At an early stage he had ostentatiously produced a book with the daunting title, *How to Run a Board Meeting in Half the Time*, and now, a few years later, he'd probably got it down to a quarter.

Jet TV was a real success story. It was just about seven years ago that, with a wing and a prayer plus a little bit of capital supplied by his business partner, Mohammed Halid, Carr had set up Jet Productions. They'd persuaded Andy Davison, a professional Glaswegian, to film a series of celebrity interviews for a small fee and a share of profits. Davison had used his contacts, and the interviews had been nothing short of sensational, particularly when he'd done an hour exclusive with the singer Rory Devlin just before he'd topped himself. Jet had sold the interview to the networks for a huge premium and Jet Productions had well and truly arrived.

Carr and Halid had then been astute enough to anticipate the impact of satellite and cable television and knew that the best was yet to come in that field. Jet Productions had spawned Jet TV, producing programmes for its own channel, seeking out bargains and opportunities, spotting the emerging talent before it emerged, now with Andy Davison as Head of Production.

Even as he spoke, Nathan Carr knew he was on to a winner and the explanation was a mere sop, a humouring of the rest of the board. Halid was travelling abroad, extricating the last of his assets from his troubled homeland, Iran. When Halid was away, Carr ran the company and the board meetings, with ruthless efficiency. He was certain that by 1998 the majority of homes would have access to extra-terrestrial broadcasts. Dishes and cables would bring the immediacy of politics, of news, of shopping into the home, a constant choice which would bring a new generation of compulsive couch-bound channel-surfers. Carr had seen the future and not only wanted to be a part of it, but also wanted to own it.

3

Jet already had the rights to one or two of the smaller football tournaments and Carr had been amazed by the viewing figures. Nathan Carr was not a man who was easily surprised and he realised that if people were prepared to watch a competition that involved teams knocked out in the third round of the FA Cup (a sort of footballing Wimbledon Plate) then how many millions more would tune in for what he now had in mind?

'The ESL, the European Super League, is right now an idea on paper in an office in Zurich; but come 1998 my sources tell me it'll be a reality. There's no point in waiting until the day before it starts to begin negotiating for the television rights. Just think about it. Whoever wins the Premier League in England goes out there and plays against the likes of AC Milan, Bayern Munich, Barcelona, Ajax, not just in the European Champions Cup, but in a proper league, the real Premier League of Europe that will put our own Championship in the shade. Forget midweek jaunts by Manchester United, or whoever, to the likes of Coventry or Southampton. They hop on a plane and they're walking the streets of Spain, not stopping off in a motorway café for fish and chips. And they're being watched by millions. I want those millions to be watching us. Now, do I have your authority to do whatever is necessary to acquire those rights?'

He looked from face to face, receiving the nods of approval as a formality.

'Minute that, will you?' he said to Alan Sykes, the company secretary, then satisfied that he, at least, had got what he wanted from the meeting, rose to go.

'There's no other business, is there?' he asked rhetorically as he pushed his chair neatly back in place. That was how he liked things, neat endings, everything in its place. Instinctively, rather than as a calculated act of deference, the other male directors got to their feet, as the secretary furiously scribbled and Alissa merely smiled. Carr towered over his fellow board members as he passed them, the physical advantage underlining the other differences between them. Only Alissa seemed unaffected by the royal exit. She remained seated, a small smile playing around her mouth. As Project Development Director she knew this was going to be her baby. Her baby. Again, the memory of the loss, although the smile she showed to the outside world did not fade. She was adept at keeping her feelings to herself. Do whatever

4

was necessary to acquire the rights, Carr had said. Left alone in the room she let her mind wander, let her imagination run riot, to try and discover exactly what it was that might indeed be necessary.

CHAPTER 1

July 1997

Mark Rossetti had learned to relax on air, and, once he'd achieved that, he really began to enjoy broadcasting. The first programme had been a nightmare. He'd sat opposite Bob Miller, the anchorman of the show, looking so frozen that he might well have just suffered a major stroke. His face was carved into a wooden expression that still managed to convey the look of a man who had seen something too horrible to describe. All the warnings not to er and um had been forgotten along with every anecdote, every joke, every expression that he had rehearsed for days in front of his bathroom mirror. All he was left with was a stammering hesitation and a barrowful of clichés that stamped him indelibly as a former professional footballer. After that it could only get better.

Much to his surprise he was given a second chance, and indeed it did improve. Bob Miller had been around for twenty years or more. He'd seen five World Cups, managers come and go, players shoot into the firmament, then crash back to earth like dying fireworks. Producers, directors, they all might change, but Bob Miller was indestructible. He'd moved stations, from BBC to Ball Park TV, but he seemed to have carried his viewing public with him. He had become a cult hero, getting fatter and fatter as his career developed; but then his size had grown into a trademark itself, a subject for discussion with whoever was the panellist at the time.

When Mark had first been invited to appear on Ball Park's Saturday lunchtime football programme he'd declined. His girlfriend, Patti Delaney, had other ideas.

'As a journalist you never turn down opportunities. If you don't try them, then you'll never know whether or not you like it, or whether you're any good.'

'Yes, but you don't have to conduct experiments like that in front of a few million strangers.'

'Cock it up, Mark, and they won't stay strange for long.'

She'd laughed and he'd kissed her and then they'd gone to bed in her flat. Despite the money she now had at her disposal from the unexpected inheritance she and Mark had received from their old friend Leopold Schneider, she had refused to move from her basement home that they affectionately called 'the Burrow'.

That had only been a few months before, just after she had fully recovered from the injuries she had received during their Russian adventure. He'd thought then of marriage, of eternity with her, but things had a habit of never standing still, of changing for the worse just when he felt he could live with them always being the same. He'd joked about it with Patti, wondering when she'd be bitten by the Boredom Bunny, but now the joke was on him, and the woman he had seen virtually every day of the week now limited his ration to the odd evening. It wasn't that they were so busy that they had no time for each other, it was rather a case of her pushing him away, distancing herself.

He'd phoned her this evening, just before he came to the studios. The answerphone was on. Whereas in the past she'd often snatch the phone off the hook once she heard his voice, interrupting her own message that said she was not at home, now he had to listen to the whole recital, the apology, the mobile number that would not be switched on, finally the request to leave a message. Leave a message. What was the point when there was every chance she was sitting there listening to what he had to say? He didn't think there was anybody else sitting with her, but he could not be sure. That was the thing with Patti, he realised, he could not be sure and perhaps he never would be sure.

He tried to clear his mind of her and concentrate on the programme ahead. The station might be covering just another nothing pre-season tournament, but it had to be made to seem important to the viewers. If the public didn't care about the result then they switched off, always assuming they had bothered to switch on in the first place.

Bob Miller settled his face into the features that were so popular with the public, his public. The resigned look that said whatever might happen on the show was out of his control, the slightly raised left eyebrow that gave the message to the viewers

7

that he was on their side in expecting the unexpected. If anything went wrong he could transform the disaster into a matter of public interest in seconds. That was the true hallmark of the professional, to deal with the unscripted with consummate ease.

'OK Mark, let's get our show on the road,' Bob said, as the producer counted down the last thirty seconds in his ear before the programme went on the air. 'It may be crap, but let's make it palatable crap.'

Even as he spoke, Bob was preparing to swivel his chair to face the camera. He liked that introductory swivel and knew from talking to viewers that they liked it too. Bob Miller was never one to complain about being recognised in public, although he feigned a gentle false modesty that anybody could be interested in asking for his autograph. Yet he also liked them to go away with the feeling that he was accessible, a genuine human being and all-round nice guy, and for the most part he succeeded. Yes, that swivel was a gesture of anticipation that something was coming that promised an afternoon full of entertainment.

'Hi, and welcome to Ball Park's exclusive presentation of the Anglo-European Cup, the friendly tournament where friendship flies out of the window.' Mark could almost see Bob wink and immediately relaxed. There were just the two of them, chatting together in a room about their favourite subject, a subject upon which they were both experts. It didn't matter that there were millions out there hanging on every work as if it were gospel.

'Looking forward to this afternoon, Mark?' Bob asked and Mark suddenly realised that indeed he was. The summer was nearly over in the kingdom of football, that ever-shrinking summer, and he was back in his real world.

'Yes,' Mark replied. 'You realise that the season's about to start when we get matches like this. I think we're going to learn a lot about Hertsmere's championship prospects. I'm not sure there's anybody in the Premier League as good as Barcelona or Munich so it's going to be a real test.'

'I can't see any of the foreign visitors taking their foot off the pedal against the European Cup Winners Champions. Let's bring in our studio guest for his views. Today, I'm sure we're all delighted to see Kenny Cunningham, the England Manager. Interesting game ahead?'

'Without a doubt,' Cunningham said. He was a television natural and he knew it. England's most capped player since the war, he'd been the favourite for the national team job from the day he retired from the game as a player. He'd cut his teeth on taking Walsend out of the First Division in his first season as manager, then revitalised the sleeping giants at Stretford United to bring them back as a real force in the game. He'd been in charge of the England team for some six months and had begun to learn it was a different ball game from club soccer management. One win (the first game), three draws and a defeat meant the honeymoon was over and at least one tabloid was already sniffing blood, if not exactly baying for it. In a month's time he had another friendly against Colombia, the last match before the World Cup qualifiers reached boiling point, and he knew he had to get it right.

'So Kenny, can you give us any clues as to which Hertsmere players might be catching your eye this afternoon?'

'Well, there's this youngster called Rossetti,' Cunningham said with the slow theatrical smile that he'd developed by rehearsing for hours in front of his bathroom mirror.

'Not so sure about the youngster bit,' Mark said, laughing, surprised that he no longer felt the pain of a missed career.

'Seriously,' Cunningham continued, 'anybody who's qualified to play for England and who puts in a good performance has got a chance. You know me, I'm open minded. As long as I've got the England job nobody's too old or too young to pull on the white shirt – as long as they're doing the business out there on the pitch.' He flashed Mark the smile again. 'So I suppose that does rule you out, unless you can get yourself back in training.'

The three of them laughed as if they were just old friends putting down a pint or two at their local.

Even at forty-five Kenny Cunningham looked very much like the man who had taken England so near to the final of the World Cup a decade before. There was a lot of grey in the curly hair, but only as much as he permitted by his decision not to tint it out. He liked to be in control of his life from the top to the bottom and the run of indifferent form that England had experienced in the last four matches had annoyed, as well as baffled, him. He adjusted his glasses, which again he had made a conscious decision to wear, although he was only a little shortsighted. He felt they added to his credibility, gave him a certain gravitas that the youthful bloom of his skin denied. He always looked clean-shaven and the slightly ruddy complexion gave a suggestion of a lad who might well have worked on a farm rather than the street-wise townie that he really was. The eyes looked straight at whoever was speaking to him, never wavering, encouraging a companion to continue with his theme even if Cunningham might think they were talking utter rubbish. He was a career sportsman in very much the same way that there were career politicians. The Football Association loved him because he brought no hint of scandal to the job, the players idolised and listened to him because they knew he had been there and done it, whilst for once the public all believed the right man had been chosen for the position.

They chatted on for a few moments more, exchanging jokes and anecdotes and then switched to their man outside the stadium talking to the incoming fans.

Off the air, Cunningham asked for a coffee and gave the assistant who brought it the sort of smile that would have done service to a five-course gourmet meal.

'Thanks love. Best station for its refreshments this one.'

'Is there anybody who doesn't love you?' Bob asked, a little enviously.

'Only those who love you more,' Cunningham fired back without hesitation.

'Sorry to interrupt this mutual admiration society,' Mark said, 'but who are you here to watch? Strictly off the record that is.'

'I might not be here to watch anybody. I might be here because I'm being paid for it, just like you.'

'No, no, Mark's not here for the money. He doesn't need to work any more. Hadn't you heard he's a man of independent means?'

Mark ignored him, knowing there was no malice in what he said, but Cunningham nodded as if this was another piece of information that needed storing in his filofax alongside his notes on the Colombian centre forward. The focus of both men switched to the pitch. A couple of the Hertsmere team were already out there. Barry Reed, the young Geordie, curled the ball past Greg Sergovitch from thirty yards. Another ball was rolled to him and he did it again. From the corner of his eye

10

WHITE LINES

Mark saw Cunningham sit forward in his chair, alert and attentive, nodding once more almost imperceptibly, and at that moment Mark knew exactly who it was that the England manager had come to observe.

CHAPTER 2

Helen Davies no longer felt as if she were a woman in a man's world. That was not to say that she felt any less feminine. Indeed, since her marriage to Rob Davies, newly promoted in the police force from sergeant to inspector, she felt more feminine every day. She thought about what she would be wearing the night before she actually wore it, bought some jewellery to match her clothes and then reflected on the effect of it all. She had become a far cry from the large, almost ungainly, girl who'd got into football because she was a groupie who loved the sport. Now she had become respected as one of the most efficient chief executives in the Premier League and there was no doubt that David Sinclair, the Chairman of Hertsmere United, relied upon her absolutely. Yes, he might be a successful businessman in his own right; yes, other members of the board might be perfectly competent, but it was Helen Davies who ran the administration of the club from top to bottom. She missed nothing. A dirty floor in reception meant a review of the contract cleaning; the match day catering was subject to random tests and, on occasions, the replacement of the catering manager; any disappearance of kit reported by Alfred the kit-man meant the implementation of security measures that inevitably led to the discovery of the identity of the thief. It was hands-on management that led to her being at the club from early morning until late at night. With her husband taking his newfound promotion seriously it gave them little time together so it was with some surprise that the news had been confirmed to her just this morning that she was pregnant. She didn't know whether to laugh or cry. She'd come off the pill a few months earlier upon doctor's advice and their use of condoms had been fairly disciplined. However, there had been one occasion after Rob's promotion when they'd rolled home legless, couldn't wait for any protection, couldn't even wait for the bed. Although the night of passion had seemed great at the time there was an inevitable price to pay.

She was taking her time in getting used to the idea. She supposed she had another eight months or so for it to sink in fully – and after that, what? Did she give up the job she'd fought so hard to attain? Did she take her maternity leave and then get back to work? Or did she drop the little creature in a convenient paddy field and be at her desk the same afternoon? The real problem was going to come when she had to tell David. He'd had enough trouble with the club over the last few years and she knew he was looking forward to a period of stability and consolidation.

That was what today's meeting was all about. In late July, with people not yet returning from their holidays, the previous season might seem to have ended only yesterday, the next season might appear aeons away, but in the real world of football there was no rest. Season tickets had to be sold, the decorators were still in one stand and the contract with the main sponsor was up for renegotiation. The players might have just returned from sunning themselves in Florida and Majorca, but Helen had permitted herself only one lazy weekend in Bath before returning to the fray.

She hoped and prayed she was not going to suffer from morning sickness. She couldn't recall having had a day's illness since she'd got the last of the childish ailments out of the way in her teens. She could think of more constructive things to do with her mornings than retch in the bathroom. Even as the thought crossed her mind she felt a small spasm of nausea and wondered if it were self-induced. If her life were about to go out of control then the least she could do was to restrain herself from helping it on its way.

She watched from one of the few executive boxes contained within the ground as David Sinclair made his way up the stand towards her. He had just returned from a sailing holiday in Bermuda, having cut his trip short to see Hertsmere play the day before in the fairly meaningless Anglo-European pre-season tournament. Although that had been a friendly it had given him cause for concern. Both Barcelona and Munich, in the forty-five minutes allotted to them in a round-robin competition, had wiped the floor with the English side. It was, he felt, going to be a long hard season.

The Bermudian suntan could not conceal the strain and tension in his face. Given everything that had happened to him over the last few years, it was a miracle he was still there at all and at times Helen thought it a miracle that Hertsmere were there themselves. A little club who had come through the old Southern League, up into the Fourth Division via the Conference, then all the way to the Premiership. And, despite everything and every dire warning, they had survived. Not merely survived, but triumphed in Europe.

Yet this season, playing again automatically as holders of the European Cup Winners Cup was not enough. The money would be useful, but the real pot of gold had been moved further out of reach, beyond the existing rainbow's end. Until this year the jackpot was the European Champions League, open only to the winners of the individual championships of Europe. But now the powers that be had decided that in itself was not enough. There was to be a full league programme in Europe over the entire season, the ESL, the European Super League.

In order to accommodate the extra fixtures, the Premier League would be reduced by four clubs, with another four going the season after. It was the ultimate in elitism. Only the strong would survive.

On this July morning, however, it wasn't mere survival that David Sinclair had in mind. It was the ultimate victory, the Premiership itself, and with it entry for Hertsmere into the ESL. Their brand new fifty-thousand seat stadium would be ready by then, of that he was sure. He'd been to see it just an hour or so before and had visualised it filled to capacity as Hertsmere challenged for the European title. He wanted visiting chairmen from France, Italy and Spain to return to their countries talking not just of Hertsmere's prowess on the field, but of their facilities.

He remembered going to the Olympic Stadium in Rome with his beloved daughter. From the outside it looked good, it looked great, but then the reality set in and hit you in the face. The absence of any printed match day programme, the battle for an expensive cup of coffee, and Holly's ultimate complaint – that the ladies' toilets were little more than a hole in the ground. There would be no chance of any of those areas being overlooked at Hertsmere's new home. Although they did not have a limitless budget, with the help of the local authority and the Football

Trust they were going to create a state-of-the-art theatre of sport. The sadness was that his daughter had not lived to share in the triumph, because without her, it was a hollow one indeed.

'Morning, Helen,' Sinclair said, his tall frame filling the doorway momentarily as he entered the box. Helen smiled, half at the memory of how once her chairman's very presence could have turned her legs to jelly. Now only her husband did that for her, although she sensed that it had taken her marriage for David Sinclair to realise she was, in fact, a woman.

'Hello, David? Been down to Disneyland?'

That was their private code for the new stadium being constructed some five miles from the city centre. There was still some argument raging over its ultimate nomenclature and, having been present at some of the more heated discussions, both David and Helen could bear witness to the fact that Disneyland was as near to the truth as anything could ever be.

'Everything's fine in the Magic Kingdom. It's Park Crescent that worries me,' Sinclair said gesturing around their existing home. 'Obviously, if we're moving, I don't want to spend too much money on this place, but on the other hand we've got our European campaign to worry about.'

'We managed last season,' Helen said.

'Managed is very nearly the right word,' he replied, then seeing the expression on her face, quickly added, 'not that I've any complaints about what you achieved. You did a great job but quite frankly even Michelangelo couldn't turn this particular sow's ear into a silk purse. Somehow it looks even tackier twelve months on. I've seen the bill from the painters and I can't really believe we've had any value for money.'

'Trust me, David. I got that quote down to the wire. To get anything cheaper we'd have had to have the local primary school out with their paint brushes. Everything costs a fortune nowadays. You only have to look at the specs and costings for Disneyland.'

'Yes, but at least that's an investment for the future. What do you think the council will do when we move out? They're not going to turn it into a shrine or a museum, that's for sure. The bulldozers will be in and new housing development, here we come. In a year's time nobody will even remember where the clock was situated.'

'What are you trying to say, David?' Helen asked, gently

sensing the frustration in the chairman's tone.

'I'm not sure. It's just that we've got past the point where Park Crescent was a horrible little place that all the big boys hated to visit. If we beat them then they blamed the playing surface, the size of the ground, the proximity of the crowd, the lack of hot water in the showers . . . Whatever. It was never the fact that Hertsmere United may – and only may – that we may just have played better football than them. I didn't want it to be like that second time around. We've won the FA Cup, we won a European trophy, now I want to go for the big one.'

His eyes misted over a little as he gazed around his beloved ground, a ground now empty of spectators, but filled with so many memories. The terraces where he'd stood as a kid were no longer there, but were banked with seats. The fans had hated that and when matches became exciting the stewards found it virtually impossible to get them to remain seated. There were times when Sinclair felt he was the star of an English *Field of Dreams*. If he rebuilt the club then they would come, the ghosts of the past. The great ones he remembered from his childhood. Of course, they'd not really been great, merely better than the rest in those lower divisions. But time played tricks on the memory and he was quite happy to believe that the Hertsmere side which won promotion from the Conference into the League just over a decade before had enjoyed skills to compare with those of the Manchester United team who perished at Munich. Yes, if he built it they would come. Costner in the movie had built the stadium for his dead father, and Sinclair was building it for his dead daughter. Only nobody would understand that, except perhaps Helen. He had no other woman in his life, there had not been one for a long time. He just made sure that he was too busy for any involvement that might cause him pain. He had suffered enough pain already in his lifetime.

Helen Davies, like David Sinclair, had always been a Hertsmere fan, only the sharp end of the business side of the club had caused her rose-tinted spectacles to mist over.

'David, we struggled in the League last season. In some ways we're lucky still to be in the Premier. We've signed nobody of note in the close season. What makes you think we have any chance of the title? Why should it be different this time around just because you want it to be?'

Sinclair's strong mouth took on a steely set of determination. 'It'll be different because we'll make it different. And no, we won't win the Premiership just because I want us to, but because we have to.'

Another woman might have laughed at his stubborn illogicality, but Helen Davies was not another woman. She also wanted it to happen. The only difference was that, unlike David Sinclair, she did not truly believe it was possible.

CHAPTER 3

Mark Rossetti knew Patti Delaney well enough by now to realise when she was unhappy and even before they had gone into dinner he knew she was not a contented lady.

'You really didn't have to drag me all the way out here to prove that we've money to spend. I've looked at the prices on the menu as well as the room rates and we'll be burning money rather than spending it.'

It had been Mark's idea to take her away for a romantic weekend. The Compleat Angler in Marlow, he'd thought, would be perfect. Lovely setting by the Thames, good food, not too far to travel, pretty countryside all around.

The expedition had not even begun well. The M25 and then the M40 had been solid with traffic, all heading out of town for the weekend. They'd had to phone ahead three times from the car, on each occasion pushing back the time of their dinner a little.

'We might as well make a booking for breakfast at this rate,' she'd grumbled, lighting up a cigarette and challenging him to argue because she knew he hated her smoking in the car. He'd indulged himself by buying a Mercedes with a sun roof, but with the temperature edging up into the eighties even as the evening drew in, he found himself relying on the air-conditioning as they edged along the motorway inch by inch. He tried to make light conversation, but she obviously wasn't in the mood.

'I feel as if I'm in a car park,' he said.

'You can get out of a car park if you've got a ticket,' she replied, looking ahead to the solid line of traffic snaking its way up the hill as far as the eye could see. A sign appeared informing them that the roadworks which were causing the tailback did not actually begin until a mile ahead. Still less encouraging was a flashing message saying that there were no emergency telephones for miles and that anybody breaking down would have to stay

18

with their vehicles. All that was missing was a little face sticking out its tongue and mouthing, 'Yah, boosucks.'

After about an hour, during which they'd progressed about two miles, she rolled down the window, letting in the mix of stuffy air and diesel fumes and lit another cigarette. She flicked the ash out of the window, sure that the ashtrays in the car were virginal. Again she challenged him to complain and he made the mistake of trying to joke it off.

'I don't know why you don't staple your fags together – you could smoke yourself to death twice as fast.'

'Not funny,' she snapped. 'You tried to drink yourself to death. That was acceptable behaviour, was it? If you want to tell me to stop smoking why don't you have the guts to come straight out with it?'

'And if I did?' He knew he was being drawn into an argument but he seemed to have no choice but to continue riding into the valley of death.

'Then I'd tell you to mind your own business.'

'I worry about you,' he said softly.

'You needn't.'

'Look, Patti, you had a really close call with that bullet wound,' he said.

'That's what I get for trying to rescue your daughter,' she replied without a trace of the humour she would normally have injected into such a statement. He should have shut up then, but he couldn't stand the silence from somebody he so needed to talk to.

'All I'm saying is that you'd have had to have the constitution of an ox to have made a full recovery already. I can't believe your doctor knows you're still smoking.'

'Oh, you'd better believe it. He knows. I told him.'

'And he approved?'

'No. But he's less devious than you – and he also knows he can do fuck all about it.'

She blew smoke out of the window and, despite the fact that none of it drifted back into the interior of the car, Mark found himself instinctively coughing. Patti clearly thought it was a gesture, an affectation calculated to annoy her. She took one last drag and then reluctantly tossed half a cigarette into the road, hesitated for a moment then lit up a third. She'd once told him she only smoked because she was bored, and he had seen what happened when she became bored at earlier stages in their relationship. Whatever it was that was on her mind she was not ready to share the burden with Mark.

In the elegant dining room they ate together in almost complete silence. Normally she drank little when she was with him. She realised how difficult it was for an ex-alcoholic to be around people drinking wine. Tonight, however, she finished a bottle on her own. Again he could do nothing to stop her without incurring her wrath. Yet, as glass after glass disappeared, the waiter finally dismissed as she emptied the bottle herself, so she became more and more aggressive. He'd seen her in these moods before. Not frequently, but often enough to know that he should be careful to give her no cause for an onslaught. He did not love her any the less in the long term but for the moment he was treading on egg-shells.

They were seated by the window and even in the darkness of the night he could see clearly the white water of the weir tumbling outside. Wild water that man tried to control. Patti was like that. You could swim in her, cool off beside her, but she was untameable. Sitting with her as she struggled for life in the hospital bed he had asked her to marry him. But she had been unconscious and it didn't work like it did in romantic novels. Her eyes had not opened wide at the sound of his voice, but rather she had slumped deeper into her coma, a coma from which for a time it had seemed she would never emerge. When she did finally surface into the daylight he had not had the courage to put the question again. They did not even live together on a permanent basis as she wanted to retain the independence that the Burrow gave her.

'If I want to sleep alone then I can sleep alone. And if I want to wake up beside you then I can always call you to come over. And if I fancy a change then I can find a dishy footballer to shag.' She'd smiled then, but he wondered at this moment whether or not in his absence she did always sleep alone. He did have a set of keys to the Burrow but on the one occasion he'd gone around there uninvited and let himself in she had gone ballistic even though she had been quite on her own.

He'd not repeated the mistake. Sometimes he wondered why he did not stand up to her more. He knew the fact that he simply did not argue drove her crazy at times, but he had had enough dissent in his life. It was easier to remain silent and he was becoming increasingly good at it. In his mind he justified his failure to propose by a reluctance to put any pressure on her as she returned to health. In the real world, however, it was an act of cowardice, a surprising response from a man who had faced death and destruction on more than one occasion.

The church clock across the river struck eleven. He yawned, and a shadow of irritation flickered across her face making her seem far older than her years. Her red hair was pulled straight off her face and tied severely at the back, giving her a look of sophistication that contrasted starkly with the mischievous expression he'd first seen in her eyes some two years before. Two years. It seemed incredible that they'd only known each other for such a relatively brief period of time. He could scarcely remember pre-Patti days, PP as they called the period in their happier times together. But, given his intake of alcohol at the time, his loss of memory was hardly surprising. He'd fought hard for her during the relationship, not just for her but for himself too, and he would not be giving it up without a struggle.

'Are you trying to tell me it's time for bed?' she asked.

'I'm ready if you're ready,' he replied.

'I'm ready for sleep.' She looked him straight in the eye. 'And I mean sleep. Don't even think about anything else. Lay one finger on me and I'll move to the settee.'

Mark said nothing. She had a remarkable talent at times for making him feel cheap. As if by taking her to an expensive hotel he was trying to buy sexual favours. His silence seemed to annoy her more. She had an inner anger that the drink had fuelled rather than subdued and for a moment he thought she was going to storm out of the room and cause a scene in front of the few remaining diners. Instead she rose a little unsteadily to her feet, waving away the waiter who solicitously made to pull back her chair. She swayed for a moment, then steadied herself, finally leaning on Mark for support with obvious reluctance. Together they made their way up the narrow staircase to their room which also overlooked the river. Mark stood at the window admiring the view, reluctant to draw the curtains and remove it from sight.

Behind him he could hear Patti undressing for bed, her clothes dropped in a casual heap on the carpet.

'What is it, Patti? What's wrong?' he asked without turning around.

'I'm tired and I don't want to talk about it now.'

'When then?' he persisted, knowing he should not push the point at this time of night, but also certain that he would not sleep unless they made some progress in their conversation.

'Mark, I don't want to talk. About this mysterious "it", or anything. OK? Or do you need a translator?'

Again he did not answer. He understood all too well. Instead he watched the lights of the hotel play on the river, dancing with the restless current. He stood for a long time. The church clock struck midnight and when he finally undressed and went to bed, Patti was so deeply asleep that she did not stir and he did not try to touch her.

CHAPTER 4

Mohammed Halid did not feel his age. This year he would be fifty and, with his son Nabil now twenty-three and his daughter Dominique eighteen, he would seem to have every reason to start counting the grey hairs in the mirror; that was if he could bring himself to look into the mirror.

Susie had changed all that. She was nearly twenty years younger and she had given him Jason just a year ago and, with a young wife and an infant son in his life, he was beginning to count backwards. He was also actually spending more time in front of the mirror than he could recall since his teens. Susie had rekindled the pride in his appearance that had threatened to vanish for ever after twenty-five years of marriage to his first wife, Yasmin. Both he and Yasmin had been young and slim when they'd met in pre-revolutionary Tehran. The city was beautiful then and they were part of the beautiful set of people themselves. Yet as Halid prospered so Yasmin had gradually become a less significant part of his life, and to compensate she had begun to eat. She ate steadily and relentlessly until the young attractive girl she had been was as much a part of history as Tehran's five star hotels.

It did not take too long for Mohammed to realise that his future and that of his family lay beyond his native Iran. Many of his countrymen were moving to the States but Mohammed decided to make London his base. He had a double expertise. He'd trained in communications and he was a natural salesman. He'd already established a business in Tehran. Cables, satellites, mobile phones, they were all a dream of the future when he started out, but he anticipated them all. When they were still close Yasmin had described him proudly as 'my own H.G. Wells'. She liked to read English classics and as her husband became more and more entwined in his business so she read more and more. And always by her side as she devoured English literature

23

was a box of chocolates, a plate of biscuits or a bag of cakes. Halid liked London. The cosmopolitan nature of the city reminded him of home although he found it less class conscious. Here a man was judged by what he achieved, not who his family had been, or at least so it appeared in the day-to-day world of Halid's business. Later he learned of all the prejudices of the City, and realised that to the bankers and brokers it did not matter how much money he had, he was still just another grubby Arab clawing his way up the social ladder. Arabs and Jews: there might be an eternal conflict between the two races, but as far as the anti-Semites were concerned they were both equal targets. And so it was with a certain inevitability that Halid met Nathan Carr. Nathan was London born and bred although hardly English through and through. His parents had been born in England but his grandparents had escaped the pogroms of Russia and Poland to seek a new life in what they thought would be the tolerant world of Edwardian Britain. En route Nathan's grandfather had changed his name from Cohen to Carr in honour of the first motor vehicle he had ever seen.

Curiously enough they had met through one of the bankers that Halid came so to despise. They'd both been invited to a lunch at Granby's in Frogmorton Street. Halid's company was being courted by more than one merchant bank as a potential target for a flotation. Carr was more into the world of media and entertainment. Halid never discovered whether or not Granby's believed there was a genuine synergy between the two companies or whether they simply did not want to impose the two outsiders on their more prestigious clientele.

However, the fact of the matter was that Halid and Carr hit it off immediately. In looks they could not have been more different. Halid was of average height, his hair already grey and the nose aquiline. At times he looked more like a Red Indian Chief than a Middle Eastern trader. He dressed, subtly, traditionally; sombre suits, delicate, pearl-grey ties. His voice was as soft as his hands, well modulated, the accent there for all to hear, although difficult to place. He had seen what gluttony had done to his wife and he was beginning to make the effort to keep himself trim. He had taken on a personal trainer who worked with him every morning and the results were beginning to show.

Carr was tall, well over six feet, his large frame topped by a mass of black unruly hair that always looked in need of a trim yet was the subject of a weekly visit by the hairdresser to his office. Although he was younger than Halid he needed spectacles to see beyond his hand and had never come to terms with the use of contact lenses. Behind the glasses, the chameleon eyes had an expression of permanent, cynical amusement as if this was the only way he could tolerate the madness that was going on in the world around him. His face had a slightly lop-sided look about it, not aided by the broken nose that would have been more in place on a boxer than a successful businessman. Carr never offered an explanation for the break, preferring his rivals to believe it resulted from a fight, when in fact it had occurred on the rugby field at the public school to which his parents had sent him in the hope it would rub smooth the rough edges that he had inherited from his transient grandparents.

In fact, Carr had left the school considerably rougher than when he had joined it. He was the only Jewish boy in his class and, although he'd not thought of himself as particularly Jewish when he'd begun his education, he was left in no doubt about it by the time he finished it. One look at his circumcised penis in the changing room and he was nicknamed 'Chopper' and whilst he left school without any great educational qualifications he left with the name 'Chopper Carr' hanging around his neck like an albatross. One of the major lessons he did learn was never to try to hide one's roots, but rather to use them instead. The bullying that at times bordered on persecution had given him the identity of which his parents had deprived him. By the time Nathan Carr met Mohammed Halid he was making no attempt to hide the fact that he was Jewish and proud of it.

The host banker had found it difficult to bring the lunch to an end when Halid and Carr had met for that first time, and, indeed, as they'd left the building together, they'd gone first to a pub, then to a coffee shop and finally to a restaurant to try to discover everything there was to know about themselves. It was only some years later, after their merger, after the bitter dissolution of their partnership, that they discovered it was not possible to know everything about any other person.

Waking on this July morning Halid thought of his time with Carr. He found himself thinking more and more of him nowadays. They may have started out in different fields but they were now deadly rivals. Halid had his company, Ball Park, and Carr had been left with Jet. They were the two fastest growing production empires in the world of media and it was as inevitable that they would meet in the first place that now their paths would cross as they both targeted the same business opportunities with relentless zeal. Halid knew Carr well enough to know that if they were set on a collision course he would not be the one to change direction. He also knew that whatever partnership, whatever friendship, there had been between them was long over and was damaged beyond repair.

The woman beside Halid slept on. Her night had been disturbed by little Jason, at one year old enough to know he was having a bad dream, but not old enough to decide it was nothing more than that. It had taken her a long time to soothe him back to sleep and Halid wished that his own fears could be so easily dispelled.

He stared hard at her fair skin, her youthful complexion, the domestic and maternal strain of the day removed by sleep. She slept like an angel, with the calm serenity she had brought into his life. Susie, his love, Susie, his wife. Yes, she and Jason were indeed the reasons he did not feel his age. They had achieved the impossible by turning back the hands of time.

Yet, for every miracle there was a price. In this case it had been his friendship with his business partner. Because Susie Halid, the mother of his infant child, until she had come to live with him, had been the wife of Nathan Carr.

CHAPTER 5

It was too hot for football. As August tilted into September the sun still beat down remorselessly. It was not so much an Indian summer as a summer that seemed as if was never going to end. Even up on the television gantry Mark Rossetti sat in a T-shirt and shorts, the air still and lifeless, more like the tropics than the south of England. The match being played out beneath him was very much a reaction to the humid atmosphere, and the footballers seemed at times to be treading water. They would make quick darting runs, then pause with hands on knees, bent over like old men trying to catch their breath, their shirts clinging to their skin, sweat pouring down their faces. The coaches rose regularly from their benches to toss water bottles to the team whilst the St John's Ambulance men kept up a steady stream of journeys to rescue spectators afflicted by the heat.

For the first leg of the Coca-Cola second round cup match Hertsmere's visitors were Denley Athletic. Given that Denley had finished bottom of the Third Division and had only been saved from relegation by the shortcomings of the Conference champion's ground, it was hardly surprising that the Park Crescent ground was less than half full.

At one end some two hundred Denley faithfuls had gathered with flags and banners, obviously convinced by the fairly disastrous results this season that this was likely to be the high point of the year. They'd only progressed beyond the first round when their opponents had been reduced to nine men thanks to the efforts of an over-zealous referee and their resistance to Hertsmere had been limited to the first five minutes of the match. At least during those three hundred seconds they had progressed over the halfway line and managed a shot on target, which Greg Sergovitch in the Hertsmere goal had caught with casual ease. Now, however, as half-time approached, Hertsmere had found the back of the net three times, two of them coming from Barry

27

Reed, the other an own goal that the Denley centre-half would relive in his nightmares for the rest of his moderate footballing career.

Having built up the cushion of their lead Hertsmere had then slowed down the pace with all the experience they had gained in Europe. There was a long haul ahead of them and none of them wanted to risk injury or premature burn-out. None of them that was except Barry Reed. Nobody seemed to have told the nineteen-year-old Geordie that the match was as good as won, that they needed to do nothing more than keep a clean sheet, take the odd chance and then go to Denley for the second leg with a team of reserves.

Reed picked the ball up just inside his own half. There were moments when he looked clumsy, almost immobile. He had a huge bull of a head, his close-cropped hair giving him the look of a storm-trooper which belied his quiet, almost shy personality off the field. A casual observer might have thought him fat with his broad shoulders and barrel chest, but at the stomach there was a tapering down to the waist which was so slim as to be at odds with what went above and below. The thighs were unmistakably those of a professional footballer, the legs slightly bowed, the picture as a whole reminiscent in part of Malcolm MacDonald, in part of Paul Gascoigne.

A Denley midfielder came across to challenge and Reed cheekily nutmegged him, placing the ball between his legs with total precision. Before his opponent could turn, Reed was round and past him, drawing a couple of defenders towards him like filings to a magnet. He ran with his head erect, totally aware of what was going on around him without any need to look. Then he suddenly stopped dead. It became a scene from a silent slapstick movie. The two defenders were both in mid-flight, neither could stop and, as they cannoned into each other, Barry had time to pat each of them on the head as they fell before continuing his run. The crowd, who had seemed to be falling asleep in the heat, erupted, aware of the fact that if he scored this was going to be a goal to reminisce over during the long winter evenings for many years to come. As far as Barry Reed was concerned there was no if about him scoring. He saw another defender hurtling in from the left, kicked into top gear and left him for pace. The defender did not know whether to chase him or head for the goal-line as the keeper came out to narrow the angle. Reed pulled wide to the right, neatly side-stepped the goalie and arrogantly side-footed the ball into the net as a confused Denley player belatedly slid across.

Barry stood back and admired his work for a second, a broad grin spreading across his open face. The Hertsmere supporters behind the goal were being actively restrained by stewards as they desperately tried to get near to him to show exactly how they felt. Barry suddenly remembered what he was, who he was and where he was. Instead of clenching his fists in triumph as a reaction to their adulation, he merely gave them a shy wave and trotted back to the centre circle, shrugging off with some embarrassment the embraces of his team-mates.

From his lofty position, Mark's co-commentator, Michael Burridge, had virtually lost his voice in the excitement of his description of the goal. Hoarsely, he handed across to Mark who was watching the action replay on his monitor in some disbelief.

'I'm just trying to reassure myself that really happened. A great goal, one to stand alongside the Bests, the Laws, the Greaves. One, not just for Barry Reed's scrapbook, but for everybody's scrapbook. Forget who the opposition was. Just remember the genius of it.'

The rest of the match was an anti-climax. Hertsmere added a couple more from Tommy Wallace and, with a six goal lead, the last few moments were pure exhibition. Mark heard the producer's voice in his ear through the headphones as he continued his own commentary. He had become accustomed to these interruptions, able to concentrate on his own words while taking instructions as to what he was going to do next.

'Mark, you know young Reed well. Get down off the gantry as soon as you can. We want you to interview him and then Kenny Cunningham who's been here watching.'

'No problem,' Mark muttered as Burridge took over the last few moments of commentary on his own whilst sucking a throat lozenge.

And it was no problem. That was how far he'd come now in broadcasting experience and confidence. He could handle two off-the-cuff interviews without a moment's apprehension, when just a few months ago he'd have been struggling even with a prompt board. He just wished he was making such progress in the rest of his life.

Somehow he seemed doomed never to be able to pull all the loose ends together. Professional, emotional, they were two sides to his existence and like little weather people only one was able to appear at a time.

He caught Barry Reed at the edge of the tunnel. The relatively thin crowd seemed reluctant to disperse, reluctant to let go of the little piece of magic they had witnessed. A hard core group of supporters on what had been the old East Terrace were still chanting his name as Mark began the interview.

'What's it like to be a folk hero when you're still in your teens?'

'I'll be twenty next month. Does that mean I have to stop being a hero?' The reply and the question were given with a straight face and it took a moment for Mark to realise the player was winding him up. 'Anyway,' Barry continued, 'I'm not sure my mam thinks I'm a hero.'

'Your mother's still up in Tyneside?'

'Aye. I'd like to get her down here, but she don't like the south. Says it's a bit posh for the likes of her.'

Again Mark was not sure if the comment was tongue-in-cheek or whether it was said in all innocence. It might well be that there was more to Barry Reed than met the eye. They all started off innocent though. They came from working class backgrounds, they had no academic qualifications, they made a bit of money and then what was there to spend it on? Early marriage, kids, a house, furnish the house, buy your parents a house and furnish that, get them a car because yours is sponsored and have an expensive holiday every year in the few weeks permitted between the end of one season and the rapid approach of the next. If you were wise then the rest went into your pension fund to be available at thirty-five which the Inland Revenue in their generosity accepted as the retirement age for a professional footballer. If you were foolish there was the booze, the horses, the women, the hangers-on. They'd hoover up your money faster than any vacuum cleaner and, once the pockets were empty, well, the booze had to become cheaper, the bottles of Dom Perignon a distant memory; money had to be borrowed for the horses, for that magic bonanza that somehow never came, and the women became older, lined, world-weary before they disappeared together with the hangers-on who no longer had anything on which to hang.

'Bit of a goal that, Barry,' Mark continued.

'I'm sure you scored better, Mark,' Barry replied, 'and anyway, weren't the defences better in your day?'

Mark tried to steer him away from a mutual appreciation society that he did not think the viewers would appreciate. That was something else upon which he had become expert, the boredom threshold of his audience.

'Did you know the England manager was watching tonight?'

'Well, with respect to Denley, I think the opposition might be a tad tougher if I ever get chosen to play for England. I just went out there and did my best like I always do.'

Off the air now, Barry took in a deep breath.

'I don't know as how you can do that all the time. Just thinking about the millions watching fair makes me come out in a cold sweat.'

'You're playing in front of the same millions, even more probably, because I reckon a load of them turn off as soon as the game's finished. I did. I couldn't believe the load of crap the so-called experts spoke.'

Barry paused as if the thought of a television audience out there watching him play had just dawned upon him.

'Yeah. I suppose I am. Only when you're playing, you know, and not talking, it doesn't feel like it. You're playing for the team, for yourself, for my mam and the rest sort of fades into the background.'

'You're obviously very close to your mother,' Mark said with a tinge of envy. He wished his own mother was still alive so that he could do the sort of things for her that Barry was obviously intending for his 'mam'.

'She means the world to me. All the more so since Dad left, although I thought at the time, good riddance to bad rubbish. I reckoned she'd be happier once he'd gone, all that drinking, and the knocking her about. But whatever he was, he did finally come home at night, and when he was sober I suppose he was someone to cuddle up to in bed.'

He seemed more exhausted by the length of the speech than the effort he'd put into the previous ninety minutes.

'Look, I've got to go and get changed. Day off tomorrow and

I'm heading up to the north-east. Thanks for everything, Mark. I'll never forget how you spoke to me after the Cup Final.'

Mark Rossetti stood in the shadows and watched him disappear towards the dressing room. He could not say exactly why, but he feared for him. Feared for his innocence and the loss of it that he knew would certainly come. Feared for his talent and for those who would try to destroy it. Feared for the pressures that he knew would be imposed by the predators in the media, seeking to build him up and then knock him down. Yet, some sixth sense made him fear for him for no real reason at all. Something made Mark Rossetti believe that Barry Reed was the stuff of which victims rather than heroes were made. And it was that premonition that frightened him most of all.

CHAPTER 6

The worst phone calls always come in the middle of the night.

Mohammed Halid had never forgotten how he had been woken at two in the morning to hear the news from a distant country of his father's death. He relived that moment whenever the phone rang after midnight even though his business was of such a nature that nocturnal calls were far from unusual.

He had not been sleeping well. The long hot summer showed no sign of the sharp decline into autumn that usually occurred in England and despite the relentless heat of his childhood, Halid still found sleep hard to achieve when the temperature at night rarely fell below seventy degrees.

So he awoke with the first peal of the bedside phone. Beside him he felt and heard Susie stir in the darkness within her deep slumber, spent and satisfied by the hour of making love before she had finally closed her eyes.

'Hello,' Mohammed said softly, ready to move to his study as soon as he identified the caller.

'Mr Halid?' The voice was rough but official sounding, brusque, sufficiently trained to ensure that the formalities were properly accommodated.

'Yes, yes,' he replied impatiently, 'this is Mr Halid.'

'Mr Mohammed Halid?'

'Yes, this is he. Who is this? What do you want? Do you know what the time is?'

By now Susie was awake, sitting up beside him, the sheet drawn up over her breasts in a poor imitation of modesty. She gripped her husband's arm tightly, sensing something was wrong, even though he did not yet know the identity of the caller.

'I do know what time it is, Mr Halid, and believe me I wouldn't be disturbing you at this hour if it wasn't urgent. My name's Neil Taylor, Detective Sergeant at West Hampstead Police Station. We have a young lady here who says she belongs to you, claims to be your daughter, Dominique Halid.'

'Claims? What do you mean claims?'

'Well, sir,' the calm voice at the other end of the line continued, 'she has no identity on her as such and I'm afraid we've not been able to establish for ourselves with any great degree of certainty exactly who she is.'

'Surely she can tell you?' His voice was cold, his mind now expecting the worst. Yet, if she had been in an accident she would certainly have been in hospital not at some police station, the voice of reason whispered in his ear.

'Well she can and she can't. Let us just say she was not exactly *compos mentis* when we brought her in.'

'You mean she was drunk?' Halid asked, hoping the answer would be yes.

'No, sir, she wasn't drunk. She was very much under the influence of drugs. We're not sure exactly what drugs they were as she had a fair assortment on her person. We offered her the chance to make a phone call, but quite frankly she was hardly in any condition. This is the fifth number we've tried from the combination she gave us and, believe me, I've received more verbal abuse from the four other individuals I've woken up than in all my years on the beat. So, anyway, do I assume that I've hit the jackpot and you do have a daughter called Dominique?'

'I do.'

'And do I also assume she's not tucked up in bed in her Winnie the Pooh nightie?'

'That's correct, although I find your tone offensive.'

'Do you, Mr Halid? Well, let me tell you what I find offensive. I find it offensive when somebody your daughter's age is pushing pills to thirteen-year-olds. I find it offensive that she's so high herself that she doesn't know who she is or where she is, or even how much money she has upon her person from the same illegal pushing of pills to young kids who should be tucked up in bed.'

'In their Winnie the Pooh nighties?' Halid said, although he knew it was hardly the right response.

'I don't think this is a time for flippancy, not when your daughter is looking at quite a long stretch of jail time ahead of her.'

'You have no proof she has committed any crimes,' Mohammed said, suddenly defensive, although he had nothing

34

to support his claim of her innocence.

'Don't I, Mr Halid? Don't I indeed? Well, you're in bed in your expensive house, and I'm down here in my nasty smelly police station, so why don't you join me and we can discuss the little matter of proof. And if you want to bring your doubtless even more expensive lawyer he can join in this discussion as well.'

Halid realised the conversation was at an end and replaced the receiver with a gentleness he did not feel. He did not know Detective Sergeant Neil Taylor and had no particular desire to change that situation. Indeed, if he had met him at that moment he believed he might well have been tempted to inflict sufficient damage on his person to ensure he found himself in a cell alongside his daughter.

Dominique, his daughter, in a cell. It was not a pleasant thought, yet it was not an incredible one either. This was not the first time she had been in trouble, nor the first time that drugs had been involved. Yet, on other occasions they had been able to sort matters out, to gloss them over, to take her home leaving behind generous donations to charities or individuals and the promise that she would not be a naughty girl again. He did not think D.S. Taylor was going to be so easily satisfied. Mohammed could not understand it. She didn't need the money, that was for sure. Whatever any petty cash from drugs could have bought her, Mohammed could have given her ten-fold, a hundred-fold, so what was the appeal, what was it that was driving her on to destruction? In her absence he still thought of her as a small child, so feminine, so vulnerable. She would run to him, fall over and cry and he would hold her tight, kiss the top of her head until it was all better even when it had not been so bad to start with. She had always been closer to him than to her mother. It had been the opposite with his son, Nabil, but that was another story, another problem. Right now he had to focus on Dominique, the Dominique of today not of yesterday, the woman, not the child. Yet was there really so much of a difference? She might well be eighteen but she persisted in behaving as if she were much younger. An adolescent who had never grown up, never grown out of that painful awkward age. For a while he had convinced himself that her behaviour was just a phase; but phases ended and hers never had. He looked at the bedside clock.

Two a.m. Again that hour that brought with it such evil and malevolent spells. Quickly he told Susie what had happened. His previous marriage was just a memory and he knew he could never have spoken so openly to his first wife.

'What are you going to do, Mo?'

'Get dressed. Take the car and try and get her out.'

'No.'

'What do you mean, no?'

'I mean what I say. Leave her for the night. The police think you'll come. If she's capable of thought she thinks you'll come. Disappoint them both and stay with me.'

Halid was half out of bed, his legs on the ground, his buttocks still on the mattress, frozen into a tableau. Yes, he remembered his daughter as a child, yes he could almost feel her pain, but even more recent in his memory was the impression of his wife's fresh young flesh on his skin, the feeling of exultation, of possession, of sheer gratitude as he'd come inside her.

As if in time with his thoughts, her hand reached out to him again, circled his shoulders, his waist, then moved to between his legs.

'Come on, Mo, let's play the up-and-down game again,' she said in their private, intimate language, 'only with more of the up than the down.'

It took him but a second to spring to life beneath her hand. She stroked him gently through the fine cotton of his shorts and as he turned to her she peeled away the material and took him in her mouth.

He struggled for a moment, wondering how long the night would be for his daughter, but then as his wife sucked him fiercely, her teeth raking his sensitive skin with pleasurable pain, everything else was forgotten; and once he had come again with furious spasms he could do nothing else but go back to sleep and wait for the morning when everything would look different.

CHAPTER 7

Detective Sergeant Neil Taylor was surprised to find Dominique Halid still in the cells when he reported back for duty after a few hours snatched sleep. He had sensed her father was the sort of man who would not rest easy until his family were secure within whatever castle he called home.

Neil Taylor didn't live in a castle. He lived in a bedsit in Kilburn and had done ever since he'd returned to his semi-detached in Barnet and found his wife in bed with the decorator. From time to time he railed against the unfairness of the situation. She screwed around, he walked out, she kept the house and he was forced to live in conditions where the proverbial cat would be hard pushed to crouch let alone be swung. When the black mood took him that way then he, in turn, took it out on whoever was in his sights at the time.

He'd hoped it would be Mohammed Halid who would come to negotiate for the release of the girl, but instead he had to settle for the son. He'd never met Mohammed but he knew he'd dislike him just from the conversation he'd had the night before. He had now met Nabil Halid, the son, and he didn't like him either. There was no good reason, but then he was in a position where he needed no reason at all, good or otherwise. That was one of the great advantages of being a copper, you didn't need a reason to do anything. Seeing the father and the brother he was almost beginning to feel sorry for Dominique. Almost, but not quite. The boy didn't want to be here, didn't want to be his father's messenger and certainly didn't want to be dealing with the likes of Neil Taylor. That was tantamount to getting his hands dirty. All Nabil wanted was to see his sister, put her in the car and take her home. Only it wasn't going to be that simple. Taylor was going to make sure of that.

He could have released her in her own surety, that was within his powers. He knew now who she was, knew where she lived and was reasonably confident that she'd turn up in court in due course to face the charges; but he didn't have to let her go and truth be told he was in no mood to expedite her release. In fact he was in a particularly sour mood. He'd thought he'd cracked it with the manageress of the local wine bar, but when he'd got home the message on his answerphone had left him in no doubt he was mistaken. He didn't know how he could have forgotten that he'd agreed to pick her up at midnight to take her home. That was when he'd been sure that he'd be off duty. But that was also before they'd asked him to deal with Miss Halid, and a couple of hours dragging incoherent answers from her drugged-up lips in the presence of an impatient police doctor and a not unattractive WPC had been enough to drive Janie from his mind. The message suggested he was not to be given a second chance to recall her.

'Constable, when can I take my sister out of this place?' the young man asked, in a tone that suggested she might well catch some contagious disease if she stayed there a moment longer.

Taylor looked up slowly. He was a large, heavy man who knew he needed to shed a couple of stone to get him down to his pre-marital break-up weight. Often people said that he looked like Brian Blessed in his *Z-Cars* days and he quite liked modelling himself on the role of Fancy Smith. He could bring an expression to his eyes of bovine indifference that made whoever was addressing him despair that the message was getting through. Then, as an alternative, there was an expression of barely controlled rage that made people doubt if they were dealing with a man who was playing with a full deck. He had not really mastered any emotion in between and had not actually had the need to do so. The latter emotion came to hand for the likes of teenagers who'd been caught stealing the poor box from the local church and that was the look he now turned upon Nabil Halid, causing him to glance around to see if there was anybody within sight who might be about to witness the assault on his person that this policeman was about to launch.

'It's Detective Sergeant to you, sonny, and I'm not at all sure that your sister is going to be going home today – or for a long time for that matter. I don't like drug pushers and the court doesn't favour them either.'

'My sister isn't a drug pusher. She may have been duped into

38

taking some drugs but she has no need to sell them.'

He cast his eyes around the station, now satisfied the policeman was not about to hit him, this time as if trying to give Taylor the message that if the Halid family so desired, they could buy the whole building, the detective sergeant included. Any income from drug-trafficking would be small change indeed.

'Need doesn't always have a lot to do with things,' Taylor replied, speaking deliberately slowly, slipping into his Mr Plod mode. 'I've known the sons of millionaires kill for a hundred quid where there are drugs involved; or worse still over a girl.'

No, he thought to himself, no girl's worth killing for or else that decorator with the pecs would have gone long ago.

Nabil Halid seemed lost for words. He was a good-looking boy, there was no doubt of that, his skin mediterranean rather than middle-eastern, his eyes the colour of olives, the lashes feminine in their length, his hair dark and thick, tied back into a pony tail. There the hippie look ended as he was clean-shaven and immaculately dressed despite the early hour of the morning. Taylor had little doubt that this was not a young man who would slob out in front of the television in a tracksuit with a take-away at his side. This was a young man who regarded himself as a crown prince, as the heir-apparent to the family fortunes. So what had gone wrong with the sister? Neil Taylor wasn't one for playing amateur psychology. Normally he assumed a person was a crook because they had done something dishonest and he was none too concerned about whether or not they'd been abused as a child or were misunderstood by their nanny.

'May I make a phone call?' Nabil asked, the tone reluctantly polite.

'Of course, sir. You'll find a public telephone just along the corridor.'

Nabil bit his lip. He didn't like to ask what he now had to request but he had no choice.

'I was wondering if I could use *your* phone. I seem to have left home without any money or charge cards.'

Neil Taylor nearly smiled. This was good. This was a windfall. Not quite good enough to make him forget the lost opportunity with Janie from the wine-bar, but pretty good for all that.

'Sorry about that. I'd love to help.' He accentuated the love so that Nabil was left in no doubt that it was the last emotion he actually felt. 'I'm afraid we can't allow any private civilian calls, other than the one we allow to our invited guests – and, of course, your sister's already had the benefit of that. I'm assuming that you don't want to confess anything to encourage me to arrest you?'

He paused wanting to see the effect of his refusal on Nabil.

'Who was it that you were wanting to call?'

'Our family lawyer,' Nabil replied, unable to conceal his frustration. 'If you won't let me call perhaps you'd lend me ten pence. I trust your policeman's salary extends to that.'

It was the wrong thing to say. Taylor had, until that moment, every intention of making arrangements for Nabil to make the call, but now he decided he needed teaching a further lesson. Ostentatiously he tapped his pockets, carefully avoiding jingling the change in his jacket, then removing his wallet, flipping through the notes he'd budgeted to spend on Janie in front of Halid's face.

'Well, it doesn't look as if I've anything smaller than a twenty. So why don't you take a seat, relax and I'll let you know when I've finished with your sister. Or maybe someone will come on duty to replace me and from whom you can borrow a coin for your call – that is if you ask them nicely.'

Someone to replace him. That sounded good. He shouldn't be on duty at all. He'd done his stint last night but when Tucker had phoned in sick they'd not hesitated to rouse him out of a bed he seemed just to have tumbled into.

Nabil began to bluster. He was not used to being treated this way and he did not think a reverse charge call to his father telling him he'd not even been able to arrange a call to Henry Freeman, the family solicitor, would go down very well. Of course, he should have rung before he'd left home, his father had told him to do so, but he'd thought he'd be able to cope with it all himself once he'd got down to the station, that everybody would roll over and kow-tow to his every whim. Yet, he wasn't coping. Not at all.

'Can I at least see my sister, Detective Sergeant?' he asked, making a point of getting his rank accurate, then adding the word, 'Please.'

Taylor stood for a moment as if considering a request that

might be within his gift if he pulled a string or two and then shook his head.

'Sorry, sir. You call your solicitor when you've cracked a way of doing that, and perhaps by the time he gets here, then *he'll* be able to see her; but family visits at this moment in time? No, I don't think so. Although if you'd like to get your father down here, then obviously I'd reconsider. No promises, mind. Now, if you'll excuse me I've got some paperwork to complete on your sister's case.'

He looked at his watch. Ten in the morning. Probably too early to try and make his peace with Janie. No phone call, flowers, chocolate or champagne were likely to wangle his way into her bed.

'Yes, I've got a good few more hours yet. Overtime you understand, Mr Halid. We poor coppers need to make all the money we can . . . Down to the last ten pence.' And with that parting shot he left Nabil Halid angrily checking his Rolex watch.

CHAPTER 8

Mark Rossetti sat with his second cup of coffee of the morning. There was an odd feeling in the offices of Ball Park Productions that something monumental was about to happen. A fuse had been lit and everybody had withdrawn to avoid the explosion.

The headlines in the morning papers had all been about the arrest of Dominique Halid; but the focus of the stories had been her famous and powerful father, the media magnate who always tried to shrink back from the spotlight. One of the tabloids had obtained an old photo of the girl with her breasts virtually out of a tight dress, another had a picture of her holding her father's hand on the way to a movie premiere. Neither of them were calculated to please Mohammed Halid any more than the sensational nature of the story against the background of what were less than sensational facts.

'I can't believe the old man let it get this far,' said Nick Donaldson, the company's Head of Sport.

'What do you mean?' Mark asked, a little naively.

'She's a bit wild is our little Dominique, but she's not what you'd call really bad. There's been a bit of trouble before and our esteemed owner seems to have been able to smooth it over.'

'So what happened this time, do you reckon, Nick?'

The question was asked by Richard Conway, the company's star director. Conway had achieved a certain reputation in the business. If there was a sniff of a story then he would be on hand to direct a programme about it. If there wasn't even a sniff then he'd create a smell by making a programme in any event. He was the despair of the company's lawyers and the bogeyman of their insurers. It took a maverick like Mohammed Halid to recognise the talents of a maverick like Richard Conway and, perhaps of more significance, to tame them sufficiently to enable him to focus on his undoubted talents. It had been one of Halid's masterstrokes to have Conway work under Donaldson and then to put them both on the main board of Ball Park. They seemed to work like gin and tonic, one both diluted and complemented the other, making him less lethal but never totally removing his kick.

Nick Donaldson was a bull of a man, an Oxford rugby blue who'd probably been good enough to play for England if he'd not caught the media bug. Short cropped curly hair, a mis-shapen nose, a cheerful smile made lop-sided by the absence of a couple of teeth he'd not been vain enough to have had replaced.

Richard Conway was the complete opposite, small, wiry, totally dependent upon thick glasses which some of his camera crew delighted in hiding to give them the chance to watch him stagger around like Mr Magoo in vain search of them. Whilst Donaldson never spoke without thinking and even then slowly and carefully, Conway fired out his words in an endless stream of staccato messages, each almost inevitably upsetting someone in the target area. He seemed oblivious to this fact, just as he seemed right now to be uncaring of the minefield through which he tip-toed in extracting information about the arrest of his boss's daughter.

'What happened, Dickie?' Donaldson replied, knowing full well that Conway hated to be addressed in that luvvie-mode. 'What happened, is that our leader depended upon our junior leader and our junior leader in the shape of Nabil, fucked it up big time.'

Mark was not at the offices often enough to understand in sufficient detail the political in-fighting that seemed to be a daily way of life for the Halid family and those who worked for them.

'I'm not sure I understand,' he said, curious all the same.

'Very simple,' Donaldson continued in the concise way he would use to present a new project to the board. 'It appears, or so it is alleged, that Mohammed entrusted the immediate release of his daughter from Her Majesty's custody to his son. Within a relatively short space of time, son, one Nabil, so seriously pisses off the copper in charge, that daddy has to go down to the station himself accompanied by big-time expensive lawyer, Henry Freeman. Eventually the not-so-happy family are reunited, but that's not the end of the story. Charges are pressed, not dropped. Mo has a fight on his hands and Nabil fails the test. Somehow I don't think Mo's going to be in the best of moods when he turns up, particularly as someone seems to have tipped off the tabloids to enable Dominique to feature in the later editions.' Donaldson spread the papers out on the desk. 'In a way you have to admire these guys, getting all those details together so quickly and all before dawn breaks over the metropolis. Nice to know somebody works while London sleeps.'

'So where's Mohammed now?' Mark asked, knowing they were all due to meet later that afternoon for a scheduling brief.

It was Conway's turn to click into gossip mode.

'Well, if past history is anything to go by, he's either sulking or throwing a temper tantrum.'

The phone rang, Donaldson's direct line, to interrupt the speculation. As the noise level around him continued unabated he put his finger to his lips and mouthed the word, 'Mo' as if in the presence of a deity. It was a tribute to the personality of the company's head that one moment his staff could be chatting about his daughter, the next jumping to attention because they realised he was back in the game.

Donaldson's contribution to the telephone conversation appeared to be somewhat limited. The occasional 'sure' or 'yes' or 'certainly', but apart from that there was merely nodded acquiescence. From the expression on the face of the Head of Sport what Halid had to say was both of interest and a challenge. Eventually he replaced the receiver and puffed out both his cheeks.

'Well, Dominique or no Dominique, Mo's really going for it this time. He wants the ESL.'

'Don't we all,' said Conway, 'but wanting's not always getting as my apple-cheeked old grannie used to say.'

'It usually is where Mo is concerned. Can't remember the last failure, can you?'

'Getting his daughter off a drugs charge?' Conway retorted like a shot.

Mark looked puzzled. These men had worked together long enough almost to have their own form of communication and he was a stranger in their country still learning the language. He knew all about the ESL, the European Super League. It had been dreamed of for years and now it was about to become reality.

'I thought the rights for that were long gone,' he said.

44

'So did everybody except our Mo. He's had the lawyers working overtime and has been able to persuade the ESL management committee that they have to put it out for re-tender unless they want to be dragged through every court in Europe for the next five years.'

'Bright lawyers,' Mark commented.

'No doubt, but bright Mo as well,' Donaldson continued, 'you've never really seen him operate when he's all fired up. If the lawyers have done something it's because Mo told them; if they found something then it's because he told them to go look.'

'What does he want us to do?' Conway asked.

'Meet with him,' Donaldson replied.

'When?'

'Like now.' Donaldson's tone reflected exactly what he'd been instructed by Halid.

'So we just drop everything?' Conway asked.

'Seems so. He wants us on the boat just as soon as we can get there.'

'The boat, eh? Must be serious. All luxuries, no interruptions. Where's it berthed?'

'Nowhere glam, I'm afraid. Not for us a jolly jaunt to the Riviera. It's beautiful Southampton. He's sending the car for us right away.'

Mark had just sat and listened. If the company got the rights then obviously he'd like to be a part of the commentary team, but until then there didn't seem to be a lot he could do. He rose to his feet to leave the two men to prepare for their journey.

'I guess I'll be off then. Places to go, people to see.' It didn't sound very convincing. In fact he had nothing to do for the rest of the day and the only person he wanted to see was Patti who'd told him only that morning that she'd be out of circulation for a while, working on a new project, the details of which she had shown no inclination to confide to him. Whether it was sudden, unexpected, convenient or simply fictional, he had no idea. He had no idea at all with Patti at the moment. Were they still going out together or were they going nowhere at all? The events that had happened to them should have welded them closer together, but at the moment seemed rather to have forced them apart. Donaldson put his hand on Mark's shoulder and pushed him back into his seat.

45

'The people and the places will have to wait, Rossetti. His master commands and we must obey, just like the Daleks. The invite to the boat was for three not two. I don't know what you've done right – or some may say wrong – but you're coming with us.' He glanced at his watch. 'You've got time for one quick call, as the police say. You can call your lawyer, or your date. Either way it's to say that you're cancelling.'

Mark smiled and shrugged, pleased, yet vaguely embarrassed, to be part of the team.

'I don't need to make a call.'

'And all those pressing appointments?' Conway asked waspishly, sensing he might have found a weak spot in yet another human being, which if he probed long and hard enough would give him hours of enjoyment.

'I lied,' Mark said, taking the wind out of Conway's sails, and as Donaldson laughed, the receptionist called up to say their car was ready.

CHAPTER 9

It took him about an hour on board Mohammed Halid's boat before Mark realised just how far he had travelled. Not just that day because the ride in the car to the coast had been swift and smooth, his two companions relatively quiet, both dozing on and off in the sure knowledge their employer would expect them to be fully awake for the rest of the day. 'And probably most of the night too,' Conway had said. 'Once Mo gets hold of an idea, he's like a dog obsessed with a bone. He worries at it, and then worries at it some more, until he's buried it where nobody else can find it. Then, just when you think it's lost for ever, he digs it up and carries it around in triumph.'

The bone in question was not yet buried. The bone was Ball Park's agenda to get the television rights for the ESL and, to Mark's surprise, he was regarded by Halid as a vital component.

'You see, Mark, you have a certain status in this world of football.'

Mark couldn't resist a wry smile.

'You wouldn't have said that a couple of years ago, Mohammed.'

'Mo. Everybody calls me Mo. It's more western, more appropriate. We're all friends here. These guys only think they work for me. Really I work for them. Believe me, Mark, soon I'll be working for you. You understand football and you understand football people. Nick here is a jack of all trades. Golf, tennis, basketball, women's mud-wrestling. You name it and he knows a bit about it. A bit, mind you, not a lot. He's not an expert, not like you are when it comes to football. Richard, great with the cameras, knows exactly what his audience wants to see. But he's an artist. So, I have a dilettante and an artist; and now I also have an expert. You're my team and I expect my team to win. Not at all cost, you understand, but fairly and because you're the best.'

He poured himself a cup of Turkish coffee, so strong that it seemed the spoon might stand up in it. There was a drinks cabinet in the corner, towards which both Donaldson and Conway cast longing glances, but all that was on offer was coffee and some water. Halid wanted his men focused and alcohol was likely to blur that focus.

Mark had no proof that Halid knew of his alcoholic past, but he suspected he had done his groundwork. He guessed that he did not undertake any venture without doing all the research he felt necessary.

'What's our time frame, Mo?' Donaldson asked, realising that the quicker things progressed the quicker he could get back to a chilled glass of dry white wine and equally dry land. He had never particularly liked the sea and the slight swell that had got up since their arrival had given his cheek-bones a greenish tinge.

'It's tight,' Halid replied. 'The lawyers did their job well in prising open the window of opportunity, but we have to be in Zurich in two weeks time with both our proposal and tender.'

'Two weeks!' Conway whistled. 'You have to be joking.'

'Richard. You should know by now that if I am going to appeal to your sense of humour, I preface the attempt with the statement that I have a joke to tell you. No, I'm perfectly serious. Nick, you're not feeling too good?'

'I feel a bit queasy, Mo, to tell you the truth.'

'I hope you will always tell me the truth, Nick. I have never liked falsehoods. You should have said,' Halid continued, knowing full well that now that he, rather than Donaldson, had raised the issue, it was an acceptable one for discussion. 'Come on. We'll go up on deck and take in the fresh air. You'll soon feel better.'

Nick Donaldson almost ran up the steep steps, thinking not for the first time what a clever manipulator of men was Mohammed Halid. A small gesture, yet he had him feeling a wave of gratitude. He didn't want to think of waves at that moment. There were enough waves of nausea already running through his body. The fresh air hit them all like a smack in the face as the wind blew in from the Solent. Mark was still in the same short-sleeved polo-neck shirt in which he'd arrived at the office and he shivered with cold. It was crazy. All those years on the field and in training wearing only shorts and light shirts, years playing on frozen northern wastes on January nights and he'd never felt a hint of cold. Yet, here he was in early autumn, desperately in need of a sweater. He was getting soft and he didn't know what, if anything, he could do about it.

He'd not noticed the name on the boat as they'd stepped aboard, but now he could hardly fail to realise it was called *Susie*. The name was everywhere on the vessel. The lifebelts, the exterior of the captain's cabin, wherever there was a square inch of white paint, there was the name in a delicate shade of blue. Whosoever Susie was, Halid was determined to make public his feeling for her.

Mark did not need to wait long for an explanation.

'You like the boat, I think, Mark. We have some sweatshirts or jumpers aboard if you feel cold.'

There was not a lot Halid missed, Mark realised, and made a permanent mental note for the future.

'It is a tribute to my wife, Susie. A present from me to her on our wedding.'

Richard had shepherded Nick towards the prow of the boat to enable the wind to meet him straight in the face and a note of intimacy crept into Halid's voice. It was just he and Mark together, men who had seen and experienced the variety of emotions that life had to offer. Although Mark had worked at the station he knew little about the owner's private life, had not even known his wife's name until today. This was the first time he had been alone with Halid for more than a few casual moments in the corridor or at the coffee machine. Mark had learned enough about human nature over the past few years to recognise the symptoms of a man's need to talk, his need to confide, to recognise when a man was lonely. And Mohammed Halid at that particular moment seemed to be a lonely man with a burning desire to talk.

'She is much younger than me, my Susie, you know.'

Halid looked sideways at Mark, almost shyly, as if to satisfy himself that the other man was neither laughing at him nor embarrassed by the confidence.

'Does that matter?' Mark asked. He didn't know why people felt able to confide in him, just why they felt the urge to open up, but it had stood him in good stead in his days as a private investigator and he saw no reason to hide that talent under a bushel now that he had retired.

'I have little doubt that they gossip about it and have a laugh behind my back.'

'They may gossip, but I doubt if they laugh. I'm not sure that you're the sort of man that others laugh about.'

'You're an honest man, Mark. I'm pleased to have you on board.'

'The boat or the team?'

Halid threw back his head and laughed, delighted by his unintentional pun. Mark just smiled politely.

'I like you, Mark. You do not need to humour me. The others would have pretended to have found the joke as hilarious as me. But you do not need this job, you do not need me, so you can be true to yourself, be your own man. That is good. We are going to work well together.'

Halid paused, as if considering whether to open up fully, then the decision made as swiftly as he apparently made all decisions in his life, he plunged on with the conversation.

'We have a chance with ESL, but we do not have certainty. When Nick finishes his retching we'll get back to the drawing board and I can explain my strategy; but by opening up the race once again I have also opened a . . .' He struggled for the words, refusing to ask Mark for any assistance. He was not the sort of man to ask for any help, Mark felt, even when something far more important than an elusive English phrase was at stake. 'Yes, I have opened a Pandora's Box,' Halid said triumphantly. 'We are in the lead for these rights, but only because I have fired the starting pistol. I can hear them panting after me in pursuit. I can smell his breath on the air.'

'His?' Mark asked as the plural turned to the singular.

The question seemed to calm Halid down, to make him less dramatic in his analysis of the situation.

'Of course, I am forgetting that you never met my ex-partner, Nathan Carr. If you had met him then you would not forget either him or his name. He would make quite sure of that. Nathan Carr owns Jet TV. You've heard of it?' he asked with heavy sarcasm, knowing that anybody who was deeply involved in sport could not have failed to have heard of it.

Mark nodded and then, sensing something more was required of him, added, 'Sure. Go on. Tell me about Nathan Carr and this Pandora's Box.'

'I can see I have your attention. I can also see I'm beginning to stretch your patience with my games. That's fine too. I admire men who have a low boredom threshold. They usually have an incisive mind.' He turned and looked Mark square in the face. 'Yes, I think you have an incisive mind, Mark Rossetti.'

'I'm grateful for the compliment. Test me. I'm still curious about Nathan Carr.'

'Well, let me satisfy you. I know Carr wanted the ESL rights from way back; but when they seemed to have gone elsewhere he gave up. Now I've put them back in the ring he's going to want them all over again. He'll want them all the more badly because he'll know that I want them and anything I want he has to have.'

'He sounds a little childish.'

'Childish? No, not a word I'd use to describe Nathan Carr. Children are innocent. He never was innocent, although there was a time when I thought he was at least honest.'

'You sound as if you hate him,' Mark said quietly.

'No, I don't hate him. He hates me. He envies our success.'

'He's probably not alone in that, but that wouldn't justify the sort of depth of emotion you're describing.'

'It doesn't. The hatred stems from the fact he believes I stole his wife. You see Susie was once married to him.'

'And did you steal her?' Mark asked, wondering even as he asked whether he was probing too far.

'No, I don't think so. To steal something it has to belong to somebody else and it had been a long time since Susie belonged to Nathan if, indeed, she ever did.'

Then as suddenly as he had begun his story he decided it was at an end.

'So. If Nick is ready and cleaned up shall we go back to the cabin? We've a long two weeks ahead of us. Believe me, Carr will be working his men at Jet twenty-four hours a day.'

'So what do we do about that?' Mark asked.

'We work twenty-five,' Halid replied and, although he smiled as he spoke, Mark did not get the impression that he believed that to be in any way impossible.

CHAPTER 10

It had been a long and exhausting week since what had turned into an all-nighter on the boat. Mo Halid not only expected Nick, Richard and Mark to be working on the presentation and tender for ESL in Zurich, but also to be attending to their normal duties at the station.

'Why don't you tell him to stick his presentation where the sun doesn't shine?' Patti had asked when she'd finally found a moment to place him in her busy schedule for dinner. 'You don't need his crummy job. There are a lot more useful things you could be doing than preening yourself on the little screen or trying to get him these ELS rights.'

'ESL,' Mark corrected her.

'Whatever. It's going to be a stupid league, driven by rich people who want to be richer. Come on, Mark. You know I like football. That's how we met for Christ's sake. But it's all going mad. Wages, prices, TV exposure. Last Sunday I worked out I could have watched five matches if I'd juggled around with my set and my video. It's too much of a good thing. They'll kill the golden goose, believe me.'

'Do I detect a note of sour grapes being served with this cooked goose?' he asked. It was the wrong question.

'No, you don't. It's just that I care about you, although there are times when I wonder why. I can see what's happening. You're being sucked into a world that just isn't you.'

'How do you know what is or isn't me any more? We've hardly seen each other. You come up with some project that may or may not exist. That's fine for you. I start to get involved in something I really enjoy, something I feel I might actually be quite good at and it's like the end of the world. What is this all of a sudden? You're Mother Teresa and I'm Attila the Hun?'

He was angry with himself for becoming angry when he'd made a private promise that they'd just have a pleasant evening out at one of their old haunts. But she was pushing him, had been pushing him since the evening began and he was tired, too tired to maintain the control he desired. And now she had pushed him just beyond the edge. He'd intended staying the night at the Burrow, but as he double-parked his car outside, she slammed the door shut with machine-rattling force and stamped down the steps leading to her flat before he could tell her he thought it might be better if they slept alone. He was so tired and he felt that if they spent much longer in each other's company they would both say something they would regret for ever. Yet, as soon as the decision had been taken by her he felt deprived, felt as if the night no longer held anything for him, dreaded the thought of rolling into his own bed and finding no comfort without the warmth of her body next to him. At that moment he was lost with her and lost without her.

That had happened a couple of days after his visit to Southampton and had given him the excuse to throw himself body and soul into the project if, indeed, he needed an excuse.

To add to his work burden Kenny Cunningham had pulled Barry Reed into his squad for the friendly match against Colombia. The experienced Steve Mercer had cried off with a knee injury and the England manager had clearly been impressed by what he had seen when watching Hertsmere's Geordie midfielder. Halid was never one to miss an opportunity and knowing of Mark's relationship with the latest addition to the England ranks, had delegated to him the responsibility of obtaining an interview.

'Mo, I'm not sure I've really got the time. Nick and I have a meeting scheduled with the accountants, Richard's screaming at us to sit down with him on a production budget, I'm still not convinced I know what the hell I'm doing . . .'

Halid cut him short.

'Don't be so modest, Mark. You're a natural at this. I saw your amendments to Nick's initial draft introduction to the presentation. All good points, things the others just wouldn't have thought of.'

'But I don't understand the economics of broadcasting. I'm an ex-professional footballer, sometime private investigator. Neither of those make me much of an expert on how we convince the powers that be that it should be *your* TV station that shows the ESL matches exclusively; nor how we pitch our bid.'

Mo was having none of it.

'My son Nabil's not an expert either, but he thinks he is. That hasn't stopped him getting involved.'

Mark knew that to his cost. Nabil was involved in everything, but then Nabil thought he knew everything. Nabil Halid could be told nothing. Already one secretary had been fired on the spot for giggling a little too loudly over the story of his efforts to bail his sister out of the police station. That had been a failure and, like his father, Nabil did not take kindly to failure.

'In fact,' Halid continued, 'why not take Nabil with you when you do the interview? It'll get him out of Nick and Richard's hair.'

'And into mine,' Mark thought, but kept his counsel. He had got to know Mo well enough in a remarkably short space of time to realise it would be a waste of breath. It may have sounded like an inspirational idea, but he would have thought it all through carefully before saying anything. Nick and Richard's assignments were now more important than anything Mark could achieve so he could be more usefully employed by interviewing Barry Reed. If he took Nabil with him then it would make life easier for the other two to complete their tasks. That was the way Mo operated. Move the pieces logically around your own private chess-board and in the greater game even his son was just a pawn.

'Fine,' Mark said aloud, 'I'll call Jenny right now and see when would be a good time for the interview.'

Jenny Cooper was the Deputy Press Officer at the Football Association and Mark knew that although he could easily have rung the young Geordie directly in his room at the team's England base, that action would have blown his chances and those of his station for future interviews with any other members of the squad. Jenny was both renowned and feared for her aggressive protection of the players from the media. She was never scared to be rude to anybody, including certain senior FA officials which was probably why she had remained as Deputy Press Officer for the last five years even though the main job had fallen vacant twice within that period.

'Don't ask, Mark, tell her. I want this item on air tonight,' Halid said with an air of confidence that in a man of lesser personality would have been construed as arrogance. It simply did not occur to him that either Mark or Barry Reed might have other arrangements and even less that Jenny Cooper might refuse the request.

'I'll do what I can do, Mo. Where will I find Nabil to tell him he's coming with me?'

'He's down at Studio 3. And you don't need to tell him. He knows already.' Halid smiled, as if he were just letting Mark in on what had been a neatly planned joke.

Mark looked at his watch. It was already eleven, which meant the players were in their morning session at Bisham Abbey. He brought up Jenny Cooper's mobile number on his personal computer, dialled and to his surprise got through first time. The cellular telephone system had never proved particularly user friendly as far as he was concerned. The woman's voice at the other end sounded both harassed and distant as if too many people had been able to get through that morning.

'Mark, hi. Been a bit crazy down here today. The Press just got on to the story that Inter-Milan have bid eighteen million quid for Gary Davies.'

'Eighteen?'

'Exactly. A million for each goal he's scored for England, as one of the journos told me he was going to put it within the pages of his scummy little tabloid. Anyway, Kenny's been going mad trying to get the lads focused on this Colombian match, but the locusts don't want to know. They're clambering all over the place looking for any angle from what Gary has for breakfast to whether or not he's ever had an affair with anybody from the female club physio to the mongrel who passes for the club mascot. After all that it's nice to hear from a human being.'

'I'm afraid I'm phoning as a journalist rather than a human being,' Mark said apologetically.

'Isn't that the function of your other half?' Jenny asked. Her tone made Mark hesitate. There was no doubt that Jenny was attractive. Small and slim, she was probably just the wrong side of thirty, her hair cropped close like a street-urchin's, eyes of china-blue usually concealed behind pebble glasses, but with a wonderful peaches and cream complexion, and a generous smile. She had a reputation for moodiness and the smile was hard to raise but once achieved was worth the effort, a slow dawn bursting into a full glorious sunrise. Now, for the first time Mark felt she had some genuine interest in him as a person, rather than merely somebody she had to deal with as part of her job. It had been a long while since Mark had even thought of a woman other than Patti, but the use of the words, 'other half', had struck a discordant note.

'I'm not sure the beautiful Miss Delaney is talking to me at the moment.'

'More fool her,' Jenny said, this time leaving Mark in no doubt that if he had any interest in her, then she, in turn, was readily available.

'What can I do for you, anyway?' she asked, the tone still flirtatious.

'I need to bring the cameras down to interview Barry Reed for Ball Park. Any chances?'

'For anyone else two, Bob Hope and no hope. But for you, I'll see what I can do. When do you want it? We've a general Press call today at four. Barry's not up for that one as far as I'm aware.'

She was referring to the manager's practice of putting up just two or three players for each official session with the Press rather than exposing the whole squad and in particular those players that the media felt might provide a real story. It meant spreading the duties and the publicity opportunities around as well as keeping the more controversial figures out of the spotlight.

'Can I call you back in ten minutes?' Jenny asked.

'Sure.'

'And you'll be doing the interview yourself? I'm sure that will make some difference to Kenny.'

Mark smiled to himself. It was clear that the England manager was already flexing his muscles in ensuring everybody from the Press upwards knew exactly who was boss.

'Yes, I'm doing the interview myself,' Mark replied, omitting to add that he would have the boss's son for company. Even as he spoke he was certain that Jenny Cooper was going to make sure that Kenny Cunningham's answer to his request was going to be in the affirmative.

CHAPTER 11

If Dominique Halid had any cause to show the least sign of gratitude towards her brother and father for getting her out on bail she did not show it. She had lived away from home and she had lived under her father's roof and there was no doubt in her mind that away was better. The only trouble about away was that it meant no money. No money, in turn, usually meant crashing out on the floor of some squalid flat, without any recollection of how she had got there, no knowledge of where she was and no real plan for how she was going to get home, where the circle would begin all over again.

All her family said she had a drug problem. She thought she had a family problem and the drugs were a way of making her forget it. She didn't like any of them, but then there weren't many people she did like. There was one, of course, but he was a problem as well. Not him, exactly, but the fact she had to find some way of telling him that she was pregnant.

They'd not known each other that long and she wasn't sure how he was going to react. Not only that, but she wasn't even sure that she should bother to tell him. She'd had one abortion before, but then the father could have been any one of half a dozen she'd slept with in the month before. This time around she'd been remarkably faithful. She liked him, perhaps in her moments of greater clarity even loved him, yet, despite that, she couldn't quite quit her habit.

If the police thought she was a supplier then they were wrong. Sure, she'd give stuff to her friends; but then for the most part they couldn't afford to pay for it and if they had to buy it then they'd steal and at least what she got for them was good quality stuff. There were times when she felt a hell of a sight older than her eighteen years. There were times when she thought she had been born as a teenager, that the normal formative years, the years of going out with her parents as a family, of sitting on her

57

father's lap, of being tossed in the air by loving grandparents, those years had never been experienced by her. Was that true? She could barely remember her mother. Even before her father's involvement with Susie Carr, her mother had long vanished from the scene. She could recall the day she had left, her bags packed and ready, ready for a return to Tehran, despite all the troubles in that troubled land.

'Your mother's going home,' was all that her father had said. No more than that. And after that, silence. No phone calls, no postcards, not even any cards or presents on her birthday. It was as if she did not exist, as if her mother had never existed. It was only when she got a little older that it occurred to her that it was her father who was denying her existence.

That was her father's way. He had probably paid her mother off, bought her a large house, given her an allowance, all signed and sealed and delivered by his clever lawyers, all subject to the condition that she did not trouble him again, that she did not contact her daughter. There was nothing her father could not resolve with money, or so he believed. Money and charm, because there could be no doubting that he was a charming man when he wanted to be. Yet neither of those commodities cut any ice with Dominique. He could neither buy her, nor win her around with his honeyed words. She had backed herself into a corner as far as her father was concerned and could not be seen to be coming out other than fighting. All she and her father could ever do now was fight tooth and nail, they simply had no other way of communicating. There were other considerations to be taken into account in their relationship. Nabil was going his own way and the path he trod had no appeal for his sister. Whereas Dominique wanted to be as different from her father as possible, Nabil's world was built around his efforts to emulate Mohammed. When she confronted him with the truth, he denied it, but then he would. How could he admit to imitating somebody he claimed to dislike when imitation was so clearly the sincerest form of flattery in the Halid family. Dominique would never flatter her father, would never give him any hint of encouragement that sometime in their relationship he might have done the right thing.

Nabil was the least of her problems. She'd grown up with him and, although they were not particularly close, at least they understood each other. Liked, no, but understood, yes. Susie she did not come close to understanding, nor did she really want to. She could not understand how somebody like her had married Nathan Carr in the first place and certainly could not believe she saw anything in her father other than an open cheque book. Her father was more successful than his ex-partner, that was for sure, so there was one reason for a younger woman to leave one for the other. But was that enough? Living with her father as man and wife was bad enough, but having his baby as well was disgusting. It was all too much for her to bear. For seventeen years Dominique had been the baby of the family herself and although that did not mean as much as it would in a normal family it did, at least, count for something. Yet, a year ago, her father had even taken that from her. He couldn't remove Nabil's birthright, that was sacrosanct, but the little she had, the flotsam she clung to from the shipwreck, well, all that could go in one night of conception.

The birth of Jason had not been a happy day for Dominique. The little bastard was just over a year old now. Wrapped in his golden fleece, his birth had signalled a new wave of excessive behaviour from Dominique. That was until she'd met the man who was the father of her child or who would be the father if she permitted it to be born. If she permitted . . . The power of life and death. Normally that was a gift only in the possession of gods and authors. And murderers too. Never forget the killers. She let her mind dwell for a moment on the man. She'd met him indirectly through her father. There was something rather dramatic about that although whether it was comic or tragic only time would tell. Susie had tried to be friendly in the early days of her relationship with Mo, but Dominique would have none of that 'let's all be girls together' nonsense. Thank goodness she'd never tried to come on strong as a mother-substitute. If she had done then Dominique would have just told her to fuck off. The approaches for a friendly chat she just froze out, just as she brushed away any of Susie's pitiful attempts to get her involved in her newfound motherhood. And now she was pregnant herself and Susie would have been the natural person to talk to about it. There was a chance, just a chance, she might not only understand, but actually help.

There were times when, despite herself, Dominique was very much like her father. For the most part things were carefully planned. She'd launched forth on her campaign of drug abuse in the full knowledge of the effect it would have on her father who, unlike many of his contemporary compatriots, would have nothing to do with drugs. He got his kicks, reached his highs, from succeeding in business. There were times when his particular road to achievement left more carnage than any batch of cocaine. Yet he could not see that, would never see that, so if Dominique was going to discuss her situation with anyone at all, the answer still came back to Susie. There was no way she was going to tell her father at this stage. Oddly enough one of the reasons was that she felt it wouldn't be fair on him, particularly as this pregnancy had been another deliberate ploy of hers, another example of planning things out. She'd told him she was on the pill, which was true when they'd started their relationship. She'd not lied to him, she'd merely omitted to tell him that she'd come off it. She'd not been able to get enough of him, had been frustrated by the fact they couldn't see each other every day and as ever she had over-compensated.

Quite what happened now she wasn't sure. There were moments when she thought she'd quite like to settle down with him for the rest of her life, raise this baby, raise a few more. OK so she was only eighteen, but her mother had been younger than that when Nabil had been born. Sixteen, in fact. That was the way of things in the Middle East her father had once said. Well, perhaps it was, but at sixteen could her mother ever have envisaged her life some twenty-three years later, separated from her husband and both her children? Not even Sophie's choice, no choice at all.

Dominique lay back on her bed, her hands behind her head. It was a large, sunny room in the Halid house near Henley. She always claimed it was the best room in the house and however long she might be away she always regarded it as her room and guarded it ferociously. She'd picked it for the view of the river, seen off her brother when he'd tried to claim it during the year she'd back-packed around Asia. That trip had brought one or two close calls. In Bangkok when she'd left her stash in her hotel room whilst she'd taken the fire escape out of the building; in Kuala Lumpur when her contact had tipped her off by telling her where a car would be waiting to get her out of the city. Either of those could have seen her facing a death squad or at least a lengthy prison sentence in surroundings from which death could have been a merciful relief. There would have been nothing her father could have done for her there.

She'd never, in fact, asked him to do anything for her anywhere, but he had and he did. A chief constable with whom he played golf had called off his lads when she'd run into a spot of local bother. An inspector in France, whose sister her father employed in Paris, had arranged for her to be escorted on to the first flight home when by rights she should have been looking at the bare walls of a French prison cell; but this last occasion seemed to have exhausted his patience and his tolerance. It was as if by sending Nabil, rather than rolling out of bed himself or despatching his solicitor, he was sending her a message that he could not relay in words. The message was one of total despair. He was, as ever, killing two birds with one stone by washing his hands of her and setting her brother a new challenge. That was what their whole life with their father had been, a series of challenges.

The music of Nas played at full volume passed over her in a wave. She liked black music, just as she had liked black men in the past. Their size was no myth. She remembered teasing one semi-respectable white boyfriend, fresh from university, who'd fancied himself both for his performance in bed and the length of his tackle.

'Hung like a horse. I don't think so. More like My Little Pony.' And off he'd gone in a strop, never to be slept with or even to be seen again. They could all be disposed of like that, all of them. Replaceable like batteries when they wore out, the buzz only coming at the start when their power was at its peak. They were a means to an end, a means to satisfy her when she needed satisfaction. None of them realised they were being used until she told them, and then they left, tails and pricks between their legs.

She had no true friends, not since she had been expelled from her first senior school at the age of fourteen. She had acquaintances with whom she mixed, often druggies like herself. Some she liked more than others, some she pitied, some she feared. At eighteen years of age, Dominique Halid was intelligent enough to realise she was at the crossroads, bright enough to be frightened by what was in store. Pregnant, on bail, feeling terribly lonely, she decided in that instant to confide in her step-mother, Susie, and rolled her legs off the bed. A line from Shakespeare flashed through her mind, probably inaccurate but as close as it needed to be. If 'twere done then were best done quickly. She liked the classical theatre, although even that she would not admit to her father. She did not know if she was doing the right thing, but it was the only game in town short of topping herself, and, curiously for someone with such low self-esteem, that had never seemed a viable option. She opened her bedroom door and called down.

'Susie? Susie? Are you there? Can we talk for a minute?' And then she was taking the steps two at a time with the effortless confidence of the teenager she really was.

CHAPTER 12

Mark had never expressed any real desire to visit Bogota and now, as the plane circled its sprawling chaos for the third time, he saw no reason to change his mind. He was old enough to remember the framing of Bobby Moore, the scurrilous allegations that the late, lamented England captain had stolen a bracelet when he could probably have afforded to buy the whole shop.

He couldn't quite believe he was making this trip. So much had happened in the last seventy-two hours, so much to confuse him, to inspire his confidence, to make him wonder just who or what he had become.

It was the interview with Barry Reed that had made it inevitable that he would be despatched to work on Ball Park's coverage of the international against Colombia. Jenny Cooper had been true to her word. She'd asked him to drive to the rear entrance of the hotel and then allocated him, the cameraman and the sound recordist a private suite. She'd put her fingers to her lips as she led them in to signal the conspiracy of silence.

'Not a word, Mark. Kenny's banned all the rest of the media after the Press con for the next forty-eight hours. He says it's all becoming a circus.' She deepened her voice into a passable impression of Cunningham's semi-cockney tone, 'If one more agent rings one of my players on a mobile to arrange some kind of product placement then I'm going to take both the phone and the product and stuff them up his fucking arse.'

Mark applauded in appreciation of the performance and Jenny gave him a mock curtsey. She seemed hyped – as if the secrecy had lit a fire deep within her. It was hard at that moment to recognise her as the hard-boiled career woman that she was reputed to be.

'I do appreciate this, Jenny. I'm sure Mo does too.'

She smiled and wiped ten years off her age.

'I did it for you, Mark, not your boss. From what I hear I

don't know why you need to have a boss at all.'

'I don't need one. I just enjoy the work. And you're sounding like Patti.'

She made a little moue of her lips.

'So that's what it's all about. She finds you in the gutter, does the big philanthropic trip, and now you're back on level terms she can't cut it.'

It was a fair summary, but Mark did not particularly like the way it was put. This woman shouldn't have known him at all. They were friendly when they'd met, had shared the odd cup of coffee, yet, she seemed to know him far too well.

'Anyway, Mark, I'll love you and leave you.' Again the smile. 'I hope you'll have time for a drink before you leave. Tea, if nothing else.' She knew that too, knew about his alcoholic past, but then there weren't too many people in the game who didn't know that by now.

'I have to catch a lift from the crew. They brought the jeep and I left my car.'

'That's no problem. I have to drive into town tonight. I'll give you a ride.' She waved a stern finger at him. 'Now, I'm not going to take no for an answer. A bit of company on that grotty drive down the M40 is a small price to pay for the sort of facilities I've provided.' She paused, then added, 'And might yet provide.'

Mark couldn't argue with that and certainly didn't want to upset a woman who could make life difficult for a television company. He rather liked her anyway. He took her as he found her rather than listening to the comments that went on behind her back.

'You've twisted my arm.'

'I'm disappointed that I needed to. My room number's 201. I'll see you later.'

The interview itself had been difficult and Mark quickly realised that if it had been anybody else but himself the boy would have refused to give it. He put the youngster's reluctance down to the pressure of it all having happened to him so quickly, yet even now, as the plane began its final descent, he was not entirely sure there was not something more to it, something deeper and darker.

A teenager like Barry Reed, suddenly pushed into the spotlight of the England squad could have reacted in one of two ways. He could have been delighted by his promotion, determined to savour every moment of it, to ensure that everything was retained in his mind for his scrapbook of memories; or he could have gone the way Barry Reed had done, his face pale and strained, dark shadows under his eyes, testifying to a lack of sleep, his gaze forever wandering as the camera rolled, looking for some invisible escape route. Mark signalled to the two men from Ball Park to stop their filming and recording.

'What's up, Barry? You look about as confident as a one-legged striker. It's not like you.'

'I don't know, Mark. If I were given the chance to go back home then I might just take it up. There's so many good players here, so experienced. I'm looking about us in training and I'm freezing. I'm not trying things I know I can do in case they don't work, and I'm scared they will work in case they think I'm flash.'

'Can you leave us alone for a few minutes?' Mark said to the two technicians, who nodded their assent, pleased to be able to get a drink at the hotel bar on what had become a humid day, more suited to the height of the summer than the early autumn. Barry looked grateful for the break himself, the tension momentarily easing from his jaw. As the door closed behind them Mark thought he was going to open up, but instead the player merely inspected his fingernails as if they held the answer to the mystery of life.

'You're good, Barry. You're here on merit. Believe me, if I was the England manager, I wouldn't just have you in the squad for the experience, I'd actually have you in the starting line-up. You're a Geordie. There's a history of your folk succeeding for England. It's not only the barmy army who'll be supporting you when you pull on that white shirt for the first time, it'll be the whole of the north-east and they'll make more noise than the entire population of England put together. I've played up at St James's Park and I know.'

'I know too, I suppose. Yeah, you're right, Mark. Get the lads back before they get too many in and can't focus. Let's get the interview over so I can get a bit of kip. I'm that tired. By the way, the gaffer said he didn't want us talking to no one so when's this going to be shown?'

'Tonight, I guess. But only on Ball Park. He won't know when we filmed it. Don't worry, I won't land you in it.'

And he hadn't. The rest of the interview had gone like a dream and persuaded Mo that Mark should go to Colombia and then on to Zurich. Yes, the interview had been fine, but the rest of the day had been a nightmare.

He'd knocked on the door of room 201 when the rest of his team had departed with the film in the can.

'It's open,' Jenny had called, her voice a little slurred, suggesting she had not waited for him to start in on the drink that she knew he would not be sharing. He knew that tone of voice, had heard it in his own head a thousand times. It had always meant trouble then and he had no doubt it meant trouble now. He didn't know why he should be feeling any guilt. He had given Patti every chance to make the two of them a couple for ever, and it was she who had pushed him away, was still pushing him away. He didn't know what he had done, any more than he knew what he could do. He did not even know if she wanted him to do anything, or if he could raise the energy to do any more himself.

Jenny was lying on the bed towards one side, where a bottle of champagne was open and two-thirds empty. On the other side was an incongruously neatly laid-out tea-pot, cup, strainer, milk jug and sugar bowl. From the state of her, whatever else was going to happen Jenny Cooper was not going to be driving Mark back to London.

'I've got your tea ready,' Jenny said. She was wearing only a T-shirt and panties and he could see the colour in her face, sense the anticipation and excitement in her voice, in her body. It was not going to be an easy few moments, but he kept his own voice calm and measured.

'The interview went well. I could do with a good cuppa now.' He was determined to keep it deliberately chatty, neutral, normal. They both had to come out of this with their dignity intact.

'Fuck the interview. Fuck the cuppa. Fuck me.'

She was there for the taking. Her boyish breasts rose and fell beneath the blue cotton. He could see her nipples erect through the material, fancied he could see a damp patch on the white silk of her G-string. Despite his determination to remain untouched he knew he was becoming aroused and saw her eyes focus on the bulge at the front of his jeans. She moved her gaze up his body until she was staring straight into his eyes.

'Are you hard for me, Mark? Do you remember what to do or

66

has that little journalist of yours chopped off your balls and put them in a jar of preservative?'

'I don't think this is a good idea, Jenny.'

'I'm not asking you to think. I'm asking you to get undressed and shag me. I'm tired of having these little babies around me, all making bets as to which of them can be the first to get into my knickers. If I'm going to shag a footballer I'd rather he was at least retired from the game – like you.'

Mark sat on the edge of the bed, feeling stupid as he leaned across her to pour himself a cup of tea. He didn't want just to walk out of the door and as long as he had the cup of steaming liquid in his hand he didn't think she was likely to leap upon him. He was wrong. She sat bolt upright, one hand on his mouth to still his protests, the other pulling his head towards her. She released her hold and her tongue was raking his teeth, trying to prise his tongue into her mouth. Just for a second he was lost, was ready to take what was on offer, but then he pulled away and gently put the cup down on the bedside table.

'I'll call a cab, Jenny. Another time, when you've not had a head start on me, perhaps we can have dinner, try and see if a relationship will work. From a level playing field that is.'

He'd judged it to perfection and he breathed a sigh of relief as she rolled away.

'You're a good man, Mark. Someone else would have screwed me and left. We'll have that dinner and I'll arrange the cab.'

Suddenly she was sober and they could both get on with their lives.

And he was on his way to Colombia where they would inevitably meet up again. As the plane dropped its undercarriage he wondered whether he should have just given in to his desires. Who would have been hurt? Jenny had wanted it, he had needed it and Patti would never have known. There were times when he wondered just by whose standards he was trying to live. He'd found her attractive, been attracted to her, and although he might have closed the chapter on that particular afternoon he felt that Jenny Cooper was a book that at some time in his life he might actually get to read.

CHAPTER 13

Patti Delaney replayed in her mind the last conversation she'd had with Mark and mouthed an obscenity aimed only at herself. She could not understand what was going wrong with their relationship, yet she was sure it was down to her rather than to him.

In the Burrow she lit another cigarette, studiously ignoring the unemptied ashtray, knowing exactly what Mark would have said if he'd been around. She hated his habit of washing up her ashtrays whenever she turned her back.

'They don't taste the same when you smoke them from a clean ashtray,' she said, only half joking.

There was no doubt he had an influence on her life, although that had fallen short of being able to get her to kick the habit.

'I'll stop when I want to stop, not when someone gives me a look of disapproval every time I light up a fag. My flat, my Burrow, my lungs, my life.'

And now she did want to stop and she couldn't. She couldn't because she was missing Mark and all there was to fill in the gap between the evening and the night was the rapidly diminishing bottle of wine and equally rapidly filling ashtray. When she'd discovered that both she and Mark were comfortably, if not seriously, rich after their inheritance, she had believed it was the beginning rather than the end. He did not need to work, she did not either, yet they were both driven on by some devilish ego that made them see even less of each other.

She knew Mark did not believe her when she said she was not jealous, that she genuinely disapproved of his involvement at Ball Park – and he was half right. She was jealous; but she also knew enough about Mohammed Halid to disapprove. Yet, Mark would not listen so there was no point in trying to explain that the man was a chancer, an opportunist who was not selective in whom he used to promote his business. Maybe that in itself was

68

no good reason to condemn a person. Hadn't she been like that herself when she had first met Mark? So, who was she to be so judgmental?

She didn't enjoy holding the high moral ground that was so hard to take, but she also knew her attitude upset Mark and sometimes that was enough. She wanted it to anger him, but he was hard to anger and that angered her as well. There were times when she thought she might be losing it, might be in need of psychiatric care, but that in itself would be admitting defeat, acknowledging weakness and she was certainly not a weak person.

If Mark did not believe that she was not jealous then he also did not seem to believe that she was on to a story; but she was. And a big one at that, possibly the biggest of her career and also perhaps the most dangerous. Like most good stories it had come to her by chance. She'd bumped into Jessica Brown at Marks and Spencer's in Brent Cross, inevitably in the underwear department. She'd not seen Jessica since they had left school and it was hard to believe that they were the same age. She'd been a pretty girl back then, English rose pretty, biscuit tin pretty; but those days were long behind her. Now the blonde hair needed a wash whilst the china-blue eyes were themselves washed of all their colour. Her skin was greasy and blemished and she could not have weighed more than seven stone. There had been a time when if Patti had been forced to name a best friend the name of Jessica Brown would have leapt to her lips. They'd lost their virginity on the same night to a couple of policemen they'd picked up in a club that didn't ask too many questions about the ages of its clientele and that had been enough for a bit of mutual bonding for a year or so. Then Jessica had moved upwards and onwards from the clubbing, the drinking, the sexual adventures and the smoking. That was to say she still smoked, but she had discovered drugs and drugs had discovered Jessica. Drugs had sunk their teeth into Jessica Brown and would not release their grip and, as her old friend told Patti over a glass of wine, she was dying. She told her in a calm matter-of-fact way in a little bistro in Fortune Green Road, but even as she told the story the calm ebbed away and it was clear that Jessica was angry and Jessica wanted revenge.

'I don't think I believe in fate, but if I did then I'd be confident today's meeting with you didn't happen by chance. You know ever since I discovered that I was HIV positive I've been thinking of two things. How did it happen and what can I do to those who made it happen? I'm not sure I'll ever be able to suss out the first. So many needles, so many men, who the hell knows which was infected; but the second? For the last month or so I've been wondering who I could tell. You may or may not believe me, Patti, but your name has been on my mind more than once. I'd lost your phone number and, although I'm sure I could have traced you, it would all have been too much effort.'

She held up the empty glass and twirled it around until it caught a glint of sunlight making it seem far more precious than it really was.

'Sun and wine. If only it could have ended there. If only. Can't live your life on if onlys my mother always used to say and now I can't live my life at all. My mother's going to outlive me. That's not the way it should be, that's not the natural order, and I've not been able to tell her that I won't be around for too long. She rang last week and started asking if I had any plans for Christmas. Plans for Christmas? It's September now and if I get to Christmas it'll be a miracle and not one I'm really praying for. If I'm still around I'll be in some hospice with a bunch of nuns and do-gooders bringing me presents I'll never be able to use. Or singing carols I've no interest in hearing and encouraging me to join in and sing along for baby Jesus. Christ Almighty!'

She banged the glass so violently on the table that the stem broke off in her hand. A young waiter came swiftly over to clear away the debris.

'What's a girl got to do to get a drink around here?' she asked. The waiter smiled helpfully despite her tone and Patti nodded her consent to him bringing another bottle.

'Have you got a fag, Pat, or better still a packet? I was just window-shopping at M & S, or perhaps looking for the chance to nick a pair of new knickers. It's been a while since I worked, the benefit's not much and I've just about run out of credit with most of my friends. Those who've not turned their backs on me in disgust.'

Patti obliged by taking the last two packets of duty free that she had in her bag and shoving them across the table.

'Here you are then. I know somebody who would approve of that particular piece of beneficence.'

'Fellow?'

'Sort of.'

'Serious?'

'Could have been.'

'Could have? Over then, is it?'

'No, not over. Might still be serious.'

'Whose call?'

'Mine.'

For a few moments they were two schoolgirls again, swapping their experiences, the first fondle of their breasts, the first French kiss, and that night they'd both staggered home, leaning on each other for support, wondering which of them would be the first to admit they'd not really enjoyed what passed for proper sex, worrying as to how long it would be before they could be sure they weren't pregnant.

'I'm so sorry we sort of fell out of touch, Patti. I suppose you didn't really want to mix with a loser like me, and I can understand that. I've read your articles from time to time. I think you're a really good writer, but then you always were. Why don't you have a go at a book?'

'I'm not so sure I'm ready. I've got to find the right subject.'

'I can give you the right subject,' Jessica said urgently, leaning towards Patti in a sudden puppet-like jerk of a movement. There were beads of sweat on her brow, her skin was so translucent that her cheekbones carved clear lines through them giving her white face the quality of a skull, a preview of her imminent passing.

Patti was beginning to regret the invitation to a drink. It was all becoming too intense. She felt sorry for the woman, but right now she didn't need any additional emotional baggage. She was looking to shed her own overboard, rather than reload. She wondered if Jessica was quite in her senses. She could hardly be blamed if she'd lost them, but the last thing Patti wanted was a wild goose chase for a story or novel just because an old schoolfriend thought there was some drama in her sad life. The other woman sensed her change of mood, her desire to be away from there, to be back in the Burrow, in the shower, washing away both the dirt and the guilt. It was clearly something that she had seen and felt before.

'I'm sorry, you're obviously not interested.' Jessica rose to leave.

'It's been good seeing you again. Just show me where I get the bus for Kilburn and I'll be off.'

If it was a calculated act then it was a good one. Patti reached out her hand and gently pushed her down into her seat.

'No, Jessica, it's me who should be sorry. I've got all the time in the world to listen and I understand . . .'

'That I've not got all the time in the world to talk?'

'I wasn't going to say that.'

'No, but you were certainly thinking it. Don't worry. I'm almost beyond hurt when it comes to acceptance of my own mortality. Just hear me out, Patti. I'll tell you what I know. You're a journalist. You may make more sense of it than I can. All I know is that I know something important, something that's a vital part of a bigger picture. It's as if I've got the last couple of pieces of a jigsaw but can't find the shop that sells the bloody puzzle.'

And when Jessica told her, Patti realised exactly what she meant. It was dark by the time they parted and Patti insisted on ordering a taxi on her account for her old friend.

'Listen, Patti, who knows if we'll see each other again, but keep in touch. Let me know if what I've told you leads anywhere. Maybe if you get there quickly then I'll be able to read all about it.'

'If there's anything I can do for you, Jessica, financial or otherwise let me know. Here's my number.'

Jessica looked at the card in her hands as if it were the permanent key to the Magic Kingdom and for a moment Patti was sure she was going to hit her for a loan.

'There is one thing,' Jessica said. 'Lend me your pen for a minute. I don't seem to be able to keep one on me for very long. I keep putting them down and forgetting where.'

She ripped a piece of paper off the corner of the menu and received a baleful stare from the waiter who'd replaced the broken glass. She waved at him gaily and in that instant Patti could see again the girl that Jessica once had been.

'Don't worry, garçon. Plenty more where that came from and I'm sure you'll be revising them tomorrow. Be a crummy restaurant if you serve the same thing two days running.'

Her breath became a little laboured as she turned her attention to Patti, the weariness winning over the ravaged body.

'This is my parents' number. At the end I'll get a message to you. Will you let them know? I'd rather it didn't come from a total stranger. And they always liked you. They thought you were a good influence on me.'

'How wrong could they be? I was always the wild one,' Patti said with a rueful smile.

'Yeah, yeah, yeah. And doesn't it show now? Anyway, do you mind?'

'No, of course not. It's cheap at the price, after what you've told me.'

They'd said their goodbyes and ever since then Patti had been unable to think of anything else. Certainly she'd not been able to concentrate on her relationship with Mark and so he had been the unwitting victim of her obsession.

The drug route. It had an end with people like Jessica. The victims. It had a middle as it came in through Europe. And it had a beginning as well. A fortnight on from her chance encounter, the right people questioned and both the story and the geography were beginning to take shape.

There had been a message from Mark after the conversation. An invitation only a couple of days ago.

'I'm on my way to beautiful Colombia. I don't like travelling without you. Why not come with me?'

He never gave up. Perhaps she was relying on that. Testing him out to see how far he could be pushed before he broke. Well, maybe she'd pushed far and hard enough. She looked at her watch. It was nearly two in the afternoon. She hit the code on her phone that got her through to her travel agent.

'Hello, Gerry. Patti Delaney. When's the next flight to Bogota and what's the availability?'

Gerry checked.

'Tomorrow at ten twenty-five. Nothing in economy, I'm afraid. Club or first class.'

She didn't hesitate.

'Make it first.'

She had the money and she needed the time and comfort to ensure that when she arrived she had her story and mood just right for Mark and whoever or whatever else waited at the end of the flight.

CHAPTER 14

The England team camp might have been some ten minutes from the centre of town, but Mark's hotel was bang in the heart of it. Nowhere he'd ever been had prepared him for Bogota. There may have been traffic signals and controls but for the great majority of the drivers it was as if they did not exist. They had three colours as they did in England – green, amber and red – but none of them had any individual significance to the Colombian drivers, or indeed the pedestrians. It was car versus man and it was a minor miracle that most of the contestants survived to fight another day.

He had never regarded himself as having any bronchial problems, but the altitude mingled with the air pollution, fuelled by so many ancient vehicles, and he could hear himself wheezing within a few minutes of leaving his hotel. The couple of days he had spent there had been windless and the clouds of smoke relentlessly pushed out of the rears of the cars, taxis, buses and *collectivos* was murderous. Mark's parents had told him tales of the old London smogs, the pea-soupers where you could not see your hand in front of your face, but they must have been a veritable health farm compared to a bad day in Bogota.

As he recorded his first report back to Ball Park, he couldn't help but be critical.

'Whoever arranged this fixture just after the start of our domestic season must need their brains tested. There are moments and places of beauty about this city and this country, but hell far outweighs heaven. It's hard to walk the street without being offered drugs. The noise is everywhere, blasting out of the bars, from the cars, the houses, the ghetto blasters. I travelled on a bus yesterday for the experience and was subjected to at least six different radio stations all played at full volume from separate parts of the vehicle. Even in the first class hotels you don't go into the television lounge without ear-plugs. When we

74

were allowed to attend the squad training session yesterday we could see several of the players struggling with their breathing. And this is the so-called dry season. It's a wonder that the bumbling administrators who decided on this match, more for the media money than the experience, didn't decide to make the trip in the rainy season. Then we could have arranged a joint tour with our international swimmers and water polo team.'

Two days still to go before the match, two days of acclimatisation for the players, but stretching endlessly ahead of him. Yet he was lucky compared to some. A few of the journos on tight budgets were staying on the fringes of the red-light area of town. The rest of them had already heard a sample of the horror stories. Hookers and drug-addicts thronging the steps of their hotels, walls made of paper-thin plywood sawn through during the day and their rooms stripped bare of all their possessions. Then there were those who thought they were more streetwise than the rest and felt they were safe if they fell into the Colombian way of life. They'd accepted invitations at bars to *rumbas*, the traditional all-night parties. They rarely ended before dawn and had left them walletless and with a sickening headache from the local beer and the ear-splitting noise that, again, was so much a part of the Colombian way of life.

He felt even luckier now that Patti had arrived. He'd found her, spread out on his bed, fast asleep, when he'd arrived back from the training ground the previous day. He'd allowed her to crash out for as long as she needed even though he'd longed to throw his arms around her, kiss her half-awake and then make love to her until she was fully aroused.

He'd had his reward for his patience. She'd eventually come to, stretched and yawned with that feline gesture that he loved so much, then opened her arms to invite him towards her.

'If you can stand the smell, Mark, I can live with you having your wicked way with me.'

She'd not really smelled badly. First class travellers were not permitted to arrive looking as if they had been anything else than thoroughly spoiled on their journey. Making love had been like the first time. It seemed so long ago that they had shared their bodies that Mark went on a voyage of discovery, seemingly working by instinct to discover what it was that she really sought from a man's body, from a man's touch. His tongue ran its way over her long nipples until they were erect, then worked its way down to the valley of her breasts, down until it found the fine hair-line, until finally it entered the damp, welcoming crevice between her legs.

'If you can live in a Burrow, then I can live in one too,' he'd once said in the dawn of their relationship, as he eased himself into her, feeling her nails digging into his back, urging him ever deeper. As they came together in this hot room in Colombia, all the pain, all the harsh words were dispelled from his mind.

'Whew, I feel awake now. First a shower and then you can show me the town, big boy.'

'I'm not so sure you really want to see the town, Patti. Quite frankly the sooner I'm out of here, the happier I'll be. It's like Sodom, Gomorrah, New York and Piccadilly Circus all rolled into one.'

'I thought they were all one,' she replied. 'Come on Mark, it can't be that bad.'

'Were you unconscious on the way in from the airport?'

'I was pretty tired.'

'You have to be pretty dead not to notice.' He paused and took a notional step back to look her up and down.

'Sorry. Just checking that you are for real. What *are* you doing here? Why didn't you let me know you were coming? I'd have got us a better room.'

'This'll do just fine. And as for letting you know, it was a spur of the moment thing.' She sought for the right words, then, mindful of the fact their bodies had been intertwined just a moment before, said, 'I was missing you.'

'I'm glad.' He opened his mouth to continue, but she put her finger to his lips.

'Leave it at that, darling. I'm not in the mood for serious analysis of what might or might not have gone wrong with our relationship. It's all right now.'

She kissed him long and slowly, leaving him in no doubt that she meant what she said. Mark watched her walk towards the shower and shook his head in wonderment at the ways of women. It seemed neither possible, nor fair, that they should have the power both to wound and to heal, for them to change the rules of the game without rhyme, reason or warning; but for all that he was pleased to have her here, pleased that once more they would seem to be a couple, ready to take on the world.

She returned to the room, still naked save for a towel wrapped around her head.

'Toss us my bag, Mark. I've lost all track of time, but I'm dying for a morning fag.'

'It's not morning,' Mark replied.

'It is somewhere,' Patti countered, and reluctantly Mark handed across the voluminous hold-all that had the dimensions and capacity of the Tardis. She rummaged around and produced a two hundred pack of duty-free Silk Cut.

'Don't worry, I'll smoke on the balcony,' she said. 'I can see the look of disapproval. Just don't start.'

There was a light note to her tone, but Mark knew from experience that could change in a heart-beat and he didn't push the joke too far.

She leaned over the balustrade which overhung a huge swimming pool and took a deep drag from her cigarette.

'That's better. This place doesn't look too bad to me.'

'It shouldn't. We're paying for the privilege. Or at least Ball Park is. We're up in the north of the city. From what I understand that's comparatively fine. There are certain no-go areas. The *tugurios* are definitely out.'

'What are they when they're at home?'

'Shanty towns,' he replied, 'I know you, Patti Delaney, when it comes to local colour, but forget it. If it's dangerous to walk around there by day, then it's suicide by night. And don't assume the city centre's safe, either.'

'You seem to have got yourself well prepared.'

'Matter of survival. One of the Colombian TV guys is an ex-pro who played in Europe for a while, Luis Cano. We had a drink the other night and he filled me in.'

'A drink?'

'He had a drink to be precise. I had a Coke. Don't worry, Patti, you've not driven me back to the bottle. Anyway, Luis told me some real horror stories. Fake policeman stopping you in the street, strip-searching you in a corner café, then leaving you without clothes or belongings; taxis taking off with your baggage and leaving you behind; buses hi-jacked in broad daylight, drugs planted on you so that you pay up a bribe to get rid of the charges. The list is endless.'

'Sounds a cosy sort of town. Where do the elves and pixies live?'

'Cosy? You need a bit of journalistic licence to make that word fit Bogota. We'll have to be sure to come back here for the honeymoon.'

He waited for her to see him off with a barbed comment or her usual put-down, but she had either not heard him or chose to ignore it.

'Tell me a bit more about the drugs. After all, it's Colombia's claim to fame.'

'Probably their main export as well. I'm not sure how much I really know. It's not the sort of thing you chat about over a cup of coffee. And by the way, that's the best thing here. Anyway, Luis is coming by the hotel tonight. He seems to know everything about everything. Ask him yourself.'

'Perhaps I will,' she said as a throw-away line, but Mark knew her well enough to know she was only feigning lack of interest.

She got dressed quickly, leaving him no option but to take her out, although he was ready for a siesta himself. There was another training session in the relative cool in the evening, he had today's film in the can and he could not honestly say he'd had any plans for the afternoon.

He made for the door and ushered Patti out first. A door to a room along the corridor opened almost simultaneously and he took in a deep breath as he saw the familiar figure of Jenny Cooper. She saw Patti, recognised her and ignored her in the same second, but flashed a knowing, familiar smile at Mark.

'Mark Rossetti! Are you avoiding me? We've been over forty-eight hours and I don't think you've said more than half a dozen words to me. And after you left Burnham Beeches in such a hurry . . .'

Patti seized on the reference to the team hotel and shot the Deputy Press Officer a look that would have shattered glass at fifty paces, then turned what was left of it on Mark.

'Did I interrupt something?' Jenny asked. Patti took in Jenny's tight blue jeans and clinging white T-shirt that left nothing to the imagination. Jenny gave her a pitying smile.

'No, you interrupted nothing,' Patti almost snarled. 'I'm sure you're very busy, Mark. I'll find my own way around town. Don't worry, I'm a big girl. I can look after myself, and I'll be sure to avoid all the nasty areas. Doubtless if I'm not back by tomorrow you and your friend can send a search party out for me. That is if you're not too tied up with other things.'

She danced past Jenny and, without giving him the chance to reply, she was gone; and Mark was left in the corridor with Jenny, key in his hand and time on his hands.

CHAPTER 15

Mark did not know what Patti had done with her time away from the hotel and she gave him no encouragement to ask. However, by the time they met up in the room in the late evening she seemed to have calmed down. He was careful to ensure that he gave Jenny a wide berth, and in a way was flattered that Patti should show such jealousy and animosity towards another woman. It was a long time since he had experienced two women fighting over him. It was interesting, but he had experienced enough things of interest in his life and he wanted it to be over.

Luis Cano had spent enough time outside his native country to have acquired a vaguely European approach to time-keeping and arrived at the hotel shortly after the appointed hour of seven.

'You see, my friend, the Colombians invented *mañana*. You know what that means?'

'Tomorrow,' Patti said with a smile, knowing that the obvious answer was also the wrong one.

Luis smiled back, a dazzling smile that suggested he kept it only for special ladies. He looked more Italian than South American. Slim, with long dark hair falling in permed rolls, his olive eyes shaded by girlish lashes, he had clearly kept himself in trim since his retirement from the game. His cheeks were covered by a designer stubble that suggested that it took more time and attention than if he had shaved every day and which contrasted sharply with the pearly-white teeth that he flashed regularly in a lazy well-rehearsed smile.

'He's the sort of man who could make you pregnant with just a handshake,' Patti said later. But at their first meeting, to Mark's growing annoyance, she seemed to hang on every word he had to say. If there were any secret messages passing between them, Mark could not decode them, and given Patti's reaction to Jenny earlier in the day he thought it best to say nothing. He was certainly not going to disclose Jenny's clumsy attempts at

80

seduction. That was the sort of incident that either merited a phone call immediately to your loved one or else should remain buried in the mists of time.

Luis focused on the *mañana* question.

'No, you are not wrong,' he said to Patti. 'But it means some time in the future as well. Maybe tomorrow if you are very lucky; but more probably in a week or so. Sometimes it means not in your life-time, but then life can be very brief.'

They gave their orders for dinner to an over-polite waiter who congratulated them on every choice as if he had cooked the meal himself, even though they followed Luis's recommendation to try the local specialty of *comida corriente*.

'We want our table in fifteen minutes,' Luis said to the waiter. 'That way I think we get it in about half an hour. That is OK?' he continued, now talking to his companions.

'That's fine,' Mark said, getting to his feet. 'Let me get some drinks. What do you want?'

'*Aguardiente*,' Luis replied. 'You've tried it?'

'Hardly. I only got in today,' Patti replied.

'The *cristal* is our local spirit. It's flavoured with anise; but for ladies we have *mistela*.'

'Which is?' Patti asked with suspicion.

'It's a home-made liquor. We put fruit and herbs into the *aguardiente* to make it sweet for the women.'

'I'll stick with whatever the men have,' Patti said grimly. 'I'll give your *mistela* a miss. It sounds like the sort of thing that you get at a vicarage tea-party.'

Luis had clearly never been to a tea-party, let alone one at a vicarage, but he got the message. In a near-perfect imitation of his accent Patti placed the order for the drinks with another hovering waiter. Without even asking, she ordered Mark a Diet Coke. Luis nodded admiringly at her accent.

'You speak Spanish well.'

'I learned at school. I've not used it for a while. I guess I can get by.'

'I guess you can get by at most things. Come, there's a table near the window. We must appreciate the miracle of something happening on time. The boy will bring over the drinks.'

They settled down and clinked glasses.

'To a good match,' Luis said. 'I think you will be surprised by our team. This is not the same bunch of strangers who gave up without a fight back in '94.'

'I remember that,' Patti said, knocking back the drink in one gulp. 'Didn't one of your players get shot?'

'They take their football seriously here. And, as I said, life can sometimes be short. Particularly if you miss a penalty.'

'Not so much the goalkeeper's fear of the penalty then, as the man taking it,' Patti said, but her reference to the German film passed both of her companions by. There were times that she forgot that whatever Mark meant to her he was still an ex-professional footballer. She had tried to drag him screaming into the world of culture, but with only partial success. He still preferred musicals to straight plays, still watched little on television that wasn't sport and rarely picked up a book when a magazine would do. Still at least she'd got him out of the habit of ordering steak and chips wherever he went.

'Christ! Waddle, Pearce and Southgate can thank their lucky stars they play for England and not Colombia,' Mark said. Patti yawned a warning.

'Look, if you boys are going to talk football all night maybe I should leave you and turn in early. I'm really not that hungry and it's been a long, long day.'

'No, no,' Luis said quickly. 'We had only just begun about football and we will stop although Mark tells me you are a woman who likes and understands the game. We are being rude and we could not think of spending the evening without you decorating our table.'

'I do like football. But I prefer it in the stadium to around the dinner table. And if you think I'm no more than a decoration, then think again.'

Luis made a mock bow from the waist down without rising from the chair and gave her his most winning smile.

'My dear, you are not like our Colombian women. I can see that now. I promise to treat you like a man.'

'Believe me,' Mark added, seeing the expression on Patti's face, 'you couldn't get a greater compliment from a Latin American.'

'Can I have another of those drinks, if somebody can spare the time from this mutual admiration society? Maybe I could get to like this place.'

She glanced around the room, satisfied herself that there was a smoker at almost every table and lit up. Belatedly she offered one to Luis from the packet and he took it without hesitation, leaning forward to take his light from her cigarette rather than the lighter.

'I'm no longer a trained athlete, and I don't have the dedication of your friend Mark. Together we will smoke him out.'

Mark forced an expression to his face that was meant to signify that he took the joke in good part, but instead made him look as if the food before him on the plate was causing him severe gastric pain. In fact he was having difficulty with the meal and he noticed that Patti, too was playing with her portion to make it look as if she had eaten more than was actually the case. The soup that had started them off could have been anything, but the main course was recognisable as some kind of fish, with rice, pasta, red beans and lentils, some fried plantains and a mixed salad.

'You are not enjoying our local food, I can see,' Luis said. 'I must tell you that your native Colombian has this every day, twice a day, only his portions are smaller, sometimes so small as to be invisible.'

'I think they're the lucky ones,' Patti said, pushing her plate aside. 'No offence, you understand.'

'None taken,' Luis replied. 'So we drink together and we smoke together, and next time we eat together we eat European. And always football is off the menu. So, Patti, it is your choice. What would you like to talk about? Some part of our Colombian culture other than food perhaps?'

'That'll do,' she said, lighting another cigarette to add to the four already stubbed out in the ashtray. 'How about drugs? They're a great part of your culture, aren't they?'

Luis smiled again, only this time it was as forced as Mark's effort a few moments earlier, and there was no laughter in his voice as he answered.

'Part of our life, yes, unfortunately. Our culture, no. I don't think so. We export drugs, rather than use them at home. Why should drugs interest you? And forgive me, I am not intending to be . . .' He sought for the word, although his English was virtually perfect.

'Condescending?' Patti offered.

'Exactly. You have given me the word, but not the answer.'

'I'm interested in everything. I'm a journalist.'

'Ah yes, Mark told me last night. That can be a very dangerous occupation in this country. Everybody reads the papers, but nobody likes the people who write them. The politicians, the police, our guerrillas, yes, even our drug barons, they stand together on only one issue; that journalists are the enemy. Sometimes, they are killed. Newspaper buildings are bombed.'

'And who does that?'

'Who knows? Maybe the drug barons, maybe the guerrillas, maybe the police and the politicians, or any combination. There are odd alliances in Colombia.'

'Nobody seemed to take any notice when I came into the country. They stamped my passport and it says what I do for a living.'

'You were lucky to arrive here at the time of the football. This week we have many journalists. If you are here then they assume you have something to do with the match. But let me give you a little word of advice. We have not met before tonight. Mark and I have only spent a little time together but it is enough for me to call him a friend. Patti, I like you too, even though you try very hard to behave like a man and to be like the porcupine. If you do not want me to come close, then that is fine. I won't come close.'

'The advice?' Patti said impatiently, in a tone that Mark knew spelled trouble.

'The advice. We Colombians, we like to make speeches, to take our time in coming to the point. So I will try to be English and be direct, because I think you need to be advised, to be advised to be cautious. I do not know why you have come here, but let everybody continue to believe that you are here for the football, even if you have to chat about it over dinner. If you are not here for the football then be here for Mark, for the coffee, for me if you prefer, but whatever, don't be here to write a story about the drugs. Do not draw any attention to yourself. I will tell you what you want to know, but do not ever ask anybody else.'

He was obviously deadly serious and even Patti, with a couple of local drinks inside her, knew better than to try and joke it off.

'Do we have a deal?' Luis asked.

Mark had said little, and was only now wondering whether

84

Patti had been totally honest when she had told him that she had come on an impulse.

'Answer the man, Patti. Does he have a deal?'

'Of course,' she said just a little too promptly for his satisfaction, lifting her empty glass as if to drink to the bargain. 'When have you ever known me to put my life on the line?'

'I hope you don't actually want me to answer that,' Mark replied.

The waiter brought over the dessert trolley and they all declined, settling instead for strong, black coffee.

'I thought you wanted to sleep tonight, Patti,' Mark said as she refilled her cup.

'I'm that tired I doubt if even this amount of caffeine will keep me up.' The bill arrived and the two men briefly tussled over it with Mark winning.

'One nil to England,' Luis said after he had thanked him, 'I think it is the only win you will get this week.'

They all rose to leave and parted with kisses and embraces in the foyer of the hotel. Mark realised as he and Patti rode the lift up to their room that he did not like the way the night had gone. Patti was half-Irish, was totally stubborn and most of all she was a journalist. He knew her well enough to be sure that she had not brought up the subject of drugs out of casual interest, nor did he think the potted history that Luis had supplied would satisfy her. Although Luis may have thought that she would keep to the bargain, Mark was convinced that whatever it was she was after, the pursuit had only just begun.

CHAPTER 16

If this was a friendly then Mark would have hated to have sat in this stadium with the visiting fans when the result really mattered. For once England's barmy army of support was almost unnoticeable. There must have been about a thousand of them, the usual hard core who followed the team anywhere, visas and deportation permitting, a sprinkling of holiday-makers and back-packers, plus the local ex-patriates. They'd tried their usual trick of booing the opposition national anthem and had been on the receiving end of a water-cannon from the local police who had been warned what to expect. After that, they kept their xenophobia to themselves.

The stadium must have held one hundred thousand. Mark knew from one of the roving reporters that there were some seventy thousand inside, yet it was by no means full. All the cheaper seats were filled, but the price of some of the more expensive was equal to about a week's average salary and there were big gaps in the comfort of the stands. The game was being broadcast live on national television and doubtless the local bars were doing the business that the match promoters had lost.

The big news as far as Mark was concerned was that Kenny Cunningham had chosen Barry Reed in his starting line-up. The lad had again seemed more than a little withdrawn when besieged by the reporters anxious for a heart-warming story to transmit home. They were ready for a new hero, eager for a young, good-looking kid they could build up before they knocked him down. Mark, inevitably, got closer to him than anybody else.

'They all think I'm getting a fortune from Ball Park for giving you these one to ones,' Barry said, the accent sounding even more Geordie in this alien climate.

'Well then, as you're not, you shouldn't,' Mark replied, 'and quite frankly, although I'm delighted you're talking to me, you shouldn't give the rest of the media the impression you're in Ball

86

Park's pocket. It's a bit like the tabloids. If you're exclusive with one then the others will look at ways to get you, in the knowledge that your exclusive deal will try and protect you. And that way they get a few days out of a nothing story.'

'It's all a fucking game, isn't it?' Barry said, with a hint of despair in his voice.

'It's all part of the game, yes. But the main game, that's the one only you get to play,' Mark said regretfully. Being around footballers once more, it was beginning to hurt him, the knowledge that he could have achieved all this, yet it had been cruelly taken away from him. He could understand how innocent men felt when they came out of the dark back into society. Nothing could give them back what had been taken away from them. And all the lies, the conspiracy against him, which had led to his suspension from football for all those years, they were hurting more now than they had at the time. Then he had viewed life through an alcoholic haze. But these days it was all crystal clear, so clear that it hurt and dazzled his eyes. He wanted to get across to Barry just how he was feeling, but the words would not come. Or at least not words that the boy would understand.

'I'm not sure I want to be a hero, Mark. I saw what they did to Gazza.'

'Different time and different man.'

'The Boss asked if I wanted to be put up for the Press conference this afternoon. First cap and all that.'

'And you said?'

'I said, no.'

'Mistake. Go back and tell him you've changed your mind. If you don't you'll get slaughtered, particularly when they know you've done an interview with us.'

'I don't care,' he said in a tone that gave no optimism for his performance on the field.

'Maybe not now, but you will. And your family will care as well.'

A worried look crossed Barry's face and Mark realised how isolated the team was out here. There was the Boss, the lads, the medical team, the kitmen and even the media. They were all part of a walled community. The outside world did not exist, or least not until Mark had reminded Barry that it was still there.

'Yeah, you're right. I don't want my mum and dad thinking I'm too shit scared or too big for my boots. I'll tell the gaffer I've changed my mind and I'll do it.'

And he had, and he'd been fine, even cracking the odd joke against himself, apologising for his accent whilst at the same time making it broader than usual. He was fine on the pitch as well. Whatever it was that had been biting him was forgotten as he began to reproduce all the tricks that had so excited in training. The superlatives sprang to the mouths of the commentators, although Mark was more restrained. He, more than anybody, realised not only how good Barry Reed was, but how good he could be. He didn't need to be there hoisting him up on the pedestal and he would certainly not be there alongside whichever Brutus and Cassius put the knife into the player's back when the first opportunity arose.

It was totally against the run of play when Colombia took the lead.

Their giant centre-forward, Ferrera, who had spent the first half an hour of the game alone and isolated, suddenly decided that if anything was to happen for him then he would have to make it happen on his own. He tracked back, looking for the ball and, as a reward, picked up a clearance from his keeper on the halfway line. He took the ball on his chest, brought it down in a swivel, and turned Peter Ranson, the English captain with unexpected grace. Ranson was having difficulty deciding whether he should be playing as a sweeper or a conventional centre-half and was left stranded. With the two wing backs pushed up in Cunningham's preferred formation, Ferrera found himself with a clear path to goal. He was not the speediest player on the pitch, but his height and long legs gave him the benefit of huge strides that ate up the ground as Ranson and the other defenders struggled in his wake. They were several strides behind when he reached the edge of the area and the England keeper, Dave Collins, could do nothing but race off his line, spreading his body to maximise his chances of a save. Ferrera glanced up, saw exactly what he was doing and coolly chipped the ball over his body into the net.

Suddenly it was carnival time. Fireworks and Klaxons erupted and blared as in the streets outside a thousand car horns signalled the arrival of the goal. Luis Cano, in the Press Box close to

Mark, was on his feet screaming into the microphone along with the rest of them, as if they had just won the World Cup, not taken the lead in a meaningless friendly.

The English contingent, both amongst the media and on the bench, remained seated and philosophical. Kenny Cunningham signalled to his captain to forget the mistake, get on with the game and rouse the rest of the team as well. He rolled up his short sleeves in a meaningful gesture and pushed the side to respond with all they had. One or two of the more senior members of the squad were clearly struggling in the heat which seemed just as overpowering at night as it had been during the day. By half-time the game was being played at a walking pace, with Colombia delighting in possession, content to let the sweating and exhausted Englishmen chase the game.

As the whistle blew to signal the end of the first forty-five minutes, Luis, off the air for commercials, came over to Mark with a broad smile on his face.

'You see, I told you this was a good team. I think we had a bet of a hundred dollars . . .'

'In your dreams, Luis. I remember everything. I do nowadays.'

'And the beautiful Miss Delaney, she is here?'

'She is.'

'But not with your English Press.'

'She's not accredited. But I got her one of the best seats in the stand.'

Luis waved his hand.

'A woman so lovely amongst all these hot blooded Latinos. I think you will be a lucky man if she sleeps with you tonight.'

'I always feel lucky when she sleeps with me. Anyway, Patti can look after herself.'

Luis was serious again.

'I'm not so sure she can, although I hope from the bottom of my heart that she has no need to. I did not like her interest last night in our drug barons. When you leave the country after the match, make sure she goes with you.'

'I'll try. It's not easy making Patti do anything. She's half-Irish and half-Jewish and I don't know which half makes life the more difficult.'

'Ah, but no part of her is South American, so be grateful at least for that.'

Their conversation was brought to an end by the return of the teams to the field, the Colombians being greeted by a huge roar that suggested the English Christians were about to be fed to the lions. For once Mark did not welcome the restart of the match. He felt that Luis still had more to say, and although he did not think he would like it, he did feel he had to hear it all through.

Kenny Cunningham had used the interval to make a couple of changes. Josh Nicholson for Collins in goal, Darren Cartwright, who was also making his debut, replacing the seemingly evergreen Peter Dennis in midfield. Dennis who had been one of the players most badly affected by the heat and humidity in the first half, now sat on the bench, accompanied by the team doctor, taking huge gulps of oxygen, his complexion an unhealthy grey.

'He ought to be in the treatment room, not out there,' Mark said to his co-commentator, the experienced Ritchie Lennard.

'Do you want to be the one to try and tell Peter Dennis anything?' was the reply.

Barry Reed was looking as if he were the senior professional in the side, clapping the players enthusiastically to get stuck in, yelling orders to which nobody listened. Within ten minutes of the restart they were listening – and watching.

Barry played a confident one-two with Darren Cartwright, collecting the ball back from him on the left side of the halfway line, cut inside one, then two defenders and balanced himself for a shot from the edge of the penalty area. His boot was never permitted to make contact with the ball as a Colombian defender with Desperate Dan bristle on his chin brought him crashing to the ground. The tackle was so ferocious that the entire England contingent, as one man, gasped. For a moment the whole game was frozen in a pageant of horror. Barry lay there absolutely still and silent, a bad sign in itself. Mark knew that when a player rolled around in agony he was more than likely to be up on his feet in a matter of minutes, limping away a little for effect. The England physio did not wait for a signal from the referee, and nor did Kenny Cunningham. As one they ran, stride for stride, to Barry's side.

'Are you all right, son?' the manager asked, ignoring the official's efforts to remove him from the field of play. The physio shoved some smelling salts under his nose and he jerked himself upright.

'I'm fine. Although if I get my hands or my boots on that fucking defender that's not how he's going to feel.'

'I don't think you're actually going to get the chance unless you follow him home, which is probably just as well,' Cunningham said as he saw from the corner of his eye the referee first produce a red card and then point to the penalty spot.

If the crowd had gone crazy when it came to the goal, then the referee's insurers must have trebled his life premiums after his double decision. Bottles, cushions, cans and, even more threateningly, pieces of timber broken from the seats, began to rain down on the pitch. Mark did his best to maintain the commentary on the match, but one eye was in the stand where he knew Patti was seated, praying that the mini-riot would die down, that the fans would come to their senses and realise that this match had little or no significance other than what it might tell the two managers about their teams.

A rocket lit up the night sky, followed by another. Colombians had exited the bars and the sound of their blaring car horns filled the night in an unorchestrated war dance, boding ill for any foreigner trying to make it out of the stadium.

Mark turned again to Ritchie Lennard.

'It's not often I hope England lose, but this has to be the night.'

'You're not wrong, Mark. I tell you if I were taking the penalty out there I'd blast it over the bar and apply for the Colombian Congressional Medal of Honour.'

'I'm not so sure they've got a Congress here,' Mark replied, but even as he spoke, Peter Ranson was striding up to the spot, apparently oblivious to all the noise. With no apparent back-lift he coolly hit the ball into the top left corner of the net and turned to acknowledge the cheers of the small contingent of English fans, fenced into a pen in the corner. What might have been intended for their protection now seemed to expose them to danger as a hail of missiles was hurled in their direction. Cans filled with nails, odd bits of metal and even a half-filled picnic basket landed around their heads as they pulled back into a close-knit group, their celebrations brought to an early conclusion. The police force seemed indifferent to the attack. They had been warned about the hooligan element amongst the English fans, but had no instructions to lay down their lives for them.

The referee did the only thing possible and pulled the players off the pitch. An announcement came over the loudspeakers, first in Spanish and then in English.

'Please. We are all here to enjoy the match. It is only a friendly contest. Let us all be friends.'

The words were greeted with an outburst of jeers, not just from the Colombians but, incredibly, also from the English fans, who were now breaking up their own section of the ground and giving as good as they had got in the exchange of missiles. However, gradually the noise and sporadic violence subsided and was replaced by a rhythmic handclapping to signal that the crowd having paid their money now wanted to get full value. If they had chosen to interrupt for a few moments, then that had been their prerogative. Nobody had died, any wounds inflicted were superficial and could be worn as a badge of honour and there seemed no reason not to play on.

Mark shook his head in despair. The commentary had come off the air and the pundits in the studios back home were giving their deep meaningful analysis. He mouthed across to Luis, 'A bunch of kids, that's what they are.'

Luis shrugged, the Latin shrug that could have a hundred different meanings, then shouted back, words that carried all too clearly across what had suddenly become a silent Press Box.

'Sure, Mark, a bunch of kids; but what dangerous children to play with.'

But then, as the referee finally led the players back on to the field of play, anything else he had to say was lost in a wall of noise.

CHAPTER 17

Nathan Carr, sitting in the stands at the Colombian National Stadium, was one of the few English spectators to view the violence and interruption of play with any pleasure. He'd tried to get the rights to screen live England's friendly internationals played outside Wembley for Jet TV and had failed. He did not take kindly to failure and worst of all he had lost out to Ball Park. He was tired of losing to Mo Halid, his so-called former friend. It was bad enough that he had lost his wife to him without also losing every sporting contest that was on offer. This was going to be the last time.

Mo Halid was beginning to think he was unbeatable. He had money, power, connections and a track record. Even Nathan Carr could not honestly criticise the professionalism of the coverage that Ball Park gave to the game. There were always more than enough cameras, commentators and experts. They had their pick of the bunch, including the latest one Mark Rossetti. A real find, considering his past. Carr knew all about Rossetti's background. He made it a point to discover everything about anyone who was in any way connected with Halid or his company. He never knew when it might come in useful.

He'd come to Bogota because, yet again, Jet had the crumbs from the rich man's table. They were being given the chance to show recorded highlights late in the evening. Recorded highlights. What good were they? He knew exactly what the viewing figures were likely to be. Who was going to watch thirty minutes of a game on one cable channel when they could have seen all of it live on another three hours earlier? The advertisers knew what the viewing figures were going to be as well, and advertising revenue was the life-blood of his station.

He'd not come to Bogota just to supervise his team recording and editing the highlights. He still had enough people capable of doing that. He had people capable of doing everything that

Ball Park did, better probably. They just needed to be given the chance to do it. He'd come to Bogota not only to keep his station's foot in the door of televised football, but also to listen and learn.

Although this was a friendly there was enough interest in both teams for everybody who was anyone in football to be here. FIFA and UEFA administrators and officials were here in numbers and of more importance there was the fact that those who would decide upon the future of ESL in Zurich in a few weeks' time were also present.

Carr was a little more subtle than simply going up to the members of the committee and asking what it would take to bring the contract home to Jet. He'd wanted those rights since way back in 1992 when he'd first thought they'd be available. He'd seen them snatched from him in 1997 and now they were back on the table. That, too, was thanks to Halid, although he had no intention of showing him any appreciation. Indeed, he'd had a long private laugh when his arch-rival had won his battle to re-open the tender. All those legal fees, all that effort, all that manpower and he, Nathan Carr, had not had to lift a finger, not had to spend a penny. He'd had it all fed to him on a plate.

He'd made sure that he'd be staying at the same hotel as Jacques Vicheron, the Chairman of the ESL Committee, who was here merely as an interested spectator. There was no harm in him knowing that with Carr he was dealing with a man of substance. Vicheron's luxurious suite was paid for on an expense account, whilst Carr's own company was footing the bill for him. He'd brought Alissa Bland with him. Again, he was not so naive as to believe that she could seduce Vicheron into bed and guarantee success that way, but people would talk to her, confide in her, when they might look upon Carr with some suspicion. It had worked up to a point. They'd gleaned a few hints as to the sort of levels at which the tenders would need to be aimed, a few comments as to the kinds of items in the presentation that would impress. And he had every hope now that those hints would not have to be put to any meaningful use. It had certainly not been a wasted trip. He knew for certain that Ball Park and Jet were going to be the only serious bidders from the UK. That made it simple. Not easy, but simple. Nothing that involved Mo Halid was ever going to be easy and in a way Carr would have been disappointed if it was. What was the point of gaining a victory over Halid if it were easy? He wanted to work at it and knew for certain that if he was working at it, then so was Halid. And when Halid lost then he would know that he had lost something he really wanted. It wouldn't be like losing a wife though. Susie had been something he'd really wanted.

The pair of them had thought they were so generous, so sophisticated, so understanding, telling him to his face. They'd been waiting there, drinks in hand, in his own lounge when he'd come home from work. Home from a hard day's work to keep Susie in the manner to which she'd become accustomed. They'd even had a third glass on the table expecting him to drink with them, to toast the future of the woman he loved and the partner he trusted.

They'd told him the whole story, how nothing had been planned, an evening spent together when he had been travelling for the company, their company as it then was. He recalled the trip all too well. Over to Vienna for a day to land a major contract. A mad dash to the airport only to find they'd reallocated his seat. An argument with the girl on the check-in desk to no avail and by the time somebody senior had been summoned the plane was already taxiing along the runway.

Apologies to a regular first class passenger, the offer of a complimentary night in a five-star hotel. It had all seemed enough at the time as he'd luxuriated in a bath and phoned home whilst still in the water to say he'd be away for the night. Susie had sounded all charm and solicitude, amused by the sound of splashing water down the line. She did all that very well and perhaps, during the good times, for the most part, she meant it.

She'd reminded him that Mo had been coming over for dinner. Poor Mo, poor lonely Mo, who'd separated from his wife, who needed feeding up, looking after. How many times had they asked him round, listened to his problems, listened to his ambitions for the company, his dreams for all of them. They were going to go all the way. Mo, with his great ideas was going to make them seriously rich. Together they'd build the company up, float it, sell out and then do what? He could never envisage doing nothing, could not imagine Mo doing nothing either. Susie would have done it very well. She'd always liked to spend money even when it had not been there to spend. So what would she have been like if Mo's plans had reached fruition? What was she like now when doubtless she had her limitless credit cards, the keys to the most expensive shops in the world?

There were times when he could even convince himself he was well rid of her. It had not been the happiest of marriages, because he had always wanted not just to own her, but to flaunt her. She was indisputably attractive with her fair hair always looking freshly washed, her slim, boyish figure that she still persisted in squeezing into clothes at least one size too small. She was the kind of woman who turned heads in restaurants, whose bejeaned backside drew men's eyes to swivel in their heads as she walked down the street, who exhibited a clear preview in her skin-tight outfits of what she would look like totally naked. He'd been surprised when she'd had Mo's baby. He didn't think she would have wanted to risk losing her figure, didn't think she would have put up with all the mess and inconvenience that came with motherhood. Doubtless she would have done whatever was necessary to minimise the inconvenience. The best maternity hospital, nurses, nannies, all part of the supporting cast as she showed off the child in public, successfully playing the role of tender, caring mother.

When he'd first met her she'd just finished at drama school. She'd told him she was waiting for the big break, the main chance. It never came in her acting career, it only came the night he slept alone in Vienna and she slept with Mo in his matrimonial bed. He'd spurned their offer of friendship. Yes, he'd raised the glass they'd offered him from their celebratory bottle, celebrating their liberation from him. Then, just when they thought he was joining them in the toast, taking it like a gentleman, he'd thrown the liquid full into their faces. Tossing their honeyed words back in their faces, he stormed out, directionless and alone.

It was a bad move to have left his own house, his lawyer told him later. He'd not been impressed by the advice, and nowadays he used a man in whom he had total confidence. Lars Clinton was half-Swedish, half-American, English qualified and one of the leading experts in the world on communication law. Fight fire with fire. Halid was using the high-profile Ben Rubens rather than his family solicitor, Henry Freeman. Smart and Jewish. Smart enough to make it all the way up the ladder in the big City firm in which he was a partner. He'd done a good job on the re-opening of the bid. Clinton had confirmed that.

'You understand, Nathan, I'm only a lawyer who interprets regulations. I can tell you what to put in your submissions, I can't tell you how to put it.'

'You don't need to. I'm paying an arm and a leg to consultants to do just that. Anything you can do to boost up our bid, anything to undermine Ball Park.'

'We'll do our best,' Clinton had said. At nearly £500 per hour, he bloody well ought to be doing his best, Carr thought. He ought to be performing miracles for that sort of money. Still, the thing about Clinton was he did at least give the impression you were getting value for money, but only time would tell if that impression was correct.

It was with a slight feeling of disappointment that Carr saw the match resume. He had his team back in London analysing Ball Park's coverage, dissecting it clinically like a surgeon searching for a cancer that might or might not be there. If they'd focused too much on the violence then he'd home in on that. Concentrating on the wrong part of the game, sensationalizing the coverage. Surely ESL wouldn't like that.

'Do we have to stay, Nathan? I'm hot and I'm bored and I'm not sure they'll keep our table for dinner, or even if they understood that we made a reservation. This country really is the armpit of South America,' Alissa said.

'They'll keep our table until breakfast. Don't worry, they may not understand English but they certainly understood the tip I left them.'

He leaned forward in his seat trying to concentrate on the game. Despite the fact it was such a vital part of his business he really did like football. He not only liked it but when he bothered to talk about it he could also demonstrate that he was very knowledgeable. Young Barry Reed was impressing him on his debut. He looked a real find, playing with a maturity far beyond his years. Not for the first time Carr idly wondered about acquiring or establishing a sports agency within his company. It would complement the media side very nicely.

He clapped appreciatively as Reed received the ball out on the left and hit the ball cross-field to the right wing with a startling accurate volley. The focus and the pressure off him, he began to make ground towards the Colombian goal and instinctively was in the right position when the ball was returned to him some three passes later. He took it on his left foot, hit it first time and there was just a blur as it flashed past the keeper to put England in the lead.

Even the Colombian supporters for the most part reacted with applause. They had already shown the violent side of their nature by venting their spleen on the referee, now it was time to show that they could also appreciate a piece of footballing genius.

'What a great goal,' Alissa said, forgetting her boredom.

'Wonderful,' replied Carr, but within seconds the moment of euphoria that arose from being there when something special occurred had passed. All he could now contemplate was the endless showing and reshowing of the goal on Ball Park. Jet would eventually have the footage, but the instantaneous moment would have passed. He also knew that Ball Park would also get to the goalscorer. There was obviously a relationship with Mark Rossetti that the rest of the media, Jet included, could not hope to challenge.

The referee blew his whistle for the end of the match as soon as the exact ninety minutes were up on the clock. There were still a few cries of protest from the Colombians, who clearly felt he should have played on until the home team had equalised, but the referee was racing down the tunnel before they even had time to complete their arguments. He had a wife and family and wanted to see them again.

As they rose to leave, Carr saw a distinctive redhead in the row in front of him talking to a stylish man, who, in his ice-cream coloured suit, seemed totally unaffected by the heat. Carr's sharp ears picked up an English accent within the conversation that was being conducted in Spanish.

'I've told you before not to look at other women. You know it makes me jealous,' Alissa said in a bantering tone, 'and in any event she's spoken for.'

'Who is she?'

'Patti, Patti Delaney. Mark Rossetti's other half.'

Carr nodded, but continued to stare. Patti's side of the conversation was becoming animated, bordering on the heated and anybody not knowing the couple would have taken her for the South American rather than the man. She was asking for something and the man was shaking his head calmly in denial.

But Patti was evidently a woman who did not take no for an answer.

Carr caught the eye of the other man. Patti followed the direction of his gaze. Was there a hint of recognition or was it simply the bonding of two men of the world where an attractive woman was involved?

Carr had hesitated for only the briefest of moments, then held his arm back and, with a sweeping gesture, escorted Alissa out of the ground. He was tired and he was hungry and, for the moment at least, had had his fill of the world of football.

CHAPTER 18

Barry Reed sat in the medical room beneath the main stand of the stadium and tried to prepare himself to urinate. By his side was Juanito Ferrera, the Colombian goal-scorer who had already given one sample and was just waiting to give a second if the need arose.

It had taken the edge off things being selected for a random drug test. He'd left his problems behind when he'd got on to the pitch, just as Mark said he would, but sitting here waiting to pass water gave him too much time to focus, too much time to think. Yes, he'd made a goal and scored one. Not just one, but probably the best he'd ever scored in his career. But the glory of a goal didn't last for ever, however many times it was shown on the box. You were always going to be judged on what you did today not what you had done yesterday. It was a little bit like going on holiday when you were a kid. You spent months looking forward to it, and then the second half of the break realising the days were ticking away to your return. Yet a part of him wanted to talk through the performance, to sit before a video with Mark and relive the game and the goal before they shifted too far in his memory.

The FIFA official and the local doctor returned and this time Barry succeeded in giving the sample. The official, a round, squat Swiss, shook Barry's hand, whilst the doctor removed the sample for testing having carefully labelled it up with identification.

'A great goal,' the round man said, 'one about which I will be proud to tell my grandchildren. I'm sure you'll score many more in your career.'

Ferrera gave his second sample and made to leave.

'You played good. You think maybe I could play in England one day?' His English was flawed and heavily accented, but he could make himself understood.

'Too right,' Barry replied with a grin that made him look about

100

sixteen. 'You'd be a top man back home. You're built like an English striker, took your goal well. How old are you, mate?'

'Twenty-six.'

'Spot on. Do you want me to have a word with a few people?'

Ferrera looked at Barry, puzzled by the confidence in one so young.

'Do you mean agents?'

'Nah, I can't stand the fuckers.'

'You are clever for your age. Me, I don't like agents either. In South America it is hard to find an honest agent, one who works for you and not for himself. They take money from you for doing nothing and you never know how much the club pays or what you earn.'

He produced a visiting card, which, with its gold edging and embossed letters looked more suited to a private banker than a professional footballer.

'Give me a call if you think there will be interest. If I come I think you and me, we will be friends.'

'Sure,' Barry said, looking up at the Colombian with admiration as he tucked his Armani shirt into Calvin Klein jeans and adjusted the solid gold necklace around his neck. He was a big man in every sense of the word, with wide slanting eyes, a broad nose contrasting with the almost girlish lips. His complexion was remarkably fair but his hair was jet-black, worn long at the back and tied into a pony-tail. He clearly had some European or perhaps even Scandinavian blood in him somewhere, and with his stylish and sophisticated appearance, it would not have surprised Barry if he had a Harley-Davidson parked outside ready to shoot off into the night at a hundred miles per hour. Ferrera finished dressing by slipping on Gucci sneakers and finally tossing a cotton jacket over his arm with, again, the Armani label in evidence. His total outfit looked as if it must have cost more than Barry earned in a month at Hertsmere.

He'd meant it when he said he disliked agents, but he really did need to do something about revising his contract at the club. Lennie Simons had been involved last time around, he of unblessed memory. Even if he'd still been around he'd learned his lesson and wouldn't have gone back to him again. The man had screwed him for five per cent of the total value of his contract and then gone back to Hertsmere and had the gall to ask them to pay his fees as well. David Sinclair, the chairman, had given him short shrift and had made sure that Barry knew all about it.

He'd ask Mark when he gave him the post-match interview he'd promised. Mark would know, Mark knew everything. He was happy at Hertsmere, he liked the chairman and the manager, but realised their limitations in respect of the depth of their pockets. Mr Sinclair had tried to explain it all to him at their first get-together after the summer break. This could be their last season at their old ground. Moving cost money, but if they could only win the Premiership, then there'd be as much money for the players as there was at any other major club. Winning the Premiership meant entry to the ESL. Barry had never been much good at arithmetic or maths at school and he had never attempted the mysteries of economics, but even he could understand just how much was at stake this season.

Being with the England team he'd been exposed to players from the major clubs, Manchester United, Liverpool, Newcastle and the old-established London pairing of Spurs and Arsenal. There was a common language amongst professionals in which only certain subjects tended to surface; clothes, cars, women, music, football and money. The odd experienced pro was tight-lipped about what he was earning, but most of them seemed quite happy, if not proud, to boast of their achievements of their agents and all the good things they had in their contracts. Barry had sat silently and listened. At Hertsmere he was considered anything but shy, but Peter Ranson had felt the need to tell Kenny Cunningham how quiet and withdrawn he'd found the young Geordie. Yet, his silence had advantages as people began to speak around him as if he were invisible. He was learning all the time, and as a full England international with every chance of retaining his place in the squad if not the team itself, he was beginning to have a reasonably good idea of what he was worth. He just needed Mark to advise him as to how to put it all together. He was definitely going to need the money.

The doctor returned to interrupt his train of thought before it went down that particular path, a path that had given him so many sleepless nights.

'You can go now. We get the results from the laboratory tomorrow.'

'We're leaving tomorrow,' Barry said.

The doctor shrugged.

'No one will be stopping you from going. These things are a formality. Football is not like athletics. Nobody I have ever tested has been positive.'

'Always a first time, mate,' Barry said. 'Still, it's not going to be me. Sorry to have kept you waiting.'

He followed the noise and bustle and arrived back in the dressing room.

Nearly all the rest of the players were changed and ready to go. The Colombian FA in conjunction with the government had arranged an official dinner. None of the players were looking forward to it with any relish.

'Can't get pissed when you've half the old farts from a dozen or so FAs there, can you?' Dave Collins, the keeper said. When it came to hard drinking, he had a certain reputation amongst his peers.

'What time's our flight tomorrow?' Barry asked.

'Noon. You can have a bit of a lie-in,' Collins replied.

Peter Ranson put a friendly arm around Barry's shoulders.

'He'll want to get up early to read the papers even if they're all in Spanish. Probably bribe the pilot to drive faster so that he can get home in time to buy the English ones as well. We've got the coach outside, but half the world's press is waiting to talk to you. I'll get the driver to wait for ten minutes. You can use that as an excuse to bugger off if they get too persistent.'

'Thanks, Pete.' Barry looked really appreciative.

'No problem. You'll do the same for me when I'm as famous and good-looking as you, or score those sort of goals.'

Barry wasn't ready for the reception. Nothing had prepared him for the flash of cameras, the booms of the mikes, the sea of faces, the cacophony of voices all asking different questions. The Press Officer, Jim Kelly, was already at the reception, dealing with the authorities who were wondering just what time they were going to sit down and eat, or if they were ever going to see their beds that night. He'd left Jenny Cooper in charge and she was doing a pretty good job of getting the howling masses into some semblance of order, barking orders with a ferocity that belied her looks.

'Can you hold up this shirt, Barry?'

'Put the ball on your head.'

'Hold this jar of coffee.' That from somebody a little more inventive than the rest.

'Take the England flag in your left hand and punch the air with your right.'

'Just a bit to the left.'

'This way, this way, this way. And again.'

Again, and again and again. His eyes hurt from the bulbs popping in his face. His leg hurt from the tackle that had brought him down for the penalty. He wanted to get to a phone. There were people he needed to talk to.

The photographers had their five minutes and, despite their plea for more, Jenny shooed them outside. The regular travelling journos had already agreed between themselves who'd ask the questions. For the most part they were a decent bunch, hard-drinking, womanising, creative with their expense accounts, but fair with the players. A far cry from the rat-pack of feature writers and news reporters who latched on to them and were there for any dirt that might arise.

The sports journalists would all write down the same answers, only they'd be interpreted in a different way depending upon the publications in question. The TV camera crews came last. Mark held back. He had no problems. He knew Barry would talk to him, would find the time to give him the exclusive footage he'd been promised. He didn't need to fight alongside the rabble.

Ten minutes passed, then fifteen. The coach-driver impatiently sounded his horn. Barry looked anxiously at his watch and pulled away from the penultimate interviewer to make his way over to Mark, waiting patiently at the rear of the room. He'd only taken a couple of steps when Jenny intervened.

'Sorry, Barry, I've just had Jim on the phone from the reception. There's hell to pay down at the civic centre. I'm afraid you're going to have to leave it for now and get on the bus.'

'But I've promised Mark a few minutes.'

'No can do, honeychild. Be a good boy and do what mummy says.' The expression on her face and the tone of her voice were anything but maternal.

Mark, who had been standing within earshot of her, tried to control his anger.

'I didn't hear your phone ring.'

'Didn't you? Well then, I suppose you're none too good at hearing things, are you, Mark? I mean I tried to tell you something back in England and you certainly didn't hear me then either.'

'Come on, Jenny, this is business, not anything personal.'

'Everything's personal, Mark. What's that they say? All's fair in love and war.'

Mark made one last effort.

'Let the bus go and I'll bring Barry down myself.'

She shook her head, a look of triumphant power in her eyes.

'More than my job's worth to split the lads up. So sorry, Mark. Still it'll give you an extra few minutes to spend with your little journalist friend, won't it?'

Mark looked helplessly at the crew and then at Barry. For a moment he thought the boy was going to argue, but Jenny took him firmly by the arm and hurried him to the door.

'What am I going to tell the studio back in England?' It was a question to himself, but it came out louder than he intended.

'Tell them you lost yourself the right to special privileges,' she said. Then turning back towards him, she said in a whisper that only he could hear, 'Tell them you fucked *yourself*.'

And then she followed Barry out of the door, pushing him towards the waiting bus like a beautiful, porcelain shepherdess rounding up the last of her flock.

CHAPTER 19

It was two in the morning and Mark was getting really worried. He'd arranged for Patti to join him at the reception if they weren't able to meet up after the match. He'd assumed that, because of the delay in the game and the further fruitless wait for Barry, she'd simply cadged a lift down there with someone else. By midnight, it was clear that she wasn't coming and, with two telephone calls to the hotel producing no result, all the horror stories he'd heard from Luis Cano were racing through his mind.

He looked for Luis amongst the throng and it took him a good five minutes to locate him and tell him what had happened. A shadow crossed the Colombian's face before he spoke with a reassurance that was not entirely convincing.

'If she arranged to do an interview the odds are that she is still waiting for her subject to turn up. I keep telling you about time-keeping here. It bears no resemblance to what you know of in Europe.'

'I'm not so sure. Have you ever waited for an Italian?' It was a light-hearted comment, but Mark felt anything but light-hearted. 'She didn't say anything about doing an interview.'

'She tells you everything?' Luis asked in a tone that suggested he already knew the answer, but Mark gave it to him anyway.

'No, she doesn't tell me everything.'

'Then don't worry my friend. That is unless you think she is with another man. She is a very attractive lady, your Patti.'

'I don't think she's with another man. But you're the one who told me what a dangerous city this was, yet you don't seem to be in a panic.'

Luis gripped Mark's arms, and he realised that the Colombian was a little the worse for drink. If that explained his apparent calm then there was even more to worry about. Mark could stand the tension no longer and decided to give the final speeches of the evening a miss. Barry had been more than apologetic, but security had refused to allow Ball Park's cameras inside and Mark wondered whether that too was on Jenny's instructions. He'd actually been surprised to find himself on the invitation list when none of the rest of the English media party had been similarly honoured. He could only put it down to knowing Kenny Cunningham, or being potential flavour of the month with Jenny when the guest list had been drawn up.

Right now the invitation meant nothing to him. He was worried about Patti and he was also very angry with her. If she'd got herself into trouble then this was no place in which to do it. If she'd just got herself involved with something more important than meeting up with him then she could, at least, have let him know. It had not been easy arranging an extra seat for her at the dinner when he was merely a fringe guest himself. He rehearsed the sort of argument they were likely to have when she refused to admit she had behaved in anything less than a reasonable manner. He'd actually begun to miss those sort of arguments, but now that the storm clouds were once again overhead he could think of no good reason why that should be.

He was getting ready to leave when Nathan Carr and Alissa Bland came across to speak to him. They'd never been formally introduced but anybody who worked for or with Mo Halid could not fail to know exactly who they were. Carr was *bonhomie* incarnate.

'We've never had the chance to talk, you and I, Mark. But let me say how impressed I've been with your TV coverage for Ball Park. I don't think I've ever seen a natural like you. Lineker, Waddle, Hansen, Francis, they all grew into it; but you look as if you're talking directly to the bloke in the lounge in front of his TV.'

'Maybe that's because there's only one bloke watching,' Mark replied with a smile.

'Good sense of humour as well. When we get back to London I think we should meet up for a chat. When I get the ESL rights, I reckon we could find a job for you heading up the team.'

Mark's mind was racing ahead, still thinking about Patti, but he could not help but note that Carr had said when rather than if. Was he truly feeling that confident or was he just being given a message to deliver back to Mo, albeit in an oblique way?

'I'm not unhappy where I am,' Mark said, his eyes firmly fixed on an escape route through the door.

'Not unhappy? Surely you being a person of, how shall I put it, independent means? Surely you're entitled to be deliriously happy if you're going to work at all. Otherwise, why bother?'

'Look, Mr Carr . . .'

'Nathan, please.'

'Nathan,' Mark responded, not wishing to argue, 'I'm sure you've got my best interests at heart, but I really don't have time for a philosophical conversation at the moment.'

'Ah, of course, you want to be hurrying back to the lovely Patti Delaney. Alissa and I saw her after the match, although we didn't have the opportunity to speak to her. She appeared to be otherwise engaged.'

'What do you mean?' Mark asked sharply, concern and jealousy hitting the pit of his stomach simultaneously and making an uneasy combination.

'The man, Alissa, what did you say his name was?'

Alissa had dutifully complied with Nathan's instructions in the few hours since the match had ended and had found out the name of Patti's companion.

'Branco. Riccardo Branco.'

Luis appeared by Mark's side as if he knew what information was about to be related. He sparked into life, any suggestion that he might be drunk instantly wiped from his demeanour.

'Are you sure? You did say Riccardo Branco?'

The next question was how Alissa Bland had come to recognise him, but he did not bother to ask that one. His mind was several paces on. He turned to Mark and pulled him aside, out of earshot of Carr and Alissa.

'I know she is a beautiful woman, your Patti, but I did not think she could also be this stupid. All through dinner last night she asks about drugs in this country and I tell her, because she is your friend, and she is curious and everybody is curious about drugs in Colombia. You remember?'

Mark remembered only too well. Luis had told them how a relatively honest administration had gone about eliminating the Cali cartel, a group of seven men. Not the magnificent seven either, but possibly the seven most deadly criminals in the world. Six of them were now behind bars, the seventh had been killed in a shoot-out. But their disappearance from the scene had no immediate impact on the drug trade. Instead of the sophistication of the computer-organised cartel there were now hundreds of splinter groups all producing cocaine within the camouflage of the jungle. The terrain was a natural. The eastern region of Guaviare consisted of some 26,000 square miles of savannah and jungle reachable only through the airfields operated by the traffickers. And out of the chaos that the destruction of the cartel had left behind, sprang up Second Division leaders all fighting for their share of the cocaine market that supplied some 80 per cent of the world's demand. And of all the Second Division leaders the one who had emerged triumphant, who had shot to the top of the Premier League, who perhaps merited the title of drug baron more than any of his predecessors, was Riccardo Branco.

'I made an error,' Luis continued. 'I did not ask your friend if her curiosity was merely idle or a matter of professional interest.'

'Luis,' Mark interrupted, 'do you want to tell me what's happening? Why's Patti chatting up this mobster?'

Luis put a finger to his lips.

'I do not think it a good idea to be calling Branco a mobster. He has many friends.'

'He doesn't sound a friendly sort of guy.'

'Maybe the word friends is wrong. Maybe I should just say that he has many people who fear him, who would do anything for him.'

Nathan Carr and Alissa were drawn back to the scene by the men's anxiously raised voices.

'Is there anything I can do to help?' Nathan asked.

'No, I do not think this is a matter for anybody but a Colombian,' Luis replied dismissively. 'Perhaps it's not too late. Perhaps I can still do something. Listen, Mark, go back to your hotel. Go to your room, lock the door and stay there until I call or come.'

'I want to come with you.'

As they argued, the two men were walking and now stood on the marble steps of the building.

'No, believe me, I am not being dramatic and I am not trying to be a hero, but I know this city, I know Branco. If I try to take a gringo with me, then certain places will be barred to me, certain questions will not only go unanswered, but it will be as if they had never been asked.'

'Tell me more about Branco then. Just tell me that and I'll do what you say.'

'Time may not be on our side, or on Patti's side. This is not the moment for a history lesson. Enough to say that he is a bad man. He wants to be the new king of Bogota, maybe of all Colombia. As things stand he is the most powerful criminal since Escobar. If your Patti thinks she can handle him like some petty English criminal then she is very wrong. And your other English friend and his lady . . . who are they?'

'They're in the same business as my boss.'

'And they know Branco. I think they too may be looking to cause trouble; but I'll leave the English troublemakers to you.'

He paused for breath.

'Don't hail a cab in the street. Ask the man on the door to get you one. At least that way you have a ninety per cent chance of arriving safely at your destination.'

'What sort of country is this, Luis?' Mark asked with a hint of desperation in his voice.

'Sometimes, my friend, even I do not know,' the Colombian replied and the last Mark saw of him was as he headed towards the telephone booths in the corner of the lobby.

CHAPTER 20

At two in the morning, standing on a corner of the Plaza de Bolivar in the heart of Bogota, Patti Delaney was beginning to think she may have made a mistake. In fact, she had probably made several mistakes, like deciding to follow up on Jessica's leads, like coming to Bogota, like not confiding in Mark and not listening to Luis Cano's words of warning. She just hoped that they were all remediable. Arranging to meet a man like Riccardo Branco in the early hours of the morning, when nobody else knew where the hell you were, could very well be the last mistake she ever made. She cursed her Irish-Jewish genes, that combination of curiosity and stubbornness that always seemed to get her into trouble. And on this occasion she was not too sure how she could possibly rely upon Mark to bail her out.

It had all seemed so simple, so straightforward, but then it always did. A couple of names from Jessica, a map, the coincidence that Mark was going to be in the very country where it all started. Luis had been helpful. He'd thought he'd been telling her what he wanted, when in reality he'd been answering her questions, questions she'd prepared carefully before she'd left England. She wasn't quite ready to go on *Mastermind* with Colombian Drug Exports as her specialist subject, but she wasn't far off it. Taxis cruised by, taxis that might well take her back to the safety of the hotel and a bed to be shared with Mark. But she resisted the temptation to hail one, justifying her decision with the threat of kidnap or robbery of which Luis had warned. She forced herself to concentrate on what she knew in an attempt to blot out the situation in which she now found herself, and blot out the time, blot out the men who ogled her from afar. One or two had tried to approach her, but she had seen them off with a hail of obscene Spanish. She ran through the history, as she knew it, in her mind, the same sort of mental exercise she had

111

used in the past, often when her mother was in one of her more incoherent modes.

It wasn't all about cocaine, although Colombia might well have been the leader in that particular product. But it was also third in the marijuana stakes and roaring up the charts with heroin since it started growing opium poppies in the late 1980s. The States may have been the main recipient of its produce, but the mule routes were just as effective in getting the stuff into Europe. Yes, they began here and they ended with a young woman like Jessica dying in an English hospice. Only they didn't end. They began again. It was ceaseless, this treadmill of death. As long as the men who built the machinery, who held the whips, were making their obscene profits, then it would continue.

The old cartels might be dead and buried, but the regional mafia was still there, and now there was also the Branco cartel. No need to hide the name; everybody, including the rest of the mafia, the police and the government, knew who was behind it. It was almost as if the last two had exhausted their energies in clearing out the old guard and had no stomach for a fresh fight.

The chief of police had done a great job over the last few years, but perhaps Branco had learned from those who came before him, or else he was just naturally more clever. Nothing could be linked directly to him. A Minister of Justice had come close, but he had been a passenger in a plane blown up over the mountains, taking him, his investigators and forty other innocent souls to kingdom come. A judge who refused to yield to the pressures to dismiss a seemingly water-tight case against Branco's nephew, was machine-gunned down on his way from church, killed in a state of grace along with two children, a grandmother and a passing stray dog.

The war between law enforcers and pliers of the trade had been long and violent. Back in 1983 Tranquiland was established on the banks of the Rio Yari in Los Llanos as the largest cocaine factory in history. A strange name for an industry that brought with it death rather than tranquillity. It became a town of its own, with roads, sleeping quarters and, of necessity, its own airstrip. With its fourteen laboratories, its own water and electricity supply, it operated as a community in every sense of the word, lacking only a political infrastructure. When you were producing some 3,500 kilos of purest cocaine every month, there was no need for politicians.

Rodrigo Bonilla had been appointed Minister of Justice back in August 1983 and launched a serious spearhead attack on the drug barons, Jorge Ochoa, Gonzalo Gacha, Carlos Lehder and, perhaps most powerful and renowned of them all back then, Pablo Escobar. Eventually a group of police and undercover agents were formed who were as incorruptible as it was possible to be amidst the corruption that was Colombia itself. In the spring of 1984, in the midst of the rainy season, the crack squad raided Tranquiland and arrested everybody they found. Needless to say they were able to detain only scientists and artisans. The men in charge had flown, leaving behind seven aircraft, enough weaponry and military vehicles to equip a small army and a river with fourteen tonnes of cocaine floating downstream filled with dead or dying fish who had overdosed.

All the cartel bosses moved to neighbouring Panama except for Lehder, who had some political ambitions, which he pursued by founding his own newspaper and his own political party, the MNL, of which, perhaps not surprisingly, he was the first (unelected) leader. He did, however, get himself elected to Congress from which position of power he claimed immunity from prosecution, a contention that he was able to maintain for some considerable time. His argument found particular support amongst those members of the judiciary who were either rewarded by his generosity or blackmailed by his knowledge.

The emigrés pined for their homeland and were actually missed by a large section of the population who had benefited from their industry either by employment or charity. Escobar, with his estimated wealth of two billion US dollars, could afford to be generous. Not only did he finance the construction of a *barrio* for 200 poor families in Medellin, for which he earned the title of Robin Hood Paisa, but he also offered to invest his capital in a national development programme. More inventive was a joint offer with the other drug barons to pay off the entire Colombian National Debt of 13 billion dollars.

When that offer was refused they reverted to type, buying land and industries through nominees, creating their own private armies, and finally in 1984 assassinating their main enemy, Justice Minister Rodrigo Bonilla. The war had entered a new phase.

The government began to issue extradition orders, assassinations became daily events, bombings were no longer a rarity. Newspaper headquarters were destroyed and even the National Police Agency in Bogota was not spared a bomb attack so powerful that buildings twenty blocks away collapsed.

The government stepped up its efforts and one by one the old cartel leaders were either killed or so persecuted that they surrendered to save their lives and their wealth. The Ocheas and Pablo Escobar finally struck a deal. They pleaded guilty to a minor charge and were guaranteed that they would neither be extradited nor sent to one of the unspeakable Colombian jails that housed the common criminals. In fact Escobar insisted on a new jail being built just for him, low security, high luxury, situated in his home town of Envigado, just outside Medellin.

For several years Escobar ran his business from the jail with all the home comforts required. But without his ability to travel, his teeth were no longer so sharp, his name was no longer so feared. The market became fragmented as young Turks made inroads into his territory, and by 1992 his patience was exhausted. Anticipating a governmental step to move him to more secure surroundings he decided to escape. His freedom lasted nearly a year and a half. For the most part his reputation was sufficient to guarantee sanctuary wherever he sought it, but he had still made enough enemies in his life to watch helplessly as his aides and bodyguards were picked off one by one. The American Drug Enforcement officers were particularly interested in Escobar and in December 1993 he was tracked down to his jungle hide-out and killed. It may have quietened down but it was not over. There was too much at stake for it to be over. The Carli cartel was led by the Rodriguez Orejuela brothers and for a while they seemed to have learned from their predecessors' mistakes. Within a year, moving in a smoothly sophisticated way, they had the major share of the New York cocaine market under their control. This time around there were no bombings, no assassinations and very little violence. Instead, they used lawyers. In place of cash there was a whole pyramid of companies set up for the purpose of money-laundering. It was another industry like any other. In 1995 Rosso José Serrano was appointed Chief of Police. He began with the police force itself, cleansing it of over 6,000 officers, nearly one third of the nation's force. It was he who had seen off the Carli cartel and it was he who had methodically set about the destruction of the laboratories in the Guaviare region. The statistics were incredible. Patti loved statistics. They were the framework upon which a journalist could construct her stories: 63 airstrips destroyed, 35 aircraft captured, 57 tons of pure cocaine seized together with 783 tons of cocoa-leaf paste. Enough to turn the whole of New York into addicts, if they weren't already.

Yet, it had no real effect. The supplies of cocaine from Colombia remained constant, and as one of the Hydra's heads was cut off, another dozen sprang up to replace it. And through the chaos, out of the smoke and mist had strode Riccardo Branco. He claimed to be a relation of Escobar although nobody had ever seen any proof of that. He also claimed to have inherited the Medallin cartel with its complex network, and he also claimed to be Robin Hood reincarnated. Where Escobar had built homes for a couple of hundred, Branco built for thousands, naming the blocks after his dead aides, turning them into martyrs, when they were, in truth, just murdered gangsters who had lived and died by the gun. It did not stop with homes. He also constructed an orphanage and a hospital, although his enemies whispered that he contributed to the population of them both.

Yet, there could only be whispers about Branco. There was never any hard evidence. He appeared to have a perfectly successful and legitimate business. He was into construction, he was into the equipping of hospitals, he was into communications, he was into the media and, however hard the authorities tried to probe beneath the surface, they could never unravel the illegitimate from the legitimate.

Unlike the Cali cartel, Branco courted publicity. He wanted to be visible, wanted people to see his good works. He could never be accused of hypocrisy as he supported the open sale of drugs, although obviously always referring to the suppliers and manufacturers in the third person. That, in itself, was a clever and subtle smokescreen. Patti had read the translation of one of his speeches.

'You drive drugs underground, you drive up the prices. What do the manufacturers of cocaine do that the tobacco giants do not? Men, women and children, they smoke. My hospitals are full of them, dying of lung cancer and those are the lucky ones, for there are other painful ways of creating a living death. These tobacco giants, those who sell cheap alcohol, they advertise, they glamorise and all is fine. And what do these kings of tobacco do for their subjects? Cheap labour, poor conditions, with all the power of a government behind them anxious to claim its revenue by way of tax. And the so-called drug barons are the criminals. They give to charity, they create jobs, they worry about the quality of their product. And they are the criminals? I do not think so.'

It was that desire for publicity that had given Patti the edge, the thought that if she could persuade Branco that she could show him as a great humanitarian, then she could get an interview. After that she only had the vaguest idea of what she might do. In the past, things had the habit of falling into place, like the haphazard plotting of a thriller where all the pieces come together.

Seeing Branco at the football match was a windfall. She'd planned to stay on after Mark's departure and somehow or other get an audience. Then he'd been presented to her on a plate and she could not believe her luck. A Brownie point to Mark for getting her into the best seats. Branco hadn't wanted to know at first, saying he knew all about the English tabloids; but Patti always kept a few photocopies of her better articles for the broadsheets and upmarket magazines in her bag. She'd produced them, stretched her Spanish to its very limits and, sensing that Branco had an eye for a pretty girl, she fluttered her eyelashes, tossing her feminist ideals to the wind. He had argued. To his surprise she had argued back and, eventually, with a broad smile that seemed to invite fish to swim towards it, he agreed, but only on his terms.

'I have a commitment after the match, and tomorrow I must fly to Panama on business . . .'

'Any time, anywhere,' Patti had said, never thinking he would say between one and two in the morning and a car would collect her from opposite the Capilla del Sagraci in the Plaza de Bolivar. She'd known that he'd made this arrangement to show her not only that he was in control, but also to test her. It was an offer she could not refuse if she had any chance of completing her mission. She looked first at her watch. She'd been here an hour already. She knew Mark would be worried, but she knew that if she'd gone to the reception and told him what she had planned, there was no way he would have let her go. So she'd returned to the hotel, showered, changed, collected her dictaphone and notepad and had been there well before the appointed hour. Her eyes moved from the time on her wrist to the chapel in the shadow of the cathedral. It looked very old, maybe seventeenth century and another time she would have got out her guidebook to check its credentials; but not tonight.

The Plaza was still busy despite the lateness of the hour. This was not the heart of the hotel district, more the cultural centre, but she still felt terribly exposed. A clock, perhaps from the cathedral itself, struck the hour. One, two. She could only remember what Luis had told her about Colombian punctuality and realised that she could be standing here until dawn. Maybe Branco had only agreed to meet her to see off her persistence. Next to the information kiosk was a phone booth and she moved towards it, driven by guilt. The very least she could do was to telephone Mark, who surely by now would be back at the hotel. Unless he'd been picked up at the reception. It was odd how that jokey little thought sent a shiver down her spine. She wouldn't hurt him for the world, and she was sure that by now he must be worried sick. She'd caused him enough heartache these last few weeks with her selfish behaviour. She had taken only a couple of steps, when out of the corner of her eye, she spotted a long, dark car slowing down beside her, matching its pace to her stride. She had seen that car before as it made its first circuit of the Plaza, but had not thought it was for her. Now it most certainly was. It never quite stopped, but just in front of her it pulled in to the kerb, a door opened and a voice said, 'Ah, Miss Delaney, I have found you,' and then a pair of strong, male hands pulled her off her feet and into the dark air-conditioned interior.

CHAPTER 21

'I can't believe you did what you did,' Mark erupted. She was back in the hotel room, shaking from head to toe and he realised that if he continued the tirade for a moment more she would burst into tears. It had been just ten minutes before that there had been a knock on the hotel door. He'd hesitated about opening it, then heard Luis's voice. He'd sensed he wasn't alone and had used the security spy-hole before releasing both locks. Luis half pushed, half carried Patti into the room. He seemed overcome by disbelief.

'I find her, Mark, I find her standing in the streets of Bogota in the early hours of the morning. I watch her for a few minutes before I pick her up and see the driver of every other car that drives around the Plaza also watching her and wondering why an expensive girl like her is standing on a street corner, wondering whether they can afford her.'

'How the hell did you know where to look?' Mark asked.

'I have friends. When I hear that she is talking to Branco I make a few calls, people who know Branco.'

'The police?'

'Some of them. But more than that. There are people in this city who make it their business to know every time that Branco goes to the toilet. And so they also know he has agreed to meet an English journalist. They know that for the moment he is amused by her, but Branco's moods change wildly. Now the English journalist is also a matter of interest. They think they know where he is to meet her, but I get there first.'

'Did she argue?' Mark asked as he heard Patti retching in the bathroom. She returned to the room with a toothbrush in her mouth and a tube of toothpaste in her hand, a hand that was still trembling.

'No, I didn't argue,' she said and threw herself into Mark's arms. He tried to kiss her, but the toothbrush got absurdly in the way and he settled for holding her close against him. 'I was terrified. I was just about to call you when Luis showed up.'

'I'm grateful,' Mark said, wondering for the first time how an ex-footballer, a sports commentator, had the sort of contacts that Luis so obviously possessed.

'You should be, my friend.'

'You don't think Branco would have given the interview, do you? He may have interviewed you to discover what you were really after, but he always has his own agenda. Who knows what he would have done? If he thought you were harmless then he would probably have given you a drink, asked you to sleep with him and when you said no, his pride would have insisted he delivered you back to your hotel.'

'And if he didn't think I was harmless?'

'If you had asked the wrong questions, then he would not have hesitated to force you tell him exactly what you were after.'

'Forced?'

'You want another word?' Luis asked. 'Tortured, maybe raped. He will treat all women well, but you lose your sex when you become an enemy. To his enemies Branco will show no mercy.'

'Isn't this all a bit dramatic?' Patti had poured herself a whisky from the minibar and was quickly recovering her composure. 'This is the end of the twentieth century, not the middle of the sixteenth. I think you're just trying to scare me.'

Luis frowned.

'I can see that you are beginning to lose the fear you felt when I found you.' He looked at the glass of scotch in her hand which she had topped up from the rapidly diminishing minibar.

'Drink can make heroes of us all.' She smiled and took another swallow.

'I am not joking. Ask Amnesty International about Colombian jails. They are the official punishment areas. Can you imagine what the unofficial ones are like? Believe me. Go to sleep now. Get on a flight in the morning with Mark. I don't know what really brought you to this place, but don't come back. How do they say it in English? They have your card marked now.'

It was hard to tell whether or not Patti had taken his advice but, after he left, she did at least collapse on the bed, her red hair contrasting sharply with the crisp white of the pillows. Her dress rode up over her pale freckled legs and Mark, despite the situation, or perhaps because of it, felt at once the rising of desire and the more passive desire to protect her, now and for always. But, it was never going to be easy to protect someone as wild and free as Patti. He lay down beside her without undressing and, as she rolled over on her side, he put his arms around her in a loving spoon and they fell into a deep sleep almost immediately.

He awoke with a start at six, the alarm clock beneath his hand blaring out some local station. Reluctantly, he realised that he had a plane to catch and there was no question of going back to sleep. The alarm had made no impression on Patti and he left her sleeping for an hour or so whilst he made a few calls to satisfy himself that there was a spare seat on the plane which could be reallocated to her. She was never at her best in the morning and as he tried for the fifth time to wake her, he wondered how someone who had been through such a trauma could suddenly switch off when it came to sleep. Eventually he got her to open her eyes and, incapable of speech, she pointed with her right index finger to her left wrist.

'It's eight o'clock,' he said giving her eight rapid, little kisses. 'We have to get packed and out of here before you get into any more hot water. I've got you on the same flight as me.'

'Too early, too early,' she muttered, burying her head under the pillow in the vain hope that Mark would leave her alone.

'Come on, Patti. You heard what I said about not getting into hot water. But I will run you a bath. Very hot, lots of bubbles, just the way you like it.'

'No. Come back to bed, Mark. I'm sorry about last night. It was really dumb.'

'I guess you're just one dumb broad,' he said in a mid-Atlantic accent. 'I'd love to come back to bed, but we can't right now. And, as for last night, I'm sure you had a perfectly good reason which you'll tell me about when you're ready. But you have to get up, have a bath and then we have to go catch a plane.'

Somehow or other he got her ready, throwing her clothes into the case without folding them, pushing down the lid and enjoying hearing the click of the lock, as if it signalled the end of their stay in Colombia.

They arrived at the airport about ten minutes before the England team coach and by the time they had checked in they found themselves in the midst of the main party. The journalists who were privileged to be flying on the same plane were still buzzing around Barry Reed in the same way as they would normally have gathered around a hotel bar for a free drink. Barry saw Mark and his face lit up.

'I'm sorry about last night's interview, but that cow never gave me a chance.'

'Don't worry about it. You already apologised last night. It's my day for receiving apologies. Anyway, there'll be lots more chances for interviews, I'm sure.'

At Passport Control Mark handed in his passport and the moustachioed official looked at it as if it were a certain forgery. After an interminable pause he begrudgingly waved him through. Barry stood back to let Patti go next. The same officer took her passport and scanned it with even more interest than he had accorded Mark's. Eventually, he grunted, then lifted the phone and spoke swiftly in Spanish. She stood there, trying to grasp what was being said, understanding one word in three, her A-Level Grade A of no use to her in an hour of real need. All she could appreciate was that this was not a diversion, not a call from the man's wife to see what time he might be home for dinner. This was a discussion about her. Mark realising something was wrong, tried to make it back to her side. Another official, taller, more menacing, flashes on his uniform indicating some form of seniority, blocked his path.

'One only,' he said in his own tongue and even Mark could understand the message and was forced to stay where he was, in a kind of no-man's land between Colombia and the British Airways plane.

Meanwhile, the official behind the desk had received some instructions.

'Señorita Delaney,' he placed the accent on the first three syllables, but she was left in no doubt that he was addressing her. 'You will follow me, please.' The last was an afterthought. She looked pleadingly at Mark, the same look that relatives must have given to friends left behind on the platform as the cattle trucks took them away to the death camps.

'What do I do?' she called out. It was an odd question from a woman who in the past had always known what to do, who would have regarded as a sign of weakness any reliance on others.

'Go with them. Don't argue,' he shouted back, without

121

hesitation. He knew her all too well and was concerned that some violent reaction could see her thrown into a local jail on a trumped-up assault charge. Arrest without trial was always the threat in countries like this.

'Don't worry,' he continued encouragingly, 'I won't let the plane leave without you.'

He sounded more reassuring than he felt. When it came down to the wire there was little or nothing he could do to affect the timetable of an airline. With or without Patti Delaney on board the plane would leave for London, even if he managed to hold it up for a little while on the pretext of avoiding an international incident.

The official with the moustache returned without Patti and stared at Mark belligerently as if to question why he was still there. The second man, who had barred his path, grabbed Mark by the arm and began to push him towards the departure lounge.

'You go. You go now. You leave on your plane.'

The queue behind Barry was increasing in length all the time, a mumble of concern snaking its way through the ranks of those waiting as vital duty-free purchasing time was frittered away. Already a few of the journalists were sensing a story and creating rumours in the ranks. A photographer, who Mark recognised, unslung his camera in anticipation of an exclusive and a man in a military uniform immediately came across to him and angrily pointed to a sign stating that photography was forbidden.

Mark hesitated. He could wait and hope that Patti was going to talk her way out of whatever it was they wanted to question her about. Or he could report the matter to the airline and get them to phone the British Embassy. He realised that he didn't even know if there was an ambassador or a consul, and if he had known then he was none too sure what exactly was the difference.

He made his way into the departure lounge, passing by familiar faces as if they weren't there. At least that would get him near to a phone. He assumed Barry was following close behind, but the youngster wasn't his immediate problem. In fact, if he'd glanced back he would have seen that the Geordie was undergoing the same sort of suspicious treatment that had been accorded to Patti. Once again Moustache was on the phone, his gaze not leaving Barry's face, the eyes accusing him of some unknown crime.

'Señor Reed, you too will follow me.' He did not accord him a please, perhaps because now he was dealing with a man rather than a lady. Kenny Cunningham was only a place or two behind his player in the line. He saw Barry being led away, and leapt forward to restrain him as if claiming a piece of stolen property.

'What's going on? I'm the England manager and that kid there is in my care.'

A man emerged from a side-office, drawn by the commotion. The journalists now had their pencils at the ready. The photographer had surreptitiously produced a tiny camera which he could conceal in his hand, thinking that the opportunity was worth the risk. The Colombian looked cool in his neatly-pressed uniform, despite the lack of air-conditioning in the terminal building. He was tall and slim, his shirt so white as to be fluorescent, the creases in his trousers like knives. His grey hair was cut short in military style and the ramrod backbone also suggested that he had been used to the parade ground at some time in his career. As soon as he spoke, in near-perfect English, he exuded an air of authority that the other two officials had lacked.

'We know who you are, Mr Cunningham, and we know who your player is as well. And he is not in your care. He is in my care, or custody as the case may be.'

'Then if you know, what the hell are you playing at? And what do you mean by talking about custody?' Cunningham asked, unable to conceal his anger, aware by now that whatever happened, this story would be the next day's headlines back in England.

'We are not playing. This is not a football stadium. My name is Fernando Diaz and I am in charge of our anti-drug squad in Bogota.'

'I'm delighted to meet you,' Cunningham said with heated sarcasm. 'Now perhaps you'd tell me what drugs have to do with this young man.'

'It is all very simple, Mr Cunningham. This young man, as you describe him, has tested positive for drugs after last night's match. That in itself is evidence that he has been using illegal substances in our country. I do not think that your British government would take kindly to one of our nationals using drugs in London, so why should we? Now, if you would release his arm, we can take him away for interrogation.'

Barry Reed was the colour of Diaz's shirt, suddenly looking too small for the England blazer that he had been wearing so proudly. He followed Diaz like a man being led to his execution, pausing only to look back at the stormy face of his manager.

'I didn't do anything, boss, honestly. I didn't take anything.' But his words echoed down the corridor like an exit line from a play spoken to an empty theatre.

CHAPTER 22

Patti knew she was in big trouble this time around. The previous night, waiting in the street, was merely a prelude. Now there was no Luis to come to her rescue and she did not see what Mark could do on foreign, seemingly hostile, soil. She was playing away and the officials in charge of the game had been bought off.

There had been two men questioning her when she'd been brought into this tiny office. Even as a smoker she found the nicotine-thick air disgusting. The room was little more than a cell, six feet by eight, with one skylight window and one battered desk occupying most of the floor space. An ancient fan creaked asthmatically overhead disturbing the contents of an ashtray filled to overflowing with cigarette butts.

They had left her alone after a while and she was still none the wiser as to why she was being detained. Yes, she was a journalist; yes, she had only been in the country a few days; yes, she'd lied, she had come just for the football match because her fiancé (she didn't think Mark would mind his elevation) was a commentator for a television station. And yes, she was due to be on board a plane heading home in less than an hour.

It was as if they had been sent in as advance troops, to upset her balance, to turn her upside down, like the crocodile dealing with its prey, making her lose her bearings. Breathe out and follow the bubbles, she'd been told once on a trip to Africa. That'll take you to the surface. She felt as if she were underwater right now, but breathing out would not help her. Breathing in was causing her a problem as the lack of air caused a tightening of her chest. If only she could have a cigarette then she might be able to forget the haze of smoke around her. It seemed to penetrate her clothing like an old-fashioned London fog. But they had removed her bag and presumably were ripping it apart at this very moment searching for goodness knew what. She just hoped they didn't destroy her tampons because she knew her period was due any time now. Apart from that the bag didn't concern her. It was replaceable. All she wanted was to get out of the country and get out fast.

The door opened and she half rose to her feet, then slumped back on to the hard, rickety chair with its uneven legs, feigning boredom. Keep cool, she told herself, don't let them realise they've got you rattled. This time it was only one man. She bit her lip. She had seen this man before, spoken to him just the once. He was immaculately dressed in a pale-blue light-weight cotton suit, a blue silk tie, white button-down shirt, the sort of man who would certainly brush the seat before he risked placing his posterior upon it. He was not really tall, yet he gave the impression of height because of his slender build. His dark hair was combed, swept back in the style of a Latin 1950s movie star. The face was good-looking in a classical way, straight Roman nose, dark eyebrows carefully trimmed, a full mouth topping off a chin with a Kirk Douglas dimple. She had not had the opportunity to look at Riccardo Branco when she had met him in the gloomy light of the stand at the match, but she had every opportunity to do so now with his face just a few inches from hers.

'My dear Miss Delaney. I do apologise for the surroundings in which you find yourself. They are definitely not suited to a lady of your background and resources. But you disappointed me by failing to keep our appointment last night, or should I say this morning. Ever since I was a little boy I have not liked to be disappointed. After our first encounter I was so looking forward to talking to you, to getting to know you a little better.'

'And now you are,' Patti said, with a bravado she did not feel.

'And now I am.' His tone suddenly changed and he brought his fist down on the desk so violently that Patti thought it might collapse there and then. 'But what I truly wish to know is why you wanted to know *me* a little better.'

Patti hesitated. Here was a man who according to everything she'd learned about him was Public Enemy Number One. Yet he seemed to have been able to take over government resources for his own purposes with consummate ease. A powerful man that was for sure, a chameleon who could run with the hare and

126

bribe the hounds. He looked at his watch and made sure that Patti saw it was a solid gold Cartier. A man who needed others to notice him. She could have afforded to buy such a watch herself, but she still preferred the Disney one she wore whenever she travelled, with Minnie Mouse's hands telling the time. It gave her a feeling of security, her own comfort blanket on her wrist, and she needed all the security she could get.

'So. A few questions,' Branco said, his voice once more calm and friendly.

'And if I give a few answers?'

'Depending upon the quality of the answers then you will be on your plane.'

'And if the answers are wrong?'

'Ah.' He inspected his fingernails as if he had written the reply there earlier in the day as a crib. 'If the answers are wrong, then I am afraid we have to flunk you in the exam, as our American brothers say, and I have to implement my reserve plan.'

'You've told me the prize for success, what do I get for failure?' She couldn't believe what she was saying, but somehow she felt she had to keep the man talking. What was that they said about hijackers? Try and humanise yourself to them and it makes it harder for them to kill you.

'Allow me to ask the questions and then all will be revealed.' He looked at his watch again. 'We do not have all the time in the world. There are some individuals in the airport who do not welcome me with open arms, a regrettable state of affairs.'

Patti tried to sit back on the hard upright chair and look as relaxed as she could in the circumstances. She would have killed for a cigarette but did not want to give Branco the satisfaction of asking for one.

'So,' he began, all business. 'Our meeting at the football match was planned?'

'I don't have to answer your questions. You're not the police.'

'No. I am not. But, believe me, I am far more powerful than them. Now, let's begin again. Was our meeting at the stadium planned?'

Although he had, as yet, not laid a finger upon her, she could feel the goose bumps rising on her flesh, could sense that she was trying to withdraw away from him as far as the confines of the room would permit.

'No,' she replied in a voice that did not seem to belong to her.

'Who gave you the ticket for the match?'

'My friend.'

'Who is?'

'Mark Rossetti.' Was that a betrayal or was she helping him by demonstrating that she had nothing to hide?

'Your lover?'

'Mind your own fucking business.'

Branco shook his head in mock disapproval.

'In my country our women do not swear unless they are whores. They cook and they clean and they have babies. They are faithful and devoted to their men. They are more often than not virgins when they marry and before and after marriage they go to church and they light candles. Are you a whore, Miss Delaney?'

'No, I'm not.'

'Good. We have a straight answer to a question. Perhaps we can build upon that start. So, you say you didn't plan to meet me at the match.'

Patti glanced at her watch. Forty-five minutes to take-off.

'This is getting really boring.'

'Fine. Let me make it more interesting. If you didn't plan to meet me, then how did you know who I was?'

'I'd been told about you. I'd seen photographs.'

'You read the Colombian newspapers?'

'No, but I read the international press. I surf the internet. I'm a journalist. It's my job. If I'm visiting somewhere I have to make it my business to discover as much as I can about that country in case the opportunity arises to write something.'

He nodded, digesting the reply, analysing it like a spider dissecting the prey that is caught in its web.

'You were here to write a story about drugs?'

She realised that all of his questions were also statements as if he were going through the motions to demonstrate that she was being given a fair trial, but as judge and jury he knew all the answers already.

'No, I wasn't originally here to write a story about drugs. I was here to be with Mark and to watch a football match. I saw you, I recognised you and I thought it might be an opportunity.'

'A woman and football?'

128

'Not unusual any more, at least not in our country. That's how I first met Mark, when I tried to interview him.'

She bit her lip, annoyed that she was confiding in this man, when she had been determined to answer in monosyllables if she were to answer at all.

'Do you go to bed with everybody you interview?'

She did not give him the satisfaction of answering that one and, having made what he thought was a joke, he did not press her for one.

'So, your decision to ask me for an interview was on the spur of the moment?'

'Yes.'

'And if we had not seen each other then you would have just watched the match, cheered your team on, gone to the reception, returned to the hotel, made love with your man and then gone back to England with fond memories of Colombia?'

'Couldn't have put it better myself. Now can I please go and catch my plane?'

Branco pursed his mouth in anticipation of a nasty taste.

'You're not telling the truth, Miss Delaney, you're not being honest at all. I know when you bought your ticket to come here. I know you had no hotel reservation. I know you had an open return ticket and that Mr Rossetti got you on the plane that is about to depart. I think it will depart without you. I have seen your filofax. A great invention the filofax, far preferable to the computer with its code words and frustrating inaccessibility. You had notes in there, notes I think you had written in England. So all in all I do not think your story stacks up.'

Patti hesitated, wondering whether to come clean or bluff it out. He could be bluffing himself. Surely he could do nothing to her in the heart of an international airport? But he'd got himself in this room, he had obviously bought off the first few officials she had seen, so who was to say that he could not do exactly as he desired?

She decided to take her chances on the bluff.

'How do you know I made my notes about you in England? I've admitted I'd heard your name before I saw you at the match. It had cropped up in conversation the night before over dinner. So I wrote a few things down. It occurred to me that it – you – might make for an interesting article. Maybe, if I had stayed on a few days then I would have contacted you; but it was coincidence that we sat near each other at the match and I just seized the opportunity. As for me not having a hotel or a return date, well things hadn't been going too well between me and Mark. Of course, I hoped we'd make it up and he'd want me to share his room, but if things hadn't worked out then I planned to fly to New York for a few days where I used to work and where I've got friends to crash out with.'

Branco seemed to lose concentration as she rambled on. Something had caught his fancy earlier in the speech and he was homing in on it.

'You seized the opportunity. Or perhaps the nettle, or the poisoned chalice. You see I know these English sayings.'

She didn't think right then was the moment to congratulate him on his English.

'The opportunity, the nettle, the chalice, whatever. Can I go now?'

She thought she'd pitched it right. She'd held back the information out of a combination of pride, stubbornness and fear, then she'd explained the half-truth and felt she had been convincing, hoped she had got away with it.

Branco was not yet finished.

'This dinner conversation the night before. Who were your dining companions?'

In itself this was the most difficult question of all. If he was going to let her go then she would be safe, at home, in London, but Luis would be here, and she did not think that Branco would take kindly to being the subject of idle gossip. And anyway it would not be fair. Luis had not volunteered the information to her. It was she who had pestered him.

'There were loads of people at the bar in the hotel. Mark knew a few of them. I just picked up on the chat and must have asked one of them as the evening wore on.'

'Names?'

'I honestly don't know. I was exhausted by the flight and I'd had a fair bit to drink by then.'

'Ah yes, the drink. I am told that Mr Rossetti does not. Or at least cannot. So you drink for two. But you know, Miss Delaney, earlier on you said you had been told over dinner. Were all these acquaintances of Mr Rossetti with you at dinner?'

He didn't miss a trick and she wasn't thinking as clearly as she would have liked. She said nothing. She had probably said too much already. There was no point in digging the hole any bigger. If he wanted to insult her or Mark then he could do that until the cows came home.

'You see,' Branco continued, 'if people talk about me, then I assume they know me and, irrational as you may think it, I like to know who knows me and who chooses to talk about me.'

'They may just know of you. I'm told you're a very charitable person.'

Branco looked carefully into her eyes. She realised that his eyes had absolutely no expression in them. They were hard, dark rocks, there purely for utilitarian purposes, not to show emotion. If the eyes were the window of the soul, then this man had no soul. They bore into her, seeking a hint of sarcasm, but she looked absolutely straight back at him, with an expression that would have looked genuine on a choirboy.

'Now, let us sum up. Let us see what we have got. On an impulse you fly thousands of miles to South America just to go to bed with a man you can sleep with whenever you want and to watch a meaningless, friendly football match. A casual acquaintance, whose name you do not know, mentions my name and you make the effort to write me up in your little black book. Chance throws us together and with your photographic, journalistic memory you immediately recognise me and ask for an interview. And then you get cold feet and do not turn up, but instead go off with Luis Cano.' She took in an involuntary gasp of air, and broke into a coughing fit as the stale smoke filled her lungs.

'I can see you did not realise we were watching you. Did you really think I would turn up for an assignation with a total stranger without taking some basic precautions? Was it Cano who told you about me and then the same Cano who prevented us from meeting?'

His voice dropped to a whisper, as if the question were addressed to himself rather than to her.

'No, I am sorry, the answers are not good enough. I think we have to spend more time working on them, perhaps together, perhaps not.'

'What do you mean?' she asked, trying to keep the fear from

her voice, trying to keep back the tears that were beginning to build up within her.

'I mentioned a reserve plan. I do believe we now have to bring that into play.'

He pressed a small bell by the side of the door that she had not previously noticed. The two men who had begun the interview returned with a battered cardboard box containing her belongings. The three of them spoke rapidly and so great was her panic that she could barely understand a single word, although she heard Delaney a few times. Finally Branco turned to her.

'We are being very rude, speaking as if you were not here about matters that concern you so greatly. You see, these gentlemen are here to charge you.'

'Charge me with what?' she asked, her voice rising on the last word, near to hysteria.

'Narcotics smuggling, or at least attempted narcotics smuggling,' and with that he pulled a small bag of pure cocaine from her handbag, and held it up in the air like child triumphant in a game of hunt the slipper.

CHAPTER 23

Mark felt himself a man divided, unable to cope with one crisis, let alone two. If ever he had needed a drink in the past, then he needed one now, although he also knew with absolute certainty that if he fell off the wagon he would never be able to climb back on. They'd taken both Patti and Barry off to the central police station. Mark had arranged for his and Patti's baggage to be taken off the plane, but Kenny Cunningham had indicated that he had no intention of missing the flight.

'Don't you think you should stay?' Mark asked him.

The England manager shrugged.

'I can't believe the lad's let the side down like this. He's got himself into this mess, there's not a lot I can do to get him out of it.'

'So you're going home and abandoning him to his fate?'

'What else am I supposed to do, Mark? I've got the rest of the team to think of. Can you imagine what the Press are going to do when they get back? I'm not abandoning him. One of the Football Association people here, George Mulgrave, is a solicitor. He's arranging to liaise with the British Embassy and get him a local lawyer who speaks English and can hopefully get him out as soon as possible.'

Cunningham shook Mark's hand and wished him good luck. For a few moments Mark watched from the window as the English party were led across the tarmac. He could see them all clearly as they boarded the plane, watched until the doors closed and then turned away before it began to taxi down the runway. He felt isolated enough already and the departure of so many familiar faces was not likely to help.

He needed to get Patti a lawyer, but he had to find somebody honest and competent, and he didn't think that was going to be too easy in a place like Bogota. He had the feeling that both their existence and ability to survive to make a living were rarities.

The only person he felt he could rely upon in the city was Luis, but would it be fair to involve him in something like this? He went to the phone and called the British embassy first. The man at the other end of the line whistled.

'Seems to have been a busy day at the airport. We've just despatched somebody to sort out this soccer johnny.'

Soccer, Mark thought, that's all I need, somebody who calls football soccer, a rugby-playing public-school type, who had a cushy posting and wouldn't want to do anything to upset the status quo.

'They have their own way of doing things here, and in their own time,' the man continued in plummy tones. 'When they want to let her go, then they will.'

'That's really helpful, thanks,' Mark said angrily.

'Look, old chum, I'm not being deliberately difficult. I just know my own patch. Obviously we'll send somebody down if it looks like they're going to bang her up. Lawyer and all that sort of good thing. Keep in touch, won't you?'

Barry Reed was also his concern, but not his main one. He knew the kid was asking for him, because Kenny Cunningham had told him so. He'd told him something else as well before going through to the lounge.

'Take my advice, Mark, and don't get too involved. I've got the feeling this lad's bad news. I was a bit worried about his attitude the whole time he was here.'

'He was worried, Kenny. Didn't you try and find out what was wrong?'

'All of these kids have got problems. I'm an international football manager for Christ's sake, not a samaritan. Drugs and sport. He might as well have a sign around his neck that says beware of the plague.'

'Why have you decided that he's guilty, Kenny?'

'I haven't, Mark, but look at it from our side of the fence. The lad played a blinder, scores a goal that's out of this world. Believe me, I never thought he'd turn it on like he did. I was looking for a solid hour or so and then I was going to substitute him, but he performs as if he's high on something and, lo and behold, they test him, and he is. What do you want me to say? That he's pure as the driven snow. The only snow in my mind at the moment is the stuff that Barry probably snorts up his nose. I know the sort of background he comes from. They're all at it up at the nightclubs. If he hadn't had the talent in his feet, he'd never have been able to make it in his head and he'd probably be on probation by now.'

Mark had shaken his head.

'You're supposed to be the manager. You're supposed to stand by your team.'

'And I do, Mark. Through thick and thin. First match I was in charge, don't you remember the allegations by the Swedish girl that a couple of the younger lads had taken turns with her? I looked at it, I listened, I asked questions and we discovered that one of the Sunday tabloids had paid her in advance to try and set them up. But she'd not been able to. The kids were too scared to let her in their room, let alone shag her. But this is different. We're talking hard facts, we're talking scientific tests. A doctor, a FIFA official, all the rules were followed, all the forms filled out. What can I say? What can he say?'

'What does he say?' Mark asked. 'Does he deny it?'

'Of course he fucking well denies it. He says he doesn't know anything about it. What else is he going to say? He's been caught with the scullery maid with his trousers down and he's too old to claim that they were playing doctors and nurses and hope that nobody thinks he's done anything wrong.'

Mark had to put Barry to one side for the moment and leave him to the embassy. He'd called Luis straight after speaking to the British official and arranged to be picked up by him just outside the main terminal. Luis arrived in a beat-up old mini that juddered to a halt in front of Mark.

'Sorry about the car. My Mercedes was stolen and the police have never recovered a stolen vehicle in the history of Bogota. The insurers do not rush to pay out. Last night I had a luxury limo, today I borrowed this from a friend. Life has its ups and downs. At the moment Patti is down, but we will pick her up. Come, we need somewhere to talk.'

He put the car into a car park at the terminal and they walked back to one of the bars.

'You see, this car they will not steal. It is beneath the dignity of a car thief to remove such a vehicle.'

Mark tried to raise a smile, but failed miserably. Luis ordered two coffees and they took their steaming cups into a corner.

'What's this all about, Luis?' Mark asked.

'Your friend, Patti. You are certain she would not be taking any drugs with her. She was out on the streets on her own last night. She could easily have been offered them, easily bought them.'

'No way. Of that I'm certain.'

'Maybe she has this idea to write a certain story. About how easy it is to buy drugs in Colombia. How simple it is to get them out of the country. She is a journalist. These sort of games are not unusual for her profession.'

'She is crazy at times, but she wouldn't try something like that. Apart from anything else, even if she thought she had a chance of getting it out easily at this end she wouldn't have taken her chances back home.'

Luis gave an expressive shrug that said many things.

'Maybe she doesn't bother to take them home. She's done what she wanted. She gets a photo taken here or on the plane then flushes the whole lot down the toilet mid-flight.'

'No, Luis. You're into the realms of fantasy.'

'Very well. I am only playing the lawyer to the *diablo*.'

'Devil's advocate.'

'My friend, I know she is not the devil, so maybe I am just trying to prepare the defence.'

'Hopefully she doesn't need a defence. I know she's not guilty. So, what happens now?'

Luis lit up a small cigar and inhaled thoughtfully.

'We assume she is innocent, your Patti. We then have to assume she has upset somebody here. The somebody could well be Branco. I warned you, I warned her. She is not at school now, she is playing with the big boys and they have real weapons. Maybe she already asked the wrong questions about the wrong people, so they set her up.'

'Let's talk about Branco, then,' Mark said. A man at the neighbouring table turned his head in their direction and Luis put his finger to his lips.

'It is not good to suggest that man is involved, even if it is indeed the case.'

'But you think he is behind this?'

Luis spoke so quietly that Mark had to lean across the table to catch the words.

'If Patti is innocent, then I'm sure he is behind this.'

'I've phoned the British embassy once, maybe I should call them again and warn them what this is all about. Do I rely on them to find me a lawyer or can you help?'

'There is no point in telling them anything about the man we discussed. They will be helpless. As for a lawyer anybody they find will be useless, believe me. I will find you a lawyer, a special lawyer. It will cost money, big money, I'm afraid, but he will be worth it.'

'Can we at least get her out of the hands of the police?'

'I hope so. We will at least try. I do not wish to worry you, but the inside of a Colombian prison is not a pleasant place, particularly if you are a woman used to the better things in life. Wait here a moment, I go to make a call.'

Mark stirred the dregs of his coffee around the bottom of his mug. Considering this was supposed to be the coffee centre of the world the drink had been lousy, tasting like muddy water at low tide. He could only assume they exported all the best stuff or saved it for the better hotels and restaurants. He looked around him. It was a typical airport scene, handluggage strewn all over the bar, people in transit using every available seat, the inevitable haze of smoke rising above the crush as passengers took their last drag before climbing aboard their non-smoking flights. Mark had a feeling that he was under surveillance. He could not put an exact fix on the watchers, but every time he looked up there seemed to be a different pair of eyes following his every move, yet turning away at the split second that their gaze met. Maybe he was becoming paranoid. That would not do Patti any good, any more than the bottle of whisky for which he had such a craving.

He was relieved to see Luis approaching with the smile on his face of the cat who has not only got the cream but has caught the mouse to eat with it as well.

'It is arranged,' Luis said without bothering to resume his seat. 'I have engaged for you the services of Eduardo Salazar.'

He made the announcement so proudly that Mark felt a sense of inadequacy that he had never heard of the man. Luis noted the blank expression on his face.

'His name may mean little to you, but here he is a national hero, particularly amongst those who would wish us to be a true democracy. He is a campaigner, a politician as well as a lawyer. There have been three attempts on his life.'

'And that's a recommendation? I want somebody who'll survive to see this thing to a satisfactory conclusion.'

'Don't worry,' Luis said, putting his hand on Mark's shoulder, 'he is a survivor. He does not take on every case. It has to be special.'

'And Patti's special.'

'She is innocent. That makes it special. Or so I have persuaded Salazar.'

Mark did not take a great deal of comfort from that. If Luis or the lawyer had said that this sort of thing happened all the time and you were expected to buy your way out, then he could have understood that. But they hadn't said that. They had said that the case was special and he had a sinking feeling that this sort of thing did not happen all the time and no amount of bribery would set Patti free.

Luis expressed some disappointment that the car was still there and then drove Mark to Salazar's office. It was an imposing house set in the heart of La Candelaria district. The building was of colonial style on Calle Nine, having been lovingly restored, and contrasting wildly with some of the more modern properties nearby. Salazar was obviously doing well in his practice. The reception area was filled with expensive antique furniture although the telephone manned by the well-dressed girl behind the desk was top-of-the-range technology. They waited some ten minutes and were then led through to the lawyer's own office. Luis whistled softly.

'Only ten minutes. He is taking this seriously. He has been known to keep people waiting for days.'

'What is he, a lawyer or a saint?' Mark asked, but Luis had no time to answer even if he had wanted to, because Salazar was there waiting for them at the door. If he was expensive then he was going to make his clients feel they were getting their money's worth just by his appearance. He was tall, as tall as Mark, and wearing a light Hugo Boss suit over a cream silk shirt, topped off by a perfectly tied brown cravat. Somewhere in his past there must have been some Aztec blood as he looked for all the world like a chief from that ancient tribe, waiting to receive his tribute if not his sacrifice. His skin had a burnished look about it, his sleek black hair hanging long at the back over his collar. The aquiline nose gave him a look of permanent superiority and the knowing eyes, as black as coal-dust, seemed to miss nothing.

When he spoke, Mark was surprised to hear what appeared to be an American accent.

'Mr Rossetti, I am delighted to meet you, although I would have preferred other circumstances. Please come in. I will have my secretary make us coffee and you'll tell me all about it.' He saw Mark hesitate and, as if reading his mind, said quickly, 'This coffee will be the finest you have ever tasted.'

Mark got the impression that this was a man who would always require the finest.

They chatted generally for a few moments and Mark was surprised by how much the man knew about football, not just in Colombia, but throughout the world. He learned that his American accent stemmed from a few post-graduate years at Harvard and eighteen months in exile in Washington when the threats to his life in Bogota had grown too great. His confidence rose. If anybody could set Patti free then this was the man.

'So, let's get down to business,' Salazar said. 'We have, I understand, a small problem with your lady friend. Take your time, drink your coffee and tell me everything you know about her, why she should be in this country and why she should have any interest in cocaine.'

It was at that point that Mark's confidence evaporated, because he had no answer to any of Salazar's questions.

CHAPTER 24

Eduardo Salazar wasted no time. By mid-afternoon he had pulled all the necessary strings and had arranged a court application for five p.m. to seek bail for Patti. He had also taken care to speak to the judge who would hear the application and had been assured that it would be granted.

'Will she be able to return to England whilst we sort out this nightmare?' Mark asked.

'One step at a time, my friend. First we ensure that she does not spend one single night in one of our jails.'

'And then?'

'Many people might think that was enough in Miss Delaney's situation.'

'Then I'm afraid I'm not many people.'

'So I can believe, Mr Rossetti, so I can well believe. This is a city where, despite the noise you might hear in the streets, people only talk about important matters in whispers. And amongst the whispers today I have heard your name and that of Miss Delaney on several occasions.'

'Is that a good thing?' Mark asked, wondering why on earth anybody would have heard of him, let alone be talking about him. He wondered if the lawyer was merely being dramatic to justify his fee. Salazar looked him straight in the eye and Mark was grateful he was unlikely ever to come up against this man as a witness on the stand.

'No, it is not a good thing,' Salazar replied. 'It is a dangerous thing. But I will answer your earlier question. I will do my best to get the lady out of the country, but that may not be so easy. Believe me, I do not mean to boast, but for anybody else it would be virtually impossible. Yet I will endeavour to achieve it because I truly believe that every day that she – and you – remain here, your lives are at risk. Life can be very cheap. We are a young nation. When English explorers were colonising the world we

140

simply did not exist. It takes centuries to come to respect human life and other countries have a head start over us. People vanish and even those who might be concerned as to what has become of them do not necessarily make enquiries.'

'Why not, for heaven's sake?'

'Because they value their own lives more than their curiosity.'

The accent was on the word curiosity and Luis kicked him gently to indicate that this was not a helpful path to tread in the cause of Patti's release.

They left Salazar's office just after one. Mark had four hours to kill and decided to turn his attention to Barry Reed. He was, as far as he was aware, still at the same police station as Patti, although Salazar had told him Patti would now be taken to the court to await his application and there was no point in trying to speak to her before then. Luis drove him down there, between Calle Twenty and Calle Twenty-One where he was just in time to meet the lawyer who had been found by the embassy. He extended a lazy, plump hand and his whole appearance exuded sloth and obesity. It was impossible to tell which had pre-ceeded the other. He was only a little more than five feet tall, sparse hair spread hopelessly across a greasy scalp, patches of sweat staining his shirt and none-too-clean linen suit. He looked like a cross between Peter Lorre and Danny de Vito without the redeeming features of either of them. If Salazar would never be seen dirtying his hands at the scene of an accident this little man would certainly have been running behind the ambulance.

'Manuel Lopez,' he said by way of introduction, the accent sounding as Mexican as his name. 'I am counsel for your Señor Reed.'

Mark half expected him to thump his chest with pride as he made the announcement so loudly that he might well have been appearing in a New York courtroom before a very deaf judge.

'I am Barry's friend, Mark Rossetti.'

'Yes, he is asking for you all the time. He is puzzled that you have not come to him before.'

'I'm here now. Is he in serious trouble?'

Lopez spread his arms wide and hunched his shoulders.

'It is hard to say. He tests positive for drugs. To have drugs in this country is an offence if you are going to sell them. To take them . . .' Another shrug. 'To take them, that is another thing all together. Also it is not certain that he took them here in Colombia. We are waiting for the final analysis to tell us what drug it is exactly that he took. Then we wait to see how much he took. We wait to be sure that there are no more drugs amongst his possessions. And if there is nothing, as my client assures me is the case, then I think they will let him go home. He is a very frightened boy and that is what they have set out to achieve. But you ask is he in serious trouble? I do not think it is the right thing for a professional footballer to take drugs, so as far as his career is concerned, yes, I think he is in serious trouble.'

'Are they absolutely sure that he tested positive?'

'That is not in doubt. Quite frankly my advice is to tell him to apologise for all the trouble he has caused, maybe pay a small fine, and then he will be going home.'

'Can I see him?'

Lopez shrugged yet again. It was a habit that was beginning to annoy Mark.

'It is not in my gift.'

'So who is Santa Claus in this dump?'

Luis took him by the arm.

'It is not good to start offending people. Rightly or wrongly, there is a certain national pride despite all the problems.'

Lopez looked from one to the other in bewilderment and Mark realised that the reference to Father Christmas had probably stretched his command of English beyond his limits.

'Who can arrange for me to see him?' Mark asked again.

'Only the officer in charge of the case. Now, if you excuse me, I have other clients to attend upon.'

Mark grabbed him tightly by the arm and forced him back inside the building.

'No, I don't excuse you. And I won't excuse you until you find a way to get me in to see your client.'

Luis smiled at the lawyer's discomfort, but the smile faded as they entered the outer sanctum of the police station and saw a scene of utter chaos. Tourists who had been robbed, women screaming for their husbands, a drunk in the corner vomiting on the floor. It was Hogarthian in its decadence. A man hurried by, picking his route carefully so as not to touch a soul, his black, gleaming shoes hammering a staccato rhythm on the cigarette-butt strewn floor. His left hand clutched the handle of the pistol at his side and Mark felt he was just waiting for an excuse to use it. Mark tapped him lightly on the arm as he passed him and out of the corner of his eye saw Lopez shrink back against the wall in a vain effort to make himself invisible. The police officer turned to face the Englishman, his eyes distended and blazing with rage, as if Mark had been a leper touching him in the street as he tried to beg a coin. Without even asking, Mark knew he had found the man who held Barry Reed's immediate destiny in his hand. It was too late to withdraw from the confrontation.

'My name's Rossetti, Mark Rossetti. I understand you have one of the England players here in your custody, Barry Reed.'

The officer gave Mark a stare that he probably reserved for prisoners who declined to sign confessions.

'We do not have an England player here named Reed or anything. There are no names in this place, only common criminals.'

He spoke or rather barked out the words in Spanish and a glance at Lopez told him to translate and to translate with total accuracy. Lopez obliged and Mark continued despite a warning hand from Luis.

'I was wondering if it might be possible to see him.' The police officer seemed to understand enough English to comprehend Mark's request.

'Why?' he asked, the tone clipped, indifferent now, as if whatever the answer or explanation might be it was doomed to fail in impressing him.

'Because he's a friend.'

The answer understood, the reply again in Spanish, the translation from Lopez.

'He needs a lawyer. He has no need of friends. He has a lawyer.' He nodded in the direction of Lopez who bowed as if it were a great compliment although the expression on the officer's face gave absolutely no indication that it had been intended as such. Then, as if to show exactly what he thought of the lawyer, the officer spat on the floor, leaving Mark with the certainty that he would far rather have spat in his face.

'Can I at least have your name?' Mark asked, wanting to know with whom he was dealing, drafting the official complaint in his mind. The man hesitated. He ran his tongue over nicotine-stained teeth, and touched a long scar that ran the full length of his left cheek as if it might give him inspiration to reply to a perfectly simple question.

'My name is Rodriguez. Colonel Enrico Rodriguez.'

Again Mark could see Lopez mouthing the rank in a mimed prayer. It was clear that if you lived in Bogota that the name meant something. But Mark Rossetti did not live in Bogota and had no intention of spending any more time there than was absolutely necessary to get Patti and Barry on a plane home. What happened after that to the pair of them he'd worry about at leisure. He could still hear Salazar's words in his ears. As long as he was here he was in danger. But why? What had he done as a football commentator to justify such interest? Or was it just because of his relationship with Patti? He didn't know which nerve Patti had struck but it was obviously a sensitive one.

'Well, Colonel,' Mark said, drawing himself up to his full six feet and looking down on the Colombian by a good six inches, 'perhaps I should ask to see your superior officer. Tell him Lopez, tell him what I'm saying.'

Lopez virtually sunk to his knees, terrified just to be a witness to the conversation, let alone translate it. Rodriguez turned to him, kneeing him in the stomach in the same movement, forcing him back on his plump haunches. Luis who had said nothing, supplied the translation.

Rodriguez virtually ignored him and let fly a torrent of Spanish at the figure of Lopez who had not yet risen from the floor. Lopez hung on every word with the intensity of an Israelite receiving news of the Ten Commandments from Moses, then looked up at Mark with wide-eyed astonishment.

'The colonel is impressed by your courage and persistence. He likes that in a man and is surprised to find it in a gringo. He has graciously granted you fifteen minutes with Señor Reed. Somebody will escort you to his cell.'

Rodriguez clicked his heels together, like a stage character from Evita, and for a moment Mark thought he might be about to salute him. However, he merely turned on his heel and marched along the corridor, his back as stiff as a poker, his head firmly fixed ahead to ensure that nothing further hindered his path.

Lopez pulled out a grimy handkerchief and wiped the sweat

from his brow, a hopeless task, as fresh rivulets arose almost immediately.

'You are a very lucky man, Señor Rossetti. The colonel is a powerful man within our police force. You could have found yourself in court with my client.'

Mark grinned, despite the situation.

'You know, it looks like I am about to find myself in a cell with your client. Where do I wait for my collection?'

There was no need for Lopez to answer the question as another man in uniform, this time ill-fitting and begrimed, appeared behind them and without undue ceremony pushed Mark towards a door just off the corridor. They descended a flight of stairs in silence save for the tread of their shoes on the stone steps. There was no air and the heat lay over them like a smothering blanket, its smell rancid with age and decay. From his uniform it was hard to tell if his guide was a policeman or a soldier although Mark could well believe that at times the forces were indistinguishable. They continued down into the bowels of the building, a weak light coming from half-hidden oil lamps set in the wall. Mark was reminded of visits to old English castles as a child, the imagination running wild over the thoughts of the ghosts of abandoned men who still dwelt within. The journey seemed endless and Mark had a horrible thought that perhaps Rodriguez's surrender had merely been a ruse to entice him into voluntary incarceration. As he was about to turn back and run up the stairs to light and safety the descent, ended abruptly and they came out to a level corridor looking very much like the pictures of Death Row in American jails that Mark had seen in magazines. The guard opened the second door on the left with a key, ushered Mark in and then locked the door behind him. Mark waited to hear his footsteps disappear but there was only silence from outside and he breathed a sigh of relief. If he were going to be waiting then he could only be waiting to take Mark back up to the surface as soon as his fifteen minutes were up.

Barry Reed lay on a bunk in the corner, his clothes dishevelled, his eyes red from tears, looking nothing like the young football hero who had been the darling of the English fans and media the night before. He was still wearing his England blazer, but it no longer seemed to fit him, hanging loose on his frame as if made for a bigger man. He had only been in captivity a few hours, yet it was almost as if he had shrunk into himself, had withdrawn from the reality of the situation.

He looked up as Mark entered and the expression of hope that crossed his face gave his visitor the terrible feeling that he was never going to be able to live up to his expectations, that at the end of the day all he had brought with him was a parcel of false promises.

'Thank goodness, you've come. What took you so long?'

Thinking it might help, might make him feel less isolated, Mark quickly told him of Patti's arrest. It was typical of the lad that his concern was at once redirected from himself to the journalist.

'Is she going to be all right?'

Mark made a valiant effort to sound more confident than he actually felt.

'You know my Patti, she's a survivor.'

Even as he said the words, he realised that Barry didn't know Patti. Nobody knew Patti as he knew her, as he had come to know her, and with the thought he struggled to keep his voice from breaking, struggled to keep dry-eyed.

'What's going to happen to me, Mark?' Barry asked, in tones of an eight-year-old up before his headmaster.

'I've been speaking to your lawyer. He seems very confident you'll be out of here soon, although I wouldn't be planning to take my holidays in Colombia if I were you.'

'Believe me I'm not. It's afterwards that worries me more. What happens then, what about my career?'

'You have to face the fact that there'll certainly be an inquiry, a disciplinary tribunal. They don't like drug-taking at the best of times, and, quite frankly, taking them in an England shirt is not the best of times.' He'd meant to boost the lad up, but somehow it seemed best to be honest with him, to get him to face the worst so that it could only get better.

'I didn't take any drugs, Mark. Why should I? I'm good enough without them.'

The boast sounded hollow emanating from the mouth of the slumped, sad figure.

'But you tested positive.'

'It has to be wrong. It just has to be. We have to make them test again. I must have some rights of appeal. I'm telling you,

Mark, I've never taken drugs in my life. I smoked a fag once behind the lavvies when I was at school and it made me sick.' He gave Mark the look of a wounded animal, begging its finder to cure and not destroy it. 'You believe me, don't you?'

Mark hesitated, the easy answer rising to his lips. He began to speak then changed his mind. He did not think this boy would accept the easy answer.

'I want to believe you, I really do, Barry.'

'But you don't. You're going to be like all the rest of them. You'll give me pity, but you won't give me trust. You're going to think I'm guilty even without a trial. I thought you were supposed to be innocent until you're found guilty.'

Mark was taken by surprise by the boy's eloquence, but he'd obviously had time to think things through, to prepare himself for what he had to say, not just to Mark, but to everybody.

'You've got to understand that there'll be some back home who'll say you've been proven guilty. Those tests nowadays are so sophisticated that they're virtually error-proof.'

'Virtually?' Barry echoed, clinging to the word, like a drowning man holding on to a piece of timber.

Mark shrugged.

'We'll do our best. Have the tests re-done, but . . .'

He ran out of words of comfort and Barry rose to his feet in agitation and began to pace up and down the tiny cell, three strides taking him from wall to wall.

'So, that's it then. I'm washed up. Career over before it's really begun. Thanks for the visit. Close the door behind you. There are a lot of dishonest people here and we don't want any of them breaking in.'

Mark raised his fist to knock on the judas window to get the guard's attention, then thought better of it and turned to face Barry.

'Hey, come on Barry. It's not over. The fat lady's not even warmed up yet, let alone sung. We'll get you your re-test. We'll get you the best lawyers.'

'How am I going to pay for all this? I can't see Hertsmere paying my wages if I can't play.'

'Don't worry, I'll sort it all out. We'll do everything we can to prove your innocence.'

Barry's round, honest face lit up with childish naivety, as if

Father Christmas had arrived just before breakfast on December 25th having been delayed with a puncture on his sleigh.

'Promise, Mark?' Barry asked.

'I promise,' Mark replied, knowing in his heart of hearts that it was a pledge he would find hard to keep.

CHAPTER 25

It was already cold in Zurich although it was not yet October. Snow on the mountains reflected on the lake and the citizens of the city had already taken their warm winter clothing out of storage. Compared to Bogota, anywhere was likely to feel cool to Mark both in terms of climate and existence.

He had never been so glad to say goodbye to a country, although as the jet soared into the sky away from Colombia and headed towards home, he knew with a numbing certainty he would have to return. Yet, for the moment at least, Patti had been allowed to sit on one side of him, Barry Reed on the other. One had been set free, the other only released on bail after top-level diplomatic negotiations. Which was worth less? Barry's so-called permanent freedom or Patti's potential to be rid of the charges for ever? In the end both lawyers had performed their tasks well, although Mark suspected they had both made the results seem more difficult to achieve than they really were. Somehow or other they were both determined to justify their exorbitant fees.

Lopez had negotiated a simple fine for Barry which, curiously enough, coincided with the exact amount of cash he had on his person, leaving the British Embassy to pick up the bill for Lopez upon the reluctant promise from the Football Association to reimburse them in due course. It was likely to prove a temporary financial burden as they had already fixed the date for Barry's disciplinary hearing for a couple of days after Mark's planned return from Zurich.

In the face of the evidence, and the guilty plea that had been forced upon him as part of the price to gain exit from the country, the future looked far from rosy. Mark, who had already visited that bleak treeless landscape of unjustified guilt, truly felt for him. But he felt even more for Patti. He had never known her speak less than she had done throughout the long flight home, her silence suggestive of some catatonic state of shock.

They had posted a million dollar bond in the end, utilising a large chunk of the assets they'd inherited from Leopold Schneider as security. If their old friend could see what was happening, then Mark hoped he would appreciate his bequest being put to some use. What had seemed to be a fortune in property terms was looked upon cynically by hard-nosed bankers who were advancing cash against what they perceived as a real risk. Mark had come close to screaming down the phone to the London bank when they had tried to entangle him in the red tape of mortgage documentation whilst Patti waited impatiently in her prison cell.

Salazar's first application had been successful but subject to the million dollar bail money being made available, and the time difference coupled with the bank's insistence that the formalities be observed, had not made things easy.

'You see, my dear, they do not expect you to return for trial. They get to keep the money and honour is satisfied.'

'I'm telling you, Eduardo,' Patti replied, 'If they think I'm just going to walk away from them and our money then they're in for a surprise. I don't know how much of that million will go Branco's way, but I'm telling you here and now, just like Arnie, I'll be back. And when I come back I'm going to prove my innocence and then sue your fucking government for false imprisonment.'

Salazar shrugged as if he had heard it all before, that this was all a ritual that had to be said and then forgotten.

'Of course, I understand,' he replied.

'Don't humour me, Salazar, or else I'll find another lawyer, so help me.'

'You can look, my dear lady, but I doubt if you will find another lawyer like me.'

'Are you always right, Salazar?' she asked, raising a watery smile, impressed to find a man to stand firm in the face of her invective.

'Nearly always.'

'Only nearly?'

'There are a few people in here who would say that I have my failures, that they are my failures.'

'And what do you say?'

'That I told them they would be convicted.'

The 'in here' to which the lawyer had referred was the central prison, to which she had been transferred whilst the negotiations were underway, and compared to the police station it was a four star hotel. Eduardro Salazar seemed satisfied with each small victory, although as far as Mark and Patti were concerned the spoils were minimal.

'I have arranged for her to be in a cell on her own,' he said proudly.

'And that's good?' Mark asked sarcastically, annoyed with himself because he realised deep down that the lawyer was doing his level best.

'Believe me, my dear Señor Rossetti,' Salazar persisted in the more formal address, 'this is good. The women in our prisons are as dangerous as the men, more so perhaps, because they have their nails to use as weapons. If a man wants to attack he must first conceal a knife on his person.'

Patti had looked at her own bitten-down nails when Mark had told her and said, 'Mine are more like a blunt instrument.'

It was the first time she had attempted anything like a joke since her incarceration and it gave Mark the encouragement to battle on. Eventually, when all the documentation was in order, she was released on the understanding that she would have to reappear in court in December, even though Salazar had warned both she and Mark that there was nothing finite about the Colombian court calendar. Adjournments were the norm rather than the exception and the wheels of justice creaked slowly.

'Is there anything we can do in the meantime?' Mark asked.

'Yes. Read Kafka's *The Trial*. It will prepare you for what to expect over the next few years.'

'Years!' Mark exclaimed in horror. 'They planted some drugs in her bag. What can take years about proving or disproving that?'

'In matters of this nature there are many technical steps; preliminary hearings, reviews by the judge, applications, translations, interim orders, written opinions.'

'It's a drugs rap, not bloody Nuremberg,' Patti muttered, but Salazar was in full flight and was not to be halted.

'The prosecution will wish to ensure all their witnesses are fully prepared.'

'What witnesses?' Patti asked her voice rising in barely

concealed rage. 'There are no fucking witnesses. I got pulled at the airport and some bastard planted drugs on me. All because . . .'

'Yes? Because?' Salazar asked smoothly, although she had decided to say no more.

'Because nothing. Because I'm English and a journalist and I asked the wrong questions about the wrong person. That's it.'

And neither Salazar nor Mark had been able to persuade her to say any more.

Mark had been reluctant to leave for this trip to Zurich despite its obvious importance to Mo Halid. What had seemed like a life-time in Colombia in reality had been only a little over seventy-two hours, but it had taken its toll on Patti. When she returned to the Burrow she had gone straight into the bedroom, collapsed on the bed and remained virtually comatose as if only by sleep could she purge the memory of what she had been through. She rose only to scrub herself in the shower, rubbing her skin so brutally that she had to apply cream to calm down the red roughness that she had achieved with her own hands.

She would not leave the room, let alone the flat, her eyes closing in a depressed weariness whenever Mark tried to talk to her. She had always been a good sleeper. He remembered when they had first met how she had told him that former boyfriends had said that she could 'sleep for England'. But what she was achieving now was not natural slumber, but a descent into the deepest depths of exhaustion as if only there could she be safe from the dark force that had invaded her mind. He had tried to persuade her to see a doctor, maybe even a psychiatrist, but she would have none of it.

'I'm not crazy, Mark, I'm just tired, so tired,' and then she had drifted off for another few hours. She ate enough to keep herself alive, but no more, taking no pleasure in whatever Mark provided even though he tried to give her things that she would normally have wolfed down in minutes. It was when she pushed aside a Marks and Spencer cream slice that he knew he was on a loser and he would just have to wait for her to sleep her way out of it. She did not seem irrational and had insisted on him going to Zurich, even adopting a more conciliatory approach to his involvement with Ball Park and ESL.

'Go, Mark, it'll do you good. Colombia wasn't much fun for

you either, what with me and Barry. Don't worry, I won't do anything stupid. I wouldn't give the bastards the satisfaction. Anyway, I'm not the suicidal type. I left that sort of thing to my mother.'

He'd listened to her reluctantly, but now as he hurried towards the luxurious surroundings of the Dolder Grand Hotel, where all the business of the ESL was being conducted, he could not help but wonder who exactly was the suicidal type. Her mother had certainly been and with far less cause than the daughter. Yet, when he'd tried to think of somebody he could ask to keep an eye on her, he realised just how small their social circle was, how much they had tended to keep to themselves, and how badly they missed Leo Schneider. At the end he'd decided that the best he could do was simply to keep in touch with her by phone. But so far, five out of the six calls he'd made had ended with a message on her answerphone. Just when he'd despaired of speaking to her and had been considering calling the local police, she'd cut in on her message at his last attempt, her voice as drowsy as if she'd been woken from an afternoon nap.

'Are you OK?' he asked.

'Still a bit tired, but it's getting better. Are you coming home soon? I miss you.'

'I've only just got here,' he replied, feeling a glow inside at the warmth of her voice.

'Listen, Mark. Do what you have to do. I know you mean well, but I've switched the phone off in the bedroom so, unless I'm awake, I don't hear it ringing. I'm fine, honestly. You don't need to ring every ten minutes. Why don't I call you later at the hotel and you can tell me how it's going?'

'You will call?'

'I will, I promise. Ten o'clock your time. I'll set my alarm. If you don't hear from me then, send for the fire brigade.'

He felt a sense of relief that he could push aside the responsibility for the rest of the day. Today was crucial. The presentations had been made yesterday and although they were assured they'd be taken into account, the four of them, Mark, Richard, Nick and Mo had all agreed over breakfast that the actual tenders themselves would be vital. As with everything else in life it came down to money and Mo assessed the situation with precision.

'The presentations were merely a facade, a smokescreen. Just in the extreme case that the wrong applicant bids the most money it gives the committee a way out.'

In fact, there had been five of them at the breakfast table, but Nabil Halid seemed to be in tow behind them, surplus to requirements. He said more to the waiter in ordering his food and drink than he did to the rest of them, which was hardly surprising as his earlier contributions had been summarily dismissed by his father. He wore a permanently sulky expression, avoided eye contact with any of them, and Mark suspected that his father had told him to listen, learn and behave himself, rather than waste everybody's time with his interruptions. As they entered the hotel as a group, Nabil was last through the elegant swing doors and Mark wondered, not for the first time, whether Mo really wanted his son in the business or whether he was just going through the motions of what he thought a father ought to do. As ever with Mohammed Halid it was hard to tell. When a man so palpably enjoyed posing personality conundrums it was virtually impossible to solve them.

Mark excused himself to visit the washrooms before the main session actually began. The soft carpet beneath his feet made him aware that he was in a city of wealth. The gnomes of Zurich were men with hearts of stone who even today wouldn't easily yield the secrets of their Nazi gold. He thought of Leo. How many of his relations had deposited money here before the war, believing it to be safe for those of their family who follow behind, yet not knowing that so few of those descendants would survive to collect their inheritance? He was thinking of his old friend more and more nowadays and promised himself that when he got back to England he would visit his grave. He and Patti had paid for a headstone and had attended the stone-setting ceremony a few months before. But they had struggled to find the statutory ten Jewish men to form the *minyan* to enable them to say the mourning prayer, the *kaddish*. Patti had organised all that, just as in the past she seemed to have organised his life. But now the boot was on the other foot and he had to organise her.

Mark did not notice the presence of the other man until he looked up from washing his hands to see him in the mirror standing beside him.

'Mark,' Nathan Carr said, the voice deep, the clear, precise enunciation, not quite concealing a native roughness in the tone. 'I'm delighted to meet you again, even if it's in less than social circumstances.' He dried his hands carefully, caressing his skin with soap. One ring on the second finger of his left hand gleamed brightly, polished by the soap. It was solid gold carved into the shape of some mythical bird. He turned to Mark and extended his right hand gripping Mark tightly, sucking him in with the warmth of his personality.

'Have you had the chance to think about the offer I put to you in Bogota?'

'Afraid not. I've had other things on my mind.'

'Of course. A double blow for you, girlfriend and protégé. If there's anything I can do to help I hope you'll let me know. All you need to do is ask.'

'Thanks, but I'm coping.'

'I never doubted for a moment that you would. And Mo is being supportive?'

'I never doubted for a moment that he would be,' Mark replied.

'Touché. But Mo never does the predictable. I can certainly testify to that. I never predicted he'd steal my wife.'

He checked his collar and tie in the mirror, tweaked them straight and turned to go.

'Well, we have to present ourselves to learn our fate. Why not give me a ring when we get back to London?'

He handed Mark a gold-embossed Jet Promotions card with the same emblem at the top as was on his ring.

'Why would I want to do that?' Mark asked.

'Well, Mark. I can call you Mark, can't I?' He didn't wait for an answer and continued. 'When I get the ESL rights maybe I might want to offer you a job.'

'Isn't it, if you get the rights, Mr Carr?'

'Nathan, please,' he said, then added, with a quiet certainty. 'No. It's when. I'll see you around.' And then he was gone as swiftly and silently as he had first appeared, leaving Mark with a sinking sensation of imminent defeat.

CHAPTER 26

If the men behind the ESL were going to be forced to jump through the hoops one more time then they were going to do it in style, even if the style itself was in doubtful taste. The huge banqueting hall of the hotel had been converted into a mini-football stadium. Green carpet simulated the turf, and there were goals at either end, mock floodlights and even turnstiles at the entrance. The audience had been treated to an hour of pre-match entertainment from a French chanteuse and a Swiss pop band, which had been almost drowned out by the chatter in the auditorium. The committee entered through a cleverly designed mock tunnel to the strains of 'Nessun Dorma', and the floodlights picked out the portly figure of Pavarotti at first miming to his own record then gradually taking up the words until his beautiful voice filled the room and finally brought a note of respectability to the proceedings.

Those who would sit in judgment, who doubtless had already judged, filed up to the platform. There was both money and power behind this new league and in order to recover their money and maximise their power and influence they needed television. Mark could see Mo twisting his hands nervously. It had been his challenges in the court which had brought about the re-tender and he had every reason to worry as to whether or not that might affect the committee's decision, even though he had been assured in writing that he would start with every other applicant on a level playing field.

Logically there was no reason why the ESL Committee should have held a grudge. Yes, it had cost them money, but on the other hand they had been given a massive shot of publicity when last time around the negotiations for the television rights had been conducted by lawyers behind closed doors. That had meant an opportunity missed to tell the world that the Super League had truly arrived and now they might have cause to be grateful

156

to Mo for giving them another chance to orchestrate this particular gathering in full view of the world's Press. Then there was the question of money. There could be no doubt that they were likely to achieve a higher offer this time around and, whatever else they might say, money was what it was all about.

The applicants sat in little knots, each clearly identified as a separate unit. Halid, Conway, Donaldson, Nabil and Mark were on the left. As far away from them as possible to the right were the Jet contingent. Nathan Carr, who had just joined up with them today, seemed to be a little apart from his own team. There was a small smile playing around his mouth as if he were involved in a game with infants that he knew he had to win because of his age and size. Alissa Bland was nearest to him, her blonde hair cut very short, the make-up impeccable, wearing an understated green trouser suit and looking every inch the business woman she undoubtedly was. Andy Davison, their Scottish Head of Production, had decided to make a statement. He wore a tartan suit, with a matching waistcoat and bow-tie. Nick Donaldson had passed him on the way in and had asked if he'd forgotten his red nose, but the Scotsman had not appreciated the joke. Philip King, their Finance Director, made up their quartet and he sat uncomfortably in a dark suit, like a man who'd thought he was going to a funeral, but had found himself at a wedding.

A French consortium from Canal Sept were in their places, and a group of Italians, Luna, based in Rome, consisting of an unholy alliance between two industrial rivals, made up the fourth applicant. The contracts for Western Europe had originally been awarded to a Dutch media group, but with their chairman in an Amsterdam jail, accused of financial irregularities, they had withdrawn from the contest, whilst the Berlin-based company who had acquired the rights to the East had neither the money nor the stomach for another application. The Americans who had been given the rest of the world simply did not want Europe and so all four applicants were fresh. It was odd, but at none of the meetings that Mark had attended had Ball Park taken the European bids seriously. They had focused in on Jet as if they were their sole competitor and Mark just hoped that they were not going to be the victims of Halid's obsession with Carr.

Pavarotti sat down to tumultuous applause and cries for an encore from those who regarded the whole circus as an excuse for some free drink and entertainment. Eventually, the applause subsided and a hush fell over the gathering. It was time for business. The lights in the room dimmed and a single spotlight illuminated the chairman of the committee, Jacques Vicheron. Jules Rimet may have been the man whose name was immortalised in the World Cup, but Vicheron had also dreamed his dream nearly a century later. He was an unprepossessing, portly man in his mid-fifties whose footballing claim to fame was having played for Auxerre in the early sixties whilst qualifying as a lawyer. His law firm had proved more successful than his sporting career and he had also become a leading political figure when supporting the socialist party throughout the seventies. They had come to power too late as far as he was concerned because by then he was working full-time on his own brain child, his baby, the European Super League. And now it was coming together he was relishing every moment of it.

He stood with his hands behind his back, spectacles perched on his nose and a sealed envelope in front of him on a highly-polished oak table.

'Fucking hell,' Nick said, a little too loudly, 'he thinks he's about to announce the Oscar nominations.'

The sound of Nick's voice carried across the auditorium and, although Vicheron could not possibly have understood, the noise itself was a sufficient irritant for him to look across to the Ball Park party in the manner of an irritated schoolmaster. Having regained the complete attention of his audience, the Frenchman cleared his throat and began his speech, reluctantly choosing English as his language as a concession to the majority in the room. Even most of the Press contingent seemed to be gathered from the same world-weary hacks who had been with the England team in Colombia and Mark had been studiously avoiding them to ensure they didn't get the chance to question him too closely about the situation with Barry Reed.

Vicheron was standing a little too close to the microphone and his voice reverberated round the room.

'This is a momentous moment for me and I hope for all of us. The finest clubs have played each other for many years in Europe, but it has been at random, subject to the luck of the draw either in cup competitions or in the league section of the European Champions Cup. But it has always been on a historical basis, last year's champions. Now they will play each other on merit, season after season. There will be no such thing as an "easy group" or an "easy game". Every match will be a championship contest. Soon the word "Premier" and the letter "A" will live on in the shadow of the accolade "Super". We will live up to the standards of excellence we set ourselves from the very beginning and we will achieve that in conjunction with whomsoever we choose to broadcast our matches around the globe. Today we are here to announce who will be granted those exclusive television rights. When we first approached the issue and decided to sell off the rights individually we were accused of greed. We were accused of potential breaches of cross-border regulations, we were accused like common criminals rather than the innovative businessmen that we truly are. So we have bowed to the pressures, we have paid our homage to the wiles of the lawyers . . .'

Mark sensed rather than actually saw a quick glance in the direction of Halid, but if there was indeed any pause in Vicheron's speech then it was barely perceptible.

'This time we are granting the rights for the whole of the world, including Europe, to one company. If this is to be seen as a truly European league, if Europe itself is to be seen as truly united, then each country will receive the same pictures, perceive the same image. Only the language of the commentators will differ although our dream is that just as Europe will have one league, may soon have one currency, so one day it might also have a common language. So, enough of the future, enough of our aspirations. We turn to the matter in hand. We have received four tenders in all. It may interest you to know that we originally had some forty applicants, but we have set ourselves, and them, such high standards that only the four companies now seated in the room survived the course. I urge you to congratulate them all, whatever the outcome.'

He led the applause, which was both muted and sporadic, reminding Mark of the hand given to an orchestra at the end of a musical when they finally laid down their instruments just as everybody was putting on their coats and heading for the door.

'Thank you all,' Vicheron continued, 'we have been most impressed by all their presentations, so much so that had they been the only criteria for selection we would have been unable to separate them. And so it came down to the question of money.'

'Like it was ever going to be anything else,' Richard said to the Ball Park group and everybody within earshot gave a nervous laugh.

'This time,' Vicheron said without missing a beat, moving inexorably towards the dramatic thrust of his speech, 'it may be a question of money, but hopefully time will prove that this league is not all about wealth, but about a public service. We cannot expect the fans from France to travel to England, or the Italians to travel to Germany for every match. Therefore, television takes on a far greater significance than ever before. Now we have a new responsibility, a new burden to be imposed on the television company which will produce and show the ESL to Europe and indeed the rest of the world. They may be paying us the money, but we will be placing a heavy weight on their shoulders . . .'

Halid was drumming the table impatiently and muttering to himself. 'Come on, you've already said that. Do you like the sound of your own voice so much?'

Mark could see the tension showing in his face. This meant a lot to him. He had become irrationally fond of the Iranian businessman during the relatively brief period he'd been working with him. He could see all his faults and knew that even if he pointed them all out to him, and even if Mo acknowledged them, that he would do nothing about them, probably could do nothing about them. He was what he was and Mark felt that he was a loyal and generous friend. He could not help but look across at Nathan Carr to see how Mo's rival was coping with the endless wait, but his face was impassive, expressionless, carved in stone like a presidential face on Mount Rushmore.

Vicheron had the envelope in his hand now, but had still not quite finished with his moment of personal glory.

'Even when the contract is granted we will not relinquish control. We have advised all the applicants that the contract will contain stringent penalties including our right to terminate if they fall from the high standards we are imposing upon them.'

He began to fumble with the envelope.

'Who does he think he's kidding?' Mark said. 'He obviously knows exactly what's in it.'

'He's playing to the TV audience, I reckon,' Nick replied, jerking his thumb towards the back of the room where the crews were pointing their cameras at the stage.

'So television creates television,' Mark nodded, 'not bad programming.'

Nobody seated at the table smiled. It was too close to the truth to be amusing.

Vicheron finished opening with a flourish, put down the paper-knife designed in the new ESL colours of yellow, blue and green and delicately removed one thin sheet of paper.

'And we, the committee of the new European Super League, are proud to announce that the exclusive rights to televise all matches for a period of five years goes to . . .' He paused for effect, milking the last few seconds of tension and then said in a loud, confident voice, 'Jet Productions.'

CHAPTER 27

Nathan Carr rose without a word, without any sign of triumph, shook hands with the French and Italian losers and studiously ignored his former partner and associates. He then strode up to the podium and stood side by side with Vicheron, his arm around the chairman's shoulders, posing for a thousand photographs as if it were a joint triumph.

The flashing of the cameras splayed a focus of light on the victors as Carr gestured to the rest of his team to join him in his moment of triumph. He offered Alissa a helping hand and then kissed her on both cheeks.

'Come on guys, pictures of the lady. Couldn't have done it without her and she's prettier than me.'

The main lights had now been switched on in the hall. The leader of the French contingent walked over to Halid and put a comforting arm around his shoulder, gave an expressive Gallic shrug and walked away. It was Mark who was the first to speak.

'He knew. Carr knew he was going to win.'

'What do you mean?' Halid asked. 'What are you talking about? Carr may be a crook but nobody has ever suggested Vicheron is anything other than honest. He's had attempts on his life because of his fight against the French mafia.'

'People change,' Richard said, in a tired, world-weary voice, the horrendous realisation dawning upon him that all the work, the all-nighters, the deadlines they had driven themselves to meet, had been for nothing.

'Perhaps they do,' Mo said, 'but I think you're clutching at straws, Mark. Vicheron may have been chairman but there were five others on the committee. Are you suggesting Carr had them all in his pocket?'

Nabil had sat in bored indifference throughout the proceedings, with continual glances at his watch in the vain hope that the gesture might hurry along the proceedings. Now he rose to go, almost in relief.

'Dad. It's over. We lost. It's time to go home.'

The colour drained from his father's face, then immediately flushed back into it, the crimson tide of anger clear despite the olive complexion of his skin.

'For the Halids it is never over. It's a matter of pride. Mark, why do you think that Carr knew he would win?'

For a moment, Mark regretted pointing Halid down a path that could lead anywhere. But he had followed his instinct before and it had rarely led him astray and here he had more than instinct, he had the recent conversation reverberating around his head. It was, of course, no proof. Carr may have been taunting him by sounding so supremely confident, but there had been something in his voice which suggested otherwise. First he would prise away the rights and then he would take away Halid's key staff and his aim would be to leave him only with regret that he had in turn taken away Carr's wife.

'Come on, Mark, put your money where your mouth is. Answer Mo's question,' Nick said. He had more experience of Halid's obsessions than the rest of them and seemed annoyed that Mark was encouraging his boss not to let matters rest.

'Of course, I'll answer his question. Carr collared me in the Gents . . .'

Richard sniggered.

'No, Richard, not like that.' Mark half-closed his eyes to concentrate on the memory of the moment and continued half to himself, half to the other four. 'You know, it was as if he were following me. He appeared from nowhere as if he'd been waiting for me to be alone for a few minutes.'

'You're paranoid, Rossetti,' Nabil sneered. 'Are you sure that you've not started drinking again?'

Mark rose to his full height and Nabil took a step back.

'If I didn't respect your father, I'd take you apart, you little shit, and it'd be for your own good. At least I'd leave you alive. One day, if you push your luck, somebody else might not.'

Mo listened to the pair of them and looked from one to the other. Mark thought there was a chance that he was going to receive some encouragement in how to deal with his son, but

Mo had tunnel-vision as far as Carr was concerned, and was not going to be easily diverted.

'Go on, Mark. Ignore Nabil. He can be rude and tiresome at times, but I have learned to live with it and I must ask you to do so too. If he upset you, then I apologise on his behalf.'

Mark bit his lower lip so hard that he drew blood, but he had gone so far and there could be no turning back.

'He offered me a job. And he said when Jet gets the ESL rights, not if.'

'And that's it?' Nick asked. 'You're basing this whole charge of corruption on a bit of bravado. I've heard the manager of Darlington interviewed and say when we get to the Premier. Maybe you could charge him with bribery and corruption as well.'

Mark shook his head, refusing to be shaken off the scent.

'You had to be there. It wasn't like that, it wasn't like that at all. He knew the job was going to be on offer. I'm sure of it.'

'Maybe you should take it, Mark,' Mo said quietly.

'You don't mean that, do you?' Mark replied in a hurt voice.

'No, I don't. And I hope you'll stay with us. But if Carr thought you did want to swap horses . . .'

'You've got a crazy idea, haven't you, Mo?' Richard said, giving Mark a pitying glance. 'You don't know what you're doing, Rossetti. Turn back before it's too late. Beware the mind of Mo,' he added in a mock-Shakespearean declamation.

'Supposing, just supposing, Carr does think that you want to work for him,' Halid said, staring straight into Mark's face. 'If you were in there, if you get into his confidence then I've enough faith in your ability to be sure that you'd find out exactly how he pulled off this three-card trick.'

There was a silence as Mark realised exactly what was being asked of him.

'How good an actor are you, Mark?' Nick asked.

'He can't be that bad. He's convinced Mo that he likes him and nobody can really like our leader,' Richard said with a false note of jollity.

Nabil glared at his father in disapproval.

'How can you put your trust in a man you hardly know? This is family business.' He broke into his native tongue and again Mark saw the anger appear in Mo's eyes. One day, he was sure, there would be reckoning between father and son and he had a feeling that day was not so far away.

'Speak English, Nabil. It's rude to do otherwise in front of our friends. We live in England now.'

'Oh yes,' the boy said bitterly, 'I was forgetting how English we were. How English all your friends in the City think you are. There are times when you are remarkably naive.'

'And there are times, Nabil, when you forget that I am your father. I trust Mark here implicitly, and if anything ever happens to me, so should you. What you are saying is an insult and I insist you apologise.'

'Insist away. I say what I think. I didn't inherit your two faces.'

Mo clenched his fist and Mark felt certain he was going to hit his son, but just in time he remembered they were in a public place surrounded by photographers and journalists and he restrained himself.

'We'll talk about your manners when we are alone. Meanwhile, as for it being family business, don't forget your sister is out on bail and you had difficulty even achieving that, so you must forgive me if I call upon a little outside assistance.'

He turned away from his son and put his hand upon Mark's shoulder.

'You must excuse me. I don't consider you to be an outsider, but I am disappointed and hurt and I am saying things I don't really mean. Now will you do this for me? Will you go into the enemy camp? I can see Carr looking over here. He has seen us all arguing. He may well be willing to believe that you and I have fallen out rather than there having been an unfortunate misunderstanding between my son and I.'

Mark knew that he had only a few seconds to make up his mind and again he relied on his instinct. This last year or so he'd spent too much time following his head rather than his heart. It was time to take a chance.

'Well, fuck you, Halid,' he said loudly, 'I worked my bollocks off trying to get you these bloody rights and if that's all the appreciation you can show you can take the job and shove it up your arse.'

The words sounded so out of character coming from Mark's mouth that Halid reeled back in anger, once again clenching his fists into a ball.

165

'Don't hit me, Mo,' Mark muttered without changing the expression of disgust on his face, 'I tend to bruise easily.'

The words had the desired effect. Halid jerked himself back to reality, accepted that he was a part of a masquerade of his own production, and simply turned his back on his erstwhile employee.

Nick nudged Halid. 'Well, at least we've found out what sort of actor he is.' But Mark was no longer listening, he was already halfway across the room towards the triumphant Nathan Carr.

'Is that offer of a job still on the table?' Mark asked.

'I don't withdraw an offer until it's been rejected. I don't believe I ever heard you turning it down.'

'I didn't. When do I start?'

'Don't you want to discuss terms?' Carr asked with a smile on his face.

'Same as I was getting at Ball Park plus ten per cent. I'll show you the contract so you know I'm telling you the truth. An appearance fee that we'll agree every time I do a broadcast, double that basic amount if I'm the main commentator. One year rolling contract. How does that grab you for terms?'

'Not bad for an ex-footballer. Don't you guys always have agents?'

'Not this guy. Pet hate. If I represent myself then I've only myself to blame if I sell myself short. And if I sell myself ten per cent short then I'm still breaking even by paying no commission.' Mark paused and gathered his thoughts. Carr was no fool and he had to play this exactly right or else he could be in serious trouble. He didn't think Carr was going to take lightly to industrial espionage. He decided to inject a little humour into the conversation. 'I suppose my margin of error might be fifteen per cent or even twenty. Agents are getting greedier by the day.'

'So what happened between you and my old friend Mo?' Carr asked.

'He used me and then he blamed me.'

'Sounds par for the course.' The woman standing beside Carr spoke for the first time and then extended her right hand towards Mark. He could not help but notice the long fingers, nails immaculately groomed, everything about her immaculate, the skin soft and cool beneath his fingers. She wore a Hermès scarf around her neck, a subtle bracelet, silver rather than gold, with

166

a single charm, a bird in the same design as Carr's ring. She, too, wore a ring, but only one, in delicate filigree silver, looking as if it might break if it were touched. The silver watch on her wrist had a strap with the same design. Everything about her suggested understated wealth, down to the green, perfectly cut business suit, that merely suggested the curvaceous figure that lay beneath.

'Alissa, Alissa Bland,' she said. 'You may remember we met briefly at the reception after the Colombia match. I've enjoyed watching you on the box. We're both fans, Nathan and I.'

It was a platitude, yet the way she said it suggested to Mark that she really meant it. He'd liked her handshake as well; firm, inviting rather than repulsing contact. She looked at him steadily and for the first time he wondered whether he was doing the right thing by setting them up for his betrayal. Had Judas also thought he was doing the right thing? He'd reacted instinctively in crossing the floor, but now his instinct was telling him that whatever Nathan Carr might be, Alissa Bland was an honest woman. Hard, without doubt – he knew of her reputation – but honest nevertheless. It was probably too late to turn back, and if he started disbelieving Mo he would never carry this thing through. If Alissa Bland worked as closely with her chairman as he had been led to believe then he had to regard her as the enemy, had to tar her with the same brush as her chairman.

'When are you booked to get back to England?' Carr asked.

'Tomorrow evening. I'm on the same flight as the rest of the Ball Park crew. I think they thought it would be a late night for them.'

'Well, it will be for us; but we're still flying back first thing in the morning. Got a lot on at the office anyway, even without everything that will flow from this. I'd like you to join us for dinner tonight. It's by way of celebration. I've booked us a private room at the hotel. The chef knows he's on a big bonus if he really turns it on. I'm not sure if you can use the phrase "pig out" in relation to food at the Dolder Grand, but we're sure as hell going to try.'

'Short notice,' Mark said, then immediately regretted it. The less astute Carr thought him to be the better chance he had of getting his confidence.

'I told you we were going to win. No point in being unprepared if you're confident. Welcome aboard, Mark. It's eight o'clock. Black tie.'

'I'm not sure if I should come. Won't the rest of your team think it odd? And I'm not sure if I want to rub Mo's nose in it that much. He and the rest of them will still be around tonight.'

'Your loyalty does you justice. But I know what Mo can do to people. He weaves his magic and everybody is under his spell. He makes you think he cares, he demands loyalty and says he gives it back, but you've seen the other side of him. He's a bad loser, Mark. No room in any game for poor losers.'

'I suppose so.'

'I know so. I told you we'd win and we did. Have you got a dinner suit?'

'Actually I have. Ball Park was also going to have a dinner party. Maybe they still will.'

'It'll be like a wake and ours is going to be a real celebration. I'll leave your name at the door. And don't worry. You won't have to spend the evening with a bunch of strangers. We're all one big happy family and I'll make sure you have a seat between me and Alissa.'

There was the briefest exchange of glances between the man and the woman, some kind of secret, silent language and Mark was aware that they inter-related as a couple even if there was nothing physical in the relationship. He did not know why he had agreed to step off the side of Ball Park's boat into unknown waters, but now that he had done so he wondered whether or not he might be swimming for his life.

CHAPTER 28

Mark was beginning to dread flying. London–Bogota, Bogota–London, London–Zurich and now back to Heathrow again. And what then? What did Jet hold in store for him? In the cold light of day what he had done seemed remarkably stupid. How on earth did Halid think he was going to discover any deep, dark secrets just by commentating on matches? In fact he wasn't too sure if he was even going to be commentating in the short term. The ESL would not come into being for a year or so, and Jet mainly showed highlights of league games. He'd done a few dubbed commentaries for Ball Park, without ever enjoying them. It was too easy to be wise after the event, too difficult to put any emotion into it when you knew exactly when the goals would be coming. The fact of the matter was he had no plan, did not even know what he was after or indeed whether there was anything there at all. Carr could simply have won fair and square. Yet he'd travelled down seemingly blind alleys before and sooner or later there was a turn, another turn, a curve and there you were out in the dazzling sunlight.

He tried to doze on the plane, but his mind was too active and the stewardesses too solicitous, puzzled that of all the passengers in Swiss Air's first class, he was the only one declining the endless champagne. For Carr and his associates it was just a continuation of where they had left off last night, or to be more accurate, that morning. Carr was treating Mark as a long lost brother, insisting that they sat together on the plane.

'My old mate Mo's travelling BA, I suppose?'

Mark nodded.

'Always one for flying the flag was Mo,' Carr continued. 'Wanted to be more English than the English. Not for me, I'm afraid. Everybody knows I'm Jewish. East End roots and all that. I'm not ashamed of it. Not that I bother with all that religious mumbo-jumbo, but being Jewish can open more doors than it

169

closes. Me, I always like to fly first-class. If you can afford it then why not? BA only has Club on its European runs, so I don't fly it. Simple enough. Got the money, why not spend it? Why not?'

He ended the sentence with a question addressed to himself, and Mark got the impression that he was only half talking to him, half reassuring himself that he truly was where he believed himself to be. An odd man, and yet so far Mark had no reason to understand the loathing that Mo clearly felt towards him. He could, however, sympathise with Carr's emotions. Mo had stolen his wife. Mark had undergone the same experience with one of the Hertsmere players when he'd been at the peak of his drinking sessions. It had taken a long time to accept that his wife, the mother of his daughter, was sharing a bed with another man.

He'd not enjoyed the previous evening, largely because it was no fun being one of the few sober people with a load of drunken celebrants. He'd longed to be in his bed from eleven onwards, wondering how he could have ever been locked into the twilight zone of alcohol.

Nathan Carr had not got drunk though. He could either take his drink or else made a very good show of pretending to drink along with the rest of the party. Mark did not see him decline a refill all night, but then he did not see his glass empty either. It was another piece of the jigsaw, and although Mark was already having regrets about the whole charade there was still a part of him, the investigative part, that wanted to know Carr a little better.

Alissa Bland had made no such pretence of holding back on the booze. Mark could not help but recall the last time he'd been alone with a woman who'd had more than a little to drink. He felt, no, he knew, he'd made an enemy of Jenny Cooper and he didn't want a repeat performance with a woman with whom he'd be working so closely. She was close to him all evening, with her low-cut dress and expensive perfume and it made him nervous.

For years he had no woman in his life except for the constant nagging of his ex-wife, then Patti had arrived from nowhere and now he had two women showing an interest in him in the space of a couple of weeks. He couldn't believe that he'd become more desirable, but perhaps he was just sending out messages that he could not control.

170

'Tell me about yourself,' Alissa said, her eyes holding his until he was forced to look away on the pretext of adjusting his napkin. There was just a hint of grey in her blonde hair, a few lines about her eyes, a tightness at the neck and although she was still a highly attractive woman she was under pressure in holding back the inexorable tide of time. She had to be over forty, but whatever his thoughts he always returned to her eyes, which were at once those of an innocent teenager and as old as Eve, flickering with life and with knowledge.

To his surprise he had told her all about himself; not all, of course, but more than he had told Patti in the time they'd been together. He told her about the false charges against him that had cut short his footballing career, he told her about the battle with drink, the break-up of his marriage, the temporary loss of his child. He told her about his old landlord, Leo Schneider, and the money he'd been left. He told her about Italy and Russia, about his dicing with death and he'd told her about Patti and her problems in Colombia.

She had a real talent for listening, prompting him at the right moment, showing an interest when he thought he might be boring her, asking the right questions and waiting patiently for the answers. And all the time she was drinking steadily as if encouraging him to believe that her defences were down, that anything and everything he might say would be forgotten in the morning.

On the plane, he wondered if he'd said too much, if Carr had deliberately placed her next to him to ascertain whether or not his motives for crossing the floor were, indeed, genuine. Or perhaps to go even further and see what it was that made Mark Rossetti tick. As the evening wore on she had not come on to him strongly, and there was never any suggestion that he might be obliged to sleep with her; yet as he fell into bed for the few hours sleep he could grab before he had to leave for the airport, it did occur to him that if he had asked she would not have said no. But he knew he had done the right thing by excusing himself at two a.m. Normally he would not have dreamed of phoning Patti in the middle of the night, but as she seemed to have done little but sleep since her return he hoped that she'd take the call instead of allowing her answerphone to pick up the message. She'd phoned him at ten as promised and had actually said she'd be waiting for his call. Tonight, she was his life-line to normality. She represented the real world, although the reality of calling a woman who was out on bail accused of drug-smuggling offences in Colombia was more fantastic than the rest of his present situation. To his relief she actually answered the phone at the third ring. Her voice was sleepy, but perfectly lucid.

'Hi, it's me.'

'So I gather. It was always going to be you or a dirty phone call at this unearthly hour.'

'Even a heavy breather wouldn't want to risk your wrath.'

'Have you called just to throw insults or is it important?'

'It's important.'

'So tell me.'

'I love you.'

It sounded lame, melodramatic, and Mark knew from past experience that from here on in it could go either way.

'I love you too. I'm glad you called. I'm missing you. I'm sorry about how I've been, both before and after Bogota. You must be crazy to want to hang on in there.'

'Didn't you know all footballers are crazy?'

'I thought it was only goalkeepers.'

'No, they're just crazier than the rest.'

'Did you call just to tell me you loved me?' she asked with a yawn.

'Yes.'

'Liar. I know you, Rossetti, you've something else on your mind.'

'I have, but you're not here to allow me to put it into action.'

'I'm the one with the blarney. Or is this the romantic Italian side of you that's finally coming out of the closet?'

There was a silence.

'I hope you're not paying for this call, Mark, because if you are you're not getting your money's worth. Come clean. I can hear you smiling down the line.'

'I'm not smiling, Patti, believe me. I think I've done something stupid.'

'That makes a change. If it's really stupid, then it probably makes us even. So what did you do? Put your shoes on the wrong feet? Arrange to meet some Colombian drug baron in the wee small hours of the morning and not turn up?'

''Probably worse than that. I've just agreed to work for Nathan Carr at Jet.'

'Wow. That beats Colombian drug barons.'

'That bad?'

'So they say, Mark, so they say.'

'Can you always believe what people say?' Mark asked, seeking some comfort.

'Most of the time most of the people are right. Take a long spoon if you're eating with him.'

'I already have and the cutlery was standard size.'

'Watch out for the indigestion, then. Can I go back to sleep now or are we rehearsing for a telethon?'

'One more question,' he said, reluctant to end the conversation. When she was in this sort of mood it gave him a warm glow just to hear her voice.

'Do you know anything about his first lieutenant, Alissa Bland?'

'I can find out. Carr himself has always been newsworthy, that's why I know about the company. I'd have to ask somebody who writes regular business pieces. Can it wait until you get back?'

'Sure.'

'Why are you so interested in Miss Bland? It is Miss, I assume.'

'I sat next to her at dinner.'

'Oh yes, the meal with the standard cutlery. Did you shag her?'

He could tell by the lightness of her tone that she knew he hadn't, but he answered anyway.

'If I had then she'd still be here.'

'How do I know she's not.'

'You'll have to trust me. I'd hardly be asking about her if she were still in the bed.'

'It could have been a quickie.'

'I don't think Alissa Bland is the sort of woman who'd appreciate a quickie.'

'You never know. She might quite like a bit of rough trade. Appearances can be deceptive. I do, otherwise I'd never have got involved with you. Anyway, got to go now. The bloke in the bed's getting impatient. I love you, Mark.' And then she put down the phone before he could say another word, and, indeed, there was little more to say.

He still wondered what she might come up with about Alissa. He doubted his own judgment when it came to people. He'd been wrong too many times before, yet in this case, the research he'd asked Patti to carry out made him feel a little guilty. He glanced at the woman seated across the aisle from him on the plane. She was working on her laptop, concentrating on the information on the screen, oblivious to her surroundings. And what about Nathan Carr? He had tended to take Halid's warning with a pinch of salt. He had good reason to bear a grudge. But Patti was different. She was a journalist. She knew people, had cold, hard facts at her fingertips to help her differentiate the good from the bad. On a rating system her reaction to Carr had been five-star bad.

For the last time he wondered if he could change his mind. He could tell Carr he was getting married, that he wanted to work for no one. He could wish Mo good luck and leave the pair of them to get on with their lives whilst he got on with his. He could sort out Patti, make sure she was cleared and then really settle down with her for once and for all. His life had been in two separate compartments for too long. He could shut one down for ever and devote his time to living in the one that contained the person for whom he cared most of all. Yet something told him that wasn't a real option any more, that life would not be that simple. He had to see this particular drama through to the end and, truth to tell, he could not contain his curiosity as to how it would all pan out.

CHAPTER 29

Jenny Cooper had decided on an early night. She'd told her 'just in case' that she had to wash her hair and it was true. She always thought of him as her 'just in case' and when she was with her girlfriends she called him that as well. Phil was there just in case nobody better came along. There was no set or appointed time for Mr Right to come riding by on his white steed, but she felt she'd know for sure when he was not coming and then she'd tell Phil to name the day.

She was pleased to have put the Colombian game behind her, although all the ramifications of Barry Reed's positive drug test and arrest were yet to be felt. The Colombians had gone over the top with the youngster. He'd tested positive but, given their own drugs record, you'd have thought they'd have chucked him out on the plane and been glad to see the back of him, rather than making a federal case of it all. And then she'd been shoved into the front line when the Press had launched their main attack on the team's return. She'd not been around when the England side had been accused of wrecking the Cathay Pacific plane but she couldn't believe that the pressure could have been much worse.

Every hack pulled out his soapbox from beneath his desk, placed his laptop on its high moral pedestal and let fly his spleen on the unfortunate young Geordie. Unfortunately, from Jenny Cooper's point of view, they'd virtually ignored Patti Delaney's problems. But then she was one of them and they were always going to look after one of their own. That annoyed Jenny. She would have liked that snooty cow to have got her come-uppance. She was quite sure that if she'd not been hovering in the background that Mark would have capitulated to her that afternoon. She was not convinced that Mark Rossetti was Mr Right but she would have liked the opportunity of finding out.

Jenny lived in a new development in what would once have

175

been called Bermondsey or the East End, but which was now described as a City-fringe, exclusive waterfront area.

She liked it all neat and tidy, nothing out of place, and often when she got home from work early she'd have a demonic thirty minutes of clearing up. When Phil was here he sat in amazement, watching her behaving like a human tornado, unable to sustain a conversation until she had everything in its proper place. Only then would she offer him a drink, sit beside him on the settee, allow him to put an arm around her or maybe if she was in the mood to let him take her to bed. The flat was an obsession, she realised that, but it was her home, her call and she could do whatever she liked. Perhaps that was why the other men in her life apart from Phil stood no chance whatsoever. Even those few who stayed overnight were made to feel as if they were in a hotel where there was no room service, where the guests were obliged to clear up after themselves. One stockbroker who'd been the privileged recipient of a one-night-stand had been overheard in a bar saying that he thought Jenny Cooper had expected him to make the bed before he left.

Tonight she'd brought home a stack of work. Memos, mail, documents she never seemed to have time to deal with in the office. She looked at her watch. It was well past nine o'clock already. Idly she flicked through the evening paper to see what was on TV, looking for an excuse not to start the work. She settled for the end of the news, put the kettle on to make herself a coffee and, instead of sitting at the table with her papers, stretched herself out on the couch until the kettle boiled. She used an old-fashioned steam kettle because she liked the whistle. It didn't bother her it would take a good few minutes to boil on the ancient gas cooker that had travelled with her through a succession of bedsits and which she'd not had the heart to dispose of when she'd finally decided to buy.

It was a fairly small item on the news that caught her attention. Jet Productions had won the exclusive rights in Zurich to televise live ESL matches. A picture of its chairman, Nathan Carr, flashed up on the screen. She knew him. Nobody who had anything to do with the media could have failed to have come across him, but she couldn't remember ever having seen a photo before. He was not the sort of man who pushed his own profile into the foreground like, say, Richard Branson. He preferred to let his company capture the headlines rather than his own image. Yet, there was something familiar, something nagging away at the back of her mind.

Whether or not she started the work, she promised herself she'd be in bed by ten. She was not getting enough sleep, which was another good reason not to go out, another excuse for an early night, as if she needed one. Too much on her mind, too many mistakes, unforced errors as the football commentators might say. She didn't like mistakes any more than she liked mess. But she was in the midst of the ultimate mess. She could wash up dirty coffee cups, make rumpled beds, hoover the floor, but she couldn't sort out the mess that was her life.

She went into the bedroom and changed into her nightshirt. It was her favourite, with a huge teddy bear on the front, baggy and misshapen, not just from its endless washes, but also from her habit of pulling it down beneath her knees as she slept. By the time she'd returned, the news had finished and a programme about mountain goats in the Andes had begun. It was not a subject that was close to her heart and she began to surf the channels finding little or nothing that appealed to her.

She felt remarkably awake all of a sudden and cursed the coffee she'd just drunk after the packet of crisps and glass of wine that had passed for her supper. She couldn't cook, or rather wouldn't cook, and tended to eat whatever junk food came easily to hand from her cupboards. She shopped at random, nothing she bought quite making a whole meal, nearly everything dramatically unhealthy. She knew what she did need and struggled to resist the temptation. There had been too much of that lately, and the pressure had given her a ready-made excuse.

She refilled the kettle and relit the ring on the cooker. If she was going to be awake then she might as well be properly awake and concentrate on the work although there were other ways to get her through the night. She got out her laptop, plugged it into the mains and began to work steadily through the papers she'd extracted from her briefcase. Apart from dealing with the Press her remit extended to replying to the post that came in from the general public. Pointing out that she was Deputy Press Officer and not in the public relations department had cut little ice with her bosses and she was still landed with mounds of post that for the life of her she could not see fitted into her domain. She'd given up arguing. If you wanted promotion then it was better to say yes than no and, basically, all she had to do was draft a bog-standard reply and adapt it as the circumstances required. The telephone rang and she jumped. The phone did not seem to bring her any glad tidings, but she was still rational enough to realise that was of her own making. Still, there was no point in turning back the clock. What was done was done.

She allowed the phone to ring again and again, annoyed with herself that she'd not put on the answerphone, which at least gave her the option as to whether or not she wanted to speak to the caller. It was supposed to cut in after ten rings anyway, but it had been playing up lately and the phone rang on incessantly. She finally surrendered and lifted the receiver. If it was that important to the caller to persist it seemed only fair to answer. There was nobody there, or whoever had been there cut the connection as soon as she answered. She didn't like that. She'd been burgled a couple of months earlier and had only just adjusted to sleeping with the lights off. Right now she was down to a light in the hall burning throughout the night, but these sort of calls were disturbing.

She dialled 1471 hoping it would disclose who had made the call, and that it would prove to be a girlfriend who'd simply assumed nobody was at home.

'You were called at 9.34. The number has been withheld.' She liked that even less. It meant that somebody had deliberately keyed in 141 before making the call to preserve anonymity. Somebody didn't want her to know their identity, but that same somebody wanted to ensure she was at home.

She checked the door to make sure it was securely locked, then went quickly round to satisfy herself that all the windows were also closed. She tugged with some satisfaction at the sturdy bars her insurers had insisted she fit after the last break-in. At times it was a bit like living in Fort Knox, but at least she felt relatively safe. Everything was in order. Unless someone arrived by tank they were not going to get in tonight. She shivered a little and tossed up in her mind between another glass of wine and another coffee, pushing a third option to the back of her mind. She settled for the wine as being more likely to make her relax and ultimately to ensure she slept.

She began to read the letters, trying to distract herself from the phone call. Normally she loved the view from the window, looking straight out on to the river, but tonight the creaking barges assumed more sinister shapes. When she was a child she'd loved to read Dickens, loved the idea of living in one of the decrepit warehouses he'd described so well. She'd not hesitated when she'd had the chance to buy this flat, even though the monthly mortgage repayments sometimes stretched her pay packet beyond its limits. It was a duplex, rather than a flat. An entrance hall, a flight of stairs to the lounge and the kitchen-diner, then the bedroom and bathroom up another flight of stairs.

The burglary had put a few doubts into her mind and tonight, on her own, the place seemed terribly remote. She did not even know who her neighbours were because she was never around to see or speak to them, and that added to the feeling of isolation. She would normally have called Phil but when she'd bumped him off for the evening he'd told her he was going to the cinema with some of his mates to see some awful film of gore and violence that she'd told him was simply not on their agenda.

She rose and walked over to the window again. A cloud shuffled across the moon and the water was darkened. As if to hide herself away she drew down the blinds on the picture window that led on to the small balcony. To fill a few moments she put the kettle back on for the third time that evening, although this time with the intention of making a herbal tea. She turned again to the mail as a further distraction. Amidst all the junk mail she was surprised to find one marked for her personal attention. She had no recollection of having seen it before and could only assume that her secretary had added it to her pile when she'd known that she was taking it home. The envelope said, 'strictly private and confidential' and she wondered when it had arrived in the office and how she had missed it. She looked at the postmark to see where and when it had been sent, but both pieces of information were too blurred. Intrigued she opened it, read it once, then read it again. There was an enclosure as well and she began shaking as she held it in her hand. She reached into her bag for her address book, failed to find it immediately and then tipped the contents out on to the floor. She rapidly thumbed through the pages. If there was one person who needed to know about this then it was him. He was the only person who would understand, the only one she could trust.

Three rings and then an answerphone message, one that worked. She disconnected before speaking. She needed to think this out, work it through before she spoke to a machine. Speaking to him would have been different. Another glass of wine. It was going to her head. She'd always held herself out as a hard drinker, one of the boys right from her university days. Only she wasn't. A couple of glasses of wine and although she might not be anybody's she'd certainly belonged to more than she could remember. And there were some she couldn't remember. After the sexy stage she moved into aggression. Quite a few of her relationships had ended when she'd said things that not only did she not mean but of which she had no recollection whatsoever the following morning. It had ended with Rob that way. She'd really liked him, he'd travelled a lot, called her from wherever he was whatever the distance or the time differences. She always looked forward to his calls, more than she cared or dared to admit. One night he'd rung from an airport in the States, Washington, she thought. She'd been too drunk to know, one glass of wine after work had turned into another and then a bottle and then another. She could never stop after just one glass and that frustrated her. Something her drinking companion had said must have triggered off a series of irrational thoughts because by the time Rob phoned after midnight to say he was on his way back to her loaded with presents, ready for her bed, she gave it to him with both barrels loaded. Then he told her the next day in a call from his office that he'd had enough, that it was time to call it a day, that he'd not called at great expense to be advised during the course of the conversation that he was crap in bed, that she was only using him and then in the same breath that he was a coward for not asking her to marry him . . . which she'd never do anyway. She began to fumble in her bag, but regained her self-control and looked for another way.

She lifted the phone again and pressed the redial button. But even before the anticipated answerphone cut in there was a ring at her door. Gone ten. Too late for door-to-door salesmen, wrong day for Jehovah's Witnesses. She rose unsteadily and looked through the security peephole.

'Oh, it's you. Thank goodness for that. I was getting really spooked out.'

She undid the chain, slid the bolt and turned the key. The

door crashed into her face, sending her sprawling against the wall. The first blow landed before she could get to her feet, just as the door slammed shut.

'No,' she said, 'please,' and a word she'd not had an enormous amount of time for in her lifetime was the last she spoke on earth. As the door closed behind her killer, the kettle began to boil again, a long incessant whistle.

CHAPTER 30

Inspector Rob Davies was not the most welcome of breakfast guests. It wasn't that Mark didn't like the man. He'd actually grown quite fond of him, particularly so since he'd married Helen Archer, formerly the club secretary at Hertsmere and now its chief executive. It was just that he preferred him off duty to on.

'I take it that this isn't a social call,' Mark said as he ushered him in.

'Bit early for social calling. I normally do that sort of thing in the pub at the end of the day.'

'You mean when Helen lets you,' Mark said comfortably, knowing the policeman couldn't take offence because he had only met his wife because of Rossetti himself.

'She lets me. She's as busy as I am. That's about the only time we see each other nowadays, when she comes along to the local to collect me. Nothing like a pint to round off the day,' he added, the Welsh accent becoming more pronounced as he spoke fondly about beer.

'Yeah, I used to . . .' Mark began to say with a nervous smile. He didn't like the strange expression on Davies's face. He'd dealt with him professionally before and felt he knew him well enough to recognise danger signs.

'Sorry, I forgot.'

'As long as one of us remembers, it doesn't matter. How is the beautiful Helen of Hertsmere?'

'She's fine. She'd be better if the club had got off to a better start to the season. You know what she's like. Takes every defeat as a personal insult.'

'A bit like you, I guess, Rob.'

'Suppose so. Patti well?' He seemed reluctant to get to the point of his call, almost embarrassed.

'Ups and downs. It wasn't the most pleasant experience in

182

Bogota, as you can imagine. But she's fine at the moment. It's not her you've come about, is it?'

'No, it's not her.'

Again Mark saw a cloud pass across the policeman's face.

'So what is it then? From the way you look you're about to give me a formal caution.'

Davies hesitated, like a diver about to leap from the highest board.

'Look, Mark, do you think you could make me a nice cup of tea?'

Mark laughed aloud.

'Aren't you supposed to do that when I'm shocked and shattered?'

'Yes, but this whole situation is a bit arse about face.'

Davies threw his jacket over a chair and sat down on another at the kitchen table and looked around the room. There was nothing in it to reflect Mark's character. Pine cupboards and shelves, half a dozen plain mugs, empty work surfaces and one empty flower vase. A cooker, a fridge, and that was about it. He rubbed his shoes idly on the tiled floor and gratefully accepted the mug of steaming tea.

'What, for a girl, do a fellow and kitchen tiles have in common?' he finally asked. Mark shrugged his ignorance.

'If she lays them right the first time she'll have both of them under her feet for ever.'

Mark smiled politely.

'Come on, Rob, I don't think you came all the way here to tell me bad jokes.'

'No, I didn't.' He took another sip of tea, refusing to be rushed into whatever it was he was going to say. 'I'd have thought you and Patti would have moved in together by now.'

'We would have if I had any say in the matter. But it would take a nuclear explosion to get her out of the Burrow. She's virtually built a moat and drawbridge there. Every time I think I'm getting near to permanent occupancy she fills the one with water and pulls the other up. How's the tea?'

'Not bad, considering you're not Welsh.'

'I didn't know the Welsh had cornered the tea-market.'

'Ah, we've cornered the market in a lot of things.'

'Not football.'

'No, not football, but then my idea of football has always been a bit different from yours and Helen's.'

'Yeah, you think throwing a leather-cased melon around, in between lots of overweight men leaping on top of each other with a view to causing permanent injury, is some kind of sporting entertainment. My dictionary defines a ball as round. I reckon the paying customer could get all you rugby nuts under the Trade Descriptions Act.'

Suddenly, Mark ran out of small talk.

'Why have you come, Rob? It's not about my health, it's not to tell me jokes and it's certainly not for my tea-making reputation.'

'You're right. How well did you know Jenny Cooper?'

'Ah,' Mark replied, twirling his spoon around in the mug even though he took no sugar.

'Wrong reaction, Mark. It means you have to tell me the truth.'

'Why shouldn't I?'

'Just answer the question. We're on the record now.'

'You sound just like a copper.'

'I am a copper.'

Mark rose to refill his cup although it was still three-quarters full. He just wanted to give himself a moment to collect his thoughts, to try to ascertain exactly why someone he regarded as a friend should be at his house at the crack of dawn to interrogate him. In the thirty seconds he had, he came to the conclusion he had no idea and if he had no idea then his conscience must be clean and there was no reason not to cooperate.

'I've known Jenny for a while,' he said, trying to remember just how long a while was.

'In what capacity?'

'Sort of a friend. And lately as a media contact.'

'What sort of friend?'

'What sorts are there? Not best friend, that's for sure. Just a friend, someone I'd speak to from time to time.'

'Nothing more?'

'Not from my side.'

'But from hers?'

'Maybe she wanted something more.' It was the first half-lie he'd told and he could see that Davies had seized upon the intonation in his reply like a terrier being tossed a bone.

'Did you give her that something more?'

'No.'

'When did you last see her?'

'Bogota. A week or so ago. She was with the England party.'

'Did you talk to her?'

'Not a lot.'

'I thought you just told me you were friends. Don't friends talk?'

'She was busy. So was I.'

Davies looked up from his notebook.

'Mark, don't play silly buggers with me. You're probably not in trouble at the moment, but if you don't tell me the truth I could make sure you are.'

'Are you threatening me, Rob?'

''No, I'm trying to help you. What are friends for? What was Jenny Cooper all about?'

Mark took a deep breath and decided to go for it.

'OK. She was a bit upset with me. That's why we didn't talk too much in Colombia.'

'Now we're getting somewhere,' Davies said with obvious satisfaction. 'Tell me why she was upset with you.'

'She'd come on to me pretty strongly at the team hotel in England before they flew out. She'd had a bit too much to drink and I didn't respond. Hell hath no fury . . .'

'Attractive woman. Not many men would refuse if they were offered it on a plate.'

'Well, I did. I don't know why. Maybe it was altruistic and I didn't want to take advantage of her. Maybe I didn't fancy her and maybe it was because I was thinking of Patti. Either way I didn't screw her. Now, come on, Rob. I've come clean with you, so tell me what this is all about.'

'It's about murder. She's dead, Mark. Killed in her own home.'

Mark put down his cup and examined his trembling hands as if to find them blood-stained.

'I don't believe it.'

'You'd better. Once we release the body after the post-mortem and the inquest she's going to be buried. Generally speaking the police aren't party to burying people alive.'

There was a slightly lighter tone in his voice now. He'd got what he thought to be the truth and he could revert to type.

'Who'd want to kill Jenny?' Mark asked.

'I was hoping you'd be able to tell me that.'

'Why on earth should I know? I've already told you she was only a friend. Now I come to think of it, not much more than an acquaintance.'

'Mark, honestly I don't think for one minute that you're involved. But I have to produce some paperwork to eliminate you from our inquiries.'

Mark looked puzzled.

'Why should I be in your inquiries in the first place? As far as I'm aware nobody knew about our little confrontation. I've said nothing and I doubt if Jenny wanted to blab about a drunken seduction scene where there were no takers.'

'Well, we've checked her telephone records, you see. You were the last person she tried to call before she died.'

Mark shook his head in bewilderment.

'I don't understand.'

'Nor do we. Did she speak to you last night?'

'No. Nobody did. I was with Patti. I left the answerphone on, but there were no messages.'

'Mark, you're lucky this is me here. I took it upon myself to come and talk to you. If my bosses think I'm going soft on you then they may put somebody more brutal on the case. There'll be none of this cosy chat over a cuppa. Now don't be defensive. Just think. You've been on my side of the fence in a way, so imagine you're conducting an investigation.'

Mark got to his feet and stood by the window as if looking for inspiration.

'Poor Jenny. She never seemed to be a happy lady. How did she die?'

'I was hoping you'd ask.'

'Why?'

'To encourage me to believe that you don't know.'

'Come on, Rob. You can't seriously think I had anything to do with it.'

'I don't think you did, but I don't make all the decisions.'

'So you have to eliminate me from your inquiries, as you put a moment ago.'

'Exactly.'

'Well, speak to Patti. She'll confirm . . .' Mark hesitated over the next couple of words, they sounded so absurd, '. . . my alibi.'

'I'm sure she will.'

Mark looked carefully at Davies.

'Are you being sarcastic?'

'No, just relieved. Now think, Mark, think. Who'd want to kill Jenny Cooper and why?'

Mark continued to stare out of the window. It was beginning to rain, a steady drizzle that looked set for the day. He hated the period between autumn and winter, the knowledge that there'd be no real warmth for about six months. He felt tired, regretted ever getting up and wished Rob Davies would just go away and leave him alone with his thoughts. He would have liked to have gone for a run to help him clear his head. Despite the crippling knee injury that had finished off what the false accusations against him had begun, he could still jog around the park. It was one of the pleasures of his life to go around the artificial lake once at least, twice if he felt really fit, taking on the dogs and their owners who seemed to regard him as an intruder into their domain. But that would have to wait. Inspector Rob Davies was clearly going nowhere until he had the answers to his questions. The only problem was that Mark didn't think he had the answers. He took a deep breath and made a valiant attempt.

'She was drinking, Rob. If she was drinking she was talking. Maybe she was talking too much about something she knew.'

'Or somebody?' Davies prompted.

'She was screwing as well, if her efforts to get me into bed are anything to go by. Perhaps she slept with the wrong person . . .'

'And talked about it? Or was going to talk about it? Hardly an excuse for murder in this day and age. Still you reckon that she was probably indiscreet. And the phone call to you?'

'I suppose it had to be about someone I knew, otherwise why bother? The way I'd left her, the way she reacted in Colombia, I'd be the last person she'd phone unless I was the only person she could phone.'

'You *were* the last person she phoned,' Davies said grimly. 'I think you might be selling yourself short. You have to look at yourself the way others see you. Maybe she came to terms with the fact that you acted honourably towards her. You didn't take advantage so she figures she can trust you. She tries to get hold

187

of you, fails and then poof she's dead.'

'You make it sound very simple, Rob.'

Davies shook his head.

'Death is always very simple. It's what leads up to it that's complicated. If you're right and I'm wrong then we've reduced the list of suspects to people who knew you both. You'd better be careful, Mark. I know she didn't reach you, but if the person who killed her doesn't know that, if he was able to tell who'd she'd last spoken to, then it could be that you're in danger too.'

'I'd rather be in danger than under suspicion,' Mark replied with a weak smile.

'Wish granted. Watch your back. Oh and Mark, don't try any one-man heroics. You've been lucky in the past, so don't push it.'

When Davies had gone the flat seemed empty. He'd wanted him to leave, but now he wanted someone to replace him. He realised that he'd had no calls that morning. He lifted the receiver and dialled 1471.

'You were called at 22.15. The caller withheld their number.'

He thought about it. The police had logged a call from Jenny to him. But why should she have withheld her number if she was going to talk to him? And could it be that there had been two calls? He had to ask Davies about that. An icy shiver ran down his spine as he reconstructed the scene. Jenny calling him. A ring at the door, she opens it to meet her killer. He's curious as to who she's talking to. He checks the number, maybe it's showing on the phone, maybe he presses redial. Then he blocks the number by dialling 141 and calls again. Is he calling from Jenny's place, standing by her body, or has he left and called from his home?

He suddenly realised that Davies had told him neither the time of death nor how she died. But he had warned him he might be in danger and now Mark could see why. Somehow he now felt certain that he knew whoever it was who had killed Jenny Cooper. But, even if his instinct was wrong, of one thing he felt terribly sure. That they knew him.

CHAPTER 31

It was a relief to get back to the world of English football and the familiar territory of Hertsmere's little stadium. It was also a relief just to be able to watch the football without the added responsibility of commentating on it. Pleasure was added to the relief as Hertsmere had just taken three points from bottom of the table Redstone Athletic. The pleasure was somewhat muted as the manner of victory had been hardly convincing. A single scrambled goal five minutes from the end claimed by both Aled Williams and Darren Braithwaite, who'd collided with each other whilst at the same time deflecting the ball into the net. Ray Fowler, the manager, had looked displeased despite the result, and Mark could just imagine the rollicking that he was bestowing on the players in their changing room.

David Sinclair had gone through the usual ritual with his opposite number, the Redstone chairman, and now found time to stand quietly in the corner with Mark.

'Don't say a word, Mark.'

'I wasn't going to,' he replied. Unusually, Sinclair was one businessman in control of a club who could actually appreciate the finer points of the game. If he had any criticism to make of his team, then Mark was quite happy to listen to what he had to say.

'There's nothing up front, nothing at all. And Dimitri limping off after half an hour didn't exactly help.'

'I hear Murganev's been playing really well,' Mark said referring to the Russian player who had experienced such a traumatic time when he first came to the club.

'That's more than can be said for the rest of the team. I really thought this was going to be our year for the title. And Barry Reed getting into the England team was the icing on the cake. It makes life easier to get class players to the club if you can show that being with little old unfashionable us won't stand in

189

the way of international recognition.'

'Whose decision was it not to play him tonight?' Mark asked.

'Just about everybody's. Ray didn't think it was fair to put more pressure on the kid. I didn't think his mind was going to be on the task in hand, and the media have convicted him already. Believe me I got no pleasure from leaving him out. He's probably the best prospect I've seen in all my years here, present company excepted, of course,' Sinclair said, with a weak smile.

'What did Barry feel about it all?' Mark said, his voice deadly serious.

'You know, Mark, I'm not at all sure that anybody bothered to ask him. What time's the disciplinary hearing tomorrow?'

'I have to say, David, that I'm a bit disappointed you don't know that. Isn't the club sending anybody along to give him a character reference?'

'Hold on a second, Mark. Don't put the guilt trip on my head. We offered him the services of our lawyers, the PFA said they'd represent him as well and all he's done is say that you're dealing with everything and, as he put it in his quaint Geordie manner, you're the "top man" and you've got him the "best fucking brief" in England.'

'Blind faith, I'm afraid,' Mark said, concerned that David Sinclair had put into words the sort of responsibility that Barry Reed had placed upon his shoulders. He'd been good to his word and had introduced him to his solicitor, Stanley Golding. Stanley had not been optimistic and the leading counsel he'd instructed at Mark's expense to represent Barry at the hearing was even less enthusiastic about the outcome.

The three of them, Mark, Barry and Golding, had sat in his chambers the previous day and listened to his concise analysis of the problem and his prognosis as to the outcome. George Ramsden QC was a man who had got himself a reputation of doing the impossible in cases that involved any aspect of sport. He'd got the FA to return six points deducted from Thamesmead for an alleged illegal approach, he'd arranged for a suspension to be lifted on a player to enable him to appear in a Wembley Cup Final, and he'd even taken FIFA through the European courts over a bizarre decision in relation to an international match between England and Albania where they'd ordered a replay after armed rebels had brought a match to an end with England

6-0 in the lead. As Mark had told Barry, if there was any man who could get a result for him then it was George Ramsden. However, the longer the conference continued the less likely it seemed that there was any man who could get Barry Reed off the hook.

'It's exceedingly hard for us to fly in the face of the evidence. My advice is to plead guilty, try and come up with some convincing mitigation and in any event undertake to undergo some treatment both of a psychiatric and clinical nature. That might just persuade them to go lightly.'

'What do you mean by lightly?' Mark asked as Barry looked too confused to phrase any coherent question.

'Well, the unfortunate thing is that all this occurred at international rather than club level. They may therefore feel the need to make the punishment fit how they perceive the crime.'

Barry could stand it no longer.

'I can't believe all this. I'm not a fucking criminal. And I'm not mad neither, so you can stop all this talk of head doctors. I'm not going to take the rap for something I didn't do and there's an end of it.'

There had been little more to say after that and they'd left Ramsden scratching his head and wondering not just what he was going to say in Reed's defence, but how he was going to preserve his reputation.

'So have you?' Sinclair asked, jerking Mark back to the boardroom.

'Have I what?' Mark asked.

'Got him the best effing brief in England?'

'I think so. The only problem is that he can't walk on water or turn it into wine.'

'Doesn't sound like the best brief to me, but I suppose you know what you're doing. We'll have Helen go down and keep an eye on things. If you need anybody from the club to speak on Barry's behalf, then she's as good as anybody.'

'Thanks, David. I have to tell you you're being a sight more supportive than the England camp. Kenny Cunningham has refused point blank to come out on the player's side.'

'Can you blame him? He's got to send a message to the public, to the youngsters in particular, that there'll be no messing with drugs. Look, Mark, I'm not unsympathetic to Barry. We've had

191

him here since he was a kid, but if he gets a hefty ban we're going to be the biggest losers. We lose out on him as a player and an investment. And as you've seen tonight if we want to be in there challenging at the end of the season then we need every quality player we can get. Which leads me on to my next point. I appreciate you don't have the kindest memories of Colombia, but I assume you must have developed some contacts there either through your work or in trying to sort out Patti. Ray and I rather liked that striker who scored the goal, Ferrera. The last thing we want is to start dealing through agents. I hear the South Americans are even worse than our home-grown variety. Do you think you could put out a few feelers and, if you get anything positive, go out and try and put a deal together for us? We don't expect you to do it for nothing, of course. We'd put it on a proper business footing.'

Mark made to say no, then stopped himself. He had very little to do at Jet until the ink was dry on the detailed contract for the ESL rights and he certainly wanted to do something to fill his time. Although the last thing in the world he wanted to do was to return to Colombia, he felt that was where all the answers lay, to Patti's problem, to Barry's nightmare. And rightly or wrongly it seemed to him that he was the only one who could seek out those answers. The only thing that troubled him as he told David Sinclair he would do what he asked, was that he had a nagging feeling that those answers could not be bought cheaply.

CHAPTER 32

It was not often that the Halid family sat down for a meal together. Tonight was the exception. The dining room was anything but homely. A long polished oak table, dark oil paintings on the walls, heavy draped curtains, concealed lighting casting a dim glow over the whole proceedings making them look like a reconstruction of a baronial hall in a National Trust property.

Mo sat at one end of the table, Susie to the left of him, the baby, Jason, to his right in a high-chair. He'd refused to settle down in his cot, but now that he was in company seemed far more cheerful as he stuffed piece after piece of a soggy bread roll into his gummy mouth. At the far end of the table was Nabil, seeming to want to put as much distance between himself and his father as possible, whilst Dominique positioned herself on the same side as Susie, but with an empty seat in between. She didn't know how long she could conceal her condition from her father, although it was now clear that her stepmother had respected her secret at least until now. In the very near future she would have to make a decision as to whether or not she actually had the baby. She wanted that to be a joint decision, the only problem being that she was none too sure if the father was in any position to be involved in that process. Meanwhile she just toyed with the food on her plate. She'd heard all about morning sickness, but she seemed to feel nauseous all day long. She even felt sick in bed, but whether that was her pregnancy or the nerves caused by the charges levelled against her that still had to be resolved, she did not know.

Mo had tried to be pleasant throughout the meal, but he wasn't getting any encouragement. Nabil answered him in monosyllable, Susie was clearly irritated not only by the fact that Jason was interrupting her meal, but by the very presence of her sullen stepson.

It was Nabil who triggered things off, although it was Mo who pushed him.

'Nabil, must you answer everything I say with a grunt?'

His son pushed his plate aside violently, causing a glass of wine to spill before it rolled to the edge of the table and then fell to the floor. The stem of the delicate crystal snapped off cleanly and Mo got to his feet before his son bothered to move. He picked up the broken glass, oblivious to the sharp edge which drew blood from the palm of his hand.

'You have no respect for property,' he shouted, 'these glasses cost over a hundred pounds each.'

Nabil shrugged.

'What's a hundred pounds to you unless it's for something I want? I must be the only man of my age who still has to beg pocket money from his father. And if I have no respect for property that's only because you have no respect for me.' He rose to leave the room, but his father was already by his side pushing him back into his chair with a surprising show of strength.

'You leave when I say you leave. It's bad enough I have to offer you a job because I know nobody else would want to employ you. But you can't stop at letting me down at work, no, you have to insult me in my own home.'

Nabil squirmed in his seat. He had listened to this sort of abuse from his father since he was a child, and knew that he would gradually wind down when he had run out of steam.

'I thought you would learn something from being around a man like Mark Rossetti, but perhaps you are beyond education, perhaps all the money I've spent on you, all the time I've invested has been a waste,' Mohammed continued. The baby started to cry, aroused by the sound of his father's voice and Susie took him out of his chair and on to her lap to comfort him. Nabil's face grew even sulkier as he saw the look of affection his own father gave to his half-brother.

'The one thing you didn't invest in me was love,' Nabil said, the last word coming out slowly as if he had only just thought of the concept. 'And as for Rossetti, what sort of man is it who would agree to spy for you? Maybe Carr was a better judge of character than you gave him credit for. Maybe Rossetti's gone over to the right side, the winning team. Maybe he won't be coming back.'

Dominique had sat quietly, almost indifferently, as if she was a guest at a stranger's table, but now she could stand it no longer.

'You wonder why I go away, why I prefer to doss down on the floor in a squat? Listen to yourselves. Nabil may not be the brightest person on earth, but when did you ever give him any encouragement? We're your children too you know, not just little Jason and his golden fleece.'

Nabil looked at his sister in surprise. It had been a long time since they had stood up to their father together. His first thought was to wonder if she had some hidden agenda, and his next was one of relief that she had taken him out of the spotlight. The baby's cries were reaching hysteria pitch and Susie was rocking him back and forth with such intensity that he vomited over her dress.

'Look what you've done now. I don't believe the pair of you. I've never come across such ungrateful children in my life. Your father's given you a roof over your heads, he feeds you, he clothes you and all he gets in return is abuse. And look what you've done to Jason. He's done nothing to deserve it.'

Later, Dominique had no idea why she said what she did, but by then the damage was done.

'You really are a sanctimonious cow, Susie. You weren't exactly grateful to your first husband and I bet he put more than a roof over your head. With your whining he probably had to put a bucket over your head before he could bear to fuck you . . .'

If she had anything more to say it was cut short as Mo's hand whipped across her face knocking her sideways with the force of the blow.

'That's right, Daddy. If you've no reply then hit me. That's how it's always been. I've never been allowed to have thoughts of my own.'

She remained on the floor, but the others in the room were on their feet, moving around like actors looking for their positions on the stage. Nabil pushed himself between his sister and his father, Susie rose with her baby son in her arms, her pretty face twisted into an expression of pure hatred aimed at her stepdaughter.

'So, little Dominique, since you've touched on the subject, let's continue. Let's talk about fucking. Let's talk about young girls who fuck and don't have the sense to take the proper

195

precautions, because they're like animals on heat.'

'No,' Dominique protested in horror, seeing exactly where the woman was heading. 'I'm sorry, I didn't mean it . . .'

'Sorry? Yes I do believe you are,' Susie said. The baby had stopped crying and was virtually asleep in her arms. For a moment Dominique thought that the crisis was over, that her apology had been enough, but she had miscalculated the effect of her words on the woman her father had married.

'But too little, too late,' Susie continued. 'When I married your father I didn't realise the baggage he brought with him. I'm pleased we're all together for a change, nice and cosy, because it gives me the chance to tell you a few home truths. You, Nabil, have a chip on your shoulder the size of Everest. You're not stupid, so get yourself a life. Where are all your friends of your own age? You mope about the house as if not only your father, but the world owes you a living.'

Nabil said nothing, but the expression on his face revealed everything. Until now he had tolerated his stepmother as one might tolerate a painting on the wall that one really did not like. Now he hated her. Susie had not finished. She kissed the baby who was burrowing into her shoulder, oblivious to the tension surrounding him and his parents. There was a split-second when Dominique thought she would say nothing more, but the woman was beyond rationality. She had endured the Halid family in silence as long as she could bear. Now was the time to speak and if the speech hurt, then so much the better.

'And dear little Dominique . . .'

'I'm going to my room,' the girl said.

'That's up to you. You know exactly what I'm going to say, so it doesn't matter a jot if you don't hear it this time around.'

Dominique slumped into a chair once again and put her hands over her ears, her eyes wide, looking for all the world like a mad woman from a Munch painting.

Mohammed looked from his wife to his daughter, his own anger overridden by the unexpected tirade from his wife. He couldn't even remember what had triggered off a scene of such proportions.

'What's going on here? Is there something I don't know?' He turned to Dominique, believing her distress flowed from the blow he had dealt her. 'I'm sorry, Dom, I didn't mean to hurt you. I should not have raised my hand to you.'

'Raise your hand?' his wife echoed. 'Mo, there are times when you're positively old-fashioned. That was what endeared you to me in the first place. Nathan was so very twenty-first century. Well, put this to the test of your old-fashioned values. If your daughter doesn't have an abortion, then you're going to be a grandfather.'

It took Mohammed a moment to realise exactly what his wife meant. His eyes went to his daughter's stomach, took in the slight swelling that he had been too busy to notice, then went to her face where the blazing colour, the downcast eyes confirmed the truth of what he had just been told.

'Who's the father?' was all he said, the question asked in the voice of a torturer, a voice that Dominique did not recognise. She thought she had known her father well, that she had seen him in every mood, but this was something new. She shook her head dumbly, and pulled back into the chair, anticipating another blow, but it didn't come. Mohammed was beyond rage. He was into a mode that could only be described as revenge.

'Do you not know? Are you that much of a slut?' he asked, then answered his own question. 'No, I don't think so. I think you know, but you're not saying.' He put his hand on her shoulder, not in a gesture of support, but as if to force the truth from her mouth as his grip tightened.

'Go to your room,' he said, finally, his voice without expression. It was a Victorian direction to a girl who was old enough to leave the house forever, yet she rose calmly and obeyed the instruction. She did not look back as she took the stairs two at a time, remembering how naively she had rushed the tell her stepmother the news of her pregnancy, how much better she had felt once the secret was out, how supportive the woman had appeared. She wanted to turn back the clock, to wipe the tape clean of the words she had said to wound Susie, but there was no winding back the clock. Time only went forward, just like an unwanted pregnancy. But then she had still not decided in her mind if it were unwanted or not. She did not feel in the mood to decide anything. The only thing she knew for certain was that she could now never tell Mohammed who the father of the child was, because from the tone of his voice she truly believed there was every chance he would kill him.

CHAPTER 33

The Press were there in droves outside Lancaster Gate, the headquarters of the Football Association, as Barry Reed arrived with Mark and his lawyers.

'When you get out of the car, you walk in the door, holding your head up high. Don't look cocky, but don't look sullen either. If you make a run for it, then it looks as if you've got something to be ashamed of,' Mark directed Barry.

The player nodded, but Mark felt as if the message was going into one ear and out the other and, indeed, as the car door opened and the horde of cameramen pressed ever nearer to get a better picture, Barry threw his arms out wide to push them aside and raced into the building. Mark put his hand on Stanley Golding's arm.

'Let George go in and get himself set up. I think you should say something to these vultures, so they can't write anything they want.'

The solicitor shrugged. He had enough high-profile clients to feel comfortable about dealing with the media. He paused, and turned to face the crowd, his back to the door, his hand raised for silence as the questions came at him in a babble of sound.

'I have a brief statement to make and then I hope that you can disperse and let us get on with the job in hand. Barry Reed will be pleading not guilty to the serious charges against him. He did not take any stimulants before the match against Columbia, nor has he ever taken drugs in his life. He was proud to wear an England shirt for the first time and hopes he will have the opportunity to wear one many times in the future.'

As the solicitor made to go through the front entrance he heard one cynical journalist, with a hand-rolled cigarette in the corner of his mouth, say loudly, 'The only way Reed'll wear an England shirt again is if he pulls it on before he goes to bed.'

WHITE LINES

The members of the Disciplinary Committee were already seated at a long table when Mark and Stanley arrived. George Ramsden had positioned himself and Barry at the smaller table opposite them. The barrister looked uncomfortable in his dark suit, without his wig, as if he needed the atmosphere of a real courtroom to perform at his best. Mark had only seen him seated behind his desk in his chambers, and had not realised what a huge man he was. He must have been well over six feet tall, with a bull neck supporting a massive head, which was topped with a shock of white hair, through which he ran his fingers every few minutes either to smooth it down or ruffle it up. He wore a pair of spectacles that could have been borrowed from John Lennon and which fitted uncomfortably and incongruously on the tip of his nose. Barry Reed was not diminutive by any means, he had the build of a professional athlete, but he looked like the child he really was as he stood beside his counsel. He'd been told to look smart and, following instructions, he'd worn his best suit, but with its narrow lapel and stylishly high-cut two-buttoned front he looked a little as if he was dressed for a fancy-dress party.

The chairman of the hearing was Norman Hawksmoor, a director of Heddingford, who was himself a well-respected local solicitor in the north-west. The other two members of the tribunal also had professional backgrounds, Peter Lowrey, from Whitehaven was a retired accountant, whilst Gerald Cowans was a City appointment to the board of the recently floated Breedford United. The FA had taken no chances over this hearing of any accusation that Barry Reed might not have been given a fair hearing. There had been absolutely no hesitation in agreeing to Barry having his own independent legal representation even though in most instances that right was denied, leaving the player to rely on the PFA to argue his case, or if he was lucky, a director of his own club, provided he was a lawyer.

Hawksmoor quickly explained the procedure. The Association would state its case, call its witnesses and give the player's representative his opportunity to ask any questions. They would then, in turn, have the right to call their witnesses, sum up and then be subject to the decision of the tribunal which might be given there and then or after due deliberation.

'How can there be any witnesses?' Barry asked. 'Nobody can

say anything about what I didn't do.'

Golding put his fingers to his lips to quieten the player, then whispered, 'Just sit tight, Barry and wait. Have a bit of faith in Ramsden, he knows what he's doing.'

'Is that why he suggested I plead fucking guilty?' Barry muttered, but said nothing more and confined himself to doodling a series of gallows on the notepad in front of him.

The first witness called was the England team doctor, Roger Graves, who read through the analysis of the post-match tests, described the amphetamines, traces of which had been found in Barry's urine, and claimed he had no reason to distrust the report of the FIFA official or the South American doctor. Ramsden rose to his feet and loomed over Graves.

'Did you have any cause to treat Reed on the trip?'

'Yes, he had a slight ankle injury.'

'What did you prescribe?'

'I told him to see the physiotherapist and gave him some anti-inflammatory tablets.'

'What might those have been?'

'Voltarol.'

'I see,' Ramsden said, in a tone that suggested Graves had just provided him with the perfect defence to the accusations.

'Now, these Voltarol. Do they have any side effects?'

'Yes.'

'Yes? Why not share them with us, Dr Graves.'

Hawksmoor, who had neither said nor asked anything since the start of the hearing, interrupted.

'Mr Ramsden, can I point out that we like to keep these hearings as informal as possible? You're not in the High Court cross-examining some hostile witness. Dr Graves is here to help us get at the truth.'

'I'm so sorry, milord,' Ramsden replied and, not knowing whether he was being sarcastic or forgetful of his surroundings, Hawksmoor allowed the comment to pass.

'Dr Graves, tell us about the side effects of Voltarol.' Ramsden continued, his voice booming around the room, the volume unadjusted from his more usual court room habitat.

'They can cause severe stomach cramps or, if you're an asthmatic, can trigger off an asthma attack.'

'Is Barry Reed an asthmatic?'

'I really don't know.' The words were out before Graves could realise their significance.

'You don't know? And you were happy to give a player a drug, not knowing its potential effects?'

'I assumed that if he were an asthmatic that it would be on his medical records and we'd be carrying spare Ventolin with us, or the like.'

'You assumed?' Ramsden obviously liked to toss back the words to the witness. 'Assumptions can be dangerous, Doctor. Now you've told us about the urine tests. Perhaps, you'd like to tell us about the blood tests.'

'There weren't any.'

'Really? Was it an assumption too that they would also show that Reed had taken stimulants?'

He sat down, without waiting for an answer.

'What was all that about?' Mark asked Golding.

'He's just trying to shake the substance of the expert evidence.'

'And did he?'

Golding pursed his lips and shrugged, leaving Mark with the feeling that Barry's team were only going through the motions. If that were indeed the case then this was a very expensive charade and he was paying for it.

There was a pause before the next witness appeared. Hawksmoor looked down at his notes and then called out a name that astonished Mark.

'Kenny Cunningham.'

'What the hell?' Mark said before Barry cut him short.

'No wonder the bastard wouldn't give evidence for us, he knew that he was going to be on the other side. Let's pack it all in and I'll cop a plea. If the bloody England manager reckons I'm guilty, what chance have I got?'

Mark was about to say that he'd had little or no chance from the start, but felt that was not exactly helpful.

Cunningham's evidence was brief but damning. He explained that he'd found Barry depressed and subdued for most of the trip and only on a high after the game. Yes, he'd been surprised by how well he'd played. Yes, it was one of the most impressive debuts he'd ever seen. No, he'd not been surprised at the positive drug test. Disappointed yes, but with hindsight it explained a lot of things that had concerned him about the player during the time he'd been with the squad.

Mark stared steadily at the England manager during the whole period of his evidence, but the man carefully avoided any form of eye contact, keeping his gaze firmly fixed on the members of the tribunal. As Ramsden rose to his feet, Cunningham was forced to turn in his direction and Mark tried hard to read the expression on his face. Was it malice, self-satisfaction, deceit or fear? Or was he simply telling the truth as he'd seen it whilst at the same time protecting his own position?

'Mr Cunningham, are you an expert on depression?'

'No, but I'm an expert on footballers.'

'Are you, are you indeed? Well, doubtless that qualifies you to select the England international side, but gives me little confidence as to your medical or psychiatric conclusions.'

Hawksmoor sighed.

'Mr Ramsden. Whilst I'm reluctant to use legal jargon, could you refrain from making speeches and limit yourself to asking relevant questions?'

'Certainly sir. Now Mr Cunningham, you say that Barry Reed was "high" after the match. If you were as young as Barry, getting your first England cap and you'd turned in the sort of performance he'd done, then wouldn't you also be on a high?'

'Yes, I would, but not with the assistance of drugs.'

'Doubtless. Tell us a little bit more about this so-called depression of my client.'

'He didn't mix well. He kept to his room a lot. I'd put him in with Geoff Hamilton. I thought he'd like the company of another Geordie and, of course, Geoff's been around a long time. Geoff told me all he did was watch TV and sit on the phone.'

'And that's unusual for a footballer, that's evidence that he's a habitual drug user?'

'No, it's not unusual for a footballer. It's just unusual for a kid on his first trip. I'd have expected him to mix as much as possible, not to want to miss any part of the experience. And I don't know if he's a habitual user or not. All I have to go on is that he tested positive after this game. For all I know it might have been the first time he took drugs, or the last. What I do know is that he brought his national team into disrepute, and he brought me, as its manager, into disrepute as well. He let us all down.'

'It's unfortunate that most of what you've said is up to the tribunal to decide. Obviously if you were judge and jury, as you seem to have ambitions to be, my client would even now be walking the corridor to Death Row. Thank you, Mr Cunningham, I have no further questions.'

The witnesses for the defence were very much a make-weight bunch. Helen Davies, representing Hertsmere, told how Barry had been the perfect employee, the great Billy Whelan spoke of his talent and potential, and a doctor Ramsden had used before described the potential inaccuracies of urine tests unsupported by further analysis. It wasn't a lot, and Mark could see that neither the members of the tribunal nor Barry himself were impressed.

Ramsden's summing up was its useful *tour-de-force*, using every scrap of artillery he'd been offered, appealing to the emotions where he had no hard facts.

'Gentlemen, you are asked to make a finding based upon what might at first glance appear to be a cast-iron case against my client. But what do we really have? Only the results of a test taken in some far-off land, written evidence supported by an English doctor who prescribes drugs with side effects not even knowing the entire medical background of his patient. You have an England manager who believes it to be a criminal offence for a young player not to mingle at the bar drinking with his team-mates, who thinks it reprehensible for a youth to stay in his room, talking to his family back home, preparing himself for a match with a series of early nights. Gentlemen, if you find Barry Reed guilty of these offences of which he is accused, based upon such dubious evidence, then you will have cut off a potentially glorious career in its crime. I have seated beside me a man, Mark Rossetti, who was the victim of such injustice, whose own footballing career was cut down in its youth. I urge you not to make the same mistake again.'

Hawksmoor leaned forward and, just for an instant, Mark thought he was about to burst into applause. Instead he merely said, 'Thank you Mr Ramsden. We'll now adjourn for a while to consider all that we have heard.'

Mark looked at his watch. It was nearly five in the afternoon. They'd been there for some three hours and it had seemed like ten minutes.

'What do you think?' he asked Ramsden.

The barrister poured himself a glass of water as if any question he were asked, whether it be in chambers or here, merited careful consideration.

'I think your young friend should have pleaded guilty, but then I've already told you that.'

He saw Barry's eyes begin to fill with tears and immediately regretted his response.

'We've done the best we could to make bricks without straw. But I have to say that having seen the way the case was presented against us we have an outside chance. Shall we go and get ourselves a coffee? The longer they take over their decision the more chance we have.'

They moved into a side room where tea and coffee had been thoughtfully provided.

'How do you feel, Barry?' Mark asked.

'How did you feel?' Barry responded and, as Mark Rossetti trawled back over the years, he realised that he had put his past so far behind him that he really could not remember.

CHAPTER 34

It had not been difficult to persuade Nathan Carr to allow him to head off for South America.

'Sure, take a few days, take a week. Treat it as paid holiday. The more football contacts you make the better it is for Jet. Today Europe, tomorrow the world.'

Mark felt uncomfortable with the offer of payment, and even more disconcerted by the fact that he was growing to like the man Mo Halid had painted as the Antichrist. There was no doubting his charm and charisma, and as for his dishonesty, he only had Mo's word for it. Mo himself had been less gracious.

'Mark, my friend, I need you in there. Every day is vital if I am to prove that Jet only obtained the ESL rights by corruption,' he'd said when Mark had phoned to tell him that he was going back to Colombia as a favour to Hertsmere.

'I understand, but you have to understand that David Sinclair was the man responsible for getting me back into football and it's going to take a long time before I finally pay off that particular debt.'

'I admire your loyalty and I would not expect anything else from you, but please do your best to get back as soon as possible.'

As it happened the last thing Mark wanted to do was to stay away too long. The outcome of the disciplinary hearing against Barry Reed had been only a little short of disastrous. A five year world-wide ban, compulsory rehabilitation treatment and a crippling twenty-five thousand pound fine. George Ramsden had been philosophical.

'I did say that I felt a guilty plea was appropriate even if you were sincere in your belief that you had done nothing wrong.'

'And what difference would that have made?' Barry asked bitterly.

'Very little I suspect save for the length of the ban and the amount of the fine. But we'll never know. I have the feeling that these learned gentlemen have adopted the attitude of the courts in so far as they have piled on the agony because they feel that you have wasted their time. I'm very sorry,' and with that, Ramsden had taken himself back to his chambers for a conference with a merchant banker accused of a fifty million pound fraud.

Stanley Golding had been more sympathetic.

'Perhaps you can come up with some more evidence to launch an appeal . . .' His voice had trailed off into the void of false hope.

'Where am I going to get more evidence from?' Barry asked hopelessly.

And a small voice in Mark's head had answered Colombia. If he were going to try and sign Juanito Ferrera for Hertsmere then what would be the harm in trying to rake over the traces for Barry as well? Then there was the small outstanding problem of the charges against Patti, not to mention the problem of Patti herself. When he had told her what he had been asked to do for Sinclair she had not been impressed.

'You can't say no, Mark, can you? We had enough money to live on with the income from Leo's property, but you have to get a job with Ball Park and, as if that's not bad enough, you have to get a job with Jet as well and now Sinclair's trying to take advantage of your good nature.'

'Please don't put a guilt trip on my head. I know what you're trying to say. If I hadn't been commentating then I wouldn't have gone to Bogota and you wouldn't have come and life would have been different. If my mother were a man she'd be my father as my Italian grandmother used to say. And anyway you've still not told me what the hidden agenda was for your sudden arrival.'

That had silenced her for a while, but he still wanted to know why she had really come to visit him. He knew her well enough to be certain that most things in her life were planned and if her trip had just been to see the man she loved and to show him she was sorry then that would not have rattled any cages. He knew in his heart of hearts that the true reason he had agreed to go back as an emissary for Hertsmere was not totally out of loyalty to David. Somehow or other he felt that if he were going to be able not merely to salvage his relationship with Patti, but to rebuild it so that it survived permanently, then the reconstruction had to begin in Bogota.

He decided not to stay in the same hotel and instead chose the Bogota Royal in the World Trade Centre. As he checked in he was surprised to find there was already a message for him. He'd dutifully phoned Rob Davies to tell him he was leaving the country in case he wanted to talk to him about Jenny Cooper and indeed it was Rob who'd been looking for him. He didn't wait to unpack before he made the call, simply turned on the taps in the bath and worked on the assumption that he could be through with the conversation before it overflowed. It was early evening in Bogota, but only the afternoon in London and he had no difficulty getting through to Davies at the station.

'How are things in South America?' the policeman asked, his Welsh accent sounding much stronger over the phone.

'Hot and steamy,' Mark replied, longing to soak in the foam-topped water. 'Can we get to the point, Rob? I know from experience how much these calls cost after the hotel has multiplied the base charge by a million.'

'OK, I'll make it brief. Did you have any reason to believe Jenny Cooper was doing drugs?'

Mark thought about the question. He'd known her for a while and had always found her pleasant enough if a little moody. He'd assumed that the seduction scene was down to drink, but there was no real reason why she should not have been high on something else. She'd certainly been odd in Bogota but he'd put that down to jealousy.

'I'm not sure. Now I look back I suppose she could have been. I'm not the greatest expert on drug addicts. Alkies are more in my line.'

Quickly he told Rob the reasons for his conclusion and could imagine the policeman back home scribbling furiously.

'Aren't you going to ask me why I'm asking?' Rob said.

'I didn't want to give you the pleasure of refusing to tell me. I came to the conclusion that if you wanted to let me in on the secret then you would. Will you?'

'I thought you'd never ask. But since you have, the fact of the matter is that I've just had the autopsy results. It appears that the late Miss Cooper was a habitual user of cocaine. If she drank as well, we have a fairly explosive cocktail in more senses than one.'

'What do you mean?' Mark asked.

'Murders of press officers are rare even by those they've offended. Murders of drug addicts are far more common. Other users, suppliers, you name it.'

'Broadens the field a bit,' Mark said.

'Narrows it as far as we're concerned. There was no sign of forced entry at Jenny's place. Given the time of death we've estimated she was unlikely to let a total stranger in at that time of night. That means she must have known whoever it was that killed her rather than being the victim of a casual crime. A break-in or the like.'

'Are you trying to tell me I'm back in the frame?' Mark asked nervously, hoping that the bath had an overflow.

'You were never in the frame as far as I was concerned. I had to go through the motions for my superiors. Look, Mark, it's a long-shot, but where you are is the centre of the drug trade. Jenny Cooper was there with you last time you visited. I may be guilty of putting two and two together and coming up with five, but just do me a favour and keep your eyes and ears open while you're there. You never know.'

'I think your arithmetic is more suited to journalists than the police, but obviously I'll see what I can do. Can I go and get into my bath now before I flood the whole hotel?'

'Sure. Cleanliness is next to whatever as they taught me at Sunday School. Take care.'

He nearly fell asleep in the bath, and eventually he could not tell whether or not the thoughts going round his head were part of a dream. There had to be a pattern. Or did there? Were all the events of the last few weeks mere examples of the chaos theory or were they in some way inter-linked? Patti and Barry accused of drug-related offences. Jenny Cooper, who'd known them both, brutally murdered and now proved to be a user. Drugs were the common denominator. So what else did he know? Patti had tried to interview a drug baron. Luis had told him all about the narcotic industry in the country. As he'd said to Rob Davies, drink he could understand, drugs were beyond him.

The insistent ringing of the phone jolted him awake. He'd been in the bath for so long that the water had become tepid, but he'd been too tired to care. There was an extension on the wall of the bathroom and he leaned across to answer it.

'Welcome back to Bogota,' the voice said. 'I hope this trip will be happier than your last.'

'Luis, good of you to call. You got my message, then?'

'Indeed, I did. I'm sorry not to have called you before, but I've been out of the country for a few days.'

'Anywhere exotic?' Mark asked.

'Nowhere is exotic compared to Colombia. Just football business. Argentina, Brazil, Mexico.'

'Quite the little globe-trotter, aren't we? Have you had a chance to speak to Ferrera?'

'Indeed I have. We are fortunate. He has no agent, he is his own man. Believe me this is unusual in this country. Normally each player has about six bandits claiming they represent him.'

'Not that much different in England. When can we meet?'

'If you're not too tired we can arrange it tonight.'

'Suddenly I don't feel tired any more. The sooner I can sort this out, the sooner I can get home.'

'Of course. I have assumed that you would wish to speak with Salazar as well. That is for first thing in the morning.'

'What's first thing?'

'Ten. Mornings tend to start a little later here.'

'Fine. Where are we meeting Ferrera?'

'I've booked us a table at Los Ultimas Virreyes, I think you will like it. I'll pick you up in an hour. If you can strike a deal with Ferrera and his club, maybe you can be on a plane heading home by tomorrow night.'

Mark dried himself, shaved, and put on a blue short-sleeved shirt under a light-weight cotton jacket. He turned to look at himself in the mirror, trying to see himself as others might see him. He'd put on a little weight since he'd been working for Ball Park, but he still didn't feel he'd be out of place on the football field. The ache in his knee told him differently. It had stiffened up with all the long hours on the plane and the bath had only eased it a little. He grimaced with the realisation that all he could do nowadays was commentate on football and negotiate with players.

Back on the plane tomorrow, Mark thought to himself. Hardly enough time to work on the various tasks he had been set or had set himself. He looked at his watch. Just after seven. If he only had twenty-four hours then he would have to make every second count.

CHAPTER 35

From his terrace, Branco looked down on the Laguna de Guatavita, the sacred lake. He turned to the man by his side and poured him another glass of the expensively imported French wine.

'No more, please, I have a long drive back into town.'

'And you think the police will stop you for drunken driving? This is Colombia, my friend, not Washington.'

'When do you visit DC next?' the other man asked.

'When we have finally disposed of our local problems.'

'And when will that be?'

'Very shortly, I hope. I miss civilisation. For me a meal at Sam & Harry's, a visit to an art exhibition, a meeting at Capitol Hill, perhaps even a quick flight into New York to take in the theatre, a girl for a thousand dollars for the night rather than the fifty-cent whores who surround us here, they are all signs of civilisation. Have I signed everything?'

'You have.' The other man mopped his brow even though the evening had brought a relative coolness with the sunset. He knew he could not leave until Branco gave permission, but he dreaded the drive alone back to Bogota. It would take at least an hour and the first part of the journey would be along dark, twisting dirt roads – the regular habitat of bandits. They would not realise he was an emissary of Branco until it was too late, yet he was too timid to ask his host for an escort. If he thought he needed one then doubtless he would offer.

'You know,' Branco continued, snapping his fingers for a servant to bring him another bottle of wine and a cigar, 'the Muisca Indians believed this lake to be sacred. When it was their land they would have the zipa, their *cacique*, paint himself with gold dust. He'd climb on to his ceremonial raft painted with more gold, take enough precious objects to establish a modern museum and then toss them into the lake as a sacrifice and follow

211

them into the water to renew his divine powers. And one day a Spanish gringo chanced to see what was going on and was lucky enough to get away alive and when he got back to his so-called civilisation he began the legend of El Dorado. And so they came with their weapons and diseases. Have you heard of Sepulveda, my friend?'

His friend shook his head miserably. Once Branco got on to his favourite subject of Colombian history then he knew he would be there for a while.

'Sepulveda was a wealthy Spaniard who, in the sixteenth century, actually obtained a permit from his Catholic Majesty to drain the lake. So he comes here, a civilised man, and raises a huge local labour force and cuts into one side of the volcanic crater that forms the lake, in an attempt to drain off the water. Now the locals are terrified. We now know that the crater which became the lake was formed by a huge meteor falling to earth some two thousand years ago. But the Indians believe that a golden god came down to earth, made this hole, filled it with water and then lived forever more at the bottom of the lake. So, as you can imagine, they are none too happy about this god being disturbed by some gold-crazy foreigner.'

'And what happened?' the guest asked, pretending to show some interest, sensing that this was required of him and knowing what Branco did to those who failed to meet his requirements.

'Nothing happened that the Indians did not believe would happen. At the bottom of the lake, amidst the mud, Antonio de Sepulveda, found his own destiny. The result of all his efforts was two hundred and thirty two pesos and ten grammes of fine gold. Sepulveda returned to Spain a broken man and died bankrupt. When the Indians heard of this much later they thanked the god for answering their prayers and cursing the man who had caused them so much death and destruction.'

He swirled the wine in his crystal glass and looked straight ahead at the perfect circle of the lake as if seeking some ancient truth.

'There have been many attempts since then to find El Dorado. The English, the North Americans, even our own compatriots, but to no avail.' He turned his gaze full on the man beside him, who physically shrank away from those piercing eyes.

'But I have discovered my own El Dorado and there is no way

and nobody who will take it away from me. You understand?'

The man nodded dumbly. He understood.

'And our man, he understands?'

'I think so.'

'Thinking is not good enough. There are times when I feel he believes I work for him, rather than he is working for me.'

The other man shrugged in the dark. There was silence except for the cicadas amongst the greenery mingling with the low buzz of mosquitoes hovering above the water.

'And our friends across the ocean?'

'They say they have things under control.'

'Good. I have more faith in them than our local lad.'

Branco emptied his glass and rose to go inside without any ceremony. The other man followed him obediently, his brief-case under his arm.

'Well,' Branco said, 'I suppose you must be going. I am grateful to you for the visit and the information. Be careful on the roads. They are full of dangers. This country has too many criminals.'

And, as the man descended the marble steps leading to his car, he thought he could hear the sound of Branco's laughter following him all the way.

CHAPTER 36

Mark sat with Luis on the first floor of the magnificent building of the Fundacion Gilberto Alzate Avendano at Calle Ten which housed not only the Restaurante *Los Ultimos Virreyes* but also an art gallery which contained an impressive exhibition of modern works. They looked down on the beautiful patio below, the menus in their hands, awaiting the arrival of Juanito Ferrera. Luis was on to his second Scotch, whilst Mark nursed a Diet Coke without enthusiasm. There had been too much ice to start and now he had little doubt that he was doing exactly what he'd been warned not to do, namely drinking the local water.

'I think all you need is to agree terms with Juanito. I know for a fact that his club is in desperate need of money. The player is worth five million dollars, but if you pay in cash, all in one instalment, then I am confident you can get away with just a million.'

Mark laughed.

'Just a million. This is Hertsmere I'm here for, not Juventus or Liverpool. They may have won a European title, they may be hopeful of the Premiership this season, but it's still all done on a shoe-string budget. I hope Ferrera doesn't have too many high hopes of becoming a millionaire overnight.'

It was Luis's turn to smile.

'I think Ferrera is a millionaire already. His high hopes are of proving he can be a superstar outside his own country. I truly believe this is about ambition, a new challenge, rather than money.'

Ferrera had arrived unseen and, standing behind Luis, he had overheard the last part of his speech.

'I trust you do not expect me to play for nothing. But, apart from that, I am sure that all Luis is telling you is right.'

His English was heavily accented, with a slight American drawl over some of the words. Others were almost unintelligible, as if

214

he had forgotten the translation and was slurring in the hope that nobody would notice. He looked bigger off the pitch than on it. His muscular frame swelled out his open-necked shirt, whilst his broad thighs threatened to split the tight trousers he'd affected for formal evening wear. He seemed as genial now as his posture had been aggressive throughout the match. He pulled up a chair to join them, the piece of furniture looking toy-like in his hand.

'I'm pleased I'm not playing football any more. I don't think I'd stand a chance if I got in your way.'

'Señor Rossetti, you are too modest about your talents. Everybody I have spoken to about English soccer tells me what a fine player you were.'

'Flattery will get you everywhere. The only thing it won't do is get you more money. Shall we eat first or do you want to get the business out of the way?'

Ferrera fumbled in his pocket and produced a neatly folded sheet of paper.

'I come all ready. This is what I think is fair for me at a club like yours. I have spoken with my club. You pay them two million dollars, they sell me.'

'Luis here thinks they will take half of that,' Mark said.

The smile never left the player's face but there was just a blink of the eyelids that covered any irritation he might have felt for the broadcaster's interference in his negotiations.

'Well, we shall see. Now, what about my terms?'

Mark unfolded the paper apprehensively and quickly read it through. Sinclair had given him a budget with a stern warning it was not to be exceeded under any circumstances.

'I don't want you coming back and telling me what a great player Ferrera is as an excuse for blowing our wage structure to smithereens. And in case you think you've got any room to manoeuvre, let me tell you straight away that I've already built that in,' the Hertsmere chairman had said as his parting shot.

Ferrera turned his attention to the menu as Mark digested what was before him.

'A good choice of restaurant, Luis,' the player said, 'very European. It will prepare me for England.'

'Nothing can prepare you for English food, Juanito,' Luis replied. 'Steak and kidney pie, roly-poly pudding, porridge. You

215

will come back looking like a ship.'

'A barge,' Mark interrupted. 'I don't suppose either of you have a calculator?'

To his surprise, it was the footballer who produced one out of the men's Gucci bag he had placed by the side of his chair. It was tiny but sophisticated and Mark began to realise that the man with whom he was dealing was a very different sort of footballer to those he had become accustomed to at Hertsmere.

He turned on the machine and began to press buttons with a single-minded purpose. He could already see that what the Colombian was asking was not unreasonable but that was no reason to make it easy for him.

'I'm afraid we don't pay wages net in England,' Mark said eventually.

'You mean I must pay tax?' There was a note of surprise in Ferrera's voice.

'I'm afraid so. We all do.'

Ferrera shook his head in disbelief.

'How much is the tax?'

Mark told him and the player whistled.

'No wonder this is such a poor country and you have The Beatles and Mrs Thatcher.'

Mark couldn't tell just how serious Ferrera was, but he answered anyway.

'I'm afraid we don't have either any more. Anyway, the bottom line is that we could agree your wages and signing-on fee, but you'll have to pay the tax on them.'

'Maybe,' Ferrera persisted. 'I have always found that if you want something badly enough you can find a way to get it.'

'Well, Juanito – and you must call me Mark – I must tell you that the Inland Revenue in my country will want your tax rather badly and I assure you that they have a way to get it. You see Hertsmere will take it off your wages and pay it over to them.'

'This is robbery, I think. So maybe Hertsmere pay some of my money abroad. Maybe to a company?'

'Maybe they would have done that a few years ago, but not now. Now everything is very tight. If they did that they would risk being expelled from the league.'

'Perhaps I am worth the risk,' Ferrera said, with a smile. He took back the piece of paper and removed a gold pen from his bag. He sat for a few moments thinking, then crossed out a couple of numbers and handed the sheet back to Mark.

'There, I have made changes. On those monies, if I have to pay tax, then I am happy to make your English taxman happy. It's OK?'

Mark borrowed the calculator again. It was as if Ferrera had read Sinclair's mind. The figures over a four-year period tallied almost exactly with the maximum figure Sinclair had told Mark he could spend. Assuming the Hertsmere chairman had expected him to exceed his limits, then bringing the deal home dead on budget had to be some sort of result.

He extended his hand to the Colombian who gripped it tightly.

'Juanito, welcome to Hertsmere. We've got a deal subject to my sorting things out with your club. Now who do I speak to in order to do that?'

Ferrera smiled and produced a mobile phone.

'He is awaiting our call.' He dialled the number, waited for the first ring and then handed the phone across to Mark.

'Who am I speaking to? What's his name?' he asked, but the phone had already been answered.

'Hello, this is Mark Rossetti here. Do you speak English?'

'Certainly,' said the man at the other end.

'Good. I represent Hertsmere Football Club in England.'

'And I, as you gather, represent Chingaza. You are, I believe, interested in acquiring our player Ferrera.'

'We are. I hope you don't mind, but I have him here right now.'

'And if I do mind, I think it makes no difference. The player wishes to play in England. We cannot keep an unhappy player.'

'We don't have unlimited funds. I'm authorised to offer half a million pounds sterling.'

The Chingaza chairman laughed down the phone.

'Señor Rossetti, please do not insult my intelligence. If you were to return to football then your value might be that. We may be a poor country in economic terms, but we are rich in football talent. The price is two million US dollars and if you sell him for more than that then we divide the profit equally.'

'We couldn't afford that. I'm sorry, Señor . . .?' Mark realised that he had not been told to whom he was talking, unless it had been one of the words glossed over by Ferrera. But the man did not respond and Mark was left to deal with the embarrassing silence.

'I can increase the offer slightly without speaking to the chairman back in England, but only slightly.'

'Tell me what this slightly means,' Mark was asked.

'Well, we could go to another hundred thousand, which would take us to a million dollars.'

'Then I fear that slightly is not enough. I'm sorry you've had all the trouble. Perhaps it would have been wiser to deal with this in the normal way between clubs and speak to us first. I am afraid that in the circumstances if the transaction does not proceed then I shall have to make an official complaint to FIFA and indeed your own FA about what I think is called an illegal approach. Nor, indeed, are you a licensed FIFA agent, I believe.'

Mark did not like the course the conversation was taking and cursed Sinclair for landing him in this situation. He'd assumed that he'd spoken to the club, but he'd obviously assumed wrong.

'That's blackmail.'

'No, my friend, it's called negotiating. Now I am a reasonable man, so this is what we will agree. You will pay a million dollars now. When Juanito has played twenty games or scored ten goals, which he will, then you pay another half a million. That I think is fair play as you English say. Do we have a deal?'

Mark looked down the mouthpiece of the mobile for inspiration, wondering if this was all a bluff, decided it wasn't and also decided this was an agreement he could sell to Sinclair. The season wasn't that old and already they'd proved themselves short of firepower up front.

'Very well, it's a deal.'

He could hear the other man chuckle down the phone before he said, 'I will have all the papers drawn up in readiness.'

'It has to be subject to a work permit, but there shouldn't be too much of a problem there as he's an established international.'

'You must do what you must do. Juanito knows where to find me.'

'Is it all settled?' the player asked anxiously.

'It would seem so,' Mark replied. 'He's a pretty good negotiator, your chairman or president.'

Ferrera smiled and nodded and, as they ordered their meal, Mark realised he was still none the wiser as to whom he'd been dealing with and Ferrera seemed to have no intention of telling him.

CHAPTER 37

Salazar seemed preoccupied when Mark met with him the following morning. There was the usual Kafkaesque crowd outside his offices, everyone waiting hopefully for an audience with the great man, and Mark pushed his way past, ignoring what he thought were desperate requests to pass on messages to the lawyer.

He was ushered in to Salazar's office shortly after ten, but where before the lawyer seemed to have all the time in the world for Patti's case, now he appeared almost dismissive.

'I am happy to see you, but I have no news for you.'

'I'm sorry, I don't understand. Aren't there preliminary steps we should be taking before the actual trial, if indeed we can't avoid a hearing?'

'Señor Rossetti, forgive me. I thought I had won the case when I obtained bail for your friend and permission to leave the country. I don't think you quite understand what a triumph that was.'

The lawyer was already sifting through a pile of papers from a file that bore another client's name, as if Patti Delaney and her problems were behind him and he had to move forward to bigger and more pressing matters.

'You're right, Mr Salazar, I don't understand. In my country we start applauding when the client walks free. Bail is the beginning, not the end.'

'Señor Rossetti, Mark. Let me say it simply. I think bail is the end because nobody expects to see your young lady back in this country. If she fails to show for her hearing then the bail is forfeit, there will be no sentence, no international arrest warrant and pride will be satisfied. That is why I have done no work on the case. Even if I believe Señorita Delaney's story that the drugs were planted on her, what sort of evidence do you expect me to produce? A spirit who lived inside her bag and who can testify as to what was in there or not? Perhaps the spirit had a video camera to record whoever it was that placed the offending articles in there. Take my advice and go home, count the cost of the little adventure and put it down to experience. Now you must excuse me, I have an appeal to be heard today and if I fail my client will be executed by the end of the week. I'm sure you'll realise that this is more important than a matter that hurts you in your purse.'

Before he could argue, the door was opened, and Mark was ushered into the reception area and thence into the sunshine. The queue seemed to have doubled in length in the few minutes he'd had with Salazar and all eyes turned to him as a man who had been granted an audience, the eyes filled with hope.

'Go home,' he found himself shouting at them, 'go home. He can't help you. You're in a country where no one can help you if you don't help yourselves.'

They looked at him uncomprehending, wondering if he were a madman who had been turned loose on the streets. He realised it was useless. None of them spoke English and, even if they had, he was asking them to abandon their faith in a false Messiah. He looked at his watch. It was just after ten thirty. The only plane he could catch was not until seven in the evening. The whole day stretched before him. He'd spoken to Sinclair when he'd got back to the hotel, taking some pleasure in getting him out of bed in the middle of the night. He'd been grateful for everything except the disturbance of his sleep and had told Mark that Helen Davies would take over to conclude the paperwork with both the club and the player.

'Have a few days' break on the club. Isn't there a seaside where you can get a deckchair, knot a handkerchief around your head and pretend to be an Englishman on vacation?'

'You've never been to Colombia have you, David? I reckon the deckchair would last about sixty seconds on the sand before somebody nicked it and then they'd come back and mug you for the knotted handkerchief.'

'Sounds idyllic. Well, back to sleep now and we'll see you soon.'

Mark went into a sidewalk café and ordered a coffee. He realised that he was the only foreigner in the place, but when it became apparent that he was not there for the company he was left to his own thoughts. He turned over in his mind the tenuous connections he'd made between all the events that had surrounded those around him. He had to be missing something, or was he the link himself? If that was the case then, for the life of him, he couldn't think why. Now there was a new dimension to the mystery. Why had Salazar been so offhand?

He had arranged to meet Luis for lunch and he wondered if he could provide the answer. He wondered if anybody could provide the answer or if this was how it had to end, with Barry banned from the game for the best years of his life, Patti convicted of a crime she did not commit, Jenny's murderer roaming free, and Nathan Carr with the ESL rights? All the good guys and gals losing.

The waiter came over and refilled his coffee cup without him having to ask. This was a strange country. The man in the street was friendly and yet it was dangerous to walk the streets. There was something puzzling Mark. Over the past few years he had learned to train his mind to pursue those intangible things that he heard, yet found no place for in the world of logic. It was something that had been said at the tribunal, something about Barry Reed's behaviour at the hotel. He'd stayed in his room on the phone. Anything that was out of the ordinary had to be worth following. Who could he have been phoning? And, more important, was it of any relevance to anything? He doubted it, but an inquiry would fill the gap in his morning. He didn't fancy sight-seeing. Truth be told he'd already seen enough of Bogota to last him a couple of lifetimes. He finished his coffee, paid his bill and gave the waiter an over generous tip that immediately made him a valued customer.

It was a fair walk to the hotel, but he didn't fancy a cab, didn't think the exercise would do him any harm and began to stride out through the ever-increasing heat. He didn't know how people lived in it but he supposed it was the old maxim that in time you got used to anything. He knew he was being paranoid but he began to duck and dive in and out of shops, making sharp turns in the street, glancing back to see if he could pick out the same faces behind him in the crowd, a recognisable car in the road, but there was nothing and nobody. He tried to convince himself he was of no interest to anybody in this country. He had come here to do a job and he had completed the task. He'd dined with a friend, would lunch with him and would return to England none the wiser as to why or how disaster had befallen his lover and young friend. And as for Rob Davies asking him to find out what he could about Jenny Cooper, surely that was also going to be a case of whistling in the wind. Yet, she had been staying in the same hotel as he and Barry and the rest of the team. Perhaps he could kill two birds with one stone, or if not kill them, at least cause enough damage for him to have a good long hard look at them. Coming into the foyer brought back memories. The surprise of finding Patti in his room, the pleasure of rediscovery of her body, the worry when he could not find her, the speed of their initial departure and then the days and nights he had spent alone trying to secure her freedom. He struck lucky immediately when the receptionist recognised him.

'Señor Rossetti, you are back to stay with us, perhaps?'

'No just passing through,' he replied, thinking it wiser not to say that he had sought alternative accommodation.

'A pity. Can I help you with anything . . . while you pass through?'

Mark returned the man's knowing look. Doubtless he had a whole deal going with a bunch of hookers, but he didn't want to insult the man by an outright refusal.

'Thanks, but I'm afraid I've a plane to catch. Maybe next time when I have a whole night to spare. There is something you can do for me though. When I was here last you'll recall the England team and officials were staying as well.'

'How could I forget a famous victory? Although I think one of your players has a little help. So it is fortunate it is a friendly otherwise I think we would be asking for a replay.'

'I'm sure you would, and you'd be getting it. There's a place for everything, including drugs, but not on the football field.'

The receptionist, whose name Mark could see from his badge was Carlos, nodded wisely as if the very mention of drug abuse had shocked him into silence.

'Well, there's been a bit of a problem about some of the expenses that have been claimed by certain members of the party, including the certain player of whom we were speaking. I've been asked to get duplicates of their accounts, particularly their phone bills, and I was wondering if you keep them for any length of time.'

Carlos looked insulted.

'Of course we keep them. We have the finest computer system

of all the hotels in South America. Tell me the names you want and the dates and I will print them out again for you.'

'Barry Reed and Jenny Cooper are the names, and the dates would be the whole period of their stay.' He produced a fifty-dollar bill just in case Carlos was looking for the permission of any superior to provide the information Mark was seeking and the man pocketed it smoothly with well-practised discretion.

It took him about five minutes to retrieve the information, leaving Mark waiting and watching the seething hive of humanity passing through, just as he had said that he was. He still could not shake off the feeling that he was being watched, but it would have taken the CIA to pick out an observer amidst the crowd. Carlos returned with the printouts and Mark literally grabbed them and hurried out even though he still had an hour to spare before he met up with Luis. He tucked the papers into his pocket. They could wait until the plane. Somehow he'd feel safer if he were to read them in mid-flight, away from any Colombian eyes.

He left the hotel without looking back and once again was hit by the oven-like heat. It was unfortunate he did not stop to retrace his steps because, if he had done so, he would have seen another man approach Carlos and obtain from him, without payment of any money whatsoever, exactly the same information he had just provided for Mark Rossetti.

CHAPTER 38

He went straight from the airport to the Burrow. He'd been missing Patti more than he could say and he wanted, needed, to try and put his feelings into words. He wanted to dispel her view that he would rather do anything than focus on his emotional responsibilities. He knew it was a case of the pot calling the kettle black, but didn't think it would go down particularly well if he told her so.

Whatever instinct had guided him to Patti's side was totally vindicated. She was sitting on the couch, a filled ashtray by her side, a bottle of wine down to the last dregs on the table. He knew something was wrong the minute he hit the silence that filled the room. Patti was hooked on television and, if she wasn't watching it live, then she was watching a recording of one of the soaps with which she had, as it seemed to Mark, an irrational obsession.

He'd let himself in with the keys she'd given him so long ago with the warning that he should never call unexpectedly. He'd known why then. There were still other men in her life. Now, of one thing he was sure, that whatever moods took her she was faithful to him. Faithful that was, as far as other men were concerned. Whether her fidelity extended to total honesty and trust concerning her own lifestyle, he could still not be sure. What he had to decide was whether or not he should continue with his efforts to push her into agreeing to marry him, or whether those same efforts could result in pushing them further apart.

As it was, he had never seen her so pleased to see him. She practically launched herself off the couch and into his arms and, the minute her body touched his, she broke into huge, shuddering sobs.

'Oh, Mark, thank heavens you're back.'

'Hey, hey, what is it?' he said, holding her tight, feeling the tension begin to ease out of her as the tears fell.

'It's my mother . . .' Mark knew exactly what she was going to say even before she began to tell him. Patti's Jewish mother had been in and out of one clinic or another ever since he'd known her. Her Irish husband had died when Patti was young and, according to Patti, Mrs Valerie Delaney held herself solely responsible for his death. She had tried drink, tried drugs, and this time she had succeeded where she'd failed before, with a combination of them both.

'I thought she was getting better, I really did. She seemed to have been coping with life on her own.'

'You can't blame yourself, Patti, she only ever wanted to see you to make you feel guilty.'

'How do you know?'

'I know because I could see what you were like when you came back from visiting her.'

'I should have given her more time. I've been sitting here thinking about my life. I never give the people I love enough time. I never give them enough trust to want to share my life with them.'

She began to cry again and Mark took what was left of the bottle of wine over to the sink and poured it away. He filled the kettle, tossed a couple of tea-bags into the absurdly small tea-pot that was hardly enough for two cups. In a way that was symbolic of Patti's life. If you could only make tea for one then it meant that if anybody wanted to move in you'd think long and hard about it. A new, larger tea-pot would be a major investment.

He waited by the sink for the kettle to boil, then neatly divided the contents of the tea-pot between two cups, filling each one about half way.

'Here have a cuppa . . . or a proportion of one,' he said, wondering what he could say to comfort her, terrified to say the wrong thing when the right could mean so much, not just for now but for the rest of their lives.

'Mark, I need you. I'm so sorry. I've been a real cow. Even when I came out to Bogota I lied about the real reason. I was there for a story from the start.'

She took the tea in her shaking hands and sat herself down again on the two-seater settee.

'Come and sit with me, please. I want to tell you all about it.'

Mark obeyed and remained silent whilst she told him all about

226

her schoolfriend and her chance meeting and how that had set her off on such a crazy quest.

'It seems so silly now. All she told me was that there was a route out of Colombia, via Europe into England. She couldn't even give me names. Or at least no names here; but somehow or other she knew the name Branco and I got the impression that he was so powerful that he didn't even care if people knew what he did. I always intended to interview him and I couldn't believe my luck when he was sitting a row in front of me at the football match. Then it all went pear-shaped. I started firing questions at him there and then, and at first he wouldn't answer, got quite angry in fact. Then he suddenly became the perfect gentleman, apologised, said he was suspicious of all journalists, and didn't like being button-holed when he was out for a social evening. Then came the real dozy bit as far as I was concerned. He said that as I was English he would give me an interview. There were two conditions. One was that I didn't publish in Colombia and the other was that as he was leaving first thing in the morning for Brazil that I'd have to see him at some unholy hour. And like a thicko I believed him. The only plea I can give in mitigation is that I was jet-lagged.'

'Listen, Pat, it's all going to work out. I can understand why you're feeling like you are about your mother, and there's not a lot I can do about it right now other than just be here for you. As for Branco, you have to think. What was it that so rattled his cage that when you didn't turn up to meet him he felt the need to frame you, to discredit you?'

'You know, Mark, I've been asking myself that very question. I can only assume he never intended to give me the interview. That he only wanted to see me to discover how much I knew and perhaps what I was going to do about it, whether or not I posed a real security risk. It may have been that I didn't ask anything specific, but he was just not taking any chances.'

'Don't you have any notes that you prepared for the interview? It's not like you to go in unprepared.'

'That's the problem. I wasn't ready. It all happened so quickly that I didn't have time to think. I had to wing it. Unfortunately I didn't wing it very well. Christ knows what I said to him in the stand at the match. I was dog-tired and I was thinking on my feet, saying anything that came into my head to get him sufficiently curious to talk to me.'

'OK. Leave it be. It's the sort of thing that'll pop into your head when you're least expecting it. Let's talk about more important things. When did your mother die?'

'Last night. It was horrible. I was here on my own when I got the call and by then it was too late. I haven't even been to the hospital to make a formal identification. And the police say there'll have to be a post-mortem and an inquest and I can't do anything about the funeral until they're through with all that. Even then I'm not sure what to do. She was Jewish but to say she wasn't observant is an understatement. Can you bury Jewish suicides who marry Irish Catholics in Jewish cemeteries?'

She paused to light another cigarette.

'I'm sorry, Mark, I know you hate it and the Burrow must smell like the inside of an incinerator and as soon as all this is over I'm going to give up, I promise, but right now if I don't keep on having fag after fag I'm not sure if I can get through all this.'

'It's all right. I'll live with it, although I'm not sure my lungs will. We'll sort out your mother's funeral. You made all the arrangements for Leo, remember. This can't be much different. How's the tea?'

'Good. It was always one of your talents.'

'I had a lot of time to practice, and don't forget my dad had the café.'

'I know. And I know you've also suffered a lot of pain over losing your parents the way you did. It's just this . . . my mother . . . was the last link with the past. I suppose we're both orphans now.'

'I suppose we are. What are orphans supposed to do?' he asked, hoping for the right answer.

'Look after each other. Do you think you could stay here for a few days?'

'As long as you like. I'll just go home and throw a few things together.'

'Do you mind if I come with you? I'm not sure I really want to be here on my own. I keep thinking about what happened to Jenny Cooper.'

Mark bit his lower lip, not knowing whether this was the right time to tell Patti his theories.

'Yes, poor Jenny. I suppose you can consider yourself lucky that you only got arrested and not murdered.'

'Not funny, Mark. You think there's some connection as well, don't you?'

'Some connection with what?'

'Everything, everything that's happening to us, around us. It's as if we're a catalyst for tragedy, or at least I am. What do they call it in a book or a play? Deus ex machina? Or is it a McGuffin? I have to confess that, educated as I am, I tend to get confused between the two.'

'What do I know? I'm just a burned-out ex-professional footballer.'

She went into the bathroom to repair her face and as soon as she did that he knew she would survive. She cared about what the outside world might think of how she looked and that meant survival. They were both survivors, they had proved that in the past. He used the time to phone David Sinclair at the club to make sure there had been no hitches on the Ferrera transfer. Sinclair was in a meeting and he found himself speaking with Helen Davies.

'Sorry about my husband. He takes his job seriously. I told him not to bother you and he told me not to interfere,' she said.

It was typical of her to go straight into a conversation without any niceties and Mark appreciated her practical approach to life. That was what he needed at the moment. Practical people who could find their way through the maze of problems that was his life and, more particularly, Patti's.

'Don't worry,' Mark said, 'I didn't take offence. I get suspected of violent crime most days of the week.'

'Do you have to speak to David or will I do?' Helen asked.

'I'm sure you'll do. Is everything in order with the Ferrera transfer?'

'Absolutely. You did a great job. He arrives the day after tomorrow, work permit permitting. We've pulled a few strings and it should be through by then. You'll have to come down and see him. I hear he's pretty impressive.'

'Yes, he is. And thanks for the invitation.'

'Send us your expenses as well. I'll sort it out straight away. See you soon. Rob hopes so as well, socially that is.'

Mark and Patti drove to his flat in Barnet in companionable

silence. She had stopped crying and had agreed that as soon as Mark had packed he would take her down to the hospital to deal with the formalities. As he entered his living room he saw that the green message light on his phone was flashing. He pressed the play button and was surprised to hear Luis's voice as he had left him only the previous evening.

'Marco, I hope you got back in one piece. Ferrera is on his way, but I have some interesting news for you about your young friend Barry Reed. Maybe you can call me. I know you have no fond memories of our country, but I think when you hear what I have to say then you will want to pay us one last visit.'

Mark looked at Patti, the very thought of another long haul flight making him feel exhausted. She stroked the side of his face.

'Whatever he wants, leave it until tomorrow to call back. Get your things together, take me down to the hospital and then let's go to bed.'

He nodded. He knew that this time bed meant sleep, but sleep with her arms entwined around him seemed the most attractive option in the world.

CHAPTER 39

Golder's Green Crematorium was not the sort of place to linger and, as soon as the ashes of Valerie Delaney had been consigned to their plot, Patti hurried away towards Mark's car. It had taken three days to make all the arrangements. Patti had despaired of the obstacles that had been put in her way by the United Synagogue and had eventually arranged for a Reform Rabbi to officiate at what had been a brief and sparsely attended ceremony.

'Thanks for coming, Mark,' she said. She had shed no tears and he wondered how long she would manage to keep her emotions in check.

'At least I understood more of what was going on than I did at Leo's funeral. Who were the rest of the people there?' He made no complaint that he had not been introduced, accepting that Patti herself was a stranger to most of her relations on her mother's side.

'My aunt, my mother's sister, recognised me, although the only way I could tell she was related was by the eyes. It was spooky. Like my mother was looking at me through her eyes.'

He drove towards Golders Green itself, wondering at the microcosm of Jewish life; the men in their long dark coats, the women with their covered heads, the young boys made old before their time, with their black trilby hats tipped at rakish angles, the children with their yarmulkas. He envied them their faith, wondered if it were worth trying. But he knew Patti would laugh in his face if he even suggested it. Or would she on this day of all days?

'Do you fancy a coffee?' he asked, nervous in case she should think he was suggesting any kind of celebration of her mother's passing.

'Why not? You know, Mark, for the first time since I heard of her death, I feel hungry. I know it sounds strange, but I almost enjoyed that ceremony. I think she might have done as well. She

231

wasn't always like she was at the end. When I was little, when my dad was still there, she'd always be springing surprises. Little things, like making me gingerbread men, a new dress for my favourite doll, a cheap brooch. It didn't matter what they cost. It was enough that she thought about me, enough that she cared.'

Parking was a nightmare. Nobody seemed to be paying any attention to the restrictions and cars were not merely double parked, but at times even three in a line, the wardens coping with the same efficiency as the little Dutch boy with his finger in the dyke. Mark joined in the fray and slotted into a space which had been claimed by a large lady in a battered Volvo with innumerable children crammed into every seat of her vehicle. She yelled at him in a language he did not understand, and when he showed no inclination to make way for her she simply manoeuvred her car alongside his and left it there, oblivious to the fact that he could not get out even if he wanted to.

They found a coffee shop that was half filled with lady shoppers and elderly men.

Patti looked at the array of cakes behind the counter.

'Do you think it would be too terrible to indulge myself?' she asked.

'I think it would show a lot of courage. Go for it. And I'll have an eclair while you're at it.'

The cappuccinos came with chocolate and cream on top and the waiter stood back, admiring his work and challenging them to get through both the drinks and the cakes. Almost as if he sensed Patti's need he had selected the largest slice of Black Forest gâteau he could find, oozing chocolate and alcohol.

Patti lifted her cup in a toast.

'May she rest in peace.'

Mark said nothing, but clinked his cup against hers and took a sip of the steaming liquid.

'What happens now?' she asked.

'What do you want to happen?' he replied.

'I'll tell you want I don't want to happen. I don't want to be alone tonight.'

'Just tonight?' he asked cautiously, having gone down that road before and been beaten back.

'Perhaps not.' She leaned across the table and stroked the side of his face with the back of her hand, raising a smile from a grizzled old man at the next table and a look of disapproval from an elderly woman with the skin of a prune.

'Listen, Patti, I didn't want to say anything before the funeral, but I've got to go back to Colombia.'

'That call from Luis?'

'That call from Luis,' he replied apologetically.

'Can you tell me what he said that makes it so urgent for you to return so quickly?'

'I'd like to say that he'd got hold of something that would clear you, but I'm afraid it's about Barry.'

She said nothing and he thought for a moment that she was about to launch into him once again for putting himself on the line for somebody else. But Patti was in no mood for an argument.

'Have you told him?'

'No, I didn't want to raise any hopes?'

'But obviously you think there's some hope, otherwise you wouldn't be going.'

She didn't push him to tell her, but he didn't want to miss the opportunity of proving that there were no secrets between them.

'I'm not sure. I'm not even sure whether it's worth the trip, but if I don't go then I'll always feel I left some stone unturned.'

'And you couldn't do that, could you?'

He searched her face for a hint of sarcasm, an element of criticism, but he could see nothing but sincerity there.

'No, I couldn't do that.' He felt like a parrot, but could think of nothing else to say and didn't want the flow of the conversation to end. Patti lit up a cigarette and blew a cloud of smoke into the air. She watched it rise and disappear and that was when she began to cry as she thought of the smoke at the crematorium – the fire and the smoke that had left behind nothing but ashes of a person's sad and wasted life.

The frowning prune-like woman tapped her on the arm and pointed to a no-smoking sign on the wall. Mark got to his feet and grabbed Patti by the arm. He tossed a note on the table to cover the bill. As they got to the door he turned and went back to the woman's table.

'We've come straight from her mother's funeral,' he said, loudly enough for everybody in the room to hear and, without waiting for a reply or a reaction, walked out of the café, leaving the woman open-mouthed.

By the time they reached the car, their exit had cleared and he drove down the Finchley Road towards Hampstead.

'I have to go down to meet Mo Halid and report on my couple of days at Jet. I feel like somebody from M15.'

'You're not devious enough to be a spy, Mark,' she said.

He didn't reply, but realised that he still did not fully understand himslf what Luis had suggested he might learn in Bogota.

CHAPTER 40

He had little to tell Mohammed Halid and he was beginning to think that the whole charade was a waste of time. Yet the man hung on his every word, asking question upon question, as if he were preparing himself for some examination.

'Alissa. Tell me about Alissa. Is she still in love with that bastard, Carr?'

'I'll ask her, shall I Mo?' Mark replied, deciding he could no longer take the matter seriously.

'Sometimes, I think Alissa is the brains behind the company,' Mo said, ignoring Mark's levity.

'I rather like her,' Mark said, immediately realising he had said the wrong thing as it would only serve to set Halid off on another tirade.

'I'm sure you do. Most men would. She's a very attractive woman. But she's dangerous, believe me. The sort of woman who would eat a man after she had allowed him to make love to her.'

Mark was about to say that he could live with being eaten by Alissa Bland, but decided that would only encourage Mo further.

'I have established one thing,' Mark said.

Halid looked up, his face positively glistening with anticipation. 'Which is?'

'I saw a schedule of the tenders. Carr had left them on his desk.'

'Careless,' Mo said half to himself, 'or maybe deliberate. I wonder if I was right in putting you in there. Believe me, Mark, the last thing I would want is for you to be in any danger. You're quite sure that Carr has no idea that you're still on our payroll?'

'I'm certain of it. He talks quite freely around me. The only thing is that I'm not sure that anything much he says is of great interest.'

'The tenders, were they interesting?'

'Could be. Jet beat Ball Park by a mere $10,000.'

Halid's eyes narrowed as the significance of that sunk in.

'Only ten thousand. What about the others?'

'Miles behind. It was a two-horse race. They needn't have bothered to saddle up.'

'He must have known what we'd offered. He must have. But how?' Mo mused, pacing the room with the intensity of a Sherlock Holmes.

'What's more to the point, how did he get hold of the tenders?' Mark added.

'You have to find that out.' Halid was becoming animated. 'You see, I told you it would not be a waste of time, you going into Jet.'

Mark smiled.

'When do you pull me out, as they say in espionage terms? This particular spy would quite like to come in from the cold.'

'Soon, soon.'

But soon was not soon enough. It was evident that Mark would have to return to Bogota as an employee of Jet, which posed him a problem. It was one thing flying off when Carr had told him there was little to do, but quite another to find an excuse when producers and editors wanted him for pilot shows, wanted to try him out with co-commentators, even wanted to see what he was like fronting a chat show.

'Nathan, I'm sorry, but I have an understanding with Hertsmere. David Sinclair and I go back a long way. He wants me to go and iron out a few wrinkles on the Ferrera deal.'

He was getting used to lying and that worried him. What worried him even more was the fact that he was getting good at it.

'I thought it was a done deal,' Carr said.

'So did Hertsmere, but you know what South Americans are like to deal with.'

Carr had nodded as if he were faced with problems from that part of the world every day of the week.

'Maybe we could send out a camera crew with you and you could shoot a story on the transfer.'

Mark hesitated. He realised that there was every chance that he wouldn't even see Ferrera if his work permit came through

236

and that might be a little hard to explain to whoever Carr sent with him.

'I'd have to ask David. I'm not too sure he'd be happy about any of the financial details leaking out. I know for a fact that what he's agreed to pay Ferrera is going to blow the wage structure at the club to smithereens.'

He was getting used to thinking on his feet as well. He held his breath while Carr thought about it and had to fight to conceal his relief when he finally replied.

'I guess it'd be expensive for what we'd get out of it. It's not like it's one of the big clubs. I have to say that our viewers are still not entirely convinced by Hertsmere.'

'I'll tell the chairman when I see him. I'm sure he'll want to speak to you to discover exactly what it is that your viewers are after.'

Mark spoke with a smile and Carr laughed in response, but the former Hertsmere player was not amused. It had been a long, hard struggle for the club to come from non-league obscurity to a European title. The Cup Winners Cup was not easily come by and, although they may not have made the most impressive start to the season, there was still a long way to go. With a player like Juanito Ferrera in their ranks they had every chance of being in there at the death. Still, if the insult meant that he had a few days off to follow Luis's leads, it was worth taking.

The immigration official at the airport in Bogota frowned as he checked Mark's passport.

'You are a regular visitor, Señor Rossetti.'

Mark could understand why anybody should find that surprising, but didn't think such a comment would ease his entry into the country.

'I'm hoping to establish some business contacts here.'

'We are always interested in European business. What exactly do you do, senor?'

The queue behind Mark was becoming impatient, but the official seemed oblivious to them. Mark realised that his passport still described him as a professional footballer and just hoped that the man was genuinely curious and not about to take issue with his story.

'I'm involved with the media. With a TV company that specialises in sport.'

The reply elicited a broad smile.

'Ah yes, we love our sport here. I have watched the international a few weeks ago.' He examined the passport again, 'I see you were here also. It was an exciting match.'

'Yes, yes, it was,' Mark said. He felt tired and dirty and hoped the man's English was not going to stretch to a kick by kick recounting of the contest.

In fact, the man stamped Mark into the country with a theatrical flourish and, as Mark collected his luggage, he could see the welcoming face of Luis standing just beyond the hall. It occurred to him that he had become very dependent upon Luis. But then this country made its visitors dependent. He didn't know who the minister of tourism was, but he had about as easy a job as a man selling condoms in the Vatican.

Luis had acquired a new car, a gleaming Toyota. Two small boys stood proudly by it in the car park and Luis peeled off a couple of US dollar bills from a roll in his pocket and gave them one each. They bowed gravely and ran away laughing.

'Security guards are getting younger and younger,' Mark said, as Luis drove away at a speed that threatened take-off.

'A good investment. Nobody steals my car and they do not damage it. Everybody is happy.'

'What have you got for me that will make me happy? To say you were enigmatic on the phone is an understatement.'

Luis frowned as he wrestled with Mark's English.

'For an old professional footballer, you have learned some fancy words.'

'It comes of living with a writer. She's educated me in more ways than one.'

'How is the beautiful Patti? Has she come to terms with her lawyer's advice?'

'Oh, she's come to terms with it, all right. She's ignoring it.'

'You mean she still intends coming here to prove her innocence?'

'She does. But her mother died. That's why I delayed coming.'

Luis hit the horn on the car and a few stray dogs and derelicts leapt to the side of the road for safety.

'Is it the money? If you lose the bail will you be broke?'

'No, it's not the money and we won't be broke. It's just that she doesn't fancy getting a criminal record for something she didn't do.'

'Maybe I will talk to Salazar. Perhaps he can persuade the court to reduce the amount of the bail. The judge might be sympathetic to the death of her mother. Then you can persuade Patti to accept the inevitable.'

Before Mark could reply, Luis pulled into the drive of an apartment block.

'I thought this time, as I have invited you, that you would be my guest. I have a spare room.'

Mark realised then just how little he knew about Luis. He didn't even know whether or not he was married, whether he had any kids, or whether he was gay. As if reading his thoughts, Luis volunteered the information that Mark sought.

'My wife left me a year ago. She took our only son with her. I welcome any company. I miss them both.'

'I know how you feel,' Mark said with genuine emotion, recalling how he had felt when Sally had left with their daughter, Emma.

When Luis's wife had abandoned him she had not gone empty-handed. Mark could not believe that any married couple with a child could have lived in such minimalist surroundings. There was nothing wrong with the apartment itself. It was large and sunny, the air-conditioning successfully defeating the stifling heat that hung over the city like a threatening cloud of poison dust. Yet, from the picture window that led on to the balcony to the doors that led through to the bedrooms and kitchen there was virtually nothing. The walls were plain white emulsion, free of pictures or indeed anything. The floor was polished wood without any carpet to soften the look. A television and video were in one corner, opposite a single armchair. The bookshelves were virtually empty and were bereft of any vases or ornaments. The telephone was on the floor, and that was it.

Luis flung out his arm.

'It is simple, I know, but I am rarely home.'

He saw the expression on Mark's face.

'And I rarely have visitors,' he added by way of explanation, 'but I do have a bathroom.'

'Do I smell that bad?' Mark asked.

'Not at all. And if you did then I would be too polite to tell you. But I travel enough to know exactly how you feel at the end of a long flight. Please, relax in the bath and, when you are ready, we will talk. Tonight we eat here. However hard you try there is always a chance that somebody will overhear at a restaurant.'

Mark would have spent longer luxuriating in the hot water, but he needed to know what Luis had dragged him all these miles to tell him, and he needed to know with the minimum of delay. As he dried himself and put on a clean shirt and a pair of light trousers, something Patti had said as she had dropped him off at the airport suddenly struck home. 'I'll use the time you're away to make some inquiries of my own.'

He couldn't believe that he'd not reacted there and then, that he hadn't given a thought to it on the plane. What inquiries was she talking about? The last time she'd gone off on her own had led to her arrest in this city. He shook his head in irritation. He'd been so tied up with Barry's problems and Mo's intrigue that he'd taken his eye off the ball when it came to Patti. He'd hesitated over leaving her because he thought she was still mourning her mother, but he should have been hesitating because, whatever her attitude to him, she wasn't going to give up her pursuit of a story. She might be the woman he had every intention of marrying, but she was still a journalist. He looked at his watch. It was ten in the evening, still afternoon in London.

He came back into the main room which was now filled with the smell of cooking from the adjoining kitchen. Luis put his head round the door and nodded approvingly.

'You look much better.'

'I feel much better. Luis, much as I'm dying to know what you have to tell me, do you mind if I phone Patti first?'

'Of course, I was forgetting her loss. Did you pass on my condolences?'

'She was grateful. There weren't a lot of people around to support her.'

There was a sizzling sound from the kitchen and Luis moved speedily back to his culinary tasks, only pausing to shout back, 'Close the door if it is private.'

Mark thought it would be rude to accept the invitation and knelt on the floor to make the call. It took him three attempts to make the connection and, while redialling, he looked out through the window at the sprawling lights of Bogota. There were secrets out there and there were answers. There were the men who had planted the drugs on Patti, there were the men who had conspired to frame Barry Reed, and he wondered if there were also those who were guilty of the murder of Jenny Cooper.

The phone in the Burrow rang three times and then the answerphone cut in.

'Hi, it's me, I am at Luis's flat.' He rattled off the number, then paused whilst the tape kept recording. 'I love you. take care.' But he knew that the last two words of his message were a waste of time.

CHAPTER 41

Another day, another plane, another country. Mark Rossetti was beginning to feel like an American tourist. This was Tuesday and therefore it had to be Brazil. Some song-writer had described it as a whimsical fancy to go to Rio and here he was indulging in his own little piece of whimsy. Luis had offered him a slender thread towards the truth, but he was using it to climb the side of the building, hoping he could haul himself up to the locked room, enter by the window and discover the secrets within.

There could be no doubting that Luis was a better commentator than he was a cook and it did not need much of a story to distract Mark from the largely unidentifiable meal that was placed before him in a kitchen that also contained only the bare necessities of life.

'You are wondering why I should have dragged you back to a country for which you justifiably have so little regard.'

'It had crossed my mind,' Mark said, shuffling the food around his plate so that it would look as if he had at least eaten something. It did not fool Luis.

'Don't worry, my friend, you don't need to be polite. I know my limitations as a cook.'

'I ate on the plane,' Mark said.

'I'm sure you did, but as I say there is no need to be polite. I'll make us a coffee. At least I have a certain skill there. You can have the chair and I'll have the floor.'

'When all of this is over,' Mark said from the relative comfort of the armchair, 'I'll treat you to another chair.'

Luis took a sip of the scalding coffee and lit a cigarette without any apology to his visitor.

'Ah, when this is over. That is why I wanted to see you. I have discovered something that is not quite right. You must make of it what you will.'

Mark leaned forward in his seat, trying to urge the Colombian

242

on with his story, but he had decided on a way of telling it, of squeezing the full drama out of something which only might prove to be dramatic.

'After the match against England, Barry Reed was selected for a random drug test. There were two doctors present, the FIFA official observer and a local man, Dr Felipe Guerra. It is the local man who does most of the work and prepares the report. And the report finds Reed positive. Poof goes his career.'

'Yes,' Mark said impatiently, 'we know all that. What's your point?'

'When you left the first time I tried to do some detective work. For your lady, there is nothing I can do, she has upset important people, dangerous people. How or why I do not know, but I do know that I do not care to walk down that road on my own.'

He drained the coffee and Mark, who had burned his lips with the first taste, wondered if his mouth were made of asbestos.

'You want another cup?'

'No,' Mark replied, impatiently, 'I just want you to cut to the chase.' He saw the look of puzzlement on Luis's face and decided that this was not the moment to start explaining colloquialisms. 'Get to the point, Luis, or else I might do some violence on your person.'

'The point is, that I went to see Dr Guerra and he wasn't there.'

'So? I can't believe that you've brought me all this way to tell me that a doctor was out visiting his patients.'

Luis smiled. He was obviously enjoying the evening, even if Mark was not.

'No, I do not think he was out on his acts of mercy. When you were here on the Ferrera deal I went to see him again.'

'Don't tell me, he was visiting a sick patent again.'

'No, I don't think so. He wasn't there, but then he hadn't been there since my first visit. His housekeeper was not a happy woman. She had been trying to cope with a whole stream of angry patients, not to mention the fact she had no idea where her wages were coming from. She thought I was just another discontented patient looking for his doctor, so she told me where to look.'

Luis had told Mark, and Mark was on his way to Brazil to see Felipe Guerra. Luis had his contacts in Brazil, he seemed to have his contacts everywhere, and it had taken him only a few calls to discover the whereabouts of the missing doctor. Mark had asked him to come with him, but Luis had been forced to decline.

'We have an important league match here tomorrow, and I must cover it. If you would like to wait until the weekend, then I will be happy to accompany you.'

Mark had not been prepared to wait. He wanted to get this over, to discover if there was anything in this tenuous link, and then to get back to England and Patti. He'd called again before he'd left and, judging by the number of beeps on the tape, he guessed that she'd not been home to pick up her messages. He'd decided that if he still couldn't get hold of her when he reached Brazil then he'd call Rob Davies. Assuming she was safe, she wouldn't thank him for involving the police, but her safety and well-being were not something he took for granted.

He had no real idea what to do when he caught up with the doctor. Luis had told him that the wealthy, residential area in which Guerra was living was only a thirty-minute ride from the airport and, when he'd booked his tickets for him, he'd arranged a seat on the last flight back to Bogota which left at seven in the evening.

'I apologise for the airline before you fly. It is one of our local carriers, but my travel agent has a good relationship with them and I was able to get you there and back in the cheapest way possible.'

Mark was therefore travelling light, a small hold-all with a photo of Barry Reed, a dictaphone borrowed from Luis, and one change of clothing, in the knowledge that by the end of the day what he had worn would be soaked in sweat.

Luis had been right about the plane. It carried about sixty passengers, most of whom looked as if they had exhausted the possibilities of begging on the streets of Bogota and were looking to try pastures new in Rio. There were one or two businessmen in well-cut lightweight suits, with briefcases rather than bundles, but they had been shepherded together in the first three rows, although the seats looked no more comfortable than those in the rest of the cabin. Some of the upholstery was torn and patched, most of it did not match and Mark had noticed on take-off that the crew had rushed through the safety instructions as if embarrassed by the fact that there were several seatbelts missing. Mark had to resist the temptation to check to see if there were a life-jacket under his seat. Even if there were it was unlikely that the body of the plane would hold together well enough actually to get to the ground or the water.

As he came through the airport he was besieged by unofficial taxi drivers all trying to persuade him to hire them before he got to the official rank. One of them was more persistent than the others and once he discovered Mark was English seemed so anxious to demonstrate his command of the language that Mark relented and was led, almost by the hand, to his beat-up vehicle.

'Señor, you will be very happy with me as your driver. My name is José. I love England. Bobby Charlton, yes? Gazza, yes? Princess Diana, yes?'

'Yes,' Mark replied. If his driver was going to finish every sentence with a yes, then it should turn out to be a very positive day.

José did his best to act as a tour guide as he drove recklessly towards the address Mark had given him. The car seemed incapable of reaching a speed over forty miles an hour, but the way that José threw it into bends, overtook bicycles and donkeys and ignored any traffic signals made it feel as if he were breaking the sound barrier. As they progressed it became apparent that his conversation with Mark at the airport had been about the limit of his English and eventually Mark simply switched off and concentrated on his approach to the doctor. Somehow or other he had to persuade him to speak to him, to talk him through the events of the night minute by minute.

When they finally arrived at the doctor's house, Mark took in a deep breath. His surgery had been in a fairly respectable area of Bogota, but what was facing him was pure luxury. There were huge iron gates with a security intercom and beyond them a long gravel drive leading up to the sprawling hacienda. A sprinkler was playing on the carefully tended lawns and, behind the main building, Mark could just see the diving board of a swimming pool.

'I didn't know that medicine in Bogota was such a profitable trade,' he said aloud.

'Yes,' said José although he could not have understood a word.

'Yes, indeed,' Mark said to himself and pressed the buzzer to the left of the gate.

A woman's voice answered in what Mark took to be either Spanish or Portuguese. Either way he couldn't understand a word.

'Dr Guerra, is he home?' he asked.

There was some confusion when she heard his accent and then the sound of feet on wood and a male voice.

'Si. Dr Guerra, that is me.'

'My name is Mark Rossetti. I'm from England. I'm sorry to arrive without any warning. I wonder if I could talk to you. It's rather important.'

'What is this about, Señor Rossetti?'

There seemed to be little point in lying. He had little doubt that if the man could afford a house like this then he could also afford the security men to go with it and they would have no hesitation in throwing him out if his presence was unwelcome.

'It's about a drug test you carried out on an English footballer after the match against Colombia.'

There was a deathly silence at the other end. Mark looked up at the house, trying to visualise the expression on the man's face. He was so near, yet so far.

Eventually the doctor replied.

'I have nothing to say to you. Or anybody. Now, this road is private so I must ask you to leave my property.'

Mark took out his camera and photographed the house and as much of the estate as he could see. The doctor had refused to meet with him to reply to his questions, but the house and his silence had spoken volumes in themselves.

CHAPTER 42

Although neither of them would have known it, Juanito Ferrera and Mark Rossetti had quite possibly crossed in mid-air. Now, whilst Mark sweated in the Brazilian sunshine, the Colombian was shivering in an English November mist. Ray Fowler had wasted no time in getting him out on the training ground. He'd had his reservations when his chairman had suggested they try to buy him. He was a class player, there was no doubt of that, but he could not help but recall the problems they had experienced with foreign imports in the past. Admittedly, Dimitri Murganev was coming good, and there had just that week been a five-million pound bid for him from Juventus, but that had taken time and no little heartache on the way.

He had put Ferrera under Stuart Macdonald's wing. His captain and most experienced player would look after him, of that he was sure. He would also report back accurately to Fowler. Macdonald's career was coming to an end and he was a natural for a coaching position at the club. Other men might have hesitated over appointing such a popular figure and natural successor, but Fowler was always going to do what was best for the club. He knew in his mind that he had never fully recovered from the appalling injuries he'd suffered in an attack a couple of years back and he was finding it harder and harder to keep up with the pressures of the modern game. He'd never thought he would ever look forward to a time when he was no longer involved in football, but the headaches that were now a constant companion were giving him the message that his days were probably numbered. When he retired he could not think of anyone better to take over the reins than Stuart Macdonald.

Ferrera seemed to have settled in remarkably well. They had put him in the local four-star hotel they always used whilst a player was looking for somewhere to live and he appeared to be quite content there.

'He's no trouble, this one,' Macdonald had reported. 'He's in most nights, watching telly although I have to tell you I dread the phone bill we're going to get. Every time I pop in or try to call he's on the line. He seems to know quite a few people here already.'

'Do you think I should take a chance and play him tonight?' Fowler asked. There was a mid-week fixture against Colborough Town at Hertsmere that evening and he was bringing Macdonald into his selection decisions more and more.

'I would. Maybe as sub with a view to giving him a run out if we get a hold on the game.'

As it was, Tommy Wallace had pulled a hamstring in training and Fowler decided to throw Ferrera in at the deep end. It was a choice that the Colombian totally vindicated in the first five minutes. A long clearance by Liam O'Donnell was nodded down by Aled Williams. Ferrera fed off him as if they had been playing together for years, took the ball on his chest and turned away from his marker in one movement. He flicked the ball back to Williams who played a perfect one-two with him, leaving Ferrera with a clear run to goal. The Colborough keeper decided to come off his line and spread himself, but to no avail as the Hertsmere man simply clipped the ball over him and into the net with a sublimely delicate chip.

He ran to take the accolades of the crowd behind the goal who greeted their new hero with a single chant, 'Juan, Juan, Juanito, there's only one Juanito.' It didn't end there. Just before half-time he received the ball on the halfway line from Macdonald, ran some twenty yards until the ball bobbled in front of him. Instead of trying to regain control he simply hit the ball on the volley and was already turning back to the centre circle as the net bulged for another goal.

Some twenty minutes from the end he began to tire but by then Hertsmere were already four up and were assured of the three points that would take them into the top six for the first time in the campaign. Fowler enthusiastically threw an arm around the huge striker as he insisted he pull on a tracksuit top to protect him from the evening's chill.

'Great stuff,' the manager said, and those who knew him would have been amazed by his unqualified praise.

But Ferrera had already taken his mobile phone out of his

bag and was speaking rapidly in Spanish. Fowler couldn't bring himself to reprimand the player. He had banned mobiles from both the training ground and the dressing room when he'd first taken charge at the club. He was tired of players talking to their agents about deals when they should have been listening to him talking about tactics. If he'd been the Colombian then he would also have wanted to phone home to tell them about his accomplishments.

At the post-match Press conference all the talk was of Ferrera.

'I've not seen a better debut,' Fowler told the scribbling group of journalists, 'but there were ten others out there tonight who all played their parts. I think this is the turning point of our season.'

'Do you think you'll miss Barry Reed as the season goes on?' asked Dennis Stratton of the *Post*.

'He's not available, so we'll have to make do,' Fowler replied diplomatically and then felt a terrible guilt as he realised that he had not given the banned Geordie a single thought throughout the match.

He returned to the dressing room, but most of the players had left. Only Stuart Macdonald was there, combing his hair carefully to conceal the bald patch that showed his advancing years.

'Where's Ferrera?' the manager asked.

Macdonald smiled.

'He seems to have made himself at home. I offered him a lift, but someone phoned him and he said he was going out for a meal.'

'I've never seen anybody settle in so quickly,' Fowler commented.

'You're right there, boss. I saw him from the window in the car park. He was picked up by a Porsche.'

'Not bad transport.'

'Not a bad chauffeur either. Blonde, long-haired and definitely female.'

'I thought married men weren't supposed to notice things like that.'

Macdonald had married Sally, Mark Rossetti's ex-wife, some years ago and both Fowler and her second husband knew that she would not take lightly to infidelity, even if it were only cerebral.

'I can notice. I just can't do anything. Anyway, I'm off. I'll see you Friday, assuming we've still got the day off tomorrow.'

'Oh aye, you've earned it. See you Mac.'

Fowler was left alone in the dressing room. He picked up a shirt that was folded in the corner, unused. It was the number eight, with the name Reed printed on the back. He held it out in front of him, as if satisfying himself it would still fit the absent player, then carefully refolded it and placed it gently in the kit basket.

'Of course we'll fucking miss him,' he said out loud, giving a belated answer to the reporter's question.

CHAPTER 43

Mark was almost at the airport when he decided to try again with the doctor. Not tonight, perhaps in the morning. If only he could see him face to face then he might have a chance. Either the man had won the lottery, inherited a fortune from a rich relation, or else he had been paid off. Given that only the last would have encouraged him to leave his native country, Mark was more convinced than ever that Luis had been right to point him in the direction of Guerra.

'José, can you recommend a hotel?'

'Hotel, yes. Very good, yes. Belongs to my friend.'

'I thought it just might,' Mark muttered to himself, but was pleasantly surprised when José drove up to a perfectly respectable establishment just outside the bustling centre of the city.

He was quoted a rate that seemed very cheap but doubtless included a commission for José. He didn't bother to negotiate. The man had been a real find and he asked him to return at eight the following morning. The furniture in the room was simple, but functional, made largely of cane. The bed was a double, the linen crisp and clean. There was a shower, but no bath, a satellite television, a Gideon Bible in English in the drawer and a telephone. He wanted the phone more than the Bible or the shower. He didn't even bother to consider the time in England. He just phoned Patti's number and to his enormous relief she picked it up herself.

'Patti, where have you been? Is everything all right?'

'Of course. I got your desperate messages. I phoned you back at Luis', but he said you'd gone off to Brazil on a jaunt. Are you looking for the boys or the girls? If it's the former beware of Nazis, if the latter look out for AIDS.'

He didn't get her literary allusion, but he immediately protested her suggestion about any women and related to her exactly what Luis had told him and what he had discovered so far.

251

'You should have said you were a journalist. That often gets you past the front door because they're either curious about what you know or else can't resist the thought of seeing their names in print.'

'Perhaps I'll disguise my voice and try that tomorrow, although I think he must have had a good look at me with the video camera. Anyway, what have you been up to that's kept you out to all hours?'

'Maybe I've been shagging other men,' she said teasingly. A few months earlier he might have thought that she was finding a light way to tell him the truth, but now he was certain she was teasing, and in an odd way that gave him a warm glow deep inside.

'Any complaints from the customers?' he asked.

'None at all. They all sent you their regards and said you were a lucky bloke to have me whenever you wanted. Listen, Mark, we have to be serious for a moment. I went to see my friend, Jessica Brown, you know the girl who does have AIDS. I just thought she'd like to know that I hadn't forgotten her, that I had done something towards writing her story, even though I'd managed to get myself arrested in the process.'

'What did she say to that?' Mark asked, uncaring about the length of the call or the doubtless astronomic cost.

'She laughed, Mark. And I laughed along with her. I don't think anything or anybody had made her laugh for a long while.'

'Did she have anything new to tell you?'

'Sort of. I'm not sure if it was helpful, but I suppose everything's relevant. She said that at the clubs where the drugs were being pushed, there were often footballers. She seemed to think that there were more than one or two of them hooked. Maybe Barry isn't telling you the truth.'

'I think he is, Patti.'

'Yeah, but you're a lousy judge of character. You liked Barlucci. You even liked your wife.'

'I did.'

'Well, this probably isn't the time or place. The other thing I've been doing has been for you.'

'Oh yes. What's that, hiring me a morning suit for the wedding?'

'More practical. Making sure you're in one piece in case there is a wedding. Nathan Carr has a bit of a reputation you know.

Everybody I speak to says that you have to be careful of him. So I've done a little bit of investigation.'

'Great. You don't even begin to investigate Branco and you get thrown in jail. Who knows what Carr might do if he finds out.'

'There's no way he can find out. I started at Company's House. It's amazing what you can discover simply from what the records of a company don't say.'

'And what didn't Jet's records say?' Mark asked.

'They don't say who owns the company.'

'I thought that was Nathan and Alissa.'

'Ooh, so it's Nathan and Alissa now rather than Carr and Bland. Don't go soft on this job, Mark. I really believe you're dealing with hard people.'

'You warned me against going in with Mo and he turned out to be a good guy.'

'Everything's relative. Anyway about Jet. Your Nathan and little Alissa only own a half of the shares in the company.'

'So who owns the rest?' Mark said, now hooked on the line that Patti had cast into the waters.

'That I don't yet know, but I'm working on it. They're registered to an off-shore trust. But we've come across those before and if you know the right people and strike lucky you can sometimes get behind the smokescreen.'

Sometimes you can get burned as well, Mark thought, but he said nothing. He couldn't see any connection between one of his current employers and his immediate problems, but if it was keeping Patti busy and out of trouble then he was happy for her to continue her investigations. He was sure that by the time she discovered whatever pay-dirt she was digging for, he would be long gone from the organisation.

'When are you coming home?' she asked in a gentle tone.

'As soon as I can. Believe me, I've had my fill of South America.'

'I believe you.'

She blew him a kiss down the line and she was gone. He picked up the phone and called Luis to tell him he'd be staying. The Colombian sounded surprised to hear from him.

'I thought you could not bear to be away from your lady for a day longer than was necessary?'

'That was before I saw your doctor's new house. You were absolutely right about him, I'm sure. All I have to do is find a way to get him to speak to me.'

'Brute force is not a bad idea. I can arrange that through some friends if you like.'

'I don't like. He's probably got his own garrison in the place if the security outside was anything to go by. If I try to fight fire with fire then I could set off a whole range war. I'll keep you posted.'

As soon as he cut off from Luis he realised that he'd not given him the number at the hotel, but then he wasn't expecting any calls so it hardly mattered and certainly didn't justify another call. Now he did glance at his watch. His stomach was empty which was hardly surprising. It was gone eight in the evening. There had been no breakfast on the plane and all he'd had all day was a coffee and a stale roll that José had insisted they buy at a wayside stall which probably belonged to another of José's friends or relations. He didn't know quite where the day had gone, but he was determined to end it with a meal. He wandered downstairs and noticed that there was a small café next door, which could be entered from a side door leading from the hotel's reception.

The place was largely deserted. One elderly man was seated alone at a table, an empty plate by his side, a coffee cup in front of him. A waiter looked up as he came in, a look of mild annoyance crossing his face as the promise of an early night disappeared with the new trade. The man behind the bar must have been the proprietor because his reaction was the total opposite to his employee.

He indicated to Mark that he could choose whatever table he desired and signalled the waiter over. The menu was entirely in Portuguese but Mark recognised the odd familiar word and ordered what he thought was a hamburger with chips. The waiter poured him a glass of water and Mark mimed a request for a bottle. The owner obligingly brought over a beer and Mark left it on the table for a while, wondering whether he could risk just the one or whether it might lead to another and yet another. Eventually he took it over to the bar and pointed to a bottle of carbonated water. The barman shrugged as if to indicate that he could not understand how anybody could prefer water to beer, but made the exchange in any event.

The television was on in a corner and Mark's attention was caught by an announcer's anguished tones. There was a picture of a plane crash on the screen followed by live pictures from the local airport, with a woman in hysterics. Mark had a horrible premonition. He hadn't yet discovered whether or not anybody in the establishment spoke English, but he tried a question anyway.

'The plane. Where was it going to?'

It was the old man who answered, his voice husky and guttural, the accent more mid-European than South American.

'Bogota. It was going to Bogota,' and Mark did not need to ask what time it had taken off or if everybody on board had been killed. He knew that already and he was left to wonder whether any innocent passenger had filled his empty seat.

CHAPTER 44

He could not sleep. He had found it impossible to eat after he had seen the news of the crash and if he had found a way to contact José he would have had him drive him back to Guerra's home there and then, despite the lateness of the hour. He had watched the television in his room, found CNN and everything he had feared was confirmed. The plane had taken off on time out of Rio and some twenty minutes into the flight people on the ground reported seeing it turn into a ball of fire. A bomb was suspected and all fifty-nine passengers had died instantly. Fifty-nine. It was an odd number so maybe nobody had taken his seat after all. The police were scanning the passenger list carefully to see whether there was a motive for killing anybody on board. Well, they wouldn't find his name, but they might discover that he'd cancelled his ticket. If they did, would they want to speak to him to discover the reason why? He had a nasty feeling that they would.

Eventually he nodded off in the chair and awoke at four in the morning stiff and aching, his stomach growling with hunger. The hotel did not run to a minibar and a search of his pockets produced only a half packet of Polos. They were better than nothing and he chewed them one after another. He had arranged for José to collect him at eight in the morning and he hoped that breakfast was served before then. The hours he had to wait dragged by. He was tired of the television news, he had brought nothing with him to read and a call to Patti to tell her he was not a victim of the disaster only brought forth her answerphone. He thought of phoning his daughter, Emma, but she would have had no idea that he'd been booked on to the flight and there was little purpose in shocking her after the event.

In desperation he turned to the Bible. It had been a long time since he'd opened the pages, but now he found himself hooked on the story of the Creation, the Fall, the Flood, Abraham's

256

Sacrifice of Isaac, Moses and the Flight from Egypt, all Old Testament tales which formed the basis of the religion of the race to which Patti belonged, for better or worse, the inheritance passed down to her by her mother. He wished he could have some faith. During the dark days of his drinking there had been nothing for him to turn to and now that he had come so close to death there was nobody for him to thank. He could only read these stories of long ago as fables, and think that it was fate that had forced him to turn back, rather than some careless divinity dealing cards of life or death at random.

It was the phone which woke him after he had nodded off again, the Bible falling from his lap to the floor. José had arrived half an hour early, presumably in case Mark had any idea of dispensing with his services. Mark showered quickly, rubbed the stubble on his cheek and chin and wondered if it was worthwhile trying to buy a razor and some shaving foam to make himself look less threatening for his proposed visit. He decided that a threatening appearance might even be more effective, gathered his few possessions together and went downstairs to meet his driver.

José, at least, seemed pleased to see him, and was not in the least put out when Mark insisted on going into the café for a coffee and whatever he could find to eat. To his surprise they had some fresh croissants and he ordered four, offered one to José and devoured the other three himself, feeling the acidity subside as the food hit the lining of his stomach. He bought a bottle of water to take with him and climbed into the car which, if at all possible, seemed even more decrepit than the day before. The traffic was against them all the way and if he had been in a regular cab with a meter he would have had to mortgage his flat to pay for the ride. He looked at his watch obviously and José simply shrugged his shoulders to indicate there was nothing to do about the Rio de Janeiro rush-hour but to sit back and tolerate it even if one could hardly enjoy it.

It was gone ten by the time they arrived at Guerra's property. Mark told José to draw up the car and to wait until he could see some evidence of life beyond the gates. An hour passed, the sun rose higher in the sky and Mark half emptied the water and wished he'd bought two bottles. Then he got the break he was waiting for. A middle-aged man came out of the main building and began to walk around the garden, making notes as he went. He looked too well-dressed to be the gardener and Mark could only presume that the master of the house had a keen interest in horticulture. He began to work his way up the path, oblivious to the parked car. He was about twenty yards from the front gate when Mark called out to him.

'Dr Guerra. I spoke to you yesterday. You have to listen to me today, you have to. Over fifty innocent people died yesterday. I don't know if it was because of you or because of me, but either way we were involved and we have to talk.'

Guerra hesitated, then began to turn and walk back to the house.

'For crying out loud,' Mark yelled at the top of his voice, 'you're a doctor, you're supposed to save lives, not take them.'

It came from the heart and it worked more effectively than anything he had planned to say throughout the long sleepless night and the endless journey out in the car. Guerra turned again to face him, saw the car parked with the lone driver and approached the gate.

He looked Mark up and down, wrestled with his conscience and then pressed a button. The gate swung slowly open.

'You'd better come up to the house,' Guerra said. 'It is fortunate that I studied in Miami, otherwise your words would have been in vain. I will send one of my men out with a drink for your driver. It's going to be a hot day.'

He led him into the cool of the hacienda. The packing cases scattered around suggested to Mark that he had only just moved in. They went into a huge lounge, the walls covered with Aztec designs, the floor strewn with brightly coloured woven rags. Guerra took a jug in his hand and poured two glasses of the liquid.

'Lemonade,' he said by way of explanation. 'Now you tell me about these people we are supposed to have killed.'

'That plane that blew up last night. The flight to Bogota. I was booked on it. I changed my mind and decided to come back one more time to try to talk to you. I'm certain that the only reason all those innocent passengers died was because it would have covered up my own death. I don't know if it's something I've learned already or it's something they thought you might tell me, but in any event it's obviously something that they want to keep a deeply hidden secret.'

Guerra hesitated and walked over to the window, glass in hand.

'You know, when you have some money, but not enough, and somebody offers you enough not to work again, then you truly believe that this money will buy you happiness.'

'And does it?'

'No. It only buys this house. You know I was waiting for someone to come along. I did not know who they would be. They might have been the police, or an investigator, or one of those who made it possible for me to be here, but instead it is you. Who are you, Mr Rossetti?'

'Me? I'm just a played-out ex-footballer who thinks a promising young player got the rough end of the stick. I'm not the police and although I used to be an investigator I'm not really here in that role. I think I may be your conscience.'

'And you think I have one?'

'Now that I've met you, yes I think you do. Now, do you want all those people to have died for nothing, or will you tell me exactly what happened?'

Guerra scratched his neck and slapped his arm to kill an invisible insect.

'Yes, I will tell you, but do not expect me to testify in court. I have not unpacked and I think it is best if I do not. I have nothing to keep me here. My wife died of cancer two years ago. We had no children. Once you know, once the burden is off me and on to you, then I will move on and you will not find me. Nor I hope will those who paid me. Are you ready, Mr Rossetti?'

Mark fumbled in his pocket for Luis' tape recorder and switched it on without asking Guerra's consent.

'Yes, Doctor,' he said, 'I'm ready now.'

CHAPTER 45

He didn't expect Patti to meet him at the airport, but he was pleased to see her all the same. She virtually threw herself into his arms as he came through customs, ignoring the three days' growth of beard and the sweat-stained shirt.

'When I got your message, when I thought just how close I'd been to losing you, then suddenly it seemed kind of urgent that I saw you as soon as I could.'

Mark put his arm around her waist as she led him to her car in the short-stay car park and tossed his bag on to the back seat.

'Where do you want me to take you, milord?' Patti asked.

Mark wasn't sure. He'd thought he'd had it all figured out on the plane, but then he'd not calculated on being met at the airport. What Guerra had told him had been dynamite and he was not sure if he wanted Patti to be with him when he lit the fuse. What he had decided was that he could no longer lead a double life. He could not understand what had possessed him in the first place to agree to do Mo's dirty work. Perhaps it was because he had felt he was on the side of the angels and perhaps he was, but he did not really fancy being a part of any heavenly choir.

'I tell you what, Pat, let's go to see Mo first. That'll be a nice gentle introduction to what I think could be a long, hard day. Do you happen to have your mobile so that I can make sure he's there? I'll charge mine up as we drive.'

'Are you sure you don't want to go home and change first?'

He shook his head as he waited for them to exit from the tunnel at Heathrow before making his call.

'I just want to get on. You'll understand.'

'Aren't you going to tell me what happened? I thought we had this thing of mutual exchange of information.'

'Does that mean you've got something to tell me?' he asked.

'Perhaps,' she replied, a mischievous smile appearing around her mouth. Before he could reply, she added, 'Oh, and before I forget, Luis asked you to call him urgently. He called last night wanting to know where you were staying in Rio and I told him you were on your way back. He says not to worry about the time difference. It didn't matter when you called, he just needed to speak to you.'

He had forgotten about Luis in his haste to get back home, yet now something ticked away in the back of his mind, but before he could forge the thought into something concrete, Patti was talking again. She seemed years younger, delighted and relieved to see him, the troubles of her arrest and the death of her mother dark moments in the past.

'Jet. I have to tell you about your new little playmates. You know I told you that Carr and the beautiful Alissa weren't in total control.' She didn't wait for an answer and, as if to force Mark to concentrate, she roared on to the M4 and pushed the needle up towards ninety totally oblivious to the speed cameras waiting to entrap her. 'Well who's a clever girl then? Patti's a clever girl. I saw the other shares were held in the name of Guernsey nominees. Now you may think that was where the trail would end . . .'

'Patti, if you don't slow down the trail for both of us is about to end,' Mark said, sitting bolt upright in his seat, hoping that his apparent fear might curb her speed.

'But you would be wrong,' she continued gaily. 'Your Patti has friends everywhere. It just so happens that one of my exes is an accountant on the island, so I rang him up and asked him to make a few discreet inquiries. Now our off-shore dwellers are very sensitive to any scandal, so I just sort of insinuated that there might be some money-laundering involved and that, as a favour, my friend should tip off the trustees if he knew them. And he did know them, and he did tip them off and they were very grateful. So grateful in fact that they resigned and after they resigned they took my friend out for a few drinks. Now my friend can hold his booze. Many's the time he'd have to put me to bed while I was fetching up and he'd go downstairs and balance a few books . . .' She saw the look on Mark's face. 'You're not enjoying this story are you? Is that the little green god of jealousy I see? I do believe it is.'

'Concentrate on the road, Patti, please,' he said desperately. He did feel jealous. Every time she exposed a little of her past it swept over him. He knew that she was not some convent-fresh innocent, but it hurt nevertheless.

'The story,' she continued, unperturbed. 'Where did we leave it? Oh yes, my sober friend amidst a group of drunken off-shore corporate managers. A dangerous combination. Let me tell you, Mark, if you are ever tempted to rely upon the discretion of men, do not do so. They are not to be trusted.'

He was tempted to tell her to hurry up, but feared that in her playful mood she might take him literally and drive even faster. Instead, he stared straight ahead, which he had once been told was a perfect cure for car-sickness, and he hoped that, on that occasion at least, the man had not lied.

'So one of those untrustworthy men told my sober friend all about the concerns they'd always had about the beneficial owners of the other half of the stake in Jet. It had been some kind of administrative oversight that had restrained these honourable men from taking any action until they had wind of an investigation and clouds appeared on the horizon of their cosy existence.'

'And the beneficial owner?' Mark asked, curious despite himself.

'Well, there's the coincidence. I started off trying to protect your back and it seems I may end up saving my own.'

'What do you mean, Patti? Either that flight took more out of me than I thought or else you've had some raw alcohol for breakfast. Which may well explain the way you're driving.'

'I mean that the true owner of the other fifty per cent of the shares in Jet is none other than your friend and mine, Riccardo Branco.'

CHAPTER 46

Mark had thought he was getting near to the truth, yet Patti's revelation about Branco's interest in Jet had only succeeded in confusing him. He had worked on the assumption that the problems Barry and Patti had encountered in Colombia, and his own near encounter with death, had been entirely separate issues from the task that had been set for him by Mohammed Halid. Now he was not so sure. It was like a spider's web, the strands seemingly unconnected, yet all spun from the same central thread. He had to stand back and see the whole picture, and for that he needed time. He had got off the plane with a schedule in his mind, but perhaps it needed to be rethought.

'Are we still going to see Mo?' she asked.

He hesitated. Should he just drop in for a chat to tell him that he was off the case or should he tell him what they had discovered about his bitter rival? And if they told him what difference would it make? It certainly made Carr's capture of the ESL rights more sinister, more threatening, and if Carr had told his partner, Branco, that Mark was working for him then it made Mark's position even more dangerous. But why should Carr have reported the fact to Branco? Why should he even be aware that there was any connection between the Englishman and the drug baron? Even if Mark decided to end the subterfuge then he had already taken one hell of a risk and he had to decide whether Mo Halid had been worth taking it for. He just wished he wasn't feeling so tired, so in need of a transfusion of black coffee into his bloodstream.

He called ahead to make sure Halid was there but his secretary informed him that her boss was still at home.

'I'm sure he won't mind if you call him there, Mr Rossetti. I know he's been waiting to hear from you. Do you have the number?'

Mark did and immediately redialled. Mo answered.

263

'My friend, it's good to hear from you, and to know that you're back in one piece.'

Mark paused before replying. Should he read anything into that or was he becoming paranoid? He was beginning to doubt whether anybody was who they seemed to be, whether there was a single person in his life, apart from Patti and his daughter, that he could trust entirely.

'Mo, I was going to come into the office before I went home to bed. I gather you're not in.'

'As ever you are perceptive. I'll be at home all morning. Why don't you come here?'

'I'm in Patti's car on the motorway.'

'She too is welcome. Get her to turn around and I will have the oranges squeezed and the coffee ground by the time you get here.'

He was as good as his word, better in fact, because as well as the juice and coffee there were warm, crisp rolls, croissants and bagels.

'I didn't know you owned a bakery as well as a media empire,' Mark said, having made the introductions.

'If you don't help me get the ESL rights away from Carr then I might well be baking for a living,' Mo replied.

Mark was tempted to tell him there and then what Patti had discovered about the ownership of Jet, but he could not yet see exactly how it was going to help. So the company was half-owned by a crook. So what? Probably half the companies trading on the stock market had villains for shareholders. He had to see how the information he'd gleaned from Dr Guerra fitted in to the picture, if indeed there was a picture at all.

Susie came in, with the baby on her hip, looking fresh and vibrant despite the disturbed night she began to relate to them in detail.

'Can I hold him?' Patti asked and Jason gave a little cry of pleasure and snuggled into Patti's neck like a burrowing animal. Mo looked at his son and the woman gave Mark an affectionate hug.

'She looks good with a baby. Maybe you should try it for yourselves. They're always more fun when you don't have to give them back.'

The kitchen door opened and Dominique appeared. She

looked tired and drawn as if she, rather than her stepmother, had experienced the sleepless night. Mark did not need telling that this was Nabil's sister. There was the same sullen expression around the eyes, although he could see that this girl could be attractive if she tried. But she was clearly not trying. She looked defeated, a wild animal who had been broken, and Mark wondered what had happened to control her spirits. She gave Mark a desultory nod and poured herself a coffee. Patti reluctantly handed Jason back to his mother and turned her journalistic eye on the interrelationship between the three members of the Halid family. Her nose told her there was some secret they shared, even if they did not share it willingly.

'Mark, come into my study, let's leave the women to talk about women's things.'

Mark made no eye contact with Patti, which was fortunate as she might well have killed him with her expression, and she was left to stare daggers at his back and wonder exactly what it was that Mark was up to. She had been oddly euphoric at her discovery, momentarily convinced that her troubles were over just because she had found that the man who had caused them was an anonymous investor in an English company. Mark's cool reaction had disappointed and disillusioned her. Nothing had really changed. She was still out on bail on criminal charges, even if it was her choice as to whether or not she needed to return to face them. She knew Mark, though, knew him well enough to realise that he was not telling her everything. That hurt her as much as her recollections of past affairs had hurt Mark. Patti wondered if he were simply punishing her for her dishonesty about her reasons for going to Bogota in the first place. As if she hadn't been punished enough.

Susie made her excuses and left to change Jason, with Patti declining the offer to watch. It was one thing to cuddle a baby, quite another to look inside a dirty nappy. She just hoped that Mark had a stronger stomach and then found herself surprised that the thought had even passed through her mind.

Dominique, who until then had hardly acknowledged Patti's existence, now sat down at the table opposite her and stared into her coffee cup as if seeking the meaning of life amongst its dark contents.

'How long have you known your fellow?' the girl asked.

'Known him or known of him?' Patti replied, hoping the conversation could be drawn out, could be made to lead somewhere so that she could satisfy her curiosity.

'Is there a difference?'

'Sure. I knew he'd been a bit of a footballer in his day, but I met him for the first time when I tried to interview him a couple of years ago and I suppose we've been together ever since.'

'Are you going to marry him?' Dominique's face seemed to have become more animated, leaving Patti in no doubt that the exchange really interested her.

'You know I really think I may,' she said. 'But for heaven's sake don't tell him.'

Halid's daughter laughed and momentarily she was any young girl pleased at having the chance to talk to an older woman who might actually come close to understanding her.

'Do you think it's hard to be hitched to someone famous?' Dominique said, continuing with her inquiries as if she, rather than Patti, were the journalist.

'Oh, I don't think Mark's famous any more. I think your father's better known than he is.'

A shadow crossed the girl's face at the mention of her father.

'Nobody really knows my father.'

'You sound as if you don't like him,' Patti said in an understanding voice.

'I don't.'

'But do you love him?'

Dominique shrugged.

'I'm not sure. Sometimes he acts like the Islamic fundamentalist he isn't. He uses his money as power. I've left home before and he banks on my always coming back.'

'Sounds as if it never quite worked out when you left,' Patti said perceptively.

'No, it didn't. Look, Patti, I read a bit about your problems in the papers. We've got a lot in common. I'm also out on bail. Drug bust,' she added quickly to answer the question before it was asked.

'I'm sure your father's being supportive.'

'Yeah, so supportive that he couldn't even be bothered to come down to the station himself to get me out. He sent my brother who inevitably made a fuck-up out of it.'

'You don't like your brother either?'

'He's not easy to like. Ask Mark, he's had to work with him for a while. If he's as bad to work with as he is to live with then I pity your bloke.'

Patti's 'bloke' was finding it hard going with Mo. It had all seemed so easy on the plane. Go into Mo's office, close the door, tell him you'd understand if he decides that he doesn't even want you as a commentator at Ball Park, but that you want out from Jet. And then also ask him about certain phone calls that had been made to his home from Bogota. That was what Barry Reed's phone bill had revealed, a whole string of calls to Mo, a man he had no reason to know, let alone speak with. Then had come Patti's news. But far worse was Mo's enthusiasm for what little he had so far achieved.

'You're getting close. All you have to do is find out who told him what we were going to bid so that he could offer just enough, so he could beat us without it costing too much.'

Mark opened his mouth, but before he could launch into his speech there was an insistent ring at the door, as if someone were leaning on the bell. Mo looked puzzled, but there was no respite from the insistent noise.

'Excuse me, Susie is upstairs with the baby, and obviously my daughter and your lady are getting on like a house on fire.'

He rose and went to the door and Mark could see that he had aged in the few months he had known him. He shuffled across the room, his feet hardly leaving the ground, into the hall and before he opened the door grumbled aloud, 'All right, all right, I heard you. What's so important?'

Then he pulled the door fully open, and anything else he had to say was cut off by a cry of horror as the bruised and blood-stained body of his son fell into his arms.

CHAPTER 47

It was over two hours before Mark and Patti were back in her car, this time heading for the Hertsmere training ground. An ambulance had taken Nabil to the nearest hospital, accompanied by his father, who had sat cradling the boy until the medical team arrived to take over. Dominique had wanted to go with them, and it was hard to believe that a family divided could be so firmly bonded together by the vicious assault upon one of them. It was Susie and Jason who were now the outsiders, even more than Mark and Patti.

The visitors had stayed with Dominique until her father phoned from the hospital to say that Nabil would pull through, but either couldn't or wouldn't identify his assailants. Patti tried to resume her conversation with the troubled girl where it had been interrupted by the arrival of her brother in such a horrific state, but Dominique, not surprisingly, was distraught and distracted. Just as Patti made to leave in Mark's wake, Dominique had pulled herself together and asked if she could speak to her again some time. Patti had not hesitated to give her the phone number at the Burrow and Dominique had carefully written it down in a battered diary.

'She's not a bad kid,' Patti said to Mark as they stopped and started their way around the M25 on their way to Hertsmere.

'Seems a typically spoiled brat to me,' Mark commented, his mood beginning to be affected by the tiredness.

'Look who's talking. The man who'd never give his daughter anything . . . I don't think.'

'Just drive,' he replied and closed his eyes, still trying to get his thoughts in order, but failing desperately as he drifted in and out of sleep.

They'd phoned ahead to Hertsmere and the girl on the phone had put them through to Helen Davies without being asked.

'Mark, Rob thought you might contact us. He's left any

number of messages on your answerphone at home. He heard about the plane crash in Brazil and he's worried you might be wanting to run the show on your own.'

'Me? When did I ever do that?'

'Whenever you have the chance? He says there are enough corpses lying around the world without you adding to their number. Please call him, if only to get him off my back. He seems to think I've some permanent way of getting through to you. I told him I had more chance of a direct line to the Almighty . . .'

'Don't tell me, Helen,' Mark said wearily, 'he's a cop and he doesn't trust anybody, including his wife. I'll get in touch with him, but just do me a favour, don't tell him I'm heading for the training ground. I've got an agenda for the day, I'll put your husband on it, but I have to do things in my order. If he asks, say I told you to tell him to trust me.'

There was a muffled laugh down the line.

'Yeah, sure, that'll do it all right. When you've finished with whatever you think you need to do down at the training ground, pop in and see us. It sounds like you've got a busy day, but I'm sure David would love to see you. From the tone of your voice, it might well be his last chance.'

There was a note of genuine concern and affection in her voice and Mark felt almost guilty at the knowledge that he was going to ignore her pleas, ignore her husband's advice and pursue his lonely furrow wherever it might take him.

Whenever Mark watched footballers in action, whether it was on the field or in training, he felt a terrible sense of loss. Of course, he could strip off, pull on a pair of trainers, shorts, a shirt sufficiently loose to hide the hint of a paunch; but once out there he knew there would be no first touch, no pace. He would be yet another volunteer for the sad regiment of yesterday's heroes.

He knew every one of the Hertsmere team out there, going through their paces, knew their strengths and knew their weaknesses. If they all played up to their potential, they had a real chance of grabbing the title, but football was all about ifs and maybes. If the referee had given a penalty, if he'd not given a penalty, if the ball had bounced down over the line after hitting the crossbar, if the keeper hadn't fumbled, if the striker hadn't spent the previous night out on the tiles. He'd sat a hundred times after matches in a hundred different dressing rooms and the talk was always of these possibilities that had failed to become facts.

David Sinclair and Ray Fowler had realised that what they needed was a big man up front, someone to replace Nicky Collier. The former Hertsmere front man had not been particularly popular with his teammates and had taken a long time to win over the fans. But he got goals and anybody who could score a guaranteed twenty a season was an automatic selection, whatever the defects in his personality. That was why Sinclair had asked Mark to get him Ferrera. He felt confident that the tall Colombian could feed off the talents of Tommy Wallace, Dimitri Murganev and the emerging talents of the teenaged South African, Mbute.

Ferrera was demonstrating his skills as Mark and Patti walked from the car park towards the first team training pitch. He was firing the ball in to Greg Sergovich, the Slav goalie who had been in the country long before the other foreign imports and who now spoke English with such a Cockney accent that only his name served as a reminder that he had not been born within the sound of Bow Bells. Time after time the Colombian beat the Slav, hitting the ball cleanly into the corner of the net, his precision shooting just escaping the keeper's outstretched hands. There was a mechanical quality about the shooting, one ball in, another rolled to him by an apprentice, cracked in, another ball rolled. Then, just for a second, Ferrera's eyes lifted and he caught a glimpse of Mark, standing some fifty yards away. He froze completely, his foot drawn back for the shot, looking for all the world like a victim at Pompeii, covered in ash for ever. Finally he completed the shot and Sergovich dived to his left and caught the ball in triumph.

'That's fifty quid you owe me, Nito,' Greg called out, reminding him of the bet they had made that the goalkeeper would not make one save out of the first twenty efforts driven at him. But Ferrera wasn't listening, Ferrera was staring at Mark as if he had seen a ghost and in that moment Mark knew that was exactly what Ferrera had expected him to be. And if that were the case then he must also know who it was who had tried to kill him.

Ferrera had collected himself together and, ignoring Greg's taunts, ignoring the fresh ball that was rolled to where he should have been, he walked towards Mark with the air of a gunfighter about to shoot down the new sheriff in town. Patti squeezed Mark's hand.

'Are you going to tell me what's going on?' she asked as he kept his eyes on the approaching figure.

'I'm not sure I need to tell you. I think you're about to find out for yourself,' he said calmly. It was not often a man came face to face with somebody who he felt had been involved in an attempt to kill him. Ferrera was within a few feet of him now. He could not possibly be armed, yet such was the menacing expression on his face that Mark's hand automatically went to his pocket in a vain hope that he might find something with which to defend himself.

Ferrera stood perfectly still, bunching his fists as if trying to decide whether to hit the Englishman or walk away. In fact he did neither, merely adopting the scornful tone of a man who had knowledge that others did not.

'So, Mark Rossetti has more than one life. But perhaps he has only two lives and we will make no mistake next time.'

It was said with such a heavy accent, that Patti could only see the absurdity of the threat not its danger.

'Let me go and call Rob Davies,' Patti urged, still not fully understanding what was happening, but starting to realise that it was something serious. Mark shook his head.

'I can handle this, don't worry.'

Patti still began to move towards the car and her phone, but Ferrera grabbed her arm.

'Listen to your man,' he said, his grip tightening painfully on the muscle between the forearm and the upper limb. In the distance Ray Fowler's voice rose and fell as, totally oblivious to the little drama being played out behind him, he cracked the whip on the rest of his squad.

'Tell me about it Juanito, just you and me. Let her go. Don't worry. She won't call anybody. And, even if she did, you've not committed any crime here.'

He had no idea of the extradition arrangements between Britain and Colombia, but he just hoped that they would not be uppermost in Ferrera's mind. There was an arrogance about the man which he had thought would serve him well as a footballer. Now he believed that could be turned to equally good use as a

way of extracting information. The player released his grip on
Patti's arm, and although she was in pain she was not prepared
to give him the satisfaction of rubbing it. She turned to Mark.

'Are you sure you'll be all right?'

'I'm sure. There's not a lot he can do in full sight of the
Hertsmere first team.'

She looked back only once, to satisfy herself that the two men
were merely talking, and then obediently made her way back to
the car.

CHAPTER 48

Mark Rossetti was on the move again, this time on his own. He had listened to Ferrera for almost half an hour, listened to his story, his boasting, his conviction that he was above the law in England. The thing was that he was probably right. He could hardly believe that even Rob Davies could piece together a case based solely upon one look of knowledge and a confession made to just one other man, a confession made more out of conceit than guilt.

His time with Ferrera had not been within his schedule, but now he was back on track with more questions than answers, with other stops on his journey to uncover the whole truth. The tentacles of the story were clawing at other players in the game, other players in his own life. He was beginning to believe that he had been looking in the wrong places, at the wrong people, that he should have been looking inward at himself as an unknowing catalyst for everything.

He was not able to leave things tidily behind him. Ferrera had told him he was leaving the country, that he would simply tell Fowler that he could not settle here and he was missing his home and family. He did not care if he could not play. Eventually somebody might buy him and get Hertsmere some of their money back.

'It is not too bad for them. They have only paid half of the money. If I want to I have enough money to buy my contract myself. I am a rich man at home, I am a powerful man.'

'I thought Branco was the power man in Bogota.'

Ferrera spat at the mention of the name.

'Branco. It is always Branco. I am not scared of him. Now Escobar, he was a man to fear and admire.'

'But Escobar's dead,' Mark said, pushing the conversation along, scared that at any moment the man might clam up on him.

273

'And one day Branco may be dead, perhaps sooner than he thinks. Escobar's only enemies were the politicians and those policemen who did not understand how good he was for our country. Branco wins his friends with the power of the gun, but he cannot win respect that way.'

'I take it you don't like Riccardo Branco.'

Ferrera sat down on his haunches and then sprawled his long frame out on the grass. To the casual observer he was just resting from his morning's exhaustions, chatting to an old friend before he recovered his breath and returned to the fray.

'I despise Branco. He thinks he command me, but I command respect. He claims to be the owner of the club I played for, and so he claims to own me, but he is wrong.'

'So it was Branco who negotiated the terms for your sale.'

'He did what I told him to do,' Ferrera said both boastfully and implausibly.

'But why should you want to come to England? I don't understand.'

Ferrera smiled and even as he did so it clicked into place in Mark's mind. Patti had told him in the car that Branco had owned half of Jet. Ferrera might not like Branco but that did not necessarily mean that the drug baron did not think the footballer competent. If he needed somebody to keep an eye on his business interests in England, then by shifting Ferrera across the water he could kill two birds with one stone. But what were Branco's interests in England and did they start and end with Jet? He doubted it. It was all becoming so much clearer. Patti had inadvertently started it all with her quest on behalf of her old schoolfriend. Christ knew how she had even heard the name of Branco. Some kind of Chinese whisper had brought it spiralling down from the higher echelons of the organisation to a pathetic user. So Patti had asked the questions. The mistake they made was in trying to ascertain which question it was that had so shaken Branco's complacency that he had begun a personal campaign to discredit Patti.

There had been no single question. The interest of an English journalist had been enough. After that he had to find out whether or not his English organisation was in any danger. So Patti had had to be taken out of the game and he'd done that neatly enough by not only discrediting her, but by thinking he had made sure she wouldn't return to Bogota. And then, he, Mark had come back blundering into the dark and threatening to knock over something of value as he stumbled about. In a way he had represented a greater threat than Patti, not merely because he was a man but presumably they knew he was not without connections. So they'd decided he must die, but the only thing was that over fifty innocent people had to die with him to make it look like an unfortunate accident, so that nobody would come probing into the incident. If there was proved to be sabotage of the plane nobody would think that the gringo aboard was the intended victim. There had to be a Colombian or Brazilian on board who was a possible target.

Ferrera seemed to be almost asleep, his eyes half closed, an irritating smile playing around his mouth, as he had clearly convinced himself that Mark accepted his inviolability. There had to be something Mark could do. He would call Luis, tell him everything, tell him to get Salazar involved, a man who would fight for all that was good in the rotten and corrupt city of Bogota.

Maybe Patti was right, maybe they should simply pass over what they knew to Rob Davies and leave him to deal with his Colombian opposite number to try and bring the guilty men to justice. Yet he could hardly conceive that anything he had been told would really tilt the balance over there on to the side of the angels. The poisoned water ran too deep to be cleansed by what Mark knew.

As if Ferrera were reading his mind, he spoke again, relaxed and defiant, his head resting back on his arms, a man at peace with himself in the autumn sunshine.

'Yes, I shall go home, and you, Mark, will do nothing, because I believe you are a man who is too haunted by the ghosts of his own past to be able to control his future. I have done nothing wrong here and if you do pluck up courage to try and do anything then take Nabil Halid as a warning. He was lucky. Perhaps you have exhausted your luck.'

That was what had thrown Mark off balance. Until then he could not see any connection between what was happening within the Halid family and the death and destruction that was coming from Colombia. As he drove he could not see it now either.

He had not returned to Patti's car, but instead had slipped round to the small office in what was little more than a hut at the training ground. If Sinclair completed his construction of the new stadium, as now seemed inevitable, then there would be a culture shock for the players as they moved into their luxurious new surroundings adjacent to the stadium and commercial complex. He'd called a cab to get him back to Hampstead where he'd left his own car outside the Burrow and written a brief note of apology which he'd left on Patti's table. She'd been exposed to enough risk and he felt confident that, despite the lack of sleep, he could finish this whole thing off on his own. She'd want to kill him for not being there at the death, and all he could hope for was that the most expensive bouquet of flowers in the world would eventually calm her down. He permitted himself a wry smile at the choice of words in his mind. At the death. There had been enough deaths. What he was doing he hoped would ensure there were no more.

He could feel the adrenaline coursing through his body as he headed out to his next destination. Broxbourne lay to the north of London, beyond the M25, sufficiently far up the A10 to be considered country by those who could afford to buy the expensive houses which littered the town and its surrounding areas. It had become a popular place for footballers to live. At one time half the Tottenham squad had snapped up anything going in the neighbourhood and now to live next door to a famous player, ex-player or indeed, manager or ex-manager was no longer a novelty.

He found the house he was looking for without difficulty, parked a little way down the road from its main entrance and sat and waited for some sign of life. He was getting accustomed to waiting outside houses. He had switched his recharged mobile off before he started out on his journey, but now he brought it back to life with a press of a button just to check for messages. There were four. First of all Rob Davies.

'Rossetti, if you don't call me I'm going to issue a warrant for your arrest so help me. And if you think I don't have any charges well, how about impeding police inquiries, withholding information? And if I feel particularly malevolent I'll throw in aiding and abetting for good measure.' Davies's welsh accent became more pronounced whenever he got excited and he was excited now, excited and angry. Mark decided it might be a good idea to let him cool down before he made any contact. From the tone of Patti's voice it would be an even better idea to let her temper abate.

'You bastard. I'm sitting here like an idiot still watching a bunch of footballers kick their balls about. And that's exactly what I intend to do to you when I see you. If I ever want to see you again. And, by the way, I don't know what you said to Ferrera, but he had a blazing row with Ray Fowler and then took off like a bat out of hell. There's the usual gaggle of sports journos down here and they couldn't have failed to notice.'

The second message was even more succinct.

'I'm at the Burrow. I'm in the process of utilising the clothes you've left here to polish the flat. If you want to treat me like the little woman then I don't see why I can't be domestic and use the first thing that comes to hand. And as you're not here to wipe the floor with, then I'm using anything of yours I can lay my hands on. If I lose out on this story then I'll create a better one. Journalist kills ex-footballer. Call me.'

Then, finally, the familiar tones of Luis,

'Mark, my friend I think you are avoiding me, I have to talk to you. I am so glad that you got back to England safely. I have important news.'

He began to flip through his filofax for Luis' number. Patti would have to stay mad with him. If he called she'd get him to tell her where he was, what he intended to do and then she'd be in hot pursuit. The same applied to Rob Davies. But if he delivered to him what he thought he could then Rob might feel slightly better.

He looked into his mirror to see if there were any movement in the house, but it was as still and silent as when he had first arrived. The property itself was a detached house built in the popular mock-Tudor style of the thirties. He counted the windows and worked out there had to be at least five bedrooms and that was only at the front. He wondered how much it cost to buy a property like that and how much more it cost to maintain it. He knew the man who owned it had made money, but had he made that much money? Ever since Dr Guerra had told him what had occurred after the international match in Bogota he had been wondering how much it had been worth. If the information he had was right, then this house and its maintenance costs gave him a good idea.

He found Luis' number and began to dial. He had just got to the last digit when he hesitated. Incredibly enough for someone who had flown through the night, who had been through the sort of traumas he had experienced, he was thinking more clearly than at any time in the last seventy-two hours. When he had called Luis to tell him he was not coming back that night, but staying over in Rio, he had intended to leave him a message of apology. Luis should have been at the airport to meet him. That was what he said he was going to do. And if he wasn't there then he must have known he wasn't going to arrive, and the only way he could have known that was if somebody had told him that the plane was going to crash. Looking back, Luis had been too good to be true, a man who had become his best friend in a matter of hours, a man who knew everybody in Bogota, who could open locked doors. A man who could arrange flights, a man who travelled around South America, who had said he had just returned from Brazil. Who had actually sent Mark to Brazil? What had been the purpose of that? Was that just to ensure that the doctor toed the line, that at any time they could betray him because quite simply he had taken the thirty pieces of silver and was in their power. Or was the intention all along to send him to his death? He remembered how easily Luis had found Patti in Bogota, her rescue. Had that too be stage-managed to gain their confidence? Quite clearly the doctor had been a worry to them. He wasn't a natural criminal as he'd demonstrated when Mark had touched his conscience with news of the deaths in the crash. Who could tell what forces had made him do what he had done? In a way Mark hoped he had fled far beyond the reaches of Branco and his mob, if indeed there was such a place. He was one of the more decent individuals Mark had met in this whole mess.

He felt certain he was right, but he needed to make one more call to be sure. Again he turned to his list of numbers. Indeed he had the business card of the man he was about to call. The phone was answered in Spanish but he knew the receptionist could speak English.

'May I speak with Señor Salazar?' he asked.

'He is busy in a meeting. He cannot be disturbed. Who shall I say has called?'

'Please tell him I am calling on behalf of Riccardo Branco

and that it is important,' Mark said.

The tone of the girl's voice changed.

'Of course, I will see if he will speak with you.'

There was a pause, just enough time for the message to be relayed and then he heard Salazar's voice at the other end of the line and the greeting, the receptionist's familiarity with the Branco name, told him all he needed to know. He cut off and thumped his fist down on the dashboard of the car so hard that the stationary vehicle actually rocked from side to side. Once again he'd been taken for a ride by somebody he had trusted. Only this would be different from the last time, this time he knew enough to be satisfied that not only was he in the driving seat, but there would be no crashes on the way. He didn't really care if Ferrera fled the country, apart from the loss to Hertsmere. But then if it all worked out according to plan he'd get Barry Reed back in their side before too long and that would certainly soften the blow. He was realistic enough to realise that there was little he could do about Branco from this side of the Atlantic. All he could hope for was that Rob could find an honest cop sufficiently high up the ladder in Bogota who'd be prepared to take on the forces of darkness.

There were still some things he did not understand. Why had Nabil Halid been beaten up? Why had Jenny Cooper telephoned him just before she was killed? He looked at his watch. It was early afternoon, but it felt as if he had been up the whole of the day. If he continued on this roll then maybe all the answers lay within the house. He pondered long and hard and then decided to make one more call. There was no point in alienating the whole world.

As he glanced again in the rear mirror, he suddenly saw the car in the drive start up. The owner must have come out of the front door whilst he had been distracted with the phone. He raced out of his own car, leaving the door swinging wide open and got to the gate just as it opened to allow out the vehicle and the driver. The man in the car looked up and immediately recognised Mark. He had a choice. Either he could accelerate and leave Mark dead or dying, or he could stop and see what he wanted. For a moment Mark thought he was a goner, that the choice would be the former. But the car stopped just in time and Mark guessed correctly that Juanito Ferrera had been too intent on getting himself out of the country to bother about calling ahead to Kenny Cunningham, the England manager, to warn him that there was the likelihood that he was about to be paid a visit by Mark Rossetti.

CHAPTER 49

If Cunningham had any idea of just how much Mark knew about him, he gave no indication.

'Hey, Mark, what's the hurry? If you wanted to see me, all you needed to do was ring.'

The usual Cunningham smile, the jack-the-lad grin that so entranced his television audiences. The expression that said, I'm one of you, I'm public property, so love me for that.

'Can we talk?' Mark asked.

'Sure. Why don't you call my secretary down at the FA? Tell her I told you to ring and give you the first open slot in my diary.' He had turned off the engine, but now he started it up again to signal the conversation was at an end as far as he was concerned.

'No, Kenny, we need to talk now.' Mark was in front of the car again. He had to take a gamble, to make certain that Cunningham was sufficiently intrigued to turn back to the house and invite him in, yet not so spooked as to try to make a run for it.

'What's it about that's so urgent?'

'Barry Reed.'

'Look, Mark, I've had enough of that loser and you shouldn't be bothering with him either. He's bad news.'

'I've got some new evidence that shows he's innocent. Surely you, as the England manager, would want to know about that? You thought he was good enough to play for his country and you must want him to play again.'

For a fleeting moment the mask dropped, the eyes that were normally crinkled with humour were lost within shadowy hoods. The face became calculating, assessing the risk of leaving against the advantage of staying and discovering just exactly how much Mark actually knew. Then he was smiling again, reversing his car and giving Mark a welcoming gesture to follow him into the house.

'Not got a lot of food in,' he said, 'the wife's away in Spain with the kids at our villa.'

'How long's she been away for?' Mark asked.

'About a month. She's got this thing about November. Gets her depressed to think that the winter's with us.'

He threw open the door to the kitchen and allowed Mark to enter ahead of him.

'I can run to coffee. Don't worry, I'm not about to offer you a drink.' Again the lop-sided grin to show that there was no malice in the comment.

'Coffee will be fine,' Mark said, sitting himself at the table without waiting for an invitation.

'That's right, make yourself at home. I'll put the kettle on and be back in a minute. I've just got to make a couple of calls to say I'll be late.'

He went out of the room and Mark took in the surroundings. He could recognise an expensive kitchen when he saw one. He'd been with Patti when she pored over Smallbone brochures, before a considerable chunk of their resources had been tied up in the bail fund. Cunningham's kitchen appeared to have the same distinctive design. Given that it was about the size of the whole Burrow he could well imagine just how much had been spent upon it. All the utensils on display, the Aga, the fridge, the sinks, had evidently not come cheap either. His eye took in a phone on the wall and he wondered why his reluctant host had felt the need to call from the other room. He retraced his footsteps, just in case he needed to make a speedy exit, momentarily regretting his decision not to utilise Patti as some kind of back-up.

However, when Cunningham returned, the look of joviality was still on his face and he gave Mark no cause to panic, and he felt that this situation was well within his capabilities.

'Right. Here's the coffee. Sorry it's instant. I can't find the percolator. Maria's got a degree in hiding things.'

Maybe she wasn't the only one in the family, Mark thought.

'Well, cosy as this is, I haven't got all day. So what's this revelation about young Barry?'

Mark risked a glance at his watch. It had been some twenty minutes since he'd left his car. He'd wanted to drag this out as long as he could, but obviously Kenny wasn't in the mood for any idle chit-chat.

'Barry. You seemed very convinced of his guilt at the hearing.'

'Hardly surprising, is it? He tests positive under FIFA guide-lines. What am I supposed to do? Stand by him and have every do-gooder in the country accusing me of condoning drug-taking in sport? Quite frankly, Mark, I reckon he got off lightly. He could have had a life-ban. He's young enough to have another bite at the cherry.'

Mark tried very hard to control his temper, but couldn't keep the confrontational tone out of his voice.

'So that's all right then.'

Cunningham leaned across to touch Mark on the arm.

'Mark, I think you're taking all this too personally. I know, everybody in football knows, that you got a raw deal. But Barry had a fair hearing. You did your best for him. You've nothing to recriminate yourself about.'

'No, I don't think I have. But I think others have.'

'What are you getting at?' Cunningham leaned back in his chair in an effort to show he was relaxed, but he was not convincing.

'I think you know what I'm getting at. Ever heard of Doctor Guerra?'

Cunningham furrowed his brow.

'Can't say that I have. Some kind of specialist is he?'

'You could say that. He specialises in switching urine samples.'

'Really? Can't make a career out of that.'

'You'd be surprised,' Mark said. If he was going in for the kill then he had to bluff.

'Surprise me then,' Cunningham said, any pretence at friendliness and charm now abandoned.

'Well, Guerra says he knows you for starters. He says you're his benefactor. Although, given the amount in question, I'm not at all sure that you came up with his specialist's fee without a third party donation.'

Cunningham suddenly leapt to his feet and grabbed Mark by the throat, throwing him across the floor in one movement. Mark was taken by surprise both by his speed and strength. He tried to get up but Cunningham's right foot, clad in a heavy shoe, caught him in the ribs and another kick sent him reeling back, spitting blood. Cunningham leaned over and expertly searched him.

283

'I'm not armed,' Mark forced out each word painfully as he realised that at best his ribs were bruised, at worst they were broken.

'I don't give a fuck if you're armed or not. I just wanted to make sure you weren't wired.'

'You could have asked,' Mark said, struggling up into a sitting position.

'I just did. Now stay where you are and I think I can promise you no more pain. Or at least not a lot. I don't know why you wanted to get yourself involved. I never had anything against you. Reed's another young yobbo without a brain in his head. Take away his football and all you've got is a waster. He'd already knocked one bird up.'

Mark couldn't hide the puzzlement on his face.

'Oh you didn't know that, did you? And not just any bird either. Your boss's daughter, or should I say one of your bosses.' Again Cunningham saw that Mark was unprepared. 'You didn't know that either. That Nathan Carr at Jet knew all about Mo Halid's idea to get you into his camp. He thought it might be helpful so he gave you enough licence. Eventually he was going to feed you information that he knew would confuse Halid. I can't believe those two and their feud. Susie's not a bad looker, but she's not worth the grief that the pair of them cause each other.'

'How do you know about me and Jet?' Mark asked. The glass on his watch had been smashed as he tried to protect himself from one of the savage kicks, but he could see it was nearly a quarter to three.

'For somebody who used to be an investigator you don't know a lot do you? It was Branco's idea to swop the samples. We had to move quickly once it was clear they were going to test Ferrera. The stupid cunt had got himself high the night before the match, sampling the product. He calls Branco on his mobile, Branco gets a message to me and I'm down into that room like a shot. I get hold of Guerra or whatever his name is. Offer him a king's ransom. He says no. So I don't mess around. I tell him he either takes the money and does what we want or we do something to his hands and that puts an end to his medical career. And suddenly he's very helpful. After that it was easy. Guerra spoke the language, the FIFA doctor didn't. The guy didn't realise what was going on. Reed tests positive, Ferrera doesn't. It was always the idea to get Juanito into England. He was a real pain in the ass, Branco told Carr. He wanted him somewhere he wouldn't be too much trouble. All I had to do was recommend him to Sinclair at Hertsmere and away we went. I have to admit I didn't think he'd get you involved in the transfer, but even that wouldn't have made any difference if you hadn't started poking your nose in where it didn't belong. Branco's got a bit of a sense of humour. He thought it was very funny that you were dealing with him as the owner of Ferrera's club and didn't even realise it.'

'Yeah, I can see that would be the sort of thing that would amuse him,' Mark said, his tongue feeling that one of his teeth was loose, the taste of blood filling his mouth.

'So there you have it. Now all we have to do is decide what to do with you.'

'You could let me go. I walk away from here and it seems to me I can't prove a thing. It'd be your word against mine.'

Cunningham seemed to consider the suggestion for a moment, then shook his head, now smiling again.

'No, I don't think so. I'm afraid this is the end of the road for you, old son.'

'I thought you promised no more pain.'

'I did and I'm a man of my word. Everybody in football knows that. The end won't be painful. Our little chat has given me some time to think about it. I'm going to be humanitarian. Put you down painlessly. First a few drinks, and everybody knows about your drinking habits, and then, when you're nice and numb, a convenient car crash. Drunk at the wheel. Mark Rossetti fell off the wagon. RIP Mark Rossetti.'

He fumbled under the sink and produced a length of rope, then reached up to a cabinet and brought down two full bottles of Scotch.

'There you are, Mark, isn't that a beautiful sight? You'd have died for some prime malt whisky a few years ago and now you're actually going to. Life's funny, ain't it?'

Mark had only a few seconds to decide what to do. He could either made a dash for it or else launch himself at Cunningham with all the force he could muster. The door was only a few feet away, but in his weakened condition it seemed like miles as he took Cunningham completely by surprise by turning and running out of the room. Cunningham came after him in an almost leisurely manner and then leaned against a wall whilst Mark turned the handle of the front door which had been firmly locked from the inside.

CHAPTER 50

He couldn't believe that he'd ever actually liked alcohol. The first taste nearly choked him, but the way he was tied and trussed, with a funnel forced between his teeth, anything would have choked him. Cunningham had pulled him away from the door with remarkable ease and within minutes two willing helpmates had arrived. Mark could not believe how naive he had been to think that Cunningham was merely delaying his meetings on the telephone. Instead he had summoned Nathan Carr and with him had come Alissa Bland. There was no question now of them being misunderstood. Now he could see exactly why Mo had regarded them with such deadly hatred, and why he had warned him about Alissa.

As part of his continuing education Patti had taken him to see *King Lear* at the National Theatre. He had found the language difficult for a while, but then the power of the story had carried him along, just as it had captured generations before him. Regan and Goneril, the names had seemed odd to him at the time, but now he could hardly fail to remember them as Alissa seemed to combine their joint malevolence in one body.

'Can't you pour that liquor down him any faster?' she said. 'We still don't know if he told anybody he was coming here.'

'It's not that easy,' Cunningham said, 'he keeps trying to spit it out, and I can't risk him choking to death. I'm not at all sure that will convince anybody. The bruises and any broken bones could be explained away by the crash and I've been careful to tie the ropes over his clothes and not leave any marks on the skin.'

Alissa took a lipstick from her bag and applied some liberally whilst looking at herself appreciatively in a small hand mirror. She made a mouth, licked her lips and then glanced down at Mark.

'You really were a very silly man. You're going to die and it's all for Halid and Reed and neither of them are worth it. If it

287

makes it any worse for you I have to tell you that if you'd asked me to go to bed with you that night in Zurich I would have. I really quite fancied you.'

Mark was trying to cling on to his sobriety, but it wasn't easy. She was already out of focus as were the two men, but he could still see, indeed see in duplicate, the annoyance on Nathan Carr's face as she spoke. There had obviously once been something between them and it could well be that Mark's assessment, that it had been Carr who had ended it, was wrong.

He tried to speak, to have the last word and tell her that he'd simply not fancied her, but all he succeeded in doing was allowing more of the whisky to go down his throat. She laughed, and kissed Carr on the cheek.

'Don't be jealous, Nathan, it would have been a one night stand. You've always liked me to be experimental.'

Cunningham held up one of the bottles which was now three-quarters empty.

'I'm not sure how much of this has gone down him, but I reckon it's enough. Can you help me carry him out? I thought one of you could drive his car and I'll stick him in the boot of mine. If he's sick, he's sick, but at least we won't have a post-mortem wondering how he managed to vomit into the boot of his own car.'

'Sounds good to me,' Alissa said, 'as long as I don't have to start heaving him around. I had my nails done yesterday. But can we please get on with it? It was an awful drive out here, particularly with Nathan fuddy-duddying around and telling me to keep within the speed limits. Honestly you'd think he was some kind of honest law-abiding citizen.'

It was all coming to Mark from a distance, sounds travelling down the thin end of the tube, voices merging into one. He wanted to sleep, he wanted to be sick, he wanted it to be over and that was the worst because it meant he was giving up. He felt himself lifted, Carr taking his legs, Cunningham his head, Alissa merely opening doors. The fresh air hit him like a slap in the face, and he realised that the few steps between the front door and the boot of Alissa's Mercedes could be the last few moments of daylight he would ever see. He kicked out as hard as he could and, more in surprise than pain, Carr released his hold and allowed his feet and the lower end of his body to hit the ground. Cunningham swore and let his head fall as well, but Mark was so numbed by the whisky that he felt no pain at all.

The two men stood up and straightened their backs, ready to continue their task. Alissa was unlocking the boot and carefully removing anything that she wanted to avoid being stained. It was then that the first shot was fired, above their heads, but the voice over the loudspeaker left them in no doubt that the next shot would be far lower and far more accurate.

Even as his head lay on the gravel path, Mark recognised the Welsh tones as those of Inspector Rob Davies. It had all seemed so long ago that he had made that last call to him and he thanked his instinct that had suggested to him that he had come far enough on his own. There were no heroics from Carr or Cunningham. The police marksmen standing just outside in the private road suggested they would be foolish. But Alissa wasn't done yet. She turned on Carr and slapped his face, raising red, angry weals.

'You bastard.' She turned towards Davies. 'Thank goodness you've arrived. You can't believe what I've been through. This animal dragged me out here, threatened my life, tried to involve me in the murder of this poor man . . .'

Carr was having none of it.

'Don't believe a word the bitch says. The only reason Jet got involved with Branco was because you allowed him to pick you up in that hotel in Cannes. After he'd fucked you he obviously thought our business had more to offer than anything you had between your legs.'

She made to hit him again, but someone caught her hand in mid-air.

'I just hate to see a man being hit by a woman,' Patti said, and pushed Alissa towards the arms of a waiting policeman. The three of them were bundled into the back of a police van as Patti knelt by Mark's side.

'I thought it was about time I reciprocated in this life-saving business. I had a deal with Rob. We agreed that whichever of us you called first would tell the other and join forces in the rescue.'

'How did you know there'd be a rescue?' Mark asked, his head muzzy and hurtling, his voice slurred.

'Just call me Mystic Meg. Come on, Mark. The days of the Lone Ranger are far behind. Everybody needs their Tonto.'

'I think I'll settle for Pocohontas,' he said, stumbling over the last word with considerable difficulty, and then his head came forward and he was violently sick.

CHAPTER 51

Juanito Ferrera relaxed in the luxury of the first class compartment of the British Airways flight to Bogota. It was a long trip. They'd left London at 10.25 and weren't due to land until 16.40 local time. He was happy to be returning home. England was not a country in which he felt he could either live or play football. The pace of life was too slow and the pace of the football was too fast.

He had stayed the night at one of the airport hotels, had called both Branco and Salazar to tell them he was coming home and they had promised to arrange for Luis to meet him. He had thought of ordering a girl for his room, but he could wait until he was back in Colombia. He thought the girls back home were more attractive and they were certainly cheaper.

He had enjoyed the flight. His fellow passengers had recognised him and asked for his autograph. He always liked that, just as he liked the champagne and the more than passable meal. He'd watched a couple of movies, finding them implausible because the bad guys never won. Not that he regarded himself as a bad guy. He had come from the slums of Bogota, his mother had brought home men to make ends meet and his father had disappeared when he was only two. His mother had made him out to be a hero who had sacrificed himself in the cause of an uprising against the brutally oppressive government. It was only when he was ten that his older sister told him that he had run off with a younger woman from Zipaquira because his wife was refusing to sleep with him after having seven children.

He had had a talent for football almost as soon as he learned to walk. He also had an imagination that allowed him to steal with impunity from his schoolmates and the other street children, whilst always having a credible alibi or excuse. It was inevitable that he would be exposed to the drug culture and, although he enjoyed the occasional snort of cocaine (like that stupid night before the England match), he soon appreciated that there was more money to be made from supplying than using. That was how Riccardo Branco had come into his life. He had been sixteen, playing already for the national youth team, when Branco had invited him to join the club he was about to buy and had promised him more money than he could have imagined in his wildest dreams. But as with everything in Branco's existence there was a hook. The sports market was a fertile field for drugs and Ferrera was required to report back to Branco as to where there was a need for distribution, although he was never asked to sell himself. He was too valuable for that. He gradually came to recognise his own value and to place a price upon it that was higher than considered by Branco.

It was then that Branco had thought it might be a good thing for him to go to England to oversee the operation there which was growing by leaps and bounds. He'd taken him into his confidence and that was fine, but there was the constant feeling in Ferrera's mind that he would always be the boy when he should be regarded as the man. Branco had told him how he had provided the funding for Jet to acquire the rights for the new European Super League, how he could use Jet to legitimise his illegal profits, a very sophisticated way of money-laundering. Well, he wouldn't be playing in the ESL now and quite frankly he found it hard to envisage how a little club like Hertsmere could hope to be England's first entrant into the competition. He was a big player and he deserved a big club. Maybe he'd play a little longer in Colombia and then move on to Italy. Branco had connections there as well. And he would like to develop his own contacts. Branco might think he was just a footballer with an above average brain for his profession but he had greater ambitions. He had made money, a considerable amount, but his wealth did not compare with the enormous fortune of Riccardo Branco. But he wanted it to.

The stewardesses made sure everything was in place for landing and removed the last glass of dry French wine from his side. It was good that Luis was coming to meet him. Luis had been a hero in his day, but it would make him realise that his day was past and now this was a young man's game and a young man's world. The plane lowered its undercarriage, the pilot made a near perfect landing and he felt the engines roar into reverse thrust.

He liked the idea of the other passengers being held back to allow the first class travellers off first, just as he liked the concept of his baggage coming first off the carousel with its first class labels attached. He saw no reason why everything in his life should not be first class from now on. He was a star and rising in the firmament.

He was whisked through immigration, his bags came obediently off the carousel and he had no trouble with customs. It was a perfect journey which ended with the sight of Luis waiting for him just as he exited through the swing doors of the air-side part of the building. He pushed his trolley over to him, they embraced out of ritual rather than affection and began to move towards the car park.

It was then that Colonel Enrico Rodriguez, accompanied by four armed policemen, approached them and arrested them both on charges of drug dealing and murder. This was Colombia, and he was going to make these charges stick – whether he had sufficient evidence or not. Luis took his mobile phone from his pocket and called Salazar's number. The telephone rang and rang in an empty office, as once again, the lawyer sat with his client Riccardo Branco on the terrace overlooking the Jaguna de Guativita, taking instruction as to how the empire was to be rebuilt.

CHAPTER 52

The name of Enrico Rodriguez had been the only one that Mark could remember to give to Rob Davies to contact in Colombia. He thought he might just be an honest man and he was right. After the introduction, Davies, as ever, had done his work well.

'He told me through an interpreter that they didn't think they'd get to Branco this time around but that Ferrera and your friend Luis would be a start. He reckoned that Branco would be prepared to sacrifice them both to keep the police and the government off his back over the airplane incident. Oh, and by the way, he also told me that they were dropping the cases against both Barry and Patti. They know your lawyer friend Salazar for what he really is.'

'Wouldn't Branco be worried that either Ferrera or Luis might try to implicate him?' Mark asked.

'I'll assume you're still under the influence if you have to ask that sort of question. Would you try to give evidence against someone like Branco? I reckon you'd have your throat cut before you got to confirm your name and address.'

'Thank goodness for English justice,' Mark said, sitting up in his hospital bed and taking notice.

'Yes, it's almost as good as Celtic justice. Which reminds me about the book I ought to be throwing at you. I can't believe you, Mark. You never seem to learn.'

'He doesn't, does he?' Patti interrupted as she picked up the bunch of grapes she'd bought him because, as she'd made quite clear, that was what you were supposed to do for sick people and anyway she rather liked grapes.

'Let's call it even all round, shall we?' Mark said. 'I brought your real villains to justice, Patti's and Barry's names are clear and I've got a headache. Now how long do I have to stay in here?'

Patti put another couple of grapes in her mouth and spat out the pips with a distasteful expression.

'The shop claimed they were seedless. Just goes to show that you can't trust anybody. The doctor says you've got mild concussion, one cracked rib, you need some dental treatment and you're also suffering from what he called, for want of a better medical term, the mother and father of all hangovers. Apart from that and an urgent need to revisit AA he says you can leave tomorrow morning. There's only one condition.'

'Which is?' Mark asked suspiciously.

'That you come back to the Burrow, that I look after you and that you don't go anywhere without telling me first.'

'Seems fair to me,' Mark replied.

'I like you in this condition,' Patti said, 'you seem agreeable to everything. You're the witness, Rob.'

Mark groaned as the painkillers began to ease off and a wave of nausea passed through his bruised and aching body.

'I'm not sure that policemen always make honest witnesses.'

'You be careful, boyo, or I'll dig out that charge sheet from the wastepaper basket.'

'How's Nabil?' Mark asked, suddenly changing the subject.

'Much better,' Patti replied and a look passed between her and Rob, which Mark caught despite his condition.

'Are you telling me the truth?' he asked.

'Oh she is,' Rob said. He hesitated and then plunged on. 'Fuck it. Knowing you you'll find out anyway. Mo wanted to come to see you. For some reason he seems to blame himself for everything that's happened. Also we've tried to quiz Nabil about his assault, but he says he'll only talk to you.'

Mark brought his hand to his face and tapped at the loose tooth as if it might give him some inspiration.

'I don't understand that. I don't think he had a civil word to say to me when we were working together.'

Patti smiled and patted him gently on the head as an indulgent schoolteacher might treat a particularly slow child.

'It seems that we're flavour of the month with the Halid children. I've had Dominique on the phone asking if she can come and have tea with me.'

Mark tried to remember what Cunningham had told him about Dominique, but his head hurt too much to think. He winced and then it came to him, and he grimaced again.

'Before you came to the house yesterday, Cunningham said something to me that didn't quite sink in at the time. He said that Barry Reed was a no-good because he'd got Dominique into trouble. I didn't understand what he was talking about at the time and, quite frankly, I was trying to work out how long you'd take to get there after I called you. By the way, why didn't you get the local boys to come to the rescue?'

Rob sighed unsympathetically, 'We reckoned that you'd need a bit of time to get Cunningham to talk to you. You can't say that we were wrong, can you?'

'No, I suppose not,' Mark replied ruefully. 'So what do you want me to do about Nabil?'

Rob Davies did a mock doubletake.

'Is this Mark Rossetti, superhero, asking the police for advice? I do believe it is. All I want you to do is tell us what you're doing. Don't go off to save the world on your own again. You may not be so lucky next time around.'

Mark lay back on the pillows and watched the retreating back of the policeman, thinking he was indeed fortunate to have him as a friend.

His parting words had a familiar ring about them, although for the life of him he couldn't recall at that moment who'd said them to him last. But then he couldn't remember very much at all and, by the time Patti gently kissed him goodbye on the forehead, he was fast asleep.

He had to be awoken in the morning, and once he hit consciousness he regretted it. Every part of him hurt, even the bits that he had no reason to believe had been injured and the cheerfulness of the nurse who brought him his tea did nothing to improve the way he felt. Yet he was determined not to complain too much. He wanted out of the hospital and he wanted out as soon as possible.

'When can I leave?' he asked.

'After the doctor's examined you,' the nurse replied in a broad Irish accent. He was waiting for a piece of Irish humour or philosophy, but fortunately it wasn't forthcoming. It was bad enough being in love with a woman called Delaney.

As it was the doctor came round before ten o'clock, suggested he have another day or so in bed, but pronounced him fit enough to travel to the bed in question. He called Patti as soon as he heard the news.

'My parole's been confirmed. When can you get here?'

'I just have to get rid of the last bloke, prepare his bill, change the bedlinen, etcetera.'

'I'm flattered,' Mark said, a smile on his face even though he knew it was going to be hell to laugh with the broken rib.

'What about? The competition?' she asked.

'No, that you're going to bother to change the bed.'

She promised to be with him within the hour and she was as good as her word, even bringing with her a welcoming change of clothing. He got out of the bed and wished he hadn't and didn't argue when she began to help him get dressed. The socks, trainers and jeans weren't too bad, but the T-shirt and sweatshirt were agony.

'Don't worry, I'll drive back to the Burrow at twenty miles an hour. You won't feel a thing.'

'We're not going to the Burrow,' he replied.

'You have to be joking. Where on earth do you want me to take you?'

And when he said that he couldn't rest until he had spoken to Nabil Halid somehow she wasn't at all surprised.

CHAPTER 53

By the time they reached Mo Halid's house, Mark had every reason to regret his decision. The painkillers the nurse had given him with his early-morning tea had worn off and he had never before noticed the state of Britain's road surfaces. He couldn't believe that Patti sought out every bump or crevice but it certainly felt that way. She kept shooting him sidelong looks, but he gave no indication of the pain he was in, other than a semi-permanent chewing of his lower lip.

They'd phoned ahead and discovered that Nabil had also been released from hospital that very morning. Mo, having satisfied himself that he was in no further danger, had gone to see his lawyers with a view to overturning the decision to award the ESL rights to Jet. That encouraged both Mark and Patti in their beliefs that the younger generation of the Halids were more likely to open up to them in their father's absence.

'Why the rush to talk to Nabil?' Patti asked as they pulled up outside the house.

'It was just the fact that Rob said he wanted to talk to me. Just because the police have got Cunningham, Carr and the beautiful Alissa in custody doesn't mean this is all over. I get the feeling that there are more than a few loose ends that need tidying up.'

'And you think Nabil can hand you the cleaning equipment? What about your promise to Rob not to go charging off on your own?'

'What promise? I don't remember any promise. I was under the influence. Nothing I said counted. Anyway, I can't see that there's any harm in my meeting up with somebody who'll only talk to me. Whatever I find out I'll share with Rob. What's the police phrase? It'll be his bust. The pain may be mine but the glory will be his.'

'That's very literate for somebody whose idea of an intellectual read is *Roy of the Rovers*.'

298

'You can be very cruel sometimes, Patti,' Mark replied, then shut himself up as he realised that he couldn't get out of the car without assistance.

'Compared to Alissa?' Patti asked, standing back for a moment and watching him struggle with sadistic amusement.

'OK, OK, you're an angel of mercy. Just put your lamp down for a second, Florence, and give me a hand.'

It took longer than he could imagine to extricate himself and walk up the path, leaning heavily on Patti's arm. It was Dominique who opened the door and both Mark and Patti looked automatically to her midriff to see if there was any evidence to support her alleged pregnancy. Somehow, given the circumstances, Mark did not think that Kenny Cunningham had been lying to him.

'It's nice of you to come. Nabil's in a bit of a state.' Not only her voice, but her whole demeanour seemed more gentle, more ladylike than on their previous visit. The Halids might not yet qualify for their own set in Happy Families, but there was a definite improvement in the atmosphere in the house.

Dominique led Mark upstairs to her brother's room, offered him a coffee which he gratefully accepted, then needed no encouragement to leave them alone so that she could talk to Patti. Nabil lay in the bed, propped up by pillows, his face pale despite its natural olive complexion. His head was still bandaged, his left arm in a sling, his right eye virtually hidden by the swelling that surrounded it, the bruising just beginning to turn from black to yellow. He waved his good hand at Mark and signalled him to sit in the chair on his left.

'Sorry, I can't see too much on the other side. Thanks for coming. I hear you've also been in the wars.'

It was hard to recognise the sulky youth who'd been assigned to Mark from his first days at Ball Park. There was no air of arrogance about him now. He was like a teenager brought back to his own bedroom after a skateboard accident, relieved to be amongst familiar things. Mark looked around the room which told him more about Nabil than he had ever learned from his weeks of working with him. There was an unlikely mixture of posters on the walls. Spice Girls next to Jimi Hendrix, Che Guevara alongside a team picture of Chelsea. If he had any taste at all it was obviously catholic in its breadth and scope.

'I never knew you supported Chelsea,' Mark said.

'You never asked me,' Nabil replied.

'You never gave me any encouragement to ask you.'

'Let's call it quits shall we?' Nabil said, his eyes half-closing at what was still clearly the considerable effort of talking.

'Mark, I don't know where to start, but I owe you an apology. I guess I owe everyone an apology, from my father down.'

'Have you told him that?' Mark asked.

'Have you ever tried telling my father anything?' Nabil said with a tired smile.

'I know what you mean,' Mark responded sympathetically, 'he's not the best or the most patient of listeners.'

'I didn't think you were either,' Nabil added.

'I'm listening now. Why do you owe me an apology, apart from being a real pain to work with? And why did you tell the police you wanted to speak to me and me alone? And while you're supplying answers why wouldn't you tell them who beat you up when you obviously knew?'

'I didn't realise there were so many questions.'

'Maybe it's because you are the only one who knows the answers. Look, Nabil you look beat as well as beaten. I just want to get back to sleep. We've given your sister enough time to bond with my girlfriend, so let's get down to the nitty-gritty.'

Nabil fumbled with the orange juice at his side, tried to pour it, failed miserably and waited for Mark to fill his glass.

'In case my throat gets dry. It's a long story. As you've probably gathered, my father and I have never got on well. My sister and I, believe it or not, were very close when we were younger. We got even closer after my father ditched our mother for Susie. Susie's not too bad really. At least she had the taste to get herself out of her marriage to Carr. But you can imagine how we felt at the time. Dominique chose to get out. She got herself involved with a bunch of drop-out druggies and we fell out over that in a big way. It made it worse that she always came crawling back when she ran out of money or when our father bailed her out of more trouble. Meanwhile, my father decided that whether I wanted to or not I was going into the family business. He has some very old-fashioned views sometimes. It's his Middle-Eastern inheritance. The children do what the father says and the women in particular know their place.'

He paused, took a sip of the orange juice, seemed to be expecting Mark to say something, but his visitor just wanted this to be over, wanted to get to the truth, and then wanted to go home.

'Anyway, little Jason comes along. He's quite sweet really, but at the time that was the breaking point for me. And I suppose Dominique as well. Not only is our inheritance threatened, but we've got another brand-new rival for Daddy's affections. I'm not saying that any of this justifies what I've done, but I hope it explains it. I just wanted to hurt him at the time and all I could think of was the business. He wanted those ESL rights and I saw a way of making sure he didn't get them. I had all the information. I was there all the time you were working on it, talking about it and all I had to do was give the information to Carr. You can imagine how delighted he was.'

'So that was how he could pitch his bid so close to Ball Park's yet be sure of beating them.'

'Exactly. There was always the risk that one of the other parties would come in and beat them both, but that was never a real possibility. And, even if they did, at least Carr would have had the satisfaction of knowing that Ball Park hadn't won through.'

'You still haven't explained why you were beaten up.'

'After Jet won in Zurich I tried to get too clever. I told Carr that as I'd helped him to get the rights the least he could do was to offer me a job. I figured that would seriously piss off my father. He said he didn't employ losers or traitors. I told him I'd come clean about how he'd won the bidding and he sent a couple of his heavies around to demonstrate what would happen if I tried to do just that.'

'Sounds as if you haven't come out of this too well. Why did you say that you'd only tell this to me?' Mark asked, feeling desperately sorry for the boy who so obviously needed the love of his father.

'I think I caused you all your problems as well.'

'You've been a busy lad. Tell me,' Mark said despondently. He thought he knew what was coming.

'I was there when my father suggested you go over to Carr. I told Nathan exactly what was happening. My father told me what happened to you at Cunningham's house. I think that just accelerated what they had in store for you.'

There were tears in his eyes and Mark handed him a tissue. It was hard to be angry with him, but there was still a way to go for the boy. He still had to tell all this to his father and, somehow, Mark did not think that was going to be terribly easy. Unless someone else told him first. Nabil's eyes looked at him pleadingly and Mark knew exactly what he was asking.

'You want me to talk to your father?'

'Will you?' He was pleading and Mark was aware from his dealings with Nabil Halid that this did not come naturally.

'Sure. Look, Nabil, let's call it a day. I'll make some arrangements to see your dad tomorrow. It'll all be fine. I'm sure of it. All you need as a family is some time and a bit of understanding. I'll need to tell the police as well, you understand that?'

'Sure, I understand. You don't think they'll make any charges against me, do you?' There was a desperation in his voice as he asked the question and relief as Mark gave the answer.

'No, I don't think industrial espionage is a crime unless the victim complains and I can't see your father lodging charges. I suppose I was just as guilty of that in my own way.'

'I don't see Carr lodging charges either . . .'

There was something about the boy's voice, the expression on his face, that suggested to Mark that he was not done.

'There's more, isn't there?'

Nabil nodded.

'In a way it's worse. I think it led to something worse.'

'What do you mean?' Mark's question hung in the air like a ghost.

'I mean Jenny Cooper's murder,' Nabil said after what seemed an eternity, and Mark Rossetti realised there and then that it would be some time before he would feel the luxury of the crisp, clean sheets on Patti Delaney's bed.

CHAPTER 54

After what Nabil told him he knew they could not go straight back to the Burrow. They had to see Inspector Rob Davies first. He owed him that at least, given that the policeman had saved his life.

He'd swallowed three aspirin before he left the Halid house and saw from the impatient tapping of her foot that Patti was as anxious to learn what he had been told as he was to hear exactly what Dominique had confided in her visitor. Patti couldn't believe it when Mark told her to head back to Hampstead CID.

'What did your last chauffeur die of? Exhaustion. We're not in training for the Monte Carlo Rally you know.'

He was tempted to tell her that she was one of the last people to whom he was prepared to entrust himself in any kind of race, but he didn't think he'd win any Brownie points or cooperation from trading insults, however light his tone.

'It was all true about Dominique and Barry,' Patti began as she threw the car around a corner, Mark's condition totally forgotten in her anxiety to get the story out first.

'How did they meet?' Mark asked.

'Ball Park had a party at the end of last season. All sorts of people from the game were there, including young Barry. Dominique was in the midst of one of her home visits. Daddy thinks it might be a good idea if she comes along, mix with a bit of normal society, if you can call footballing folk normal. She meets Barry because there aren't that many youngsters there. It all begins as a way to get back at her father. She thinks the last thing he'd want is for her to get involved with a bit of rough like Barry so she picks him up. The only thing is that they rather like each other. Bingo.'

It had all fallen into place for Mark, even as Nabil had confessed to him the rest of his story. When he'd got the printout from Barry's room at the team hotel in Colombia there had been a whole stream of calls to Mo's home number. He couldn't understand at the time why young Barry Reed should have been phoning Mo but now it was clear. He'd been phoning Dominique. His worried, distracted look had also become clear. She'd told him he was about to become a father and she'd given him the choice of whether or not she kept the baby. Branco and his crew must have discovered the same information. They knew all about Barry and Dominique and presumably they must have told Cunningham. Mark hadn't been paranoid in thinking he was being followed in Bogota on his later trip. By then Carr knew he was still working for Halid and anything Carr knew he would almost certainly tell Branco.

It took most of the drive for Mark to relate to Patti everything Nabil had told him about the betrayal of his father and they were nearly back in Hampstead by the time he got around to the second betrayal.

'It wasn't enough for Nabil to hurt Mo, he had to try and hurt Dominique and Susie too. He overheard his sister confide in Susie about her pregnancy. She thought she had to tell somebody even before she told the father-to-be.'

'So what did he do? Even his sister's not too sure.'

'He sent a letter to the Football Association accusing Barry Reed of putting his sister in the club. And one or two other things as well. He even suggested that he'd been responsible for getting her involved in drugs.'

'I don't understand. Why hasn't that letter ever come to light?' Patti asked.

'He wanted to be certain it would be read, so he addressed it to someone he was sure would read it. Even marked it strictly private and confidential, for their eyes only. The only person he knew at the FA was a contact I'd used for Ball Park.'

'Jenny Cooper.' Patti said in puzzlement.

'Exactly.'

They sat in the car outside the police station, parked on a double yellow line, oblivious to the curious looks they received from the passers-by.

'I may be thick, but I still don't understand. Why should anybody kill Jenny just because she'd got an anonymous letter telling her that one of the young England players had knocked up the daughter of the boss of a television company and was also possibly a drug addict?'

'That threw me at first, but I think I've worked it out,' Mark said triumphantly. 'Why don't we surprise Rob and share our news with him?'

Davies was less than amused when Mark told him where they'd just come from.

'You don't listen, do you? I thought I made it clear that if you were going to visit Nabil that I wanted to be there.'

'I was trying to make life easy for you. I'm sure that you've got lots to do catching speeding motorists. And anyway I doubt if he'd have been half as forthcoming if you'd been there.'

Rob led them through to a smoky interview room at the rear of the station. The walls were a depressing shade of yellow, the one window gave little natural light, the table was battered and the chairs were rickety. Mark could understand how the atmosphere could be used to gain confessions and he was glad that he and the Welsh policeman were on the same side.

'So let me into Nabil's little secrets,' Davies said resignedly, pen poised over paper.

For the second time Mark went over what he'd been told and at the end Davies looked as bewildered as Patti.

'You've obviously got something worked out in that devious mind of yours, Rossetti, so why don't you let the pair of us have a peek in there? I promise you that for somebody with a broken rib the bunks in our cells can be very uncomfortable indeed and that's where I'm tempted to cool you off for a while.'

Mark looked long and hard at Davies and saw that this time he wasn't necessarily joking.

'All right. This is what I think happened. Nabil writes to Jenny. She takes the letter home to deal with along with a load of the rest of her post. She told me she often worked at home. She reads the letter. She knows I know Barry better than anybody else so she tries to call me. I'm not there. Then she had a visitor. We suspect that she's into drugs. Let's assume it's a supplier or someone she knows can get them supplied. We know she sleeps around. Let's assume it's someone she's slept with. Either way, or maybe both ways, she lets him in. Perhaps she's become a threat to him, a danger. She's into drugs, she's into booze, she's a loose cannon so she has to be silenced. We don't know what kind of threats she's been making. He kills her. He reads the

letter and then maybe he realises that she's been on the phone.
He checks who she's been calling and finds out it's me. He takes
the letter away with him, perhaps he destroys it. Now what does
all that tell you?'

Davies and Patti were fascinated into silence and gave him no
answer.

'I'll tell you what it tells me. Whoever killed Jenny knew not
only her, but Barry and me. I think you've already got the killer
banged up on other charges. Why don't you ask Kenny
Cunningham to tell you exactly why he murdered Jenny Cooper?'

EPILOGUE

The winter had turned to spring and in the intervening months Hertsmere had steadily climbed up the Premiership. One by one their challengers had fallen away until it had become a two-horse race. Now with the last game of the season the only threat to their title ambitions came from their old rivals, Thamesmead. Thamesmead had just got their noses in front and opened up a two-point lead. All they needed to do was defend on their visit to Park Crescent and they would be the English entrants into the first year of the European Super League rather than Hertsmere for whom nothing less than victory would do.

The television companies were ecstatic. The computers had done them proud by saving the best to last. It was Liverpool against Arsenal back in 88-89 all over again. There was the added piquancy that this would be the last match ever played at Hertsmere's cramped Park Crescent stadium.

That in itself had created its own problems. The police had placed an 18,000 security limit on the crowd and, despite the live coverage of the game, the tickets could have been sold twenty times over. Helen Davies looked distraught as Mark and Patti, with Emma Rossetti in tow, passed her on their way to the seats in the Director's Box.

'If one more person turns up claiming that they know David Sinclair personally and that he's promised them a ticket then I'm going to make sure that my husband goes down there and arrests them for attempted fraud.'

'So he got the day off then?' Patti asked.

'Miracle of miracles, yes he did. Although I have to say he's been flavour of the month with his bosses ever since he closed the Jenny Cooper murder and also ended a fairly sophisticated drugs business.'

There was a smile on her harassed features as she spoke and clearly Rob had told her that he'd done very little in the operation other than sweep up behind Mark.

It had not been too difficult to break Cunningham down into a confession. Jenny Cooper had been one of the routes he'd used to sell drugs to players. She'd been becoming difficult, drinking too much, using the drugs herself too much, talking too much. She had become a threat and she had to be stopped. He seemed only too anxious to place as much of the blame as he could on Nathan Carr and Alissa. Mark had been spot on in his analysis of the night of the murder and even Patti had begun to treat him with some respect.

'When I first met you, there's no way that you'd have figured that out. Maybe you do have a vocation in the investigation business after all.'

He'd shaken his head. He really didn't want to be involved in any business. He just wanted a good long rest, wanted to spend as much of his time in Patti's company as he possibly could and certainly during the last few months she'd raised no real objection to that.

It had not all been sunshine and roses. They'd gone together to Jessica Brown's funeral, and had stood side by side as her young, ravaged body was consigned to the ground. Patti had kept her promise and had given the news to her parents face to face. It had not been easy, but when she told them what had been the effect of the journey she had begun on behalf of their daughter she felt it had eased the pain a little. She had gone to tell Jessica as well, and her old friend had listened carefully and then extracted another promise from Patti.

'You've got the story. It's my story really. You were always a better writer than me, so write it for me.'

Patti had done that single-mindedly. Like Mark she had no financial pressures on her to work and she'd sat at her screen for hours every day, made phone calls at night and allowed Mark back into her life and her bed. She never told him how much she liked to have him around, how much she needed to have him around, but then she didn't have to. It had been a mere week before this vital match that she had heard from the publishers that they would buy the book. Not only that but they thought she had a major bestseller on her hands.

'I thought I'd give most of the advance to that hospice where Jessica died. What do you think?' she'd asked. It wasn't often that she asked Mark's opinion, and he'd kissed her gently and nodded his agreement because he felt too choked to speak.

The book was almost forgotten as the match began to grip their attention. Mo and Nabil were seated a row or two behind them. Mo was particularly interested in the outcome. He'd finally succeeded in securing the rights for ESL for Ball Park and Nabil had in turn thrown himself into the company with a new enthusiasm that had even won over the cynics working around him. Susie had left Jason in the club's crèche to be with her husband and stepson and only Dominique was absent. But then there was no way that she could be there.

There were a lot of nervous spectators and the anxiety transmitted itself to the field of play. The rival fans found their voices but it was hard to whip up any genuine enthusiasm for a game so littered with fouls, free-kicks and misplaced passes. Barry Reed had almost automatically been awarded his place back in the team, but his club form had been indifferent. However, England's new coach, Jeff Niven, had kept faith with him in the national side. He'd looked particularly out of sorts throughout the afternoon and, with ten minutes to go, Ray Fowler was fumbling with the numbers to take him off.

Reed seemed to spot the imminent substitution from the corner of his eye and rolled up his sleeves with increased determination. Sergovich, who had already made a string of fine saves to keep Hertsmere in the match, threw a long ball out to him. The Geordie midfielder controlled the ball with all his natural skill and suddenly set off on a solo run. Aled Williams went with him down the left and Reed feinted past the big Thamesmead centre back and switched the ball out to the Welshman. Williams made ground himself and the crowd, instead of urging him on, held their breath in anticipation. Reed kept on running. The Thamesmead sweeper kept him onside and when Williams centred, Reed took the ball on the volley and drove it home.

There was bedlam in three-quarters of the ground. Only the Thamesmead end and the small part of the stand occupied by Thamesmead fans, were silent. Patti embraced Mark and David Sinclair kissed Emma. Helen and Rob clung to each other, reluctant to take their seats for the last ten minutes. Somehow or other Hertsmere hung on and when the final whistle blew the thin blue line of police made no real effort to restrain the jubilant home supporters from invading the pitch and grabbing whatever souvenir they could.

Amidst the noise and the triumphant confusion it was difficult to hear the mobile phone ring, but Mohammed Halid eventually reached into his pocket, answered and took the message with a smile. He whispered something to Nabil and then came over to Mark to share the message. Mark ran to the front of the box, where it overhung the pitch. Barry Reed had extricated himself from his team-mates and the well-wishers who all wanted to touch the man who had not only taken the Premiership title to the club, but had guaranteed their unique place in European footballing history. He came over towards Mark and looked up. Mark cupped his hands and yelled down the news.

'It's a boy. Mother and baby are fine.'

Barry's celebrations at scoring the goal were subdued compared to the back-flip he performed as Mark's words sunk in. It had taken time for Mo Halid to accept that he was going to have Barry Reed as a son-in-law. The fact that he was going to be a grandfather had been difficult enough to swallow, but now he had a face and a name to put to the father. The police decision to drop the prosecution of the pregnant Dominique had been welcome. But going into labour on today of all days, had hardly been impeccable timing. Fowler had offered Barry the chance to be with her, but right now he was relieved that, rightly or wrongly, Dominique had insisted that Barry put his club and career first.

'There'll be other babies,' she'd told Barry, 'and, believe me, the excuse hasn't been invented that will allow you to get out of being there when they're born.'

Mo and Nabil said their hasty farewells and dashed downstairs to the car that Mo had arranged to whisk them and Barry off to the hospital to see Dominique and her son. The box emptied out as Sinclair and Helen also made their way on to the pitch to join the celebrations, becoming indistinguishable from the other fans. Only Mark, Patti and Emma were left. Emma was sensitive enough to move away, ostensibly to get a better view of the crazy scenes on the pitch.

'I liked what you said to Barry,' Patti said.

'What did I say?' Mark asked, although he knew full well.

WHITE LINES

'It's a boy. Mother and baby are fine,' she said, linking her hand in his.

'Are you trying to tell me something?' he said with a smile.

'I do believe so,' she replied, moving closer.

'I can't guarantee it will be a boy,' Mark said, nodding in the direction of Emma, his daughter from his first marriage.

'I know,' Patti said quietly, 'it doesn't matter.' And then she kissed him long and hard.